Warriors

ALSO BY TED BELL

FICTION

Phantom

Warlord

Tsar

Spy

Pirate

Assassin

Hawke

YOUNG ADULT BOOKS

The Time Pirate

Nick of Time

Warriors

Ted Bell

HARPER LUXE

An Imprint of HarperCollins*Publishers*

For Lucinda Watson. Sometimes it takes a lifetime
to find the love of your life.

WARRIORS. Copyright © 2014 by Theodore A. Bell. All rights reserved. Printed in the United States of America. No part of this book may be used or reproduced in any manner whatsoever without written permission except in the case of brief quotations embodied in critical articles and reviews. For information address HarperCollins Publishers, 10 East 53rd Street, New York, NY 10022.

HarperCollins books may be purchased for educational, business, or sales promotional use. For information, please e-mail the Special Markets Department at SPsales@harpercollins.com.

FIRST HARPERLUXE EDITION

HarperLuxe™ is a trademark of HarperCollins Publishers

Library of Congress Cataloging-in-Publication Data is available upon request.

ISBN: 978-0-06-229863-8

14 ID/RRD 10 9 8 7 6 5 4 3 2 1

You may not be interested in war.
But war is interested in you.

LEON TROTSKY, 1919

Author's Note

The research for this book is primarily the happy result of my election as a visiting scholar and writer in residence at Cambridge University for the 2011 to 2012 term. At the university's prestigious Department of Political Science and International Studies (POLIS), I was fortunate enough to engage with perhaps the most knowledgeable group of scholars, historians, intelligence officers, assistants to heads of state, and high-ranking military officers from both the U.K. and the U.S. As it happened, the primary focus during my tenure was an in-depth study of China's political and military roles on the modern global stage. We also kept a wary eye on North Korea. I am especially indebted to the following gentlemen at Cambridge for their support and guidance: Professor Stefan Halper, Life Fellow, Magdalene College; Professor J.B.L. Mayall, Emeritus Professor of International Relations; and, finally, Sir Richard Dearlove, KCMG, OBE, Master of Pembroke College, and former chief of British Secret Intelligence Service (MI6).

Prologue

Lord Alexander Hawke rose with the dawn.

A shadowy gloom pervaded the gilded coffers of his high-ceilinged bedchamber. He lifted his arms high above his head and stretched mightily, extending his long naked body full-length, feeling his muscles and tendons come alive, one by one. Then he wiggled his toes twice for luck and sat straight up beneath the dark blue needlepoint canopy tented above his four bedposts.

His head ached; his lips were dry, and he tried to swallow. Difficult. His mouth felt, perhaps, like that of some ancient Gila monster standing in the middle of the Mojave Desert on a flat rock in the noonday sun. That tequila nightcap, perhaps? Ah, yes, that was it. A dram too far.

Fully awake now, he needed light. There was a discreet control pad on the wall above his bedside table and he reached over to press a pearly button.

A soft whir was followed by the rustle of heavy silk. As the brocade draperies on the many tall French windows drew apart, a soft rosy light began to bloom within the room. Beyond his windows, he saw the red-gold sun perched on the dark rim of the earth. He turned his face toward the sunlight and smiled.

It was going to be another beautiful day.

Beyond his windows lay his walled gardens. Most had been designed by the famous eighteenth-century landscape architect Lancelot Brown. He was a man known to history as "Capability" Brown because the talented and clever Brown slyly told all his potential clients that only their particular estates had the "great capability" to realize his genius.

Beyond the gardens, a tangle of meadows circumscribed by dry stone walls. Then endless forests, temporarily clothed in a light haze of spring green. The narrow lane winding down to the village featured a precarious haystack on a horse-drawn cart, a lone vicar on his wobbly bicycle, and an ancient crone walking stooped beneath a heavy burden. From chimneys of little stone cottages scattered hither and yon, tendrils of grey smoke rose into the pale orange sky.

He had awoken to this chilly morning in early April to watch a grey ground fog swirl up under the eaves and curl around the endless gables and chimneys of the rambling seventeenth-century manor house.

Hawkesmoor, that ancient pile was called. It had been home to his family for centuries. It was situated amid vast parklands in the gently rolling hills of the Cotswolds, a leisurely two hours' drive north of London on the M40 motorway.

Hawke slid out of bed and into the faded threadbare Levi's that lay puddled on the floor where he'd left them at midnight. He pulled an old Royal Navy T-shirt over his head and slipped his bare feet into turquoise-beaded Indian moccasins. They were a particular favorite. He'd bought them during a hunting and fishing expedition with his friends Ambrose Congreve and his fiancée, Lady Diana Mars, to a rustic camp near Flathead Lake, in Montana.

On this particular spring morning, one day before his departure for far more hostile territory, the South China Sea, of all places, Hawke was full of keen anticipation. Four hundred and fifty very powerful horses that even now were stamping their hooves, waiting for him on the apron of bricks in the stable courtyards.

"The Snake," as his new steed was called, was a 1963 Shelby AC Cobra. It was an original, set up for racing by Carroll Shelby himself. With a highly modified 427-cubic-inch engine putting out 450 horsepower, it was capable of achieving speeds nearing 180 miles per hour. It was painted in the famous Cobra racing livery, dark blue with two wide white stripes down the centerline.

It had been purchased by Hawke's man at the Barrett-Jackson auction in Scottsdale, Arizona, and flown to England, arriving by flatbed lorry late the previous afternoon. His primary mechanic, Ian Burns, a fine Irishman with hair and whiskers so blond they were white, gave him a knowing grin. Known forever as "Young Ian," the lad had been going over the Cobra all night, adjusting the timing, checking the plugs, points, and carbs, making sure all was in readiness for Hawke's maiden voyage into the surrounding countryside.

"Quite the brute y've got yerself here now, m'lord," Young Ian said as Hawke approached the car, taking long strides across the mossy brick of the courtyard. "One can see why no one could lay a finger on Dan Gurney and the old 'Snake' at Le Mans back in '64."

"You put a few miles on her this morning, did you, Young Ian?" Hawke asked, smiling and running his hands over the sleek flanks of the beast. "I thought I heard a throaty roar wafting up through the woods earlier."

"Aye, I did indeed."

"And?"

"Still trembling with excitement, m'lord. Can barely handle me socket wrench, sir."

Hawke laughed and gazed at his prize. It was truly a magnificent piece of machinery. A fine addition to his growing but highly selective collection, stored behind the long line of stable doors. A long row that featured, among others, vintage Ferraris, Jags, and Aston-Martins, a black 1956 Thunderbird convertible once owned by Ian Fleming, a spanking-new white McClaren 50, and his cherished daily driver, a steel-grey 1954 Bentley Continental he fondly called "the Locomotive."

"I did, sir. Topped off the petrol tank with avgas, which I highly recommend you use in the car, sir, aviation fuel having much higher octane, obviously. And runs cleaner, sir. The Weber carbs needed a bit of finesse, a couple of belts and hoses needed replacing, but otherwise it's in perfect running order, sir, just as advertised."

"Let's find out, shall we?" Hawke said, grinning from ear to ear.

Hawke climbed behind the wood-rimmed wheel, adjusted the close-fitting racing seat for his six-foot-plus frame, and strapped himself in, using the bright red heavy-duty Simpson racing harness. Then he switched on the ignition.

His glacial blue eyes widened at the instant roar, deafening, really, in the narrow confines of the stone-walled courtyard.

"Bloody hell, Ian!" Hawke grinned, shouting over the thundering engine. "I do believe I feel the stirrings of one falling deeply and passionately in love!"

"As long as y' don' scare the horses, m'lord."

Hawke laughed, a laugh of pure joy.

"Anything at all I should know about?"

"Just one thing, sir. Bit of a steering issue. She seems to want to pull to the right a wee bit. I'll take care of it as soon as you return. Not dangerous, really. I just wanted you to be aware of it in the twisty bits."

"Thanks. Cheerio, then."

Hawke engaged first, mashed the go pedal, popped the clutch, and smoked the squealing tires, fishtailing through the wide wrought-iron stable gates until he reached the paved drive, braked hard, and put the car into a four-wheel drift, a left-hander. He backed off the throttle for the length of the drive, slowing to a stop at the main gate to the estate. The gate was off a two-lane road that led to Chipping Campden, rarely used, and certainly not at this ungodly hour.

Burning rubber once more, he took a hard right out into the road. He had a long straightaway shot in front of him, some miles of clear sailing before the road reentered the forest. There was still a bit of ground fog, but it was blowing around a bit and he had a clear view of the road ahead. He upshifted into second and wound the revs up to redline. He was shoved hard back into his seat, and the scenery became an instant blur.

Ian had been right about the steering.

The Cobra had an annoying habit of pulling to the right. It was irksome but nothing he couldn't handle until he got her back to the stable and corrected it.

Hawke entered the dark wood, a place of blue-tinged evergreens.

The macadam road was a twisting snake, but then, he was at the wheel of the Snake. It was narrow, chock-full of inclines, switchbacks, and decreasing radius turns. It was the perfect place to see how his new prize handled. He pushed it hard, not happy unless his tyres were squealing, and the car responded beautifully, enormous torque, precision handling, wedded to splendid racing tyres. Heaven, in other words.

When he finally emerged from the wood, he charged up a rather steep hill, crested it, went fully airborne for a moment, and then sped down into the next straightaway, the engine warmed up now. He redlined third and upshifted to fourth, then down again to second for the intersection, a tight right-hander into a narrow country lane.

And that's when he heard the blare of air horns behind him.

Christ, he thought, *who the hell?*

He glanced at the rearview mirror and saw the familiar stately grille of an old Rolls-Royce filling the mirror. Right smack on his tail. He slowed, moved left onto the grassy verge, and gestured to the big silver Roller to overtake, for God's sake. He couldn't wait to get a look at the driver. What kind of a moron would even think of trying to pass on this bloody—

A woman. A beautiful woman. Bright yellow Hermès scarf wound round her neck. Silky black hair cut short, and a stunning Asian profile.

She blew the triple air horns again as she blew past, and Hawke's shouted reply surely went unheard over the wind and the combined engine roar. He saw her right arm emerge, hand raised high, ruby red nails, the middle digit extended straight up as she tucked in front of him, almost nicking his front fender.

Fucking hell.

"Balls to the wall, you crazy bitch!" he shouted at her in vain, shaking his righteous fist in disbelieving anger.

And that's when it happened.

He'd taken his right hand off the wheel for a split second, the steering had pulled hard right, and a stout and hardy chestnut tree leaped up out of the woods and smacked him good, pinging both his pride and his new and very shiny blue bonnet in one solid blow.

He forgot the stupid incident over time, but for some reason he never forgot the license plate number on that old silver Roller.

M-A-O.

As in Chairman Mao?

He had no idea. But, as it all turned out in the end, he'd been absolutely spot-on about that damn plate number.

It was Mao.

And the woman behind the wheel? Well, she was indeed one crazy bitch.

Chapter 1

Washington, D.C.
December 2009

Bill Chase picked up the phone and called 1789.

Chase had always thought a year was an odd name for a restaurant. Even for a quaint, colonial eatery in the historic heart of Georgetown. But the year, he knew, was historic: in 1789, George Washington was unanimously elected the nation's first president. In that same year, the United States Constitution went into effect. And also that year, his alma mater, Georgetown University, had been founded.

1789 had been his go-to dining spot in town since his freshman year. The place felt like home, that was all. He loved the elegant high-ceilinged, flower-filled rooms upstairs, usually filled with an eclectic potpourri of the well-heeled and the well-oiled, frenetic lobbyists, assorted besotted lovers, gay and straight, illicit and otherwise, various self-delighted junior senators with JFK haircuts, as well as the tired, the careworn, the elderly congressmen.

He liked the restaurant for its authentic colonial vibe, the simple food and subtle service, even the quaint Limoges china. Not to mention the complete absence of pretentious waiters or wine stewards who uttered absurdities like "And what will we be enjoying this evening?"

We? Really? Are you joining us for dinner? Or this little gem he'd heard just last week at Chez Panisse: "And at what temperature would you like your steak this evening, Mr. Chase?" Temperature? Sorry, forgot my meat thermometer this evening. Honestly, who came up with this crap?

1789's utter lack of haute-moderne pretension was precisely what had kept Chase coming back since his college days; those beery, cheery, halcyon days when he'd been a semipermanent habitué of the horseshoe bar at the Tombs downstairs.

Chase hung up the phone in his office, rose from his father's old partner's desk, and stood gazing out the floor-to-ceiling windows. It was late afternoon, and the cold, wintry skies over northern Virginia were laced with streaks of violet and magenta. His private office on the thirtieth floor of Lightstorm's world head-quarters had vistas overlooking the Capitol, the White House, and the Pentagon.

To his left he could see Georgetown, Washington's oldest neighborhood, and home to the Chase family for generations. The streets of town were already lost to a grey fog bank. He watched it now, rolling up from the south and over the silvery Potomac like a misty tsunami. Traffic on the Francis Scott Key bridge had become two parallel streams of haloed red and white lights flowing slowly in opposite directions.

Bill Chase had plenty of reasons to be happy despite the dull grey weather. His marriage had never been stronger or more passionate, and his new fighter aircraft prototype, the Lightstorm, had just emerged victorious in a global battle for a huge Pentagon aeronautical contract. But the best part? His two adored kids, Milo, age four, and Sarah, age seven, were healthy, happy, and thriving at school.

Today was a red-letter day. His wife's fortieth. The Big Four-Oh, as she'd been calling it recently. He had just booked a table for four upstairs at 1789. His family would be dining tonight at a cozy round table in the gracious Garden Room on the second floor, right next to the fireplace.

Bill Chase had come a long way.

In this decisive year of 2009, he was the fifty-year-old wunderkind behind Lightstorm Advanced Weapons Systems. LAWS was a global powerhouse whose rapid rise to the top in the ongoing battle for world dominance in the military tech industry was the stuff of legend. Bill himself had acquired a bit of legend.

Fortune magazine's recent cover story on him had been headlined: "One Part Gates, One Part Jobs, One Part Oppenheimer!" His portrait, shot by Annie Leibovitz, showed him smiling in the open cockpit of the new Lightstorm fighter.

The Pentagon had relied heavily on LAWS for the last decade. Chase's firm had just been awarded a massive British government contract to develop an unmanned fighter-bomber code-named Sorcerer. It was Bill's pet project: a mammoth batwing UAV capable of being launched from Royal Navy aircraft carriers. Heavy payloads, all-weather capability, extreme performance parameters, and zero risk of pilot casualty or death.

An electric crack and a heavy rumble of thunder stirred Chase out of his reverie. He looked up and gazed out his tall windows.

Steep-piled buttresses of thunderheads had towered up darkly. Another mounting bulwark of black clouds to the west, veined with white lightning, was stacking up beyond the Potomac. Big storm coming. He stood at his office window watching the first few fat drops of rain slant across his expansive windows. A stormy night, rain mixed with fog, was on the way and it was too bad.

They had planned to walk the few blocks to the restaurant from their gracious two-hundred-year-old town house just off Reservoir Road.

He wanted the evening to be special in every way. He'd bought Kat a ridiculously expensive piece of jewelry, filled their house with flowers. All day today his wife, Kathleen, had been facing down the Big Four-Oh, and, like most women, she wasn't happy about it.

Kat had been adamant about her big birthday. She'd insisted upon no fancy-pants black-tie party at the Chevy Chase Club, no shindig of any stripe, and, God forbid, not even the merest suggestion of a surprise party.

No. She wanted a quiet dinner out with her husband and their two children. Period.

No cake, no candles.

Bill was feeling celebratory, but he had acquiesced readily. It was, after all, her birthday, not his. Light-years ago, she'd fallen for his southern Bayou Teche drawl and charm; but she'd come to rely on his southern manners. True gents were somewhat in short supply in the nation's capital. And Kat, at least, believed she had found one. Besides his own career, William Lincoln Chase Jr.'s wife and family meant the world to him.

And he tried hard to let them know it, every day of his life.

Chapter 2

Georgetown

Dinner was lovely. The heavy rain had somehow held off, and they'd all walked the five blocks to the restaurant hand in hand, the evening skies a brassy shade of gold, the skeletal trees etched black against them like a Chinese watercolor Chase used to own.

Kat had worn an old black Saint Laurent cocktail dress with slit sleeves that revealed her perfect white arms. She was wearing the diamond brooch at the neckline, the one he'd given her for their twentieth anniversary. The kids, little Milo and his older sister, Sarah, had even behaved, beautifully for them, and for that he was grateful.

Kat didn't like this birthday, with its early hints of mortality, one bit. He was determined to make it a happy evening for her and their family. He'd always had a sense of occasion and he wasn't about to let this one go to waste.

And he'd loved the shine in her lively brown eyes when he gave her the birthday present. She opened the slender black velvet case, took a quick peek, and smiled across the table at him, her eyes sparkling in the candlelight.

A diamond necklace.

"It's lovely, Bill. Really, you shouldn't have. Way too extravagant."

"Do you like it?"

"What girl wouldn't, darling?"

"It's the one Audrey Hepburn wore in *Breakfast at Tiffany's*."

"What?"

"You heard me."

"Bill Chase, stop it. I know when you're teasing."

"No, Kat, really. There was an auction at Sotheby's when I was in New York last week."

"You're serious. Audrey's necklace. The one in the movie."

"Double pinkie swear, crossies don't count."

"Oh. My. God."

"Dad?" Milo said.

"Yes, Milo?"

"You're funny."

Milo and Sarah looked at each other and laughed. Double pinkie swear? They'd never heard their brainy dad speak like that before.

"Audrey Hepburn?" Kat said again, still not quite believing it. "Really?"

"Hmm," he said, "Audrey Hepburn."

It was perfect. For that one fleeting moment, it was all just perfect.

Her favorite actress. Her favorite movie. His favorite girl. The happy smiles on the faces of his two beautiful children.

He was a very, very lucky man, and he knew it.

The fog was thick when the Chase family stepped outside the flickering gaslit restaurant entrance. You could barely make out the haloed glow of streetlamps on the far side of the narrow cobblestone Georgetown street.

Bill held his daughter's hand; pausing at the top of the steps, he pulled his grey raincoat closer round his torso. It must have dropped twenty degrees while they were inside, and the fog made everything a little spooky.

They descended the few steps to the sidewalk and turned toward the river.

He could hear that melody in his head, the theme song from his favorite horror movie, *The Exorcist.* What was it called? "Tubular Bells." They'd shot part of that movie on this very same street, on a very foggy night just like this one, and maybe that's why walking back from the Tombs at night sometimes gave him the creeps.

"Let's go, kids, hurry up," Chase said, edgy for some nameless reason as they plunged into the mist.

The street was deserted, for one thing, all the curtains in the town houses drawn tight against the stormy night. He took a look over his shoulder, half expecting to see a deranged zombie dragging one leg behind him.

Nothing, of course.

He felt like an idiot. The last thing he wanted after a perfect evening was to look like a fool and alarm Kat about nothing. She and Sarah were singing "A Foggy Day in London Town" off-key, Kat loving to sing when she'd had a glass or two of her favorite sauvignon blanc.

"Damn it!" Bill cried, bending to grab his kneecap. Looking over his shoulder, he'd walked right into a fireplug, slammed his knee and upper shin against the hard iron rim. He could feel a warm dampness inside his trouser leg. The cut probably wasn't deep, but it hurt like hell.

"What is it, darling?" Kat said, taking his arm.

"Banged my damn knee, that's all. Let's just keep walking, okay? The corner is just around the corner up there somewhere, I think."

"The corner is just around the corner!" Sarah mimicked and her mother laughed.

What the hell was wrong with him? She was happy. The Big Four-Oh was officially history. And she had loved his present.

"Let's skip. All the way home," he said. "Except for Dad. For Dad, you see, has a very bum knee." Inexplicably, he felt better. Some second sense had warned him that some bad thing was waiting in the fog.

And it was just a damn fireplug.

Chapter 3

In the next block he saw a chocolate brown Mercedes-Benz 600 "Pullman" limo pulled over and stopped. It was parked at the curb about twenty feet ahead of them. The 1967 Mercedes Pullman was a classic, the most highly desired limo of the 1960s. He'd been thinking about bidding on one at auction, for Lightstorm's corporate driver.

The interior light was on in the limo, filling the car with soft yellow light. His senses were on high alert, but as he drew near he saw that the occupants were harmless. There was a liveried chauffeur leaning against the rear fender smoking a cigarette; a tiny, elderly couple was seated on the broad leather bench seat in the rear. And there was a diplomatic plate on the big car.

The Chinese delegation.

"Probably that new Chinese ambassador and his wife," he whispered to Kat. "Looks like they need help."

The passenger door was slightly ajar, and as he drew abreast of them he could see that they were plainly lost in the fogbound streets of old Georgetown. The wife, snow white hair held back in a chignon, wearing a mink stole over a black cashmere turtleneck with a strand of pearls, had a well-creased road map of D.C. spread across her lap.

Her husband was peering over her shoulder, pointing his finger at an intersection and asking the chauffeur something about the Estonian embassy.

"May I help you?" Chase asked in English, never trusting his always rusty Mandarin. He bent down to speak to the ambassador's wife.

She looked up in surprise; apparently she hadn't seen his approach in the fog.

"Oh," the elegant woman said sweetly in English, "aren't you kind, dear? We're embarrassed to say it, but we're late for a reception and completely lost. My husband, the ambassador, and I are new to Washington, you see, and haven't yet got a clue, as you Americans say. We're looking for the Estonian embassy . . . even our poor driver cannot find it."

Chase leaned down to get a closer look at her map.

"Well," he said, reaching inside to point out their location on the map. "Here you are. And here's Wisconsin Street over here and the embassy is right—"

The woman clamped her small but incredibly powerful hand around his wrist. In an instant, she had pulled him forward, off his feet, halfway into the car. The husband had something in his hand, a hypo, and he plunged it into the side of Chase's neck. He could feel a wave of nausea instantly sweep over him, tried to pull away but had no muscle power at all.

"Try to relax, Dr. Chase," the woman cooed softly. "It will all be over in a second or two."

She knew his name.

"Kat, grab Milo! Sarah! Run! Run!" Bill Chase cried over his shoulder. Kat looked at him for a second in astonishment, saw he was serious, and gathered Milo and Sarah up into her arms. And started running. He saw them run, then lost them, folding into the swirling fog.

It was the last time, he truly believed at that moment, that he would ever see them alive.

He was vaguely aware of a white van passing the limo, headed in the direction of his family. Next he was being manhandled by the chauffeur around to the rear of the Mercedes. The big man popped the massive trunk, lifted him easily, and dropped him inside.

The lid of the trunk slammed down.

All was blackness then.

Kat, who was losing her mind to terror, tried to run. But the fog, two children in her arms, and her damn Jimmy Choo heels made it all but impossible. All she wanted to do was speed-dial 911 on her cell, get the police, and—

A van swerved up to the curb just beside her. The rear doors flew open, and four large men all in black leaped to the pavement right in front of them. They were wearing ski masks, Kat saw, as one of them, his body enwreathed with fog, stepped under the hazy streetlamp to snatch Milo from her arms.

She cried out, ripping Milo away again, clutching her son's frail little body to her chest, and that's when something unbelievably hard, a ball of pain encased in steel, struck the back of her head. It made a dull, sickening noise and sent her sprawling to the ground, her pulse roaring in her ears, her face half submerged in a large puddle with fat raindrops dancing upon it.

She knew she was close to blacking out.

"Milo!" she cried out, raising her head to search for her children. "Sarah!"

But they had disappeared into the turning wisps and wraiths of fog that hovered around the white van.

And one of the four thugs had taken them from her. The one who had hit her now had her by the ankles, dragging her toward the van, her head bouncing over the cobblestones.

Just before she slipped into blackness she saw one of the men pulling her limp son up into the rear of the van. The man who was yanking Milo and Sarah inside by the arm, his face hidden by the black balaclava, was screaming at her son. Unintelligible threats in some guttural foreign language . . . Chinese, perhaps.

What in God's name was going on?

Chapter 4

South China Sea
Present Day

Midnight. No moon, no stars, the sea a flat black void a few feet beneath his wingtips. For a man streaking through the night over hostile waters approaching the speed of sound, at an altitude no sane man would even dare consider, Commander Alex Hawke was remarkably comfortable. He was piloting an F-35C Lightning. The new matte-black American-built fighter jet was one of many purchased and heavily modified by Britain's Royal Navy for under-the-radar special ops just like this one.

Lord Alexander Hawke, a former Royal Navy fighter pilot and decorated combat veteran of the latest

Gulf War, now a seasoned British intelligence officer with MI6, had to smile.

The F-35C's single seat reclined at an angle of exactly thirty degrees, transforming the deadly Lightning, Hawke thought, into something along the lines of a chaise longue. Leave it to the bloody Americans to worry about fighter pilot "comfort" during a dogfight. Still, it was comfy enough, he had to admit, smiling to himself. Rather like a supersonic Barcalounger!

His eyes flicked over the dimly lit instrument array and found nothing remotely exciting going on. Even the hazy reddish glow inside the cockpit somehow reassured him. He was less than six hundred nautical miles from his designated speck on the map, the tiny island of Xiachuan, and closing fast.

Every mile he put behind him lessened the chance of a Chinese Suchoi 33 jet interceptor or a surface-to-air missile blasting him out of the sky. Although the Lightning was equipped with the very latest antimissile defense systems, the Lightning was no stealth fighter.

He was vulnerable and he knew it.

Should he be forced to eject and be captured by the Red Chinese, he'd be tortured mercilessly before he was executed. A British intelligence officer flying an unmarked American fighter jet had no business entering Chinese airspace. But he did have business in China, very serious business, and his success might well help avert impending hostilities that could lead to regional war. At that point the chances of it expanding into a global conflict were nearly one hundred percent.

Preventing that was his mission.

In London, one week earlier, "C," as the chief of MI6 was traditionally called, had summoned Hawke to join him for lunch at his men's club, Boodle's. Lord Hawke had thought it was a purely social invitation. Usually the old man conducted serious SIS business only within the sanctum sanctorum of his private offices at 85 Albert Embankment, the headquarters for Six.

So it was that a very relaxed Alex Hawke presented himself promptly at the appointed hour of noon.

"Well, here you are at last," C said, amiably enough. The "at last" was the old boy's way of letting you know who was boss. Sir David Trulove, a gruff old party thirty years Hawke's senior, had his customary corner table at the third-floor Grill Room. Shafts of dusty sunlight pouring down from the tall leaded windows set the table crystal and silver afire, all sparkle and gleam. Above C's table, ragged tendrils of his tobacco smoke hung in wreaths and coils, turning and twisting slowly in the sunlit space.

The dining and drinking at Boodle's was, by any standard, done in one of the poshest man caves in all London.

C took a spartan sip of his gin and bitters, looked his young subordinate up and down in cursory fashion, and said, "I must say, Alex, a bit of time in the down mode becomes you. You're looking rather fit and ready for the fray. 'Steel true, blade straight,' as Conan Doyle's memorable epitaph would have it. Sit, sit."

Hawke sat. He paid scant attention to C's flattery, knowing the old man used it sparingly and only to his own advantage, usually as some prelude to another more important subject. Whatever was on his mind, he seemed jovial enough.

"Most kind of you, sir. I've been looking forward to this luncheon all week. I get bored silly sometimes, up in the country. Good being back in town. This is a much-needed interlude, I must say."

"Let's see if you still feel that way at the conclusion. What are you drinking? My club, my treat, of course," Trulove said, catching a roving waiter's eye.

"Gosling's, please. The Black Seal, neat."

Hawke sat back and smiled. It really was good to be here, a place where a man could act like a man wants to act, and do just what he pleased without encountering approbation from bloody anybody.

"So," Hawke said after C had ordered another drink and his rum, "trouble, I take it."

"No end of it, sadly."

"Spill the beans, sir. I can take it."

"The bloody Chinese again."

"Ah, my dear friends in the Forbidden City. Something new? I thought I was fairly well up to speed."

"Well, Alex, you know those inscrutable Mandarins in Beijing as well as I do. Always some new wrinkle up their embroidered red silk sleeves. It's that abominable situation in the South China Sea, I'm afraid."

"Heating up?"

"Boiling over."

Hawke's rum arrived. He took a sip of it and said, "What now, sir? Don't tell me the Reds have blockaded one of the world's busiest trade routes?"

"No, no, not yet anyway. It may come to that. Still, simply outrageous behavior. First, they unilaterally extend their territorial claims in the South China Sea hundreds of miles south and east from their most southerly province of Hainan. All done with zero regard for international maritime law, of course. And now they have established a no-fly zone over a huge U-shaped sea area that overlaps parts of Vietnam, the Malay Peninsula, the Philippines, Taiwan, and Brunei."

"Good Lord. And with what possible justification?"

"Beijing says its right to the area comes from two thousand years of history, when the Paracel and Spratly island chains were regarded as integral parts of the Chinese nation. Vietnam says, rightly, that both island chains lie entirely within its territory. That it has actively ruled over both chains since the seventeenth century and has the documents to prove it."

A flash of anger flared in Hawke's eyes.

"Bastards have created a flashpoint as dangerous as the Iranians and the Strait of Hormuz, haven't they? Clearly global conflict implications."

"Spot-on. And now they've begun insisting that every aircraft transiting these formerly wide-open routes must first ask permission of the Chinese government. Including U.S. and Royal Navy flights. Outrageous. We will not, bloody hell, ask them permission for any such thing! Nor will anyone else, I can guarantee you that."

"The result?"

"It's all a ruse to provoke a reaction. The new-generation Chinese warrior is a fervent nationalist, with militaristic veins bulging with pride. And, the Chinese are, as we speak, using their North Korean stooges to probe and prod at our will to prevail in this region, both at sea and in the air. I mean, you've got NK coastal patrols 'bumping' into the Yank's Seventh Fleet in the night, near collisions with Royal Navy vessels, that sort of thing, spoiling for a fight. The North Koreans, of course, know China will back them up in a showdown."

"An extremely dangerous game."

"To say the very least."

"And the Western countermove?"

"It gets tricky. Under President Tom McCloskey's strong leadership, the United States is taking a very hard line with China. The U.S. Navy is dramatically increasing its naval presence in the region, of course. The Seventh Fleet is en route to the Straits of Taiwan. And they've deployed U.S. Marines to Darwin, on the western coast of Australia. Meanwhile, our own PM, in a weak moment, actually had an extraordinary idea."

"He did?"

"I know, I know, no one believes it was actually his original notion, but that's the official story coming out of Number Ten Downing."

"What's his extraordinary thought?"

"He suggests the allies consider a massive convoy, Alex. Warships from the Royal Navy, Japan, Taiwan, the Philippines, Vietnam, and the Yanks with an entire carrier battle group, the USS *Theodore Roosevelt*, along with seven or eight other countries. Full steam ahead right up their bloody arses and we'll see what they bloody do about it, won't we?"

C laughed and drained his drink.

"Well, for starters," Hawke said, "the Chinese may elect to take out a massive U.S. carrier with one of their new advanced killer satellites the CIA was describing to our deputy directors and section heads just last week. It's not beyond the realm of plausibility."

"Hmm, the life of a country squire has not completely numbed your frontal lobe capacity. But you're right. That is a consideration, Alex. At any rate, right now, the prime minister's notion is only a good idea. Hardly a done deal, as they say."

"Why?"

"Simple. A few pantywaists in the U.S. Congress are thus far unwilling to go along with the PM's scheme for fear of losing one of their big billion-dollar float babies. So, alas, our convoy scheme is paralyzed at the moment. But, look, we're not going to sit around on our arses and let this stand. No, not for one blasted moment!"

"What are we going to do about it, sir?"

"You mean, what are you going to do about it, dear boy. That's why I'm springing for lunch."

"Ah, yes, of course. No free lunch, as they say."

"Damn right. Never has been. Not in this man's navy, at any rate."

"How can I help, sir? I've been sitting on the sidelines for far too long. I've got grass and flowers growing up through the soles of my shoes."

C looked around to establish whether anyone was within earshot. The aural perimeter thus secured, he said, "We at Six have established a back-channel communication with a high-ranking Chinese naval officer. Three-star admiral, in fact. Someone with a working brain in his head. Someone who does not want go to war over his own government's deliberate and insane maritime provocations any more than we do."

Hawke leaned forward. The hook, having been set, now drew him nigh to the old master.

"This sounds good."

"It is. Very."

"Congratulations, sir."

"What makes you think this one is mine, Alex?"

"A wild guess."

"Well. Nevertheless."

"So," Hawke said, "the Chinese are well aware that they cannot possibly afford to go to war with the West now. In a decade? Perhaps. But not now. They haven't got the bottle for it. And, moreover, they haven't got the arsenal."

"Of course not. According to our chaps on both sides of the pond, they are at least five to ten years behind the

West in terms of advanced weaponry. And I mean both in the air and on the sea. No, it's an obvious political ploy, albeit an extremely dangerous one."

"To what end?"

"Simple. They wish to divert attention away from their burgeoning internal domestic turmoil, particularly Tibet, and the daily insanity run rampant in their 'client state,' North Korea. Thus this bellicose show of force. Show the peasant population and the increasingly restive middle class just how big, bad, and powerful the new boys are."

"Sheer insanity."

"Our world and welcome to it. But you, and I do mean you, Alex Hawke, with a little help from me, are going to put a stop to it. Even if it's only a stopgap, temporary measure. I intend to buy us some time for diplomacy or other stratagems."

"Tell me how, sir."

"Operation Pacifist. Clever, eh? You'll be reporting solely to me on this. Any information is strictly need-to-know. I have arranged a secret rendezvous for you. You will be meeting with a high-ranking Chinese admiral, whose name is Tsang, on a small island in a remote quadrant of the South China Sea. An uninhabited bit of paradise known as Xiachuan Island. Tsang wants to talk about a way he sees out of this extraordinarily dangerous confrontation with the West. Then it will become a matter of whether or not we can get the PM and Washington to go along with whatever proposals you come home with."

"Why me?"

"Security. He said any meeting with our side had to be conducted in absolute secrecy, for obvious reasons, and that he wanted a completely untraceable contact. In a remote location known only to him and me. Together we selected Xiachuan Island. Completely deserted for years. It was home to a World War II Japanese air force base, but abandoned because of Japan's current territorial dispute with China."

"How does one visit this island paradise?"

"One flies. There is a serviceable eight-thousand-foot airstrip there that should accommodate you nicely."

"What kind of bus shall I be driving?"

"An American F-35C Lightning. One of ours. Especially modified for nighttime insertions. All the latest offensive and defensive goodies, I assure you. Kinetic energy weapons and all that. The sort of thing you enjoy."

"Lovely airplane. Always wanted another crack at one."

"Well, my boy, you'll get one. First thing tomorrow morning, in fact. I've already cleared your calendar.

You'll report at seven to Lakenheath RAF. Three days of intensive flight training in the Lightning with a USAF chief instructor off your wingtip. Courtesy of CIA and President McCloskey's White House. Then off you go into the wild blue yonder."

"Aye-aye, sir. I think McCloskey has shown rather a lot of courage in this Chinese showdown. He's a hard-liner and just what we need at present. I just hope he keeps his wits about him. These are dangerous waters we're entering, full of political mines and razor-sharp shoals."

"Indeed. The mainstream American press is hounding the president relentlessly, aren't they? Look at his poll numbers. He just needs to stand his ground against this senseless Chinese and North Korean bullying."

"Hmm. One thing if I may. This admiral, how high ranking is he, exactly? I mean to say, is he powerful enough to actually defuse this latest crisis?"

"High enough. He is the Chinese chief of naval operations."

Hawke smiled. "Start at the top and work your way up. Isn't that what you've always told me?"

"Indeed."

"And how much of a gratuity am I going to be transporting to the good admiral in return for all this assistance in defusing the global crisis from the inside?"

"One hundred million pounds sterling. Cash. In a lockbox you'll carry in the cockpit with you."

Hawke whistled and said, "That's all?"

"If you succeed, it's worth every shilling. Now, let's order some lunch and talk of more pleasant things. I understand our mutual friend, Ambrose Congreve, is to be wed next Christmas. I assume you're to be best man?"

"Well . . . to be honest, I don't really know. I would assume so. But I haven't heard from him on the subject."

"Didn't mean to step into that one."

"Not at all. Perhaps they've called the whole thing off and he simply hasn't the heart to tell me."

Sir David picked up his menu and began to study it intently.

"Well. You will find an obsessively complete dossier on Operation Pacifist waiting for you when you get home to Hawkesmoor. Motorcycle courier just dropping it off with Pelham now. Memorize it and burn it. Now, then, Alex, what will you be having for lunch?"

"Not sure, sir. What looks expensive?"

Chapter 5

The White House

President Tom McCloskey stared at the live feed from the East China Sea. He was, he knew in some secret part of him, in a state of shock. Hell, all of them were in shock—McCloskey himself; his close friend since Annapolis, Vice President David Rosow; his beautiful new and wildly popular secretary of state, Kim Oakley Case; the always reliable secretary of defense, Anson Beard; and the chairman of the Joint Chiefs, Charlie Moore.

And all the rest of the crisis team; every one of them had been staring at the Situation Room screens for over an hour.

What they were seeing up there was real-time terror. Innocent American lives were being threatened half a world away, and there was not one damn thing he or anybody else in the White House or over at State, CIA, or the Pentagon could do about it. Not one damn thing.

"Shit," he whispered under his breath. "Shit."

China and her increasingly bellicose surrogate, North Korea, as of forty-eight hours ago, were staging joint naval war games in the East China Sea. North Korea had made a big show of it for the press, trotting out their latest warships. According to his most recent CIA naval intelligence briefing, and some help from British intelligence, it was clear that China had long been planning to use the North Korean navy as a pawn in this little game of their own. Test American resolve.

But how?

Nobody at CIA, State, the Pentagon, or any other intelligence agency had prepared him for this. This was a goddamn nightmare, and it couldn't have come at a worse time. The whole country was coming unglued over a few inadvertent remarks he'd made at the G7 summit in Prague the week before. Jesus Christ. The media, no friends of his in the run-up to the damn election, were all over him for a couple of misstatements he'd made to Putin about China.

The joint press event was over and done with and he'd assumed the mikes were dead. Reasonable assumption.

They weren't.

What he'd said was innocent enough. The once-powerful Putin, now increasingly in danger of becoming China's bitch, was playing hardball with the United States over China's currency manipulations. And McCloskey hadn't come this far to be backed into a corner by the Russian's trumped-up tough-guy act, and he was planning to draw a line in the sand and call the Russian's bluff. But he wasn't going to tell Putin that, no sir. He was going to sow a few seeds of disinformation and let the Kremlin show its cards. His own wife had told him what a shrewd idea it was, f'crissakes.

So what he said to the Russian was "Prime Minister, just give me a little wiggle room here. Just enough to get through the All-Asia Conference next month. After that, I can show a lot more flexibility. Trust me."

And for that, a few offhand comments taken completely out of context, he was paying a steep price. Using up a lot of political capital to hold his fragile coalition together. Had the Senate whip and the Speaker of the House breathing down his neck, wanting him to issue a clarifying statement.

Hell, he had Tom Friedman and the *New York Times* questioning his fitness for office. The *Washington Post*! The *Post* ran a goddamn editorial in the most recent Sunday edition headlined "Is He Losing It?" Well, so be it. Politics at this level was a game for those who could take the heat, stay in the kitchen, and keep their heads in the fucking oven.

And now this!

At 0441 hours GMT, a North Korean fast-attack warship had deliberately rammed and disabled a small and lightly armed U.S. Navy surveillance vessel now taking on water in the disputed international region of the East China Sea. It was a moonless night, there was fog, but there was no conceivable excuse for the USN captain's behavior.

In a state of relatively minor duress, he had folded his cards and surrendered his vessel to the North Koreans, for God's sake. Was the U.S. skipper insane?

The U.S. boat was CIA, of course, but the captain of the North Korean vessel didn't know that. All he knew was that his claim of territorial incursion and his demand to board (backed up by overwhelming fire-power) had been granted by the U.S. skipper.

Now, the president of the United States and his team watched as four young able-bodied American seamen, bound and blindfolded, were kneeling side by side with their backs against a steel bulkhead on the foredeck of their vessel.

The American skipper and his crew were being held at gunpoint up on the bridge. God knew what was going up there, McCloskey thought, feeling a sense of impotent rage come close to overwhelming him.

An oddly tall and lean Korean officer was screaming at the four captives, bending down, getting right up into their faces.

"What's that bastard saying?" McCloskey said to the State Department translator.

He told him.

"Son of a bitch," the president muttered.

"He's got a gun!" someone at the table said.

The NK navy officer stepped in front of one of the Americans and stuck a large black automatic pistol up under his chin. The officer was red-faced and screaming at the sailor now, venting all his pent-up hatred and anger on the helpless sailor.

Everyone in the room saw the blindfolded youth working his mouth and knew instantly what would happen next.

"Don't do it, boy!" General Charles Moore, chairman of the Joint Chiefs said to the screen. "Don't give that bastard any excuse, son! None, no way, never."

"Oh, Christ," McCloskey said, "no, no, no."

The sailor spat, catching the hysterical officer square in the face.

The Korean officer recoiled in anger, using the sleeve of his uniform to wipe away the saliva.

He suddenly raised his arm and drove the pistol into the sailor's face, smashing his nose into a red pulp.

"Sonofabitch!" the president said, leaning forward, his face twisted in anger.

Further enraged by the sight of blood, the North Korean officer put the barrel of his automatic between the young American's eyes . . . and pulled the trigger.

The dead sailor slumped forward, facedown on the cold wet deck.

"Tell me I'm not seeing this," the president said, unable to tear his eyes away from the screen.

"He's going to execute all four," General Moore said in a steady voice that sounded oddly detached.

And, as they all watched in abject horror, that is exactly what he did. Head shots, at close range.

A pin could drop.

"Turn that damn thing off," the president said.

"Off, Mr. President?"

"Isn't that what I just said?"

An ashen-faced aide made a throat-cutting motion, and the monitors all went black at once.

"That's better, isn't it?" McCloskey said, propping his polished cowboy boots on an empty chair and firing up a Marlboro.

No one said a word.

"It's a bitch, ain't it?" the president said to no one in particular. "Four of our boys dead. The goddamn NKs in possession of one of our CIA shit-buckets chock-full of classified information. Damn it to hell. Somebody give me a good reason not to turn North Korea into a goddamn NK-Mart parking lot. China, too, if they dick around with our navy anymore. I'm serious. I'll tell you all one thing. I'd like to know what Admiral Wainwright has to say about all this. Tony? What the hell am I going to do now?"

A palpable pall of shocked silence hung over the room.

"Tony?" the president repeated, swiveling around, searching all the faces in the room.

Finally, someone had the guts to speak up. Secretary of State Kim Case, which surprised no one.

"Mr. President?" the slim, attractive blonde said.

"Yeah, Kim, what is it?"

"Admiral Wainwright is dead, sir. He died in the terrorist attack on the *Dreadnought* in Tripoli last May."

The president was very quiet for a long time before he looked up, staring at the secretary, his face a stone mask.

"I know that, Kim. What I said was, I'd like to know what he thought. And I would like to know that, I really would. But he's dead. Isn't he?"

"Yes, Mr. President. He is."

A stunned silence descended.

No one said a word. What more was there to say?

Emily Young, the president's lovely young personal secretary, could be heard sobbing quietly in dark corner of the room. Emily didn't think she could take much more of this. She loved the old cowboy. Actually was in love with him. It killed her to see the boss like this, a wounded stag. And all of them, the press, with their goddamn knives out . . . and, like a mule in a hailstorm, he just had to stand there and take it.

She heard the president say, "Emily, for crissakes, will you stop bawling? What the hell is wrong with everybody?"

There was no answer.

The president stood, looked around at all the upturned faces, and said, "Well, thank you everyone. We'll reconvene in one hour."

After they filed out, he sat back down again, gazing absently into the middle distance, smoking his Marlboro down to a bright orange coal. He'd never felt so lost and alone in his life.

The White House sous-chef looked beat.

It was almost midnight on a Friday night and, for Chef Tommy Chow, it had already been a very long week. First thing Monday morning, Matt Lauer and the whole damn *Today* show crew had shown up early for a live broadcast and wanted breakfast. Then the lavish state dinner for the prime minister of England, the Rose Garden luncheon the First Lady held annually for the Daughters of the American Revolution, and on and on, no rest for the weary.

And now he'd gotten a last-minute call from the ranking West Wing staffer saying the president had invited a few of his closest cabinet members for an impromptu breakfast in the morning. Talk about China and North Korea, Tommy imagined. Hell, that's all they ever talked about lately.

"Go home, Tommy," one of his guys said. "You look exhausted. We can finish the prep by ourselves."

"No. I insist. You guys head out. I promised the boss man I'd take care of this breakfast thing and I'm going to do it. Seriously, get the hell out of here and go home to your families, okay? I got no family. Not here in Washington anyway. Leave the graveyard shift to me. Okay?"

"You got it, boss. Have it your way," the pastry chef said, and they all bolted for the exits.

Chow waited until the last one had left before he began prepping tomorrow's cabinet breakfast. Huevos rancheros, the presidential favorite, home fries, frijoles refritos with melted Monterey Jack, rashers of bacon and jalapeño-flavored sausage patties, honey biscuits, and hot sauce. Tex-Mex, they called it. Hardly his idea of haute cuisine, but they didn't care for that much upstairs anymore.

A rueful smile flitted across Chow's face as he stirred what he privately referred to as his "secret sauce" into the president's eggs.

The graveyard shift, he mouthed silently.

Truer words would never be spoken.

Not in this White House, anyway.

Chapter 6

South China Sea

A loud, keening wail suddenly filled the Lightning's cockpit. Holy mother of God, Hawke thought, he'd just been painted by enemy radar!

He whipped his head around and saw the Chinese SAM missile's fiery flame signature streaking up toward his Lightning, dead on his six, homing in on the afterburner. By the speed of the incoming, he guessed it to be one of the newer Hong Qi 61s. Where the hell had it come from? Some kind of new Chinese radar-proof shore battery on a nearby atoll? None of his so-called sophisticated gadgetry had even picked the damn thing up!

He hauled back on the stick and instantly initiated a vertical climb, standing the Lightning on its tail and rocketing skyward like something launched from Canaveral in the good old days. He deployed chaff aft and switched on all the jamming devices located in the airplane's tail section. He was almost instantly at forty thousand feet and climbing, his eyes locked on the missile track displayed on his radar and thermal imaging screens. Its unverified speed, Hawke knew, was Mach 3.

It was closing fast.

The deadly little bastard blew right through his chaff field without a single degree of deviation. The Chinese weapon was not behaving in accordance with MI6 and CIA assessments of their military capability. With every passing second, his appointment with imminent death went from possible to probable. He'd have to depend on the Lightning's jamming devices and his own evasive maneuvers if he was going to survive this attack.

He nosed the F-35C over and put it into a screaming vertical dive. He was now gaining precious seconds. The Hong Qi would now have to recalculate the target, alter course, and get on his six again. He'd known from the instant the SAM missile appeared on his screen that there was only one maneuver that stood any chance at all of saving him.

A crash dive.

Straight down into the sea.

Hairy, but sometimes effective, Hawke knew from long experience. To succeed, he had to allow the deadly missile to get extraordinarily close to impacting and destroying his aircraft. So close that when he pulled out of the dive at the last possible instant, the nose of his airplane would be so near the water's surface that the missile would have zero time to correct before it hit the water at Mach 3, vaporizing on impact.

"You've got to dip your nose in the water, son," an old flight instructor had told him once about the maneuver. "That's the only way."

The missile had now nosed over in a perfect simulation of Hawke's maneuver and homed in on the diving jet. He watched it closing at a ridiculous rate of speed.

His instruments and screeching alarms were all telling him he was clearly out of his bloody mind. The deeply ingrained human instinct to run, to change course and evade, clawed around the edges of his conscious mind. But Hawke had the warrior's ability to erect a firewall around it, one that was impenetrable in times like this.

It was those few precious white-hot moments precisely like this one that Alex Hawke lived for. At his squalling birth, his father had declared him "a boy born with a heart for any fate." And, like his father and grandfather before him, he was all warrior, right down to the quick, and he was bloody good at it. His focus at this critical moment, fueled by adrenaline, was borderline supernatural . . . his altimeter display screen was a jarring blur, but he didn't see it; the collision-avoidance alarms were howling in his headphones, but he didn't hear them. His grip on the stick was featherlight, his breathing calm and measured, his hands bone-dry and surgeon steady.

His mind was now quietly calculating the differential between the seconds remaining until the missile impacted the Lightning and the seconds until the aircraft impacted the sea. Ignoring everything, the wail of the screeching sirens and the flashing electronic warnings, the pilot began his final mental countdown.

The surface of the sea raced up at him at a dizzying rate . . .

Five . . . four . . . three . . . two . . .

NOW!

He hauled back on the stick.

The nose literally splashed coming up, and he saw beads of seawater racing across the exterior of his canopy. He'd caught the crest of a wave pulling out of the dive . . . He felt the G forces building . . .

You got to dip your nose in the water, son.

Made it.

He barely registered the impact of the missile hitting the water over the roar of his afterburners. But he heard it, all right. He was in the clear and initiating a climb out as he visualized it: the SAM vaporizing upon contact with the concrete hard surface of the sea at such speed . . .

The G forces were fierce. He began his quick climb back to his former below-the-radar altitude.

And that's when his starboard wingtip caught a huge cresting wave that sent his aircraft spinning out of control. Where the hell had that come from . . . He was suddenly skimming over the sea like a winged Frisbee. He felt a series of severe jolts as the fuselage made contact, and he instinctively understood that the aircraft was seconds away from disintegrating right out from under his doomed arse . . .

He reached down to his right and grabbed the red handle, yanked it, and the canopy exploded upward into the airstream and disappeared. The set of rocket motors beneath his seat instantly propelled him up and out of the spinning cockpit and straight into the black night sky.

Seconds later, his primary chute deployed and he had a bird's-eye view of his airplane as it metamorphosed into varying sizes and shapes of scrap metal and disappeared beneath the waves.

Along with the five hundred million in the lockbox, he thought. Not only had his mission just gone straight to hell, it was a very bloody expensive failure.

He yanked the cord that disengaged him from his seat and watched it fall away as he floated down. Moments later his boots hit the water. It was cold as hell, but he started shedding gear as quickly as he could. He was unhurt, or it seemed that way, and he started treading water while his life jacket inflated. *So far, so good,* he thought, managing to keep his spirits aloft surprisingly well for a downed airman all alone in this dark world.

Normally, there'd be an EPIRB attached to his shoulder harness. Upon contact with the water, it would immediately begin broadcasting his GPS coordinates to a passing friendly satellite. Normally, he could just hang out for a while here in the South China Sea and wait for one of Her Majesty's Navy rescue choppers to come pluck him from the soup and winch him aboard. Normally. But, of course, this was a secret transit and he had no distress radio beacon, no EPIRB. He had exactly nothing.

He knew the water temperature was cold enough to kill him eventually. The thermal bodysuit he wore would stave off hypothermia long enough for him to have a slim shot at survival.

He spun his suspended body through 360 degrees. Nothing of note popped out of the darkness. No lights on the horizon, no silver planes in the sky. Nada, zip, zero. Nothing but the vastness of black stretching away in all directions . . . no EPIRB equals NO hope of immediate rescue. He was some fifty miles off the southern coast of mainland China.

If he was lucky, and he usually was, he was in a shipping channel. If not, sayonara. He looked at his dive watch, whistling a chirrupy tune about sunshine and lollypops. Five hours minimum to sunrise.

He began to whistle a song his father had taught him for use at times like this.

Nothing to do but hang here in frozen limbo and wait to see what happens next.

And maybe pray a little.

Chapter 7

The White House

"It's the president," the First Lady said, gripping the phone so tightly her knuckles shone bone white through her pink skin. "I can't seem to wake him up."

"Is he breathing?"

"Yes, I—I think so. His chest is moving."

"Don't worry. We're on our way up now. The whole team. Stay calm," Ken Beer, the White House physician, said, and the line went dead.

"Tom," she said, shaking him by the shoulders. "Tom, wake up, damn it!"

Nothing.

Had he taken something? She scoured the bedroom and medicine cabinet for empty vials. Nothing. She'd seen him depressed before, but the mood swings were getting terrifying lately. Still, suicide? No. Out of the question. He would never do that. Too narcissistic. Far too invested in his place in history and his date with destiny, the showdown with China coming up in Hong Kong next month.

It had been two days since the disastrous meeting in the Situation Room. The entire household was abuzz with rumors about what had really happened in there. Her assistants and household spies were reporting back to her with everything they were picking up. He was drunk. He was stoned on meds. He was losing his marbles. He wasn't fit to be president. *60 Minutes* was doing a segment called "The Incredible Vanishing President." He was sick. It was dangerous. He had early-onset Alzheimer's just like Ronnie Reagan. They had to rally round him. They had to protect him . . .

Blah-blah-blah.

And then her reverie was broken as the private quarters was suddenly full of people. Secret Service, medical techs with defibrillators, portable EKGs, and God knows what all. Ken Beer was running the show, which was good; she'd had total confidence in him since that incident aboard *Air Force One* the year before.

She tried to read something into Ken's expression, but he had his game face on. All business. He had taken her aside after his initial examination and asked her if she wanted a lorazepam. She'd refused, but wondered if maybe she needed one. He looked so . . . gone . . . lying there, all the IV tubes and EKG wires taped to his chest and—

"Okay," Ken said, taking her by the arm and walking her quickly into the sitting room where they could speak privately. "Here's the deal. His vitals are good. Strong. But he's in a coma. I don't think it's a stroke. No coronary issues. I'm having blood work done right now, but I don't want to wait for it. You with me?"

"Keep talking."

"Right. He's going to Walter Reed right now. Okay? That's the best thing for him. The safest, most conservative option. I've already called it in."

"Is he going to come out of it? The coma?"

"Qualified answer? Yes. He's going to come out of it. Listen. Don't you worry. We'll take good care of him. Do you want to ride in the ambulance with him?"

"Of course I do, Ken. Do you even have to ask me that?"

"Sorry. My mistake. The president's already on his way down to the South Portico. Let's go."

Tommy Chow met his U.S. handler at the Capital Grille for drinks the afternoon the president was admitted to Walter Reed Hospital. The Grille was a mecca for secretaries, staffers, lobbyists, and bureaucrats of every stripe and strata in D.C. Tommy knew one of the Chinese waiters, a guy who always made sure they got a quiet table in the back. Even if they were noticed, and it was very unlikely, a low-level staffer from State and a noncelebrity chef from 1600 having a martini or three wouldn't cause anyone's radar to light up.

"Is he dead yet, T?" George, his State Department friend, whispered to him after they'd finished one drink. George (he never used his last name) was tall and thin, with brown hair parted neatly down the middle. He had thick black eyebrows over a large straight nose, thin lips, and a receding chin. He was always nattily dressed in a three-piece Brooks Brothers suit, preppy striped bow tie. Somebody named Tucker Carlson was his fashion muse, he'd once told Tommy Chow. Tucker who?

George, ex-military, and a semi big shot at State, had one of those thin fake smiles that made you hate him instantly. He had a degree in aeronautics from Stanford and a law degree from Yale. He was also one of those guys who truly believed he was always the smartest guy in the room.

The kind of guy who usually got caught. Which was fine with Tommy, as long as he didn't take Tommy Chow down with him.

"CNN is now saying he's still fading in the ICU. Matter of hours. True? Or false?" George said with a fake quizzical expression.

"No. You know damn well he's not dying."

"So. False information. Bad, Wolf Blitzer, bad, bad, bad. Snow White's poisoned jalapeño pie didn't do the trick, huh, little Tommy? C'mon. Let's take a little stroll around the nation's capital."

"It's raining, George."

"Yeah. It does that. Man up, little buddy. You need to get out more."

Chow paid the check as always and they left the noisy Grille, now filling up with good-looking girls who'd all come to Washington from the provinces, looking for a job but down on their knees praying every night for a lobbyist or even a senator or two.

Chow was silent for the first few blocks. Now they had sought shelter under the trees near the reflecting pool. No one around.

Chow was saying, "Shit. I just don't know what happened. After the navy taster had approved the president's tray, I stirred enough bad mushroom puree into that meat sauce to kill both of us."

"Maybe it's your sense of proportion. We know you want to do this slowly and methodically. Diluted to a degree where there'd be no forensic trace. But time is running out. McCloskey is the most hawkish man to occupy the Oval Office since Reagan. He wants his Gorbachev 'tear down that wall' moment with Beijing and he wants it before he leaves office."

"Ah, the all-important legacy," Tommy muttered.

George said, "Look, McCloskey is scheduled to make a major policy statement at the All-Asia Conference in Hong Kong next month. That speech will set the tone for America's position vis-à-vis China for the balance of his term. My people think McCloskey wants an excuse for a showdown with Beijing. So you need to act. Sooner rather than later."

"Okay, fine, sooner. Just give me some time."

"As long as you understand our friends have zero desire to see this president's face at the All-Asia Conference in Hong Kong. It's next month, for God's sake, T. They want their mandate executed. As they put it. The operative word in that sentence being 'executed.' Got it?"

"You think that's news to me? You think I haven't been trying? What is this? You want me discovered?

There are mechanisms in place to protect him, navy culinary experts watching the entire kitchen staff. These are people who know the fucking difference between murder and bad shellfish, George. Is that what you want? I don't think so. Fingers pointing at me? I'm a fucking Chinese national, remember? High on the list of likely suspects? You think?"

"I think I've got news for you, my friend. Our Mandarin friends grow impatient. They want this over. Not now, but right now."

"Listen. What the hell am I supposed to do? He's in goddamn Walter Reed Hospital. Surrounded by his Secret Service agents. He's untouchable. Shit."

"Listen to me. You're a goddamn Te-Wu assassin. First in your class at the Xinbu Te-Wu Academy. That's why you got this assignment. Just do what you have to do."

"I will. When and if he gets out of ICU and recovers and comes home, I'll make sure he doesn't just get another really bad case of food poisoning. Trust me. Until next time, okay?"

"No."

"What do you mean, 'No'?"

"Not good enough, my friend. This op is only a small fragment of a far, far bigger picture. The Mandarins are . . . complicated. And the Chinese military's hatred for this goddamn country is reaching a feverish pitch. Someone's got his blood up, and that someone is General Moon."

"Yes, I know. General Moon and his grand plan. Spring Dawn and all that happy horseshit. What is it? When is it? Who the hell knows? I'm just a hired hand in the kitchen."

"Not at all, T. Your reputation and skills are deeply respected. It's just that, here, you have no need to know more. You have your mission, I have mine. Accomplish yours so I can do mine. Now. Understand?"

"Oh, I do, believe me."

"At any rate, we like this guy, Vice President Rosow. The veep seems a far more reasonable fellow than the POTUS. Amenable, let's say. You know, philosophically and politically speaking. We can work with him, is what they think. They want Rosow at that Hong Kong conference. Moreover, and more important, they want Rosow in the Oval, Tommy. ASAP. It took a very long time to get you in position down in that damn kitchen. Now it's time to act. ASAP."

"Don't be an idiot."

"What?"

"No one says ASAP anymore. It's embarrassing."

"Really, Chow? In that case, I'll put it in a phrase even you can understand . . . chop-chop!"

"Does the expression 'go fuck yourself' have any meaning for you, George? That's a question."

"Tommy. Listen to me, you stupid sonofabitch. The world clock is ticking down, little man. Tick-tock. They want this done. Take him out. You've got until noon Friday. That's what they said."

"How the hell am I supposed to get to him when he's propped up in bed over at Walter Reed? Surrounded by Secret Service. I can't fucking do it. And you damn well know it."

It was starting to rain more heavily, a hard cold rain. Unlike his friend, Tommy Chow had no umbrella. The tall, thin State Department man stepped into the street and started trying to hail a taxi, talking to Tommy out of the side of his mouth.

"Not my problem. Thanks for the cocktails, pal. Keep in touch. Oh. Your family back home in sunny Beijing? The PLA guy I work for? He says I'm supposed to tell you they're doing great. Living the good life. Make sure you keep it that way."

"You asshole."

"Yeah. Like you. I fit right in at State that way. Being an asshole, I learned early, is the perfect credential for an aspiring politician who's for sale. Oh, look. Here's my cab. See you around, T. And don't forget what I said."

He climbed inside the taxi, collapsing his umbrella as he did. As he pulled the door closed, he heard Chow's voice calling.

"Forget what?" the round little man said over the heavy rain.

The thin man stuck his head out the window, smiled, and said, "ASAP."

Chow turned and walked back to the scant cover of the trees. What he really wanted to do was walk away from the whole thing. Catch a cab to Reagan and board the next thing smoking for Bermuda. He had a bad feeling about this. He had no assurances he'd survive no matter which way this went. He was going to be an inconvenient man when it was over. He should run. Brazil, Argentina. Find a job in a good restaurant and start over. To hell with Beijing and whatever new political catastrophe they were planning . . . he could run.

And then he saw the floating faces of his wife and child. His mother.

And he started walking back to the White House in the pouring rain.

After a while, his step got lighter. He started to smile as the beginnings of the idea took on shape and substance.

A few moments later, Tommy Chow had a plan.

————

As soon as he got back to his apartment in Chevy Chase he'd call his handler in England on his encrypted sat phone. She'd help him figure out the details. Once the deed was done, he'd need a lot of cash and a method to get out of the United States and back to his old apartment in London in a hurry. How?

Chyna Moon would make certain arrangements for his speedy exit from the scene of this assassination. After the dust had cleared a bit, he'd make his way home from London, back through Hong Kong and Shanghai to Xinbu Island. Back to his beloved Te-Wu Academy. And start training for the next mission.

Georgie Porgie, that arrogant dickhead, would find out who had the brains around here soon enough.

ASAP.

Chapter 8

Near Chongjin, North Korea
Present Day

She could feel a thousand eyes upon her, and she knew not one of them shone with pity.

Kat Chase walked, stumbled, and was dragged relentlessly toward the killing ground. Her torn camp shift was ragged and bloody from the beating she'd received upon waking. When they bored of routine torture, they dragged her kicking and screaming from the cell. She knew where they were taking her. Had accepted finally that, after years of hell in a North Korean labor camp, finally, this was the end.

There was to be no heroic last-minute rescue. No white knights in black helicopters. No. And no U.S.

Cavalry at dawn, fast-roping down from the sky to save her.

The guards, who stank of fried peppers and onions, screamed at her incessantly, telling her to stop dragging her feet. She was so emotionally numb she barely registered the fists pummeling the crown of her head. She thought her nose may have been broken. It was easier not to even try to breathe through it, so she breathed through her mouth.

There were sharp stones underfoot. Her shoes had disintegrated months ago, and her bloody feet were bound with filthy rags that offered no protection. It was very near dawn, and countless torches flared in the darkness at the bottom of the hill. She could see the heaving black range of mountains rearing up on the far horizon, the sky turning a faint pink beyond them.

Her last sunrise.

At least she could take refuge in the notion that she wasn't going to hell. She was already there.

Through her tears of rage and frustration Kat could see all she needed to see: three guards were pounding a stout wooden stake into the hard stony earth. It was a wheat field, lying high near the edge of a cliff top a few hundred feet above the banks of the Yalu River. The river that marked the border with China.

A large group of ragged, emaciated but excited prisoners had gathered in a semicircle, perhaps a thousand or more, all come to witness the execution. It was a rare treat for the inmates of hell.

The camp commandant's idea of a class play.

The labor camp laws, the "Ten Commandments" laid down by "Babyface" as Kat had come to call the chubby, sadistic, cherubic commandant, forbade any assembly of more than two prisoners. This commandment was waived only for certain festive occasions like this one. Attendance was mandatory. Public killings in the labor camp and the fear they generated were considered teachable moments. Murder for the sake of the public good. She'd been in the audience many times before. Cheering and laughing lest she be shot on the spot.

Now she was the center attraction. The doomed star of the production. And a Caucasian to boot. This was a rare moment not to be missed.

As she drew near the rough-hewn post where she would die, she could hear the despicable little man in charge of the event warming up the crowd.

"This prisoner," he shouted, "this stupid woman about to die, has been offered redemption through hard labor by our dear commandant. But she has proven unworthy of his offer of mercy. She has rejected even the benevolence of our Dear Leader and the great generosity of his North Korean government . . ."

He went on in that vein, but she had stopped listening. She was determined to focus her last thoughts elsewhere. Her husband, William, whom she had loved upon first sight. Her two children, Milo and Sarah, whom she adored beyond measure. In the beginning, in the first few months, they'd allowed her regular contact with them. In the later years, none at all. She had no idea if either of her kids were still alive. Much less her husband.

Since the night long ago, the night of her goddamn fortieth birthday, when they'd all been snatched off that foggy street in Georgetown, she really knew nothing of her family. Since they'd been bundled into a black van by Chinese thugs, drugged, and secreted out of the country . . . her family had ceased to exist for her.

She'd see pictures of the two children, every so often, grainy black-and-whites, shot in a camp that very well could have been this one. They did that, she supposed, kept Milo and Sarah alive, only to force compliance with their demands. The pictures were almost worse than nothing. She hardly recognized her children anymore. Thin, hollow-eyed ghosts . . .

A few years ago, she'd managed to steal a picture of Bill from a desktop while she was being interrogated.

No idea when it had been taken, but he had more grey hair than the night they'd been abducted. His stomach more paunch than washboard.

He stood out on the deck of an aircraft carrier at sea, demonstrating something or other, surrounded by Chinese naval officers who were laughing at something he'd said. She'd lost fifty pounds. But Bill hadn't changed. If anything, he looked healthier than when he'd been working himself to death back home in Washington.

A thought so horrible it made her sick came unbidden into her mind.

Had her husband defected to China? Had he known about the black limo waiting outside the restaurant the night of her birthday? The van?

She shoved the notion aside for the delusions caused by malnutrition, physical and psychological abuse, and the simple paranoid insanity that it was. And then she blessed her beloved family, each one of them, one at a time, in her heart, and said her final good-byes.

She was tied to the stake, her arms and feet bound behind her. One of the guards pried her jaws apart while another stuffed her mouth full of pebbles from the Yalu River. This was in the revered tradition of preventing the condemned from cursing the state that was about to take her life.

Her head was covered with a filthy burlap sack that still stunk of rotted hay and the human feces they used for manure in the fields . . .

Kathleen Chase had spent the last eleven months of her five-year imprisonment in a space reserved for the lowest of the low. An underground prison within the prison. Her stinking windowless room with no table, no chair, no toilet. This was her "punishment" for refusing to admit to her crimes against the state. Admit that she was an American spy. An agent for the CIA come to sow discredit on the government and engineer revolution against the Dear Leader.

The underground prisons were built to blindfold the prying eyes of American satellites. But not hers. She'd kept her eyes open just in case she ever managed to escape. She memorized the guards who tormented her, their names, their faces, their habits.

She'd learned that for all the prisoners publicly executed in these prisons each year, thousands more were simply tortured to death or secretly murdered by guards in the underground facility where she lived. Rape was a given at any time of day or night. Most prisoners were simply worked to death. Mining coal, farming, sewing military uniforms, or making cement.

All the while subsisting on a near-starvation diet of watery corn soup, sour cabbage, and salt.

Issued a set of clothes once a year, prisoners worked and slept in filthy rags. There was no soap in her cell, no socks, no gloves, underclothes, or even toilet paper. Twelve- to fifteen-hour days were mandatory until death.

Over time, if they live long enough, prisoners lose their teeth, their gums turn black, their bones weaken. All this by the age of forty, and none had a life expectancy beyond the age of fifty.

In December, she would turn forty-five . . .

She felt the rough hands all over her body. The guards getting in one last good feel, squeezing her breasts painfully. Then she was alone at the stake. She heard their boots clomping away from her. She heard the low keening noise of the crowd beginning to reach a fevered pitch.

She took a deep breath, knowing it was her last. Finally at peace, she waited for an eternity or more for the lead slugs to pierce her flesh and find her heart.

She heard the guard captain scream the order to fire.

Fire!

Fire!

Fire!

The crowd saw her head pitch forward, her chin on her chest. A roar went up. Deafening.

But there had been no blood, no twitching corpse riddled with bullets. They'd all fired above her head. She'd heard the rounds whistle above her. She had simply fainted.

This was not the first mock execution the joyous crowd of prisoners had witnessed. They'd seen hundreds. And so they knew the appropriate response. They laughed. Wildly and insanely, letting the guards know they were in on the joke, that they appreciated the entertainment.

"Write the letter!" her tormentor screamed at her. She was back in the basement in a private room on the lowest level of hell. Kang was in rare form today, practically frothing at the mouth. He was the only one who spoke enough English to be trusted with interrogation of such a prize as the valuable American woman Kathleen Chase.

"You write! Tell your husband what happened this morning. About our Dear Leader's beneficence in sparing your life. His mercy. Tell him about your good health. About how well you are being treated here, you and your children. Hot food, good beds. If not—"

"Show me my children, damn you! Show them to me!"

"Your children are alive, we keep telling you. But they will die if you do not obey. They will watch you die before we decapitate them. They will suffer before— tell him. You write the letter now!"

"You write it, Kang. Sign it, too. And then go fuck yourself."

"Bitch!" he screamed. The he raised his fist and slammed it down, the ballpoint pen in his grip piercing her hand, nailing it to the wooden table.

She howled in pain, unable to stop it, but her cries were no longer enough for him. He started slapping her viciously across the face, whipping her head around until she thought she'd pass out again . . .

She no longer believed her two children were alive. She had not seen them in so very long . . .

She had only one hope now.

That next time, the bullets would not miss.

Chapter 9

South China Sea

Hawke didn't have to wait long.

One second all was calm, the next he felt the rippled pressure of sudden underwater movement.

He waited for what always came next.

A soft nudge in the small of his back. No pain, just the tentative probing of some large fish. Exactly just what kind of fish it might be was not a question he preferred to speculate about. But the words just wouldn't go away.

The bad one was *snout*. That's what the nudge had felt like.

Then, a minute later, there was the really bad one. *Shark.*

No mistaking it.

Minutes later, another punishing blow.

Christ. A jarring slam to the rib cage on his right side. A second later, he saw the shark's dorsal fin knifing toward him maybe two seconds before it hit him. Sharp pain now, it hurt like a bastard. Broken ribs in there for sure. He turned slowly in the water, minimizing his movements.

Even in the pitch-black darkness, he could see the dorsal fins circling lazily around him. What did they say about curiosity? Oh, yeah, curiosity killed the pilot. Right now, they weren't in dining mode. Right now they were only curious about this new object in the neighborhood. He took a deep breath, winced at the resulting pain, and let it all out slowly.

This could go either way.

They could get bored with him and just disappear.

Or, the other way, they could shred him into several bite-sized chunks, ripping away his limbs first before fighting over his torso. Staying positive in adverse conditions was one of his main strengths, so that's what he did right now.

The fact that more dorsals were appearing and encircling him, and the fact that his body was suspended, hanging there helplessly in the frigid water, well, that made it tough to stay cheery.

But Alex Hawke, it had to be said, was nothing if not one tough customer.

He closed his eyes and immobilized his body, forcing himself to concentrate on all the good things in his life. His cherished son, named Alexei by his Russian mother, now just four years old. He saw him now, running through the patches of dappled sunlight on the green meadow in Hyde Park. The child's guardian, Nell, was chasing him, laughing. Nell was more than a nanny. She was Hawke's much-loved woman. Something of a legend at Scotland Yard, and in truth, Alexei's bodyguard, Nell had saved the child's life on more than one occasion. Because of Hawke's recent activities in Russia, his son had been targeted by the KGB.

One of his deepest fears was creeping around the edges of his conscious thought. The fear that this night he was leaving his son without a father. Or even a mother. It had happened to him at age seven . . . no other pain can compare.

An hour passed. A very long hour.

For whatever reason, the roll of the dice, God's infinite mercy perhaps, the toothy beasts had left him alone, at least for the moment. Cold had begun to claw its way inside his protective armor. He was shaking now, and his teeth were chattering away, much ado about bloody nothing. It crossed his mind that freezing to death was a far, far better way to go than serving himself up as a midnight snack for the finny denizens of the deep.

He slept, God only knew how long.

And then the lights came on.

Literally.

He found himself the target of a shaft of pure white light. He looked up to his left and saw its source. A searchlight mounted high on the superstructure of a massive ship of some kind. Then another light snapped on, and another and another. Each one picking him out from a different angle.

This must be what it feels like to be some kind of star, he thought, and, cheered that he still had a shred of his sense of humor left, he smiled to himself.

And then he became aware of the deep bass thumping of helicopter rotor blades, above and to the right. He saw the hovering black shadow come closer until it was right above him. An LED spotlight in the chopper's bay winked on and picked him out.

A diver appeared, standing in the bay and looking down at him.

Could this possibly be a friendly? The odds were certainly against it, given China's recent military posturing in this cozy little corner of the world. But, still, if this had to be bad, he'd take China over North Korea in a heartbeat. The NK troops were merciless automatons who brutalized and killed anything that moved.

The diver stepped out into the air and dropped.

He splashed down about ten feet away, surfaced, and started speaking to Hawke in Mandarin Chinese. His hopes for a miracle vanished, but still, it was better than the other option. Hawke spoke enough Mandarin to know he was being told to remain calm and he did. The swimmer approached and began securing the lifting harness to Hawke's semifrozen body.

Hawke had spent a lot of time in China with his friend and companion Ambrose Congreve, the famous Scotland Yard criminalist. In addition to being a brilliant detective, Ambrose had studied languages at Cambridge. While doing a six-month stint in a Shanghai hoosegow for "subversive activities" that had never been proven, Congreve had given Hawke a basic, working knowledge of Chinese.

"In the nick of time," Hawke said to his savior in his native tongue.

"What?"

"You arrived just in time. I was slowly freezing to death."

"Silence. No conversation, please."

"Have it your way. Just trying to be friendly."

Hawke and the rescuer were winched up and into the belly of the Chinese Changhe Z-8. He lay on his back, shivering. No one aboard would talk to him. He was quite sure they knew about the unidentified aircraft that had entered their airspace and been "shot down" by one of their SAMs. So they were sensibly predisposed not to be chatty. Hell with them—he was still alive, wasn't he? He'd managed to avoid being eaten alive, had he not? Truth was, he'd gotten out of tougher scrapes than this one over the years.

Once the chopper was airborne, he got another surprise. The mammoth floating Good Samaritan, the ship that had stumbled across the downed pilot by the sheerest of luck? It was a bloody carrier! When the chopper set down on the aft deck, he saw, to his utter amazement, an advanced Chinese fighter jet, which was the spitting image of one he'd seen in a meeting at the Pentagon just two years earlier. Code-named "Critter" because of all its spindly appendages, it never went into full production because of government "cost cutting" as the White House chose to describe it.

And now there was a whole flock of the damn things out here in the South China Sea under cover of darkness.

Whatever lay ahead, the spy knew he'd hit the espionage equivalent of the jackpot.

Chapter 10

The initial interrogation aboard the Chinese aircraft carrier was short but brutal. Hawke gave up nothing, and he had gotten out of it with little more than a severely wounded left knee, a few broken ribs, a black eye, three broken fingers, and a concussion. The leg was the worst. Two gorillas had tried to break it by pulling it backward. The attempt failed, but they'd managed to snap a tendon or two. He could walk, but not far.

When they got bored with him, they told him he'd never leave the ship alive, then locked him up inside a stinking crew cabin in the bowels of the bilge with room for little more than a crappy bunk bed.

He now lay on the top berth thinking very seriously about how the hell to escape before these bastards came for him again. Tortured and killed him.

Two military policemen with automatic weapons had delivered him to this charming boudoir. He was fairly certain the same two would come for him when it was time for the more labor-intensive interrogation. They were merely thugs, those two, viciously abusive, but stupid. Just the way he liked them. He'd feigned a far worse concussion than he'd actually suffered, forcing them to half carry him down many flights of steel stairs, something they bitched about all the way down.

At one point they threw him to the deck and took turns kicking at his already damaged rib cage with their steel-toed boots. He'd passed out from the pain.

He was consciously unconscious when they returned. They slammed into the tiny space and manhandled him down from the upper bunk. As he expected, they yanked him to his feet and wrapped his arms around each of their shoulders in order to keep him moving.

He kept his head down, chin bouncing on his chest, mumbling incoherently. When the goon on the left paused to kick open the half-closed door, Hawke took advantage of the moment. His powerful arms reached out with all the speed and precision of two striking cobras as he swept the two men's heads together with sickening force. The collision of the two skulls was sufficiently forceful to cause the two men to drop like sacks of stones to the floor.

He dropped to one knee and checked.

They were dead.

"Hit them too hard," he whispered to himself.

He fished the keys to his handcuffs from one of their pockets and freed his wrists. Then he quickly stripped the uniform from the taller of the two. It fit him badly, but it might be good enough to get him safely up eight flights of metal steps to the carrier's flight deck without hindrance.

Hawke had jet-black hair, which helped, and he kept the military police cap brim pulled down over his eyes, and his face lowered. He also had the advantage of having a fully automatic rifle slung over his shoulder in case things suddenly got spicy.

He raced up as fast as he could without calling undue attention to himself.

A sailor opened a hatch in the bulkhead just as he mounted the last set of steps. He felt a cold blast of icy wind howl in from the flight deck. He waited a full sixty seconds before stepping through the hatch and out onto the flight deck.

He had no earthly idea how he was going to execute the plan he'd devised lying in his bunk, waiting to be tortured again and probably killed. The fact that he didn't know was of little concern. You had to be able to make this stuff up as you went along. He heard laughter and saw a sizable group of men approaching his position.

He retreated and quickly stepped inside the nearest open hatchway. And suddenly found himself inside a large hangar amidships on the flight deck. Unusual, to say the least. Hangars on carriers were always belowdecks. He moved back deeper into the shadows.

A huge shrouded object loomed up in the dim overhead lights.

What the hell?

There was just enough light to see. He'd already formed a pretty good idea of what lay beneath the cover before he began tugging the tarp away.

The thing took his breath away.

It was the Sorcerer!

Either the supersecret American fighter/bomber itself, or a perfect facsimile of it, the Sorcerer was a massive, bat-winged, unmanned drone. Half again as large as his F-35C Lightning, and clearly equipped not only for surveillance, but for offensive aerial combat. Slung beneath the sleek, swept-back wings, six very lethal-looking missiles, three to a side.

And, under the fuselage, a bomb the size of which he'd never seen before. A huge bunker-buster? God forbid, a nuke?

A carrier-based drone of this size would be capable of delivering massive devastation from extremely high altitudes from anywhere on the planet. It immediately occurred to him that his entire perception of the world playing field had just altered. If he could e-mail a photo of this thing back home, it would lift Langley off its foundations.

China had somehow managed to leapfrog ahead of the West in terms of military technology and hardware. He knew the U.S. Navy was contemplating a future that included carrier-based drones for combat and delivering nuclear warheads, but China was already there!

How? How in God's name had they managed it?

He heard laughter outside on the deck and rushed back to the open hatchway. He paused, calmed his racing heart, and peered out onto the deck.

Pilots.

There were eight of them, all in flight suits. Some had already donned their red-starred helmets, some were carrying them in their hands. All were kidding around, walking with that unmistakable and cocky jet-jock walk.

Their destination was obvious, Hawke thought. They were crossing the wide expanse of darkened deck, en route to the covey of eight highly advanced fighter jets parked near the starboard bow catapult.

Fighters like the one Hawke had seen when the rescue chopper landed on the deck the night before. The pilots would have to pass directly in front of his position.

They represented his only hope of survival.

Hawke remained hidden in the shadows of a massive drone hangar directly beneath the carrier's bridge looming above him. As the pilots approached, their banter continuing, Hawke stood stock-still and held his breath until the last Chinese fighter pilot was safely past him.

Hawke then stepped out of the shadows and fell in behind the lone straggler at the rear. Fortunately for him, this pilot was by far the tallest of the lot. He approached his target directly from behind, matching him stride for stride. When he was perhaps a foot behind the pilot, he shot out both hands, and used pressure from both thumbs on the carotid artery to paralyze the poor chap and yet still keep him on his feet.

Giving the main body of hotshots sufficient time to move on, he then quickly withdrew, walking the unconscious man back into the shadows of an AA battery. It was the work of a moment to zip himself inside the pilot's flight suit, don his boots and helmet, and, finally, flip the dark visor down. He then strode quickly, but not too quickly, across the deck, rapidly catching up with the jocular pilots just as they were climbing up into their respective fighters.

He made a beeline straight for the sole unoccupied fighter jet, saluting the two attending deck crewmen who stood aside for him to mount the cockpit ladder.

"Lovely night for flying, boys," he muttered in his guttural Chinese, sliding down into the seat and adjusting his safety harness. After strapping himself in, he reached forward and flipped the switch that lowered the canopy. He then took a long moment to study the instrument array and myriad illuminated controls, quickly deciding exactly what did what.

Looking at the array of aircraft instruments, Hawke was astonished for the second time since arriving up on the carrier's flight deck.

Most of the cockpit controls on the fighter looked oddly familiar. Why? Because they were almost identical to those in the prototype of the top-secret new American fighter jet he had flown, the J-2. He was amused (in one way) to see that the Chinese had stolen so much advanced aeronautical technology from the West that getting the hang of basic things here in the cockpit was embarrassingly easy.

But he had flown the first-generation F-35C Lightning off the USN's *George Washington*'s flight deck courtesy of Captain Garry White and the

U.S. Navy. And this Chinese airplane? It was vastly more sophisticated in terms of avionics, communications, and, most important, offensive and defensive weapons systems. Holy God, compared to the current F-35C, this thing was like something from another goddamn planet.

Take the cookies when they're passed, he thought, smiling.

Due to unforeseeable circumstances, a top British intelligence officer was about to take one of what had to be, up until this moment, China's most closely guarded military secrets for a little airborne test drive!

Chapter 11

Hawke gave the internationally required hand signal to the crewmen on deck below and flicked the switch that lit the candle. The sudden engine roar behind him was instant and powerful. He added power and taxied into position behind the last jet in line. The blast shield had already risen from the deck behind the lead jet in the squadron, and Hawke watched calmly as the fighter was catapulted out over the ocean, after-burners glowing white hot.

A wave of pain in his rib cage washed over him and he must have passed out because he suddenly heard the air boss screaming in his headset, telling him to get his ass moving. The aircraft directly in front of him had advanced into position and he'd not followed quickly enough for the air boss. Now he added a touch of power and tucked in where he belonged. There remained only three fighters on the deck ahead of him.

He focused for a second on what to say and how to say it. He not only had to get the Chinese right, the words, but also had to get the attitude right, a slangy mixture of swagger and humble obeisance to the air boss gods on high.

"So sorry, boss," he muttered in the time-honored traditional communicative style of fighter pilots all over the world. For a carrier pilot, the air boss is God himself.

"Don't let it happen again, Passionflower, or I'll kick your sugarcoated ass off this boat and clear back to Shanghai."

"Roger that, sir," Hawke said, advancing a few feet forward.

"You forget something in your preflight, Passionflower?"

"No, sir," Hawke said, starting to sweat a bit.

"Yeah? Check your goddamn nav lights off-on switch for me, will you? Just humor me."

Shit, he thought, flicking the nav lights switch. He'd actually forgotten to turn his bloody nav lights on! Dumb mistake, and he could not afford to be dumb at this point, not in the slightest.

"You awake down there, boy? I'm inclined to pull your ass right out of the lineup."

"Sir, no, sir! I'm good to go."

"You damn well better be. I've got my eye on you now, honey. You screw up even a little bit on this morning's mission and your ass is mine. You believe me?"

"Sir, I always believe you. Sir. But I'll come back clean, I swear it."

"Damn right you will. Now, you get the hell off my boat, Passionflower. I got more important things to deal with up here than to worry about little pissant pilots like you. Taxi into position. You're up."

Hawke throttled up and engaged the catapult hook inside the track buried in the deck. He heard the blast shield rumbling up into place behind him and looked to his left. He nodded his head, a signal to the launch chief that his aircraft was poised and ready. The chief raised his right arm and dropped it, meaning any second now.

Hawke's right hand immediately went to what fighter jocks fondly call the "oh-shit bar." It was located just inside the canopy and above the instrument display. The reason for the handhold is simple: when a pilot is violently launched into space, the gut reaction is to grab the control stick and try to climb. It's terrifying to feel out of control when the plane's wheels separate from the mother ship. In the tiny amount of time it takes a pilot to move his or her right hand from the oh-shit bar to the joystick, a nanosecond, the catapult has done its job and the pilot can safely assume control of the aircraft.

Adrenaline was pumping, flooding Hawke's veins as he gripped the bar with his right hand. A "cat shot" from a modern carrier is as close as any human being can come to the experience of being in a catastrophic automobile crash and surviving. It was that intense.

The cat fired and he was thrown violently backward, leaving the leading edge of the deck.

He stifled an intense scream of pain at the back of his throat.

He was airborne.

He craned his head around and looked back down at the deck lights of *Varyag*, the carrier growing rapidly smaller as he swiftly gained altitude. He deliberately suppressed any feelings of joy over having escaped an agonizing death at the hands of the most sophisticated torturers on the planet.

He wasn't out of the woods yet, he told himself as he climbed upward to form up with "his" squadron's flight. Their heading was a WNW course that would take them directly over the disputed Paracel Islands. Exactly the wrong direction, in other words. He needed to be on a heading north-northeast and he needed to get moving.

The rim of the earth was edged in violent pink as Hawke slipped into his designated slot at the rear of the tight formation. The squadron leader acknowledged his arrival and went quiet. There was a minimum of radio chat for which he was grateful. There was normally a lot of banter at this stage and he didn't want to hear any questions or inside wisecracks over the radio, things he couldn't respond to without sacrificing his cover.

He needed precious time to remain anonymous until he could figure out the next step of the plan he'd hatched in those few hours he spent alone and in pain. Namely, how the hell to get away from the squadron without a dogfight. A dogfight that would pit him against seven of China's top guns was a bad bet.

If he simply peeled off and made a run for it, and didn't respond to radio calls, the squadron leader would immediately radio the carrier and report what was going on. One of their pilots was behaving very strangely. It wouldn't take a second for the Chinese carrier skipper to put two and two together: the missing American pilot had somehow gotten inside one of their fighters. He was about to steal it. Blow him out of the sky.

The Chinese would then use the incident as clearcut proof the West was being deliberately provocative.

Instead of preventing a confrontation, Hawke would now be the cause of it. C, to put it mildly, would not be pleased.

They would trot out his blackened corpse and the twisted remnants of the stolen fighter jet on global TV. Use his actions to justify an even more aggressive posture in the region. Take retaliatory measures against Taiwan, Japan, Vietnam.

Next step, war.

That's how he saw it anyway. C might disagree. But C wasn't sitting in the hot seat with his ass on the line.

For the moment, he had little choice.

He flew on, maintaining his slot in the formation, flying north toward the Pacific Ocean, desperately searching for a means of escape for the second time in twelve hours.

Half an hour later, battling pain and fatigue, it came to him. It was so simple. The only reason he had not thought of it sooner was the pain of his injuries and mental fatigue. But, he thought, it just might work.

He thumbed the transmit button on his radio.

"Flight Leader, Flight Leader, this is, uh, Passionflower, over."

"Roger, Passionflower, this is Red Flight Leader. Go ahead, over."

"Experiencing mechanical difficulties, Red Flight Leader. System malfunctions, over."

"State your situation."

"I'm flying hot, sir. Engine overheat. Power loss. Cause unknown. Running override systems checks now. Doesn't look good."

"Are you declaring an emergency?"

"Negative, negative. I think I can throttle back and make it home to mother. Request permission to mission abort and return to the carrier, sir. Over."

"Uh, roger that, Passionflower. Permission to abort. Get back safely. Over."

"Roger that, Red Flight Leader. Returning to the *Varyag*, over."

Hawke peeled away from the formation, banked hard right, and went into a steep diving turn away from his flight. The sun was up now, just a sliver above the far horizon, red light streaking across the sea far below. He looked up and saw Red Flight's multiple contrails emblazoned across the dawn.

When Red Flight was completely out of visual and radar range, he corrected course to NNE and throttled up. He leveled off at 40,000 feet and took stock of his situation. By his calculations, he could reach his destination in under two hours.

He set a heading for South Korea and stepped on the gas.

His plan was simple.

Contact Kunsan Air Base in South Korea. Home of the American Eighth Fighter Wing, Thirty-Fifth Fighter Squadron, and the Eightieth Fighter Squadron. Tell them exactly who he was, identify his J-2 Chinese fighter, and beg them not to shoot him down. Land. Refuel. Contact C from a secure phone at the base commander's office and tell him his lockbox containing a few million quid were gone to the bottom of the South China Sea. Admiral Tsang would just have to wait.

But he was coming back to England's Lakenheath RAF base with one or two little surprises that might just be worth more than the contents of the lost lockbox.

Infinitely more.

Chapter 12

Washington, D.C.

"Happy birthday, darling!" the First Lady trilled. She swept into his darkened hospital room hidden behind an enormous arrangement of peonies in her favorite shade of pink. She went to the tall windows, threw open the curtains, and cleared a space for the flowers on a dresser top. Watery sunlight flooded the president's room. She considered a moment, then placed the large cut crystal vase overflowing with pink peonies where it would look best.

"What do you think? I arranged them myself."

"Beautiful, honey," the president said, glancing up at her from his slew of binders and briefing papers. "Thanks."

She looked over at him and smiled. A real smile. *Not like the old ones,* he thought, the ones that could barely mask the fear and the pity in her eyes. The ones that confirmed his own darkest nightmares and worst imaginings.

That he was dying.

"How do you feel, birthday boy?"

"Like a million bucks, baby."

"In Confederate bills?" she said, repeating an old joke between them.

"Hell, no. Bona fide U.S. greenbacks, backed by the full faith and credit of the United States government. Namely, me. Not bad for a seventy-year-old coot, sugar."

"Attaboy! You go get 'em, cowboy. There's a new sheriff in town and he's kicking ass and walking tall."

Tom McCloskey laced his fingers behind his head, leaned back against his pillows, and beamed at his lovely wife. She was wearing the sky blue Chanel suit he'd bought her on rue du Faubourg Saint-Honoré in Paris. With the halo of sunlight touching her auburn hair, she looked like an angel. Which, in his humble opinion, she truly was.

He really did feel good, damn it.

In fact, he had made a remarkable recovery since his arrival at Walter Reed Hospital. He was alert, cogent, rational, and in amazingly good humor. His eyes were clear, his skin was radiant. Whatever had been bothering him these last few months, the docs here at Walter Reed were taking care of it. Now he had one overpowering obsession. He was itching to get out of here and get the hell back to work.

The world was blowing up out there. With a lot of help from China and a little added push from North Korea, war was brewing in the Pacific. The Brits had told him they had a three-star admiral in China who'd refused the Kool-Aid. This top naval-ops guy was going to "retard the process." But so far? He hadn't seen dick.

The Middle East, as usual, was on fire. At home, too many people were out of work. The stock market was rocketing toward twenty thousand, and yet the economy still sucked the big one. And he was one of the few people on earth with balls of sufficient size and the power to fix it.

Just last night he'd done a fifteen-minute live bedside interview with Bret Baier, the evening anchor from Fox News. Hard questions, no softballs, that was Bret. China, Japan, Iran, Putin's massive war games. The recent bellicosity of the crazy North Koreans, their threat to nuke Hawaii. And he'd knocked every damn one of Bret's questions out of the park. Short, concise, cogent answers, backed up with an impressive understanding of the details underlying each issue.

Bret was the former White House chief correspondent, incredibly savvy and a hell of a nice guy. All-American kid, just the way he liked them. Clean-cut, he looked like he could have been on the White House Secret Service staff. People had been calling all morning to wish him happy birthday and report that the "Twitter-verse" was abuzz with news of the president's miraculous comeback. The *New York Post,* they said, was running a front-page photo of him smiling from his bed. They'd Photoshopped a white ten-gallon Stetson on his head. The headline underneath, they said, was "The Comeback Kid!" The copy would talk about how he had his health back, was itching to get back in the saddle, and would be riding tall when he did.

There was a commotion out in the hall, and Mary Taliaferro, one of his favorite nurses, stuck her pretty red head inside the door.

"Mr. President? Just wait till you see what all has shown up out here at the nurses' station. My gosh, you just won't believe it!"

McCloskey laughed and looked at his wife.

"All right, Bonnie, what's this all about? You know I don't like surprises."

"Oh, honey, you know I wouldn't do that. Would I?"

She crossed the room, trying to keep the smile off her face, and pulled it open.

"Oh my goodness, look who's here!"

"Who?" the president said, sitting up and straining to see over her shoulder. "Oh, my Lord, look at that!"

The first thing through the door was a massive four-tier birthday cake. It was on a rolling table, and they wheeled it right up to his bedside. It was decorated to look like his old homestead in Colorado, the Silvermine Ranch. Miniature ranch house on top, stables, paddocks, and two little figures on horseback that looked like Bonnie and him. Even the old blue Scrambler jeep he used to get around the property. Every tier was covered with tall green fir trees, cowboys, and cattle, a tiny version of everything he cherished on this earth.

"Well, boys," he said to the two smiling young Filipino White House waiters, "you guys have outdone yourselves this time. That cake is flat-out beautiful. That big black stallion there even looks just like my own El Alamein."

"Thank you, Mr. President," one of the waiters said. "We are all very proud of it. The entire kitchen and waitstaff has asked me to wish a most joyous and happy birthday . . . and a speedy recovery."

The president starting clapping, and everyone joined in the applause.

His wife bent and kissed his forehead.

"Happy birthday, you big hunk," she whispered in his ear. "You come on home and get your cute little butt back in my bed, okay?"

There was a knock at the door. She smiled, straightened up, and motioned to one of the young Secret Service guys standing just inside the door.

And the next thing he knew, his favorite country singer in the whole world walked through his door. The vice president, the White House chief of staff, and Ken Beer, his personal physician, walked in, followed by about a dozen nurses all crowded inside around his bed. All of them were grinning from ear to ear.

"You've got to be kidding me," the president said.

Damned if it wasn't Bonnie Raitt herself.

Dressed in full cowgirl regalia, Bonnie smiled at him as she walked over to his bedside and she took his hand. She sang, "Happy birthday to you, happy birthday, Mr. President," and proceeded to sing by far the best rendition of "Happy Birthday" he'd ever heard. When she finished, the room erupted into cheers and wild applause once more.

The president's eyes filled with tears.

"Miss Raitt," he said, "I'm going to tell you something. Until this moment, I thought the best version of that song had been sung by Marilyn Monroe to Jack Kennedy at Madison Square Garden. But you know what, you're not only a lot prettier than Marilyn, you're one helluva lot better singer."

Bonnie smiled, put her hands on her hips, and said, "Mr. President? Let's give 'em something to talk about."

And she bent over him and kissed him full on the lips.

Everyone in the room erupted into loud, heartfelt laughter.

"Wow. What a birthday," he said, beaming at his wife. "You are something else, honey. Thank you so much. This means the world to me."

"Let's cut the cake!" she cried.

The younger of the two waiters handed the president a silver cake knife.

The president looked at his cake, beaming. "I don't want to ruin it. Can somebody take a picture first?"

His wife got out her iPhone, started snapping shots, and said, "Go on, darling, cut the cake. You get the first bite."

He eyed one of the horses first, but said, "I never cared much for horsemeat," popping a frosted chunk into his mouth. "I'll eat the jeep."

And those were the very last words the forty-fifth president of the United States ever said.

The president's head fell forward on his chest.

Ken Beer, his face stricken, pushed his way through the crowd around the bed and bent over the unconscious president.

The president's heart had stopped.

"Nurse!" Ken yelled. "Cardiac arrest! Get the bed down flat. Check his pulse!"

"Ken, what is it?" the First Lady cried, her face a mask of horror. "What's wrong with him?"

The physician plucked a piece of uneaten frosting from the cake, held it under his nose, and sniffed it.

"It's that fucking cake," Ken Beer said, staring at the monitor, which had flatlined. "Damn it! Get the crash cart in here now! There's no cardiac output. Intubate him and start CPR immediately. Who's the head nurse in here? Get all these people out of here."

The Secret Service agent in charge got on his radio, "Rawhide is down! White House to lockdown. Secure the entire kitchen staff immediately. Nobody moves."

An older nurse stepped forward and ordered everyone out of the room except the Secret Service, nurses, doctors, and Ken Beer. "And somebody bag that cake in a HAZMAT container. It's lethal."

Half an hour later, the nurse's compressions on the president's chest ceased.

They all stared at the monitor, and Ken Beer took the president's pulse again.

He ordered shock pads. He ordered one milligram of atropine injected. He did everything he could.

"The patient is asystolic," Ken said, profound sadness inscribed all over his face. "Flatlined. No cardiac output . . ."

The nurses waited. The First Lady had her back to the scene, facing the windows and her peonies. She was visibly shaking. When she heard Ken's voice, she started sobbing silently.

"Okay. Let's call it," he said.

The president's wife looked at his profile, her heart full of regret for all the steps and missteps that had brought them so full of hope and promise to this place and time.

Thomas Winthrop McCloskey, the forty-fifth president of the United States of America, was dead.

Murdered in his own goddamned hospital bed.

"Let's give 'em something to talk about," Bonnie Raitt had said minutes ago.

Within hours, the whole world would be talking.

Chapter 13

Xinbu Island, China

It was a school for assassins.

The Te-Wu Academy, a massive square, windowless ten-story block of pure white marble, was located on Xinbu Island in a remote region of the South China Sea. An underground railway connected the building with two other massive installations. One, a submarine base, was built right on the sea. The other, the Weapons Design Center, was built near the base of the mountain range.

The high-end resort known as Xinbu had been built for China's military and political elite, and only the highest-ranking members of the CCP, the Chinese Communist Party, even knew of its existence.

Xinbu had been built on an artificial reef. The hotels, vacation resorts, and apartment buildings along the northern coast provided a convenient cover for things the men in Beijing would rather the world not see.

The prying eyes of America's spy satellites were useless here.

Xinbu Island was in fact home to some of China's most closely guarded military secrets. Most prominent was the newest one, an ultra-top-secret subterranean submarine pen. Its very existence was known only to General Sun-Yat Moon, the men who had built it, and a handful of Moon's allies, all of whom were among the most powerful men in China, both in the military and the government.

Moon had ordered Xinbu Naval Station built to provide a deep underwater entrance that ensured absolute secrecy. Here, a whole new generation of radically advanced nuclear submarines now came and went without drawing the attention of satellites passing overhead or any two-eyed, two-legged spies lurking about on the surface ships of the sea.

Moon's new fleet of undersea monsters, known as Centurions, were the key to his plan for China's rapidly approaching world dominance. The Centurions, which he had named, would play a vital role in the coming drama. The general was an ardent worshipper at the throne of Caesar and his mighty legions. He had code-named his project in honor of Caesar's commanders, those warriors who were, as Caesar said, "first over the wall and first through the breach."

The Roman centurions.

And General Moon had chosen his project team brilliantly.

Under Moon's supervision, the Centurion Submariner Project had been conceived, designed, and executed by one extraordinary man. A scientific genius who, for five long years, had lived and worked deep within China's massive military complex.

His home was an office and a small room on the top floor of Xinbu's new Advanced Weapons Design facility. It had taken nearly three years to bring his vision to reality. And, surprisingly enough, the key to the enormous power of the Centurion Project was not complexity. It was simplicity itself.

The man behind this startling new concept in submarine design was none other than the legendary American scientist and Nobel laureate, Dr. William Lincoln Chase.

In order to keep himself and his family alive, and to ensure their ultimate freedom, Chase had agreed to a significant challenge coming directly from General Moon. To completely reimagine submarine warfare in the twenty-first century. The result was the futuristic four-hundred-foot Centurion-class nuclear sub. Here, wholly unbeknownst to the world's intelligence community, was a weapon so powerful and so advanced, it was already demonstrably capable of changing the worldwide balance of military power dramatically in China's favor.

In addition to the new Centurion Naval Base, Xinbu Island was home to the notorious Te-Wu Academy, created by General Sun-Yat Moon. Te-Wu was both a school and training ground for the world's best assassins. Here, only the hardest of the hard and the very brightest and best of the thousands of applicants were admitted each year. Sadly, many didn't survive the harsh training process. They were identified by numbers, not names. A towering wall inside the Academy was dedicated to those numbers who had paid the ultimate price.

The Academy was one of the Chinese government's best kept secrets. Graduates of the Academy, the best-trained political assassins in the world, had, for decades, been dispersed throughout the world to carry out special executions for the MSS, or China's Ministry of State Security.

But the very best of these men and women never left Xinbu Island. They remained in place and had the honor to provide maximum security for General Moon himself and the secret military base that he commanded.

The Te-Wu "Headmaster," as he is traditionally called by students (in English, oddly enough), was perhaps the most feared man in Asia. And, for certain, he was the second most powerful man in China. If he achieved his vision, and if the gods smiled on him, he would soon become the single most powerful man in China. And, soon thereafter, perhaps, the world.

His name was General Sun-Yat Moon.

To meet him, a person would never know that the polished, dashing, and urbane gentleman was someone capable of unspeakable cruelty. A deceptively kind-looking man, the general had recently suffered a stroke, which had partially immobilized his face. To his delight, the stroke left him more feared than ever. A dangerous man with a beatific smile—and a seraphic countenance.

He was tall for a Chinese gentleman, well over six feet. His thick head of longish hair was dead straight, brilliantined to a gleaming blue-black. A thick comma of it was arranged artfully on his forehead, and his perfectly smooth skin was the familiar shade of flat light yellow. His startling eyes, pewter grey, were hooded and thickly lashed.

He kept his origins secret, but he seemed a northern type. Tibetan, some people thought, or perhaps Manchurian. Moon was lean and well muscled, someone who took extremely good care of himself. A martial arts expert, he was also a crack shot and the onetime national fencing champion of China. Educated abroad, he studied history and political science at Magdalene College, Cambridge. Even now, when he spoke English, he did so in a clipped Oxbridge accent that many in his circles found either perplexing or, privately, amusing.

Moon had fought his way up through the military and political ranks, his rise as inexorable as a waxing tide. A seasoned battlefield commander, he had presided over the slaughter of thousands of demonstrating students in Tiananmen Square in 1989. A vicious hardline Communist, Moon had been deputy chief of the much-feared Special Activities Committee of the PLA, the People's Liberation Army of China. Known even in Beijing for his extremist ideological stands, he had been in operational command of more than a million Chinese storm troopers.

Fast-forward and multiply the numbers under his command by a factor of five. And now his battle commanders presided over a new kind of army. These twenty-first-century warriors had cast off the old ways. They were fiercely nationalistic and full of fight.

They were warriors of the old school in a new century and Moon was just the powerful, good-looking, charismatic man to lead them.

One of his many responsibilities as chief of the MSS (China's secret police force) was the Te-Wu Academy he had founded on Xinbu Island. He ruled there the way he ruled the MSS. With an iron fist encased in steel mail. He was known for his brutality and reveled in it. The Te-Wu secret police graduates who moved out into the far reaches of the world seldom forgot where their sworn allegiances lay. Or how important to the homeland was the successful fulfillment of their sworn duty to the service.

And to General Moon and his capricious turns of mood. The slightest trespass could lead to a slap on the wrist. Or instant execution. Usually hanging, sometimes decapitation.

If Moon was angry, and wished to make an example of a subordinate, his beheading was videotaped and DVDs of the grisly execution were sent to his surviving family members. The final shot was always the same. A grinning General Moon, holding the victim's bloody severed head aloft for a close-up.

Moon lived and traveled in great secrecy. His primary residence was not the luxurious mountaintop compound on the island. He lived in Hong Kong aboard a vast floating palace amid the tumult and turmoil of Kowloon Harbor. Hong Kong had been his birthplace and he felt an almost gravitational pull to that place.

He had raised his three daughters there: the twins— a serving Te-Wu officer named Jet, and Li, who had been killed—and then there was the baby of the family, Chyna. Chyna Moon, trained in the shadow arts since birth, had climbed far and fast through the ranks of the MSS, graduating at the top of her class from her father's Te-Wu Academy before attending Cambridge University in England.

The trained assassin was now a full professor, a don, at the seven-hundred-year-old university. She was also a full colonel in the MSS Secret Police, living and working undercover in Great Britain at her father's old alma mater. She was running a small cadre of assassins in the United Kingdom as well as the United States. Moon's youngest daughter was his pride and joy and he trusted her, and her alone, with the most sensitive assignments.

He had not a doubt in his mind that one day Chyna Moon would rule all China in his stead. She would rule with an iron fist.

The glorious beginning of what history would long remember as the "Moon Dynasty" was the general's most cherished dream.

Chapter 14

Chyna's portrait, in a monogrammed silver Cartier frame, now stood on the vast polished walnut desk that dominated his office at the Academy. Moon reached for one of the phones and spoke to his personal assistant, Li, who, like the two armed guards on either side of the door, was related to the general. He liked, for security reasons, to fill such positions with family members.

"Has Dr. Chase arrived?" he purred. "Good. Please have him shown in, won't you?"

While he waited, he flipped through the Chase dossier his assistant had pulled for him. Recent photos of the man's wife and children caused his eyes to dilate. Hollow-eyed ghosts wandering through the hellish death camps in North Korea. Skin and bone, all three of them. The decision to send them there had been Moon's alone, and it had been a wise one.

Moon was all but certain that, one day, the Americans, the CIA or the SEALs, would come looking for Dr. Chase and his family. A long time ago he had decided that if Chase and his family were separated, if the man's wife and children were imprisoned in North Korea, well, that would make it just that much more difficult for the Americans to—

"Dr. Chase to see you, General," a voice on his intercom said.

"Show him inside, please."

The intricately carved double doors opened silently and Bill Chase entered the vast, sunlit office blinking his eyes. Chase was dressed in the loose white clothing used for tae kwon do, having just competed in an Academy competition. His face and clothing were wet with perspiration, and Moon pulled a linen handkerchief from his breast pocket and handed it to the American.

"Ah, the good doctor himself, returned from the field of battle."

Moon spoke English. To his hostage, he sounded like an Old Etonian, which, in fact, he was.

"You're in a disgustingly good humor this morning," Chase said, wearily, collapsing into a wide leather chair. He'd been up all night working on new arming and disarming codes for the Centurion missile launch system. He was utterly exhausted, as usual. He worked twelve hours a day at his desk, another six in his rooms every night. He had to. His life, and the lives of his wife and children, depended on it.

"With good reason," Moon said expansively. "One of my former star pupils, an early graduate of my Academy, executed a rather delicate mission in Washington yesterday. Extremely delicate, you see. But I had no doubt Colonel Chow would succeed. The Te-Wu Academy has much to be proud of this day."

Chase said, "Bravo. Let me guess. You finally pulled the trigger. Your archenemy, President McCloskey, is dead. Congratulations. Now you can blow up the whole fucking world without nearly as much fear of retaliation."

"True enough, Dr. Chase, true enough."

Moon, a self-satisfied expression on his face, rocked his chair back and put his boots up on his monumental teak desk. Behind the general hung a massive gilt-framed oil painting by Titian, a twelve-foot-long mural quietly removed by razor-wielding Nazi art lovers from a wall at the Musée du Louvre one dark night in the winter of 1942. Moon had acquired the priceless picture from a Japanese collector's estate in Tokyo in much the same fashion a few years ago.

Chase had spent hours studying that epic canvas, knowing how much it revealed about his captor and torturer: there were Roman legionnaires with short, bright swords, helmets and shields shining with sun-glinted gilt, a powerful conqueror in his chariot behind six rampaging white stallions, an entourage of muscular Roman centurions in their trademarked plumed helmets herding downcast captured Gauls through the streets in chains; there were Greeks in buskins and tunics of Ionian blue, coal black Egyptians in flashing desert reds with images of Isis and Osiris, black dray horses struggling to surmount a hill with a massive wooden catapult, and the recognizable faces of Hannibal, Ramses, Alexander, and, of course, Caesar.

Moon's pantheon of heroes was lacking a few icons, in Chase's opinion: Stalin, Idi Amin, Genghis Khan, Vlad the Impaler, Pol Pot, Attila the Hun, and Caligula, to name but a few.

Moon was typically dressed, Chase saw, wearing his perfectly pressed white silk mandarin jacket with Burmese white jade buttons. On his lapel, a cloisonné pin symbolic of his stature: the white crane, symbol of the first rank. Also, around his neck, a string of 108 beads like a Buddhist rosary, from which hung delicate strings of coral representing the Five Elements.

His long, finely muscled legs were encased in white sharkskin jodhpurs, and his knee-high riding boots were polished to mirrorlike mahogany perfection. He fancied himself an expert horseman, though Chase had never seen a single piece of evidence indicating the presence of even a single horse on this verdant isle.

"Did you win?" Moon said.

"Win what?"

"Your morning tae kwon do bout with the master."

"Of course I won," Chase replied, mopping his brow. "Your master is a bully and a lightweight."

"So you got your blue belt today. That is very good. I'm proud of your progress, Dr. Chase. Did they tell you the meaning of the blue belt?"

"No."

"Your new belt represents the sky or heaven. It means your tae kwon do skills are growing stronger with each passing day. Like a tall plant or a tree growing toward the blue skies of the heavens. Next you will receive the red belt. The meaning of the red belt signifies—"

"Let me guess. The planet Mars. Danger. War. Any of those?"

Moon laughed. "Please. Do sit back down. Those leather armchairs are quite comfortable, as you well know. Ah, the good doctor. Where oh where would I be without you?"

"Back in some generic office tower in Beijing, shuffling papers, I should imagine. All right. No more of your perfumed bullshit. I'm here. Let's get to it. You said you had news of my family. What? Where?"

"I do, I do. I beg you, be patient. There is a letter from your wife. It seems that all is well with your family. That is not the primary reason I wanted to see you, but I'm sure you're most anxious for a report on their recent activities."

"Understatement."

"I understand. I know this is all very difficult for you. I myself would abhor being in your position, as would any man. Unfortunately, this is war. And in war there is incalculable pain and suffering in the names of both good and evil. The good news, Dr. Chase, is that with your genius and the application of that genius, we will soon challenge and defeat the West."

"You're actually going to do it, aren't you?"

"Do it? What does that mean?"

"You're going to use the Centurions to slaughter countless millions of innocent people. Right? You are. I can see it in your eyes. You are fucking insane, Moon. Sociopath. Psychopath. You've got to know that on some level."

"Why is it, do you suppose, that, throughout history, men of destiny, men of true greatness, men like my Caesar, or even our own Chairman Mao, are always tainted with that ridiculous charge. Insanity. I don't even know what the word means."

"You consider yourself a man of destiny?"

"Of course."

"God save us from men of destiny."

Moon ignored him.

"But all great men who have gone before me have borne that badge of scorn, Dr. Chase, the false accusations of insanity. Name me one who has not."

"How about five? Jesus Christ, Buddha, George Washington, Lincoln, Churchill . . . shall I go on?"

"No."

"I could, you know."

"Watch your mouth, Chase. Don't forget that any blood I shed will be on your hands, too. You designed the Centurion on a single sheet of paper right here in this office. The most destructive weapon the world has ever seen came straight out of your head, not mine."

"For God's sake, Moon, you think I don't know that? You think I don't spend every waking minute of every day living with the knowledge of what I've wrought? My God. That's just fucking sadism. So what are you trying to tell me here? I came here because I want news of my wife and kids, not your sick fantasies of world domination, you ungodly lunatic."

"All in good time, Dr. Chase. I am merely telling you that the day when your family's suffering ends draws near. The curtains are rapidly being drawn on the Old China. The China that has suffered centuries of humiliation at the hands of the West and Japan. The foreign intervention and imperialism, the British invasion of Tibet, the Opium Wars, the loss of Taiwan, the—"

"Vengeance is mine, saith the general, so spare me the litany."

"You laugh, Dr. Chase. But I am telling you that one system of government and one culture will prevail. Mine. The New China now enters the final phase of our planned military showdown with the West. On that day, you and I will deploy the weapons that will take America and her closest allies down."

"Really? What day is that, may I ask?"

"Independence Day. Or should I call it . . . Dependence Day. Quite a good one, that, don't you think?"

"July Fourth? You take America down on its national birthday?"

"Hmm. Or, one might say, its national death day."

"And just out of curiosity, how the hell do you plan to do that?"

"The Centurion Submarine Fleet, of course. First one, then two or three more major American cities on the eastern and western seaboards will fall victim to our undersea missiles launched from the bottom of the Atlantic basin and the mid-Pacific trench. They will all disappear simultaneously. Poof! New York, Washington, San Francisco, Los Angeles, let us say. The same fate will immediately befall a few of the great cities of England. The ones that Hitler sadly failed to annihilate.

"We will then issue demands that the Seventh Fleet be withdrawn from the Pacific within seventy-two hours. And that all U.S. forces be withdrawn from South Korea, Japan, and the Philippines, et cetera. If our demands are not met within a reasonable time-line, the annihilation of more cities on both sides of the Atlantic will follow. Until the White House comes to its senses. Assuming a reeling President David Rosow is still capable of making any sense at all at that point."

"That's why you took out McCloskey. Rosow's barely had time to consolidate his government."

"Excellent deduction, Doctor! And then, with the strength and might of the entire Chinese military solidly behind me, I shall march on Beijing and arrest the current government and assume sole power."

"And then? What will you do then, O mighty Caesar?"

"Then? Why, then I shall rule the world, Dr. Chase."

The old man sat there beaming like a well-fed cat in a garden full of mice. He looked up at the beamed ceiling, eyes glazed over, like an addict pumped full of some ecstatic chemicals.

"Chase?" he said.

"Yes."

"What a lovely sentence that is, is it not? I shall rule the world."

Chapter 15

Moon struck a match and lit a long yellow cigarette. He delicately inserted it into an ebony holder and stuck it in the right corner of his mouth. He kept talking, letting it burn down without taking a drag. He was a man of peculiar habits, and this was one of the milder ones.

"You will play a key role in the final phase of my grand plan, Dr. Chase. What my officers are calling 'Spring Dawn.' And when China emerges from the coming preemptive strikes on the British and the American mainlands, victorious, of course, I shall terminate any further obligations on your part to my newly formed government. You will be reunited with your lovely wife and two children and returned to what's left of your homeland."

"You said you had news of my family. I'd like to hear it now. I insist."

Moon reached across the desk and handed him a letter.

"Read that. As always, Dr. Chase, all three are in perfect health and being well cared for. Here, read the letter from your lovely wife. They are involved in the camp tasks for which they have shown the most aptitude and pleasure. They live in relative comfort and safety. I think you can rest assured that—"

"Fuck you, I don't believe it," Chase said, his eyes skimming the banal letter of reassurance. "Kat didn't write this happy horseshit. Somebody else wrote and made her sign it. I think you're lying."

"Oh, come now. Me? Why? What possible reason would I have to lie? I'm not a monster, Dr. Chase."

"I won't even bother to address that. You listen to me, damn it to hell. I want to know where they are, General! I want to speak with them. All of them. How long has it been? How long? You told me that—"

"And you will see them. You will speak with them. All of them. Just as soon as your final mission here at Xinbu Island is nearing completion. When this is all over, your family will be generously provided for. You will be given an inordinately generous stipend for your services to my country and provided with private jet transportation anywhere in the world."

"When does this Spring Dawn commence? It's spring now, as you may have noticed."

"The clock is officially ticking. We're now going to be driven across the island to the Weapons Design Center. This is where Operation New Dawn will be headquartered. As director, you will have a spacious new corner office and sleeping accommodations on the uppermost floor of the new building. From that office, you will become an integral part of China's New Reality."

"Reality? Really, General? Here on Xinbu Island? I haven't had even a glimpse of reality since your thugs kidnapped me and my family off the streets of Georgetown, two blocks from our home."

"Better than assassinating you, I should think. A far better fate than that originally intended."

"What?"

"You may as well know. Premier Li had decreed to the Politburo and to me that you were a grave threat to our national future. That you alone were the single biggest danger to China's manifest destiny, were we to become locked into an arms struggle with the Americans. Te-Wu Academy had sent a four-man team to Washington to eliminate you and your family. They were in place, reporting to me. Watching each member of the family's every move for months."

"I felt it, damn it. I knew it. But I ignored my instincts."

"You were already dead, Dr. Chase. Nothing you could have done. The executions were to take place on the night of your wife's fortieth birthday."

"All of us, I assume. Cleaner that way."

"All of you."

"But then?"

"I hesitated. I had escaped to my home in the islands. To think. I walked the beaches all day until I had to sleep. Beaches and mountains are where I get my work done. I had been thinking about you, Dr. Chase. I'd brought along a biography of you, the one by Walter Isaacson called *New Century Man*. Fascinating. And it came to me one morning that I was about to waste one of the world's greatest natural resources. And that you were far more valuable to me alive than dead."

"A reasonable assumption."

"Yes."

"What happened?"

"I went back to Beijing and began to lay the groundwork for what was then called Early Dawn that very day. I saw that China had no need of a costly and protracted arms race with America. Look what it did to the Russians. Your Reagan brought them to their knees by outspending them at every turn."

"They underestimated Reagan's ferocity and tenacity. And the innate power of capitalism. His loathing for the evils of Communism. And Lady Thatcher's, too, God rest their souls."

"Yes. The poor, benighted Soviets could never grasp or match the U.S. war machine's inherent ability to outspend and outthink them. Reagan launched a sustained economic attack that ended Communism in Russia without a shot being fired. I did not think China had the need to repeat those lessons of history. I saw a way around this problem."

"Me?"

"You."

"Deduct me from their side of the equation and add me to yours."

"Precisely, my dear Watson."

"How close did we get that night? Tell me the truth."

"Less than an hour."

"My God."

"The basement of the 1789 restaurant had been packed to the ceiling with C-4 explosives by my people posing as electricians. We were going to reduce it to rubble. I had my epiphany and pulled the plug on that. The 'lost' Chinese ambassador and his wife were merely backup. Both Te-Wu graduates, I can tell you. I ordered them to make sure your family didn't make it home. "

"Christ."

"And now the end of all that is near. You can make all this suffering go away, Bill. You can ultimately save yourself and everyone you love. You just have to take one last step. Do you understand me? It's all on the line here."

"I understand you far more deeply than you will ever know, General Moon."

"I feel precisely the same about you, Dr. Chase. It's why we get along. Although we are adversaries and not friends, we have a great deal in common. Now, I'd like you to take a look at this. Read this dossier. Cover to cover. Take your time. The car will wait."

It was a red leather portfolio marked MOST SECRET with a thick dossier inside.

The first thing Chase came to was an aerial sat photo of a house. A large Georgian brick home, quite beautiful, located within a rolling parkland of green beeches and elms.

"What's this?"

"It's called Quarterdeck. A large manor house in the Cotswolds. England. The home of the reigning chief of MI6, Sir David Trulove. That's his picture you're looking at. A crusty old admiral who keeps getting in our way. He's been a persistent thorn in our sides, not unlike Brick Kelly, his American counterpart at CIA.

The much-heralded era of the 'special relationship' between Britain and America is now about to come to a swift conclusion. One that history will 'little note, nor long remember,' I might add."

"What's all this?"

"Satellite images of the estate. Diagrams of the security systems and armed personnel in place both on the grounds and inside the house. Architect's elevations of the house itself. Bit of an armed fortress, that house. The security measures are quite formidable."

"You want me to kill the head of MI6 in order to gain my freedom?"

"Yes."

"What about your precious Spring Fling?"

"Dawn. Don't make that mistake again. You don't have to do it personally. You need to create a team. May I suggest you start with one of our senior agents, Ku Lin. UK based, runs a cell for us there. Put him to work on this. Create or provide Ku Lin with weapons that will make the correct outcome certain. There is no budget. You've got one month."

"Is that all?"

"For now."

"I feel like I've heard that scenario somewhere before, General Moon."

"Hmm. But really, Dr. Chase, what choice do you have?"

Chase was silent for a moment.

"Let me give you a little inside information on world domination, General Moon," Chase said, "since you people are so obviously hell-bent on it."

"Oh, please. I should love to hear it."

"It ain't all it's cracked up to be, believe me. Look at Caesar or Napoleon. Better yet, look at Tojo and Hitler, God rest their souls."

Moon burst out laughing as Chase moved to the door.

"One more thing before we go," Moon said, as if he'd almost forgotten. "The J-2 project is compromised. One of the new fighters you designed has fallen into enemy hands. Stolen at sea by a British intelligence officer from a carrier deck. But the circumstances are unimportant. What is important is the fact that your fingerprints are all over that fighter."

"And your point is?"

"Somehow, somewhere, men are now going to be coming for you. So. Your usefulness to us draws to an end. You need to complete your work before the end draws near to you, my friend. And your family."

"If you have been lying to me about them . . . God help you. Because I won't. I will see you dead."

Moon laughed out loud.

"Oh! Oh, my! I shall miss you when you're gone, Chase, truly I shall. And one more thing. You might want to tune in to CNN in the morning. It promises to be a rather exciting day in Washington, my sources tell me."

That very night, as he fought valiantly for sleep, Bill Chase heard, or perhaps only imagined, the heavy sound of an old dragon's tail moving over dead leaves.

Chapter 16

Arlington National Cemetery

The day was bitter cold, cold and wet.

As the seemingly endless funeral procession wended its way across Memorial Bridge, the sleet gradually turned to snow. Arlington House, General Robert E. Lee's beautiful and historic old mansion sited at the top of the hill, was barely visible in the storm. In this light, the house looked frozen and forlorn, even a certain shade of grey, like the general's ghostly armies after Shiloh and Antietam, and Gettysburg.

It had been a long time since anyone had seen a Washington crowd so still and silent. The entire route, from St. Andrew's Church to the cemetery, was lined ten to fifteen people deep with soldiers on both sides standing at parade rest to control access to the cross streets.

As the Honor Guard and the president's caisson neared, the soldiers would snap to attention. A female major was going up and down the lines, from soldier to soldier, behind their backs, discreetly handing them sugar cubes to suck on and keep them on their feet. They'd been standing in position since long before dawn.

The First Lady had requested the horse-drawn caisson to transport the president's body from the funeral service at the church to Arlington. It was the first time one had been used since John F. Kennedy's funeral in 1963. In her heart, she knew Tom would have wanted to complete his journey accompanied by his stalwart stallion, El Alamein. Two days earlier, the president's favorite horse had been flown into Andrews from the ranch in Colorado.

The big black stallion was calm, even dignified, as he completed his last journey with the late president. A short, sad trip to the heroes' burial ground. McCloskey was a decorated war hero who'd served two combat tours as an air force pilot in the Vietnam War. He'd flown the Convair B-58, the first supersonic operational bomber, and won the DFC for heroism.

The First Lady, though distraught, was toughing it out as the day of the funeral drew nigh.

The worldwide search for her husband's assassin was ongoing, but preliminary feedback from the FBI was not encouraging. The alleged murderer, a chef in the White House kitchen, had, in all probability, slipped through the cordon around Washington and left the country.

The media was making hay twenty-four hours a day with the fact that the suspect was a Chinese national. But whether his motive was personal or political was not yet known. He had enjoyed an unblemished career, working his way up to the number two position in fairly short order. He was well liked by the staff and was one of the late president's favorites in the kitchen.

But most Washingtonians suspected the worst: a political assassination, and already chilly relations with Beijing were now at an all-time low.

In one of the prefuneral logistical meetings held in the family residence at the White House, an eager young staffer was quick to point out to the group that horse poop in public was a very unsightly thing. He then asked if not feeding the stallion for the day before the funeral would prevent that.

"Gee, Chuck, I don't know," the First Lady said, reining in her roiling emotions. "What do you think the result would be if we don't feed all the soldiers and sailors for a day before the funeral?"

"I guess that they'd probably pass right out, ma'am," the staffer said.

"That's what a horse will do, too," she said.

End of discussion.

Police officers were doing crowd control. As CNN was reporting more than a million people lining both sides of the funeral route, control was necessary. Two of the younger officers on the D.C. side of the bridge were quietly chatting up a pair of young women when their lieutenant came over and spoke to them in a deadly whisper. Then they fell silent, as hushed and stone-faced as the members of the army Honor Guard marching in the wake of the caisson now rolling slowly by.

Only a muffled tattoo, a rolling tide of martial drumbeat, reverberated through the streets of the capital. For some unknown reason, the birds in the trees were twittering wildly that day. Then, too, there was also the terribly poignant and muted clip-clop of El Alamein's hooves upon the pavement, the jingle and clink of his tack, the creaking steel rims of the caisson's large wooden wheels.

As the somber procession entered the nation's most revered military burial ground, people raised their eyes to the heavens. The air force flew a low-level Missing Man flyover, one jet missing from the formation. A few minutes later, Air Force One flew over, majestically alone. Bagpipes played martial music, music to fight by, as the president's simple mahogany casket was carried from the caisson to the gravesite.

As the cortege, the Honor Guard, and the joint military pallbearers passed by the crowd on the long incline to the gravesite, the faces of many world leaders were visible. Angela Merkel, Vladimir Putin, a now frail Queen Elizabeth and Prince Philip, the king of Spain, and the president of France were among them. The kings of Norway, Sweden, and Spain. Members of the special forces had formed an honor cordon between the crowd and the grave.

Notable in their absence was the Chinese delegation.

All had come to pay their final respects to a man who had valiantly tried to reestablish America's image around the world as a bastion of freedom and democracy. The singular country the founders had envisioned. A beacon, a shining city on a hill. It was the late president's fervent dream that America could, and would, become, once again, as the old expression had it, "The last, best hope of mankind."

And he had died trying.

The sights and sounds were muffled weeping, the mournful bagpipes, the quiet dignity of the nine-man detachment of the British Black Watch Regiment, and the snow falling softly on the huge banks of flowers arrayed by the grave, powdering the uncovered heads of the veiled and mourning, draping the gently rolling hillside in a mantle of white.

Standing at the gravesite, President David Rosow looked stricken. McCloskey had been a lifelong friend since their air force flyboy days, both in and out of politics. Now Tom was gone, and the weight of the deeply troubled world had suddenly shifted to his shoulders. He would be tested in the coming days, weeks, and months—he knew that. Tested, and not found wanting, he kept trying to reassure himself.

And silently he prayed, not only for his murdered friend, but also for strength for himself and his beleaguered nation.

His prayers were not in vain.

Suddenly, with a fiercely whispered arrival, a nightmare vision appeared from the sky.

It was a large black shadow at first, swooping down out of the dark clouds. Then it resolved itself into a large drone, with swept-back wings. It was about twice the size of a twin-engine Cessna. It dove down out of the snow-filled clouds. Some glanced up at it and quickly turned away, believing it was only part of the stringent security measures that the new president had ordered for the state funeral.

The sleek black drone swooped low over the large gathering at the gravesite, then climbed and disappeared once more into the dark storm clouds over the Capitol.

"Security cameras, that's all," someone said and, reassured by the logic of the man's statement, the crowd at the gravesite instantly and visibly relaxed.

A lone bugle began the familiar opening notes of "Taps" and the firing party raised their rifles to commence the twenty-one-gun salute—

"Air incursion!" a Secret Service agent shouted. "Repeat! Hostile air incursion at the gravesite! Immediate assistance, all sectors! Code black, code black, code black!"

And then, in that horrible instant, death rained down on many of those gathered on the hillside to mourn the fallen president.

Two missiles slammed into the hillside simultaneously about ten seconds and three hundred yards apart, exploding with devastating effect. Bodies were flung high into the air, severed limbs and body parts flew overhead, screams of pain and panic were everywhere.

The armed forces pallbearers, still bearing the weight of the mahogany casket, had the stoic courage and wisdom to remain in place, carefully lowering the president's body into the open grave and out of the line of fire before taking cover themselves.

Seeing the bright wink of multiple machine guns firing from along the leading edges of the approaching drone's swept-back wings, a quick-thinking Secret Service agent guarding the new president grabbed Rosow from behind and dove with him into the only possible cover, into the yawning grave. The two men landed hard atop the recently lowered coffin.

Many of those still remaining aboveground were mowed down by the strafing drone.

Covering the president with his own body, the agent immediately rolled onto his side and began firing up at the drone with his P90, an automatic weapon capable of firing nine hundred armor-piercing rounds per minute . . . to no apparent effect.

He quickly realized the R&D boys would have to write a new definition of "armor-piercing" when this day was over. Whatever the behemoth was made of, it bore no resemblance to anything he knew of.

The Secret Service immediately got the bereaved widow and the Speaker of the House and the vice president to the ground and covered them with their bodies. Then they opened fire on the drone with their automatic weapons, yelling at the screaming mourners to take cover, run, get down! Get down! Crouched behind gravestones all over the hillside they watched in horror as the deadly drone climbed into the safety of the clouds once more.

But the Secret Service men on the hill were not watching and waiting. They were scrambling to retaliate. They were not trained for this kind of attack, and their response was slow in coming.

"Gimme a report!" the agent in charge shouted to his men inside the two blacked-out SUVs. They were tracking the drone with radar, thermal imaging, and acoustic equipment.

"Sir! That thing's still got two laser-guided five-hundred-pound bombs under the wings! It's climbing through two thousand and banking right over the Jefferson Memorial. It's gotta be lining up for another pass, sir, a bombing run!"

Another agent stood beside one of two tactical black and armored SUVs, tracking the enemy drone with high-powered binocs as it completed its loop. He visually confirmed via radio what the men in the vans were seeing on their screens.

"It's coming back," the agent in charge said into his mike. "Deploy the air defense systems! I repeat, deploy ADS now!"

Just as the nose of the descending drone appeared through the clouds, and winking machine guns on either side of its fuselage opened up, the rooftops of the two SUVs slid open.

Immediately, twin launchers of the ADS rose from within the two oversized vehicles parked above the gravesite. These were the Stinger launch racks, hidden from sight within the blacked-out Secret Service SUVs. Each operator was capable of launching four passive surface-to-air weapons, Stinger FIM-92B, called SAMs, the infrared homing missiles carried a three-kilogram warhead with hit-to-kill penetration.

As soon as the attacking drone began yet another deadly pass over the crowds below, turning to the east and beginning its descent through the cover of cloud to circle for another attack, the launch order was given.

With a roar, two Stingers, one from each vehicle, belched white smoke and streaked heavenward in pursuit of the black drone's heat signal.

The agent in charge watched in disbelief and horror as the two missiles streaked right past the giant drone and disappeared into the clouds.

"What the hell?" he screamed at the men who'd launched the ADS missiles.

Ambulances and EMS vehicles were racing across Memorial Bridge, even now, as well as police cruisers and Bomb Squad vehicles. The nation's capital reeled, aghast at this fresh hell of tragedy wreaked upon the country. Countless millions at home were watching the slaughter of innocents unfold, knowing that this was not just an attack on the American capital. It was an attack on the entire civilized world.

In an extremely remote corner of Washington's Rock Creek Park, a large flatbed eighteen-wheeler was parked atop a hill, off the road, concealed in a thicket of snow-covered trees. On the truck's bed, a black rectangular container was secured, strapped down with steel cables.

It was large, about the size of two standard Dumpsters welded together end-to-end. On either side, the words *MATSON LINES CHINA* were stenciled in large white letters. A steamship company. On top, a number of aerials, GPS tracking cameras, and a small radar dome not visible from the ground.

The truck was positioned so as to be invisible from the road. And it was. That is, unless you were looking for it.

The two men inside the innocuous grey rental sedan that pulled into a rest stop at the foot of the hill below the truck were looking for it.

"There it is," the man who was driving said. "See it up there?"

"Oh, yeah. Good work."

They drove their vehicle behind the deserted rest-room facility, parked, and got out. They looked at each other for a moment without speaking, then began their climb up the steep hill.

They were wearing U.S. park ranger uniforms, the wide-brimmed Smokey hats pulled down over their brows. On their hips, they wore holstered pistols, .357 Colt Python revolvers. Not standard-issue weapons for rangers, nor was the powerful C-4 explosive device in one man's backpack, or the two P90 rapid-fire automatic weapons in the other.

There were also two men inside the container. It was a "control container" exactly like the ones used by the U.S. Air Force to execute drone attacks in Pakistan and Afghanistan, and wherever else people needed killing. There was a man seated before a bank of monitors, a control stick in his right hand. He was guiding the attacking craft down through the clouds for a final low-level bombing run on the presidential gravesite.

The second man, tall and thin, elegant in his three-piece suit and bow tie, was standing behind him, gazing up at the scenes of death and destruction on the ground at Arlington National. He had a wry smile on his face. This would rock the Americans back on their heels.

He was beaming a live feed of the attack to General Sun-Yat Moon on Xinbu Island. He could almost see the smile on the boss's face.

And this was just the beginning.

In an instant, the smile on the Chinese drone pilot's face faded. In that second, the attacking drone disintegrated in a massive blast of fire and light and black smoke high above Arlington. A Hellfire missile launched by an American F-18 had scored a direct hit. "What the f—?" the drone driver cried, unable to tear his eyes from the screens. "We just lost the drone!"

"Shit, you're kidding," the tall man said

Someone rapped hard on the steel door at the rear.

"What the hell?" the controller said.

"I'll get rid of them. We need to get out of here. Now!"

"Yeah."

There was a small viewing port in the door, and he unlocked it and slid it open. The tall man stood on his toes and looked through the slit.

Two park rangers. Great. Perfect timing.

"Can I help you?"

One of the rangers stepped forward and put his face up close and personal.

"National Park Service. Your truck is parked illegally. You need to move it, sir."

"Can't do that. Engine died on me."

"Sir, you have two choices. You move this truck. I mean now. Or I get on the radio and have a tow truck here in five minutes to tow your ass to the pound. Up to you."

"Officer, you do what you have to do."

The first ranger stepped back, and the second ranger appeared. "Don't worry, we will do what we have to do. ASAP."

"What? What the hell?"

"Hello, George. How are we feeling on this red-letter day?"

Unfuckingbelievable. What the hell was Tommy Chow doing here? He was supposed to be hiding out in Bermuda or somewhere.

"Here's what we're going to do next, George," Tommy said and suddenly the State Department man was staring down the mile-wide barrel of a .357 magnum Colt Python.

"Hey! There's no need— Wait a second, man, we're friends, right? I mean . . . wait!"

"No waiting," Tommy said, pulling the trigger. "ASAP."

The round, fired at such extremely close range, blew away the State Department man's face and most of his head.

"Give me the device," Chow said, smiling at his companion.

He took the IED packed with C-4 and heaved it through the port, where it clattered loudly across the floor of the steel container. The drone driver at the controls screamed and raced toward the door, grasping at his only hope, to grab the explosive device and attempt to heave it back out the opened port.

Tommy dropped the Chinese guy with a head shot before his fingertips could reach it.

As they were getting back in the car, the drone command truck blew sky-high up on the hill.

Chapter 17

London

A train whistle sounded as the Flying Scot slowed. The luxury train had chugged out of the Old Station at St. Andrews, Scotland, two days earlier, headed south. Now, at journey's end, it began the long approach to London's Euston Station, a low-slung concrete monument of 1960s architecture oft described as one of the greatest acts of postwar architectural vandalism in Britain.

But no matter.

Of the nine deluxe mahogany-paneled staterooms on board the approaching luxury train, only one was strewn with various P. G. Wodehouse paperback novels, autosport and sailing magazines, Sotheby's guide to Bermuda real estate, a bottle of Gosling's Black Seal Bermuda rum, half full, two half-empty baskets of fading fruit, the stale remains of a turkey club sandwich, an array of White Rock ginger beer bottles, bowls of melting ice. Plus, a slim gold cigarette case and a battered art deco silver cocktail shaker, both monogrammed with the initials A. H. beneath a coronet.

The top berth was lowered, piled high with sheets, down pillows, bedcovers, and blankets. Even though the setting sun indicated it was late afternoon, the room had obviously not been made up since departure from Edinburgh.

And its sole occupant?

Ah, yes, Lord Hawke himself.

Alexander Hawke stood bare chested before a steamy mirror in his en suite lavatory, trying to shave. He was dressed only in his loosely fitting, light blue pajama bottoms, these courtesy of one of his favorite tailors, Turnbull & Asser, St. James. The other, Anderson & Sheppard of Savile Row, had always provided the balance of his bespoke wardrobe.

In his left hand, he hefted a stout walking stick. His pretty nurses at the hospital in St. Andrews had presented him with the blackthorn "swagger stick" on the festive day when he'd been deemed fit for discharge.

In his right hand, he held an old-fashioned straight razor. Swaying with the motion of the railcar, he used the stick to balance himself on his widespread feet as he prepared to shave.

In the steamy mirror, he noticed he had left a lit cigarette jammed into one corner of his mouth. He snatched it out and flicked it into the johnny, where it drowned with a hiss.

"Clear the decks for action," Hawke said to himself with some gusto, lifting the gleaming ivory-handled blade toward his cheek. He was in a gay mood, delighted to be returning home at last to his family, his colleagues at MI6, and his beloved country house, Hawkesmoor.

Suddenly the railcar lurched madly. Hawke was thrown forward against the basin mirror, just missing by a fraction slicing the tip of his nose off with his straight razor. He gave himself a narrow look in the mirror, snarled at his reflection, and decided safety dictated going out into the stateroom to shave. The stick was proving highly ineffectual and he tossed it up on the berth.

The semiviolent swaying of the railcar had not abated. He had to brace himself with one hand along a wall as he made his way to the long dressing mirror hung on this side of the door opening next to the vestibule.

As he stood, poised precariously, razor at his throat once more, the compartment door was suddenly flung open from the outside. This action shoved him back against the wall, completely hidden behind the door. He stood motionless, dazed for a moment.

Whereupon Eddie Moncrief, the aged railway porter, whom Hawke had come to know and admire ever since the Flyer first chugged away from Edinburgh's Waverly Station, burst into the scene. He was looking for the last passenger still unaccounted for prior to arrival.

"Lord Hawke?" Moncrief said, puzzled, quite sure he would have found his errant passenger inside the compartment. "Are you in here, m'lord? So sorry to disturb, but . . ."

As Eddie turned to shut the door behind him, he spied his lordship. The man was frozen behind the door, jammed up against the wall, the gleaming blade of his razor at his throat, his eyes fixed in a glassy stare.

Lord Hawke, wearing the sickly sweet grin of one who has only narrowly escaped certain death, said, "Oh. Hullo there, Eddie."

"I do beg your pardon, m'lord!" the porter said, amazed at his lordship's somewhat bizarre situation. "What are you doing behind the door, if I may be so bold, sir?"

"Ah, funny, what? Just having a bit of a lark, that's all, Eddie," Hawke said, striving mightily for the air of a man of insouciant nonchalance.

"Ah. Bit of a lark, eh? Most amusing, m'lord. Hiding from me behind the door. Ho-ho! Well, I just wanted to alert you that we'll be pulling into Euston Station in less than twenty minutes, sir. May I assist you with your packing?"

Eddie retrieved a dark green velvet smoking jacket from the floor and eyed the opened and overflowing leather portmanteau on the floor.

"Splendid," Hawke said. "Heave ho!"

Hawke took the icy silver cocktail shaker in hand. Somewhat shakily, he poured the remains of his favorite highball, a frothy Dark 'n Stormy, into his glass. As he threw his head back to down the aromatic potion, he cracked the back of his skull smartly against the upper berth.

"Ouch."

"So sorry, m'lord. Are you quite all right?"

"My fault entirely," Hawke said, rubbing the back of his head ruefully. "I really can't recall when I've had a more stimulating evening aboard a train, Eddie. Unless, of course, one counts that memorable night aboard the infamous Red Star crossing Siberia when a couple of Russian thugs tried to kill my son and me."

"Kill, did you say, sir?"

"KGB vendetta. Long story, Henry. You'll have to wait for my colorful and somewhat salacious memoirs."

"Most amusing tale to tell, I'm sure, your lordship."

Hawke rubbed the throbbing bump atop the crown of his skull. "Thank you, Eddie. I am going to miss this little room of mine. I must say it's made a rather indelible impression on me."

"Indeed it has. A rather angry reminder on the top of your head, I'm afraid, sir. Shall I fetch a wet flannel and some more ice cubes?"

"No, no. Time heals all wounds."

"Indubitably, sir."

"And wounds all heels, as they say."

"Ha! Good one, sir!"

His lordship's cries were in vain.

The porter smiled at his favorite passenger.

His lordship, whom Moncrief had come to know rather well in a short time, possessed a very rare combination of strength, humanity, and humor. One he'd not seen the likes of in thirty years' service to the railroad. It was also, he had to admit, refreshing to find a man of such beauty, such fame and elevated social position, who possessed an utter lack of pretension or sense of entitlement. Upon entering the dining car, with his thick jet-black hair and intense blue eyes, the women had all stared at him as if he were a god.

"Indeed, your lordship," he said. "Shall I put the balance of these soiled clothes into this valise, sir?"

"That would be lovely. I'll help. Let's not forget my silver shaker, here. Thirtieth birthday remembrance from my pal Chief Inspector Ambrose Congreve, you see."

Hawke looked from the frosty beaker to the half-filled valise. How to pack it safely?

"Where shall we put this?"

"Not quite sure, m'lord."

"Ah. This should do the trick."

Having seen his paisley robe hanging on the back of the lavatory door, he snatched it. Then he screwed the top of the icy container on, wrapped the shaker lovingly within the robe, and buried the whole thing within the contents of the open bag, viewing the result with some enthusiasm.

"Your hat, sir," the porter said, handing him a crushed brown fedora that had been chewed within an inch of extinction. "It was on the upper berth."

"Harry! Bad dog!" Hawke exclaimed.

"Dog, sir?"

"Yes, dog. A Scottish border collie. Present for my son, you see. Been researching the breed the entire time I was incarcerated during rehab at the St. Andrews Royal Infirmary. Had the idea of getting my son a dog while I was laid up. Went to a top breeder just outside of St. Andrews the moment I was finally sprung."

"The Flying Scot does not actually permit dogs on board the train, your lordship."

"Really? Odd. I was not made aware of that," Hawke said, reaching up under a blanket, withdrawing a small animal, and placing him on the floor. "In the brochure, was it? This antidog clause you refer to? Fine print, I suppose, eh, Eddie?"

"Indeed, sir. Practically invisible."

"Well, in any event, he's not a dog, not really; he's a puppy, as you can plainly see. Handsome lad, isn't he? Handsome Harry, I call him. Good boy too, aren't you, Harry?" The happy puppy barked loudly, racing round and round the elderly porter's feet in a frantic, celebratory state of excitement.

"My word!" Moncrief said, lifting his feet to avoid the scampering creature.

"Terribly sorry, Eddie. I gave him a drop or two of rum, you see."

"Rum, sir?"

"Hmm. The Gosling's Black Seal. Just to help him sleep, of course. Seems to have gone to his head, however. Yes. I do believe Harry's drunk!"

"I won't breathe a word, sir."

"You are the very soul of discretion, Eddie. I knew it at once I met you. Harry! No! Stop that! Bad, bad dog! Should we give him some black coffee, do you think?"

"Your lordship, I believe he's about to—to—lift a leg, sir."

"Harry! No!"

His lordship's cries were in vain.

The porter looked down in dismay and shook his newly dampened trouser leg.

"You'll have to forgive us, Eddie. We have been cooped up in here for an eternity, it seems."

A small crowd stood on the station platform watching the shiny maroon-and-gold train chugging forward. Porters hurried out. Baggage handlers were waiting. As the train came to a stop, Hawke saw his greeting party. His four-year-old son, Alexei. The boy's guardian and Hawke's current romantic interest, the beautiful Nell Spooner. And, of course, his octogenarian companion since childhood, Pelham Grenville, his valet, a fellow who was currently very properly turned out in spiffy grey chauffeur's livery.

The porter put down the little stepping block and Hawke descended carefully to the platform, using his swagger stick and trying to manhandle both his valise and portmanteau while keeping the squirming puppy concealed inside his Crombie overcoat.

"Daddy!" Alexei cried and ran to his father, hugging him joyously around the knees.

"There's my boy," Hawke said, putting down his luggage and patting the top of his tousled head.

The father's keen blue eyes betrayed his overwhelming love for the boy. "How are you, son? Have you been good while I was away? Hello, Nell. I hope he hasn't been a bother. How are you? You look lovely as ever. And how are you, young Pelham? Awfully snappy in that automotive regalia. Haven't seen you in that getup in years."

"We drove in from the country, m'lord. Miss Spooner wished to drive the Bentley herself, but I'm afraid I had to insist on doing the honors. The Locomotive can be a bit of a handful on those icy country lanes, as you well know, m'lord."

Hawke nodded. He had an old battleship grey Bentley Continental, which he'd long ago nicknamed the "Locomotive." No power steering, and, with a 4.5-liter engine and an Amherst Villiers supercharger, it was an overpowered but lumbering beast on the back roads. Hawke had also installed a red nitro-launch button, as he called it, for "emergencies." Didn't especially want Nell hitting that one by mistake.

"Yes, you were quite right to do so, Pelham. Thank you."

"M'lord? How are you feeling? Fully recovered?"

"Much improved, thank you for asking."

"How's the leg? The ribs? Healing nicely?"

"Getting stronger every day."

"One thing, sir, if you don't mind."

"Yes?"

"Your bag, sir. The leather valise. It appears to be leaking."

"Leaking?"

"Indeed, sir. A spreading stain on the platform."

"Ah. A little rum fizzy, perhaps. Or perhaps my bottle of Hermès Orange Verte has broken. Nothing to worry about, Pelham, I assure you."

His son tugged at the hem of his coat. "Daddy, what's that noise?"

"What noise? I don't hear anything."

"Yes, you do. It's coming from inside your coat."

"Oh, that. It must be my tie. It is rather loud, I agree. Don't know why you let me pack it, Pelham."

Harry's shiny black button nose peeked out from a lapel.

"It's not a tie, Daddy, it's a puppy! May I see him?"

"Puppy? I don't recall any puppies stowing away inside my wardrobe . . . oh, wait . . . you were right. Yes, there is definitely a puppy in here."

Hawke handed the yipping border collie to his son. Alexei kissed the puppy all over, hugging him to his chest.

"Oh, Daddy! He's the best puppy ever, ever, ever. Is he mine?"

"Of course he's yours, Alexei. Happy birthday."

"My birthday present!" Alexei exclaimed.

"He's adorable, Alex," Nell said.

"What's his name, Daddy?"

"Harry. That was the name of a dog my grandfather gave me when I was your age. And I'll tell you a secret. When I was four, I was exactly the same age as you are now. Isn't that funny?"

"Thank you, Daddy. I love Harry more than anything in whole world. 'Cept you and Pelham and Miss Spooner, I mean."

Hawke was nearly overcome by a surging tide of emotion. Few feel the powerful desire for family more keenly than those who have lost theirs at a very young age. Alexander Hawke had lost his own dear mother and father at the tender age of seven under circumstances too brutal and painful to recall.

"It's good to be home," he said, gazing up into the shadows of the familiar station. "Yes, awfully good to be home."

And with that, this particular little family gathered itself together and made their way through the rail station's thronged masses for the journey homeward to Hawkesmoor in the Cotswolds. Hawke would insist on driving, of course; he hated being driven.

In the old days, during a few years when Pelham really was a chauffeur, Hawke would drive and Pelham would sit in the rear, reading aloud to him his favorite books. Now Pelham sat up front with him while Nell, Alexei, and little Harry had the run of the old Locomotive's cavernous rear seat.

It had begun to snow, great feathery flakes. Hawke knew by morning the countryside surrounding his rambling old family pile on the hill would be blanketed with the white stuff. Hawke suddenly felt an unerring sense of the quietude and peace he had so longed for over the years. He welcomed it to his heart. He began to whistle with contentment, so very happy to be home again.

We're going to be all right, he said to himself. *We're all going to be all right now.*

Chapter 18

At Sea, off Newport News, Virginia

The sea was in a furious mood.

Lieutenant Robert "Moose" Taylor, Annapolis and Yale Law–educated son of a legendary Denver oilman, stood outside on the starboard bridge deck. His binoculars were trained forward across the sleek bow of his ship, the guided-missile destroyer USS *Dauntless*. In his foul weather gear, the boyish officer looked even younger than his twenty-six years.

USS *Dauntless* was currently streaming through heavy seas beset with sometimes patchy but unusually dense fog, en route to her home port at Naval Station Norfolk in Virginia.

Since Taylor had assumed the watch earlier that morning at 0600 hours, the weather had continuously deteriorated. Periodic squalls of heavy rain rolled through, the sea heaved, and *Dauntless* took on a heavy roll.

Taylor paid foul weather no mind.

If anything, he reveled in it. To him, it was one of those lively atmospheric mornings tinged with brine that made a man glad as hell he'd joined the navy rather than practice corporate law in D.C. or print money down on Wall Street. The honest truth was he loved bad weather. No idea why. Had since childhood summers sailing on Nantucket. Go figure.

Standing next to the tall and slender lieutenant on the bridge wing was Ensign Stubbs Pullman, a strapping, towheaded farm boy from Prairie Flower, Texas. His aw-shucks personality was belied by his serious dark blue eyes, eyes that took in everything, eyes set within a crinkle of humor that sometimes sparkled with native plainspoken intelligence.

"Of course, all y'all know where Prairie Flower is?" Pullman liked to ask any available sailor within hearing range. Moose had learned Texan from Ensign Pullman early on. He knew that "y'all" was singular. And that "All y'all" was plural. And then, when absolutely nobody knew what the hey he was talking about, Moose'd say, "Hell, son, Prairie Flower's only just a mile or so down the road apiece from Sweetwater, Texas! All y'all didn't know that? Damn!"

After six months of pirate hunting on station off the coast of Somalia, and more recently near the Straits of Hormuz, Ensign Will Pullman and the crew of the fighting *Dauntless* were more than ready to get stateside again. With no serious weather forecast for the mid-Atlantic coast, Moose Taylor told Pullman he thought they'd be steaming into their home port at 0800 hours Saturday morning.

A good thing, too. Taylor's wife, Meg, was beaming come-hither looks at him on their Friday night Skype. Their conversations were getting more and more over-heated and pornographic by the week.

Saturday was the lieutenant's twenty-sixth birthday. And he'd be cutting his birthday cake at the little kitchen table at home and sleeping in his own bed with his beautiful bride. For all the shipboard bitching, you had to admit, sometimes even the navy got it right.

This particular homeward voyage had been hugely uneventful, with one exception. Sonar had reported a faint contact with an unidentified screw signature. A large submarine had been located running a course for this particular patch of ocean forty-eight hours earlier. Contact had been lost. Navy Ops Center had reported nothing since. So, friendly or foe-wise, the faint sonar contact was a bit of a shipboard mystery.

If that sonar blip was in fact an enemy sub, which Taylor thought unlikely, the boomer had gone deep and stayed there. But in all probability, the sonar operator, bored to tears, had simply misread some visual "noise" on his scope.

Pullman grabbed Moose by the elbow.

"You hear what just happened in D.C.? I mean, just this morning, Moose?"

"Gee, let me think. It is Saturday. The president played golf. Again."

"The president nearly got his ass dead, is what he did."

"What? Rosow? He's only been in office a week!"

"You will not effing believe this, son. There was a drone attack on McCloskey's funeral at Arlington. Not two hours ago."

"No shit? A drone at Arlington? What the hell. I mean, Jesus! Whose drone was it?"

"Beats the crap out of me. Some big-ass, batwing, stealth-type mother armed with Sidewinders, machine guns, and five-hundred-pounders. Huge. I saw video of the attack on Fox News down at the canteen not five minutes ago. Man. You talk about 'death from above.'"

"And the drone?"

"Vaporized by a Hellfire. But still."

"Casualties?"

"Hell, yeah. A ton. They can't count bodies that fast. Every ambulance within a hundred-mile radius of Arlington is en route."

"The president is unhurt, though, right? He and my dad were classmates at Annapolis. I know the guy."

"So far, that's what they're saying."

"Anybody claim responsibility?"

"Not yet. And if the Feds know who did it, they sure ain't talking about it. Man. Somebody assassinates our damn president and then tries to take out the new one at the dead one's funeral! Are things getting really weird in this country, Moose, or is it just me?"

"It's not you, brother. Things are definitely getting weird. Believe me."

"And speaking of weird . . . what the living hell is that?"

"What?"

"Swing them glasses around to port side, sir. Ten points off our port bow. Little hole in the fog, see it? Some kind of mound over there . . . rising up out of the water, you know . . . almost like a sub . . . whale, maybe . . . only . . . Holy shit!"

"A whale? Gotta be," Moose said.

"Way too big for a whale . . . wait . . . hell, no, it's gotta be some kind of a sub! But—what the hell—look at the surface angle! I mean, a submarine surfacing vertically? I don't . . . I don't . . ."

"That ain't no whale, sir," Taylor said.

An impossibly huge mushroom of water suddenly exploded upward as something grotesque and threatening rose out of the sea, shining black and silver, seeming to come endlessly out of the water, unbelievable as its length and bulk climbed into the air and seemed to hang there . . . until it fell with a power that drove the water up high and white into the sky.

This was something the likes of which neither man had ever seen before, the sheer mass of it, how it broke the surface at an impossible speed and shot straight up, actually gaining momentum, like the old Jupiter rockets at Kennedy Space Center.

"Cap'n?" Moose Taylor said into his mouthpiece. "I know visibility sucks . . . but . . . is the bridge seeing what we're seeing out there to port?"

"Hell yes, we're seeing it. But what in God's sweet name is it? All engines dead astern! Stop this goddamn boat and let's have us a little lookie-loo . . ."

Pullman grabbed the lieutenant's arm, his expression shock colored with fear.

"I'll tell you one thing, Moose, if that damn thing is some kind of new intercontinental nuke . . . hell, we're all dead, podnuh. Imagine the size of that warhead. Take out Nebraska."

The men on the bridge of *Dauntless* were witness to a historic sight that morning. Though they didn't know it at the time, they were present at the dawn of an entirely new era in the annals of naval warfare. What they were observing was an undersea weapon the likes of which would change everything.

Literally.

Wherever they were on the ship, fore or aft, whatever they were doing at that moment, sailors stood stock-still, staring openmouthed in incredulous wonder, as a behemoth sheathed in black steel rose up majestically before them. What it was, they had no earthly idea. The patchy fog, thick as cotton, shielded large segments of the silhouette from view.

But somehow the monstrosity kept rising, reaching ever higher, water pouring off its black flanks in sheets, until every last foot of it had emerged from the depths.

It paused then, for a nanosecond, seemed to lean a few fractions of a degree slightly to port. And then it fell to earth like tall timber, crashing full-length into the sea with the mighty force of towering redwood in the forest.

The result of this freakish giant's epic crash on the ocean's surface produced a minitsunami. The huge

wave rocked the navy destroyer like a toy boat, rolling her over on her beam ends before she could right
herself.

"Lieutenant Taylor, this is the captain. You're an
ex-submariner. You ever see a submarine looked anything like this one before? Because I sure as hell haven't.
I mean, forgetting about the sheer length of the damn
thing . . . look at the size of her superstructure! And
standing on her tail like that? What the hell?"

"No, sir. This thing is big. Only thing I know of that's
even remotely this size was Russian. NATO called her
'Typhoon.' 'Shark,' or 'Akula,' as the Russians called
it. She was 515 feet long with 70 feet of beam. Carried
twenty long-range ballistic nuclear missiles, sir. Largest
submarine in history. Only six ever built. Deployed in
the eighties to launch SLBMs from under the Arctic ice
cap. Mothballed a couple of years ago, I think."

"But, damn it, Lieutenant, maybe one of those goddamn Typhoons was never mothballed. Russians kept
her out of sight but still in service? Sitting on the bottom
almost in sight of our coastline? What else could it be?
You got a better explanation?"

"No, sir, I do not."

"Unless, of course, that thing is a goddamn space-
ship from Mars."

"Yes, sir. I mean, no, sir."

"And so, God help 'em, since it is a sub, there's got to be crew aboard. Not that many men could have survived a vertical surfacing at that speed. Sonar watched her entire ascent. He says she was nestled on the sandy bottom when something went haywire. Suddenly, she stood on her tail and she shot straight up from the bottom like a goddamn rocket. And even if those boys over there made it through that, hell, a hard landing like that one . . . I just don't know. We could be looking at a tremendous loss of life."

"Yes, sir. But maybe some of them were strapped in? I dunno, sir. I just can't make any sense of what I'm seeing."

"Nobody can. But I'll tell you what. I want you to lead a rescue party over there. Now. Take as many men and as much equipment as you need, son. And don't waste any time; there's a damn good chance boys are dying over there inside that big tin can."

"Aye-aye, sir."

Taylor looked at Pullman and said, "You heard the captain. Let's move. Give the order to lower away the starboard thirty-two-foot patrol boat, Stubbie. Now!"

The lieutenant moved his binocs along what he could see of the mysterious sub's hull, calculating her overall length in his head.

By his reckoning, this thing was nearly a thousand feet long.

By the time Taylor, Pullman, and the rescue crew approached the surfaced submarine in a high-speed patrol craft, a two-man team of swimmers had already managed to secure a line over from *Dauntless* on the thing. That feat was a lot harder than it looked because there were no handholds on the exterior of the hull.

And in the thick, swirling fog bank, her deck loomed about thirty to forty feet above their heads. And when the two swimmers finally got up on the sub's deck? They'd had a hell of a time finding anything to secure a line to until they discovered cleats that popped up out of the hull when they stepped on them.

The sub finally secure, the two sailors hung a rope ladder over the side of the hull to make life easier for the rescue boat now approaching dead slow from astern.

Since the seas were rolling, but relatively calm, the giant was riding easily on her waterline. Which, for Taylor and the boys from *Dauntless,* would make scrambling up the dangling ladder a whole lot easier. At the last minute, since he had no clue what he would find aboard this thing, Lieutenant Robert Taylor had ordered all the men to wear sidearms. And two of them were carrying MP9 machine guns and packing smoke and flash-bang grenades to disorient any unfriendlies they might encounter.

Because of the thick fog, Taylor and his men were getting the first real close-up look at the strange vessel.

"No flag painted on her flank," Moose said quietly, putting the patrol boat's helm hard a'port on an angle to pull alongside the sub.

"Yeah. No flag. No ID anywhere, Skipper. I noticed that. "

"No anything anywhere, Stubbie. A sub without a country."

"Yeah."

"I'm thinkin' . . . no, I'm almost thinking . . . UFO."

"Stubbs. Come on."

"Well, okay, then what the hell is it? Is it a Russian Akula class?"

"Hell, no. This thing dwarfs the Akula."

"So what the hell is it?"

"Let's go find out. I'm going up the ladder first. Secure this vessel any way you can, then get the men started up and bring up the rear."

"Aye, sir."

"And, Stubbs? Keep that machine gun of yours on full auto, okay? Something I really don't like about this. Doesn't feel right."

"Yeah. Remember on the bridge when I said I thought things were getting a little weird?"

"Yep."

"Well, right now this thing is really creeping me out, sir."

"Yeah. See you up on deck."

"Aye-aye, sir."

Taylor started up the ladder, mumbling to himself.

. . . The fucking Mount Everest of submarines . . .

Chapter 19

Miami

Stokely Jones and his business partner Luis Gonzales-Gonzales were huddled over a small table in the rear of the joint, a notorious Miami waterfront dive called Marker 9. This was one week after the attack on Arlington, and they were waiting for Harry Brock. Brock, like every other CIA operative on the planet, had been called back to Langley for briefings on the ongoing search to identify the perpetrators.

He'd arrived back in Miami two days ago but was mum on the subject of the drone attack whenever Stoke asked him about it. Just gave him a look of *Don't go there, man.*

Stoke didn't take that as a sign of progress. He glanced at his watch. Harry was CIA, yeah, okay, but his track record for promptness, Stoke had long believed, was sketchy.

At one point in its shady history, Marker 9 had been a wildly popular mob bar. Capo di tutti capo fatti Santo Trafficante out of Tampa ruled his South Florida roost from a bar stool there for nearly a decade. Then in the 1950s it was a cop joint. Crooked cops mostly. A big corruption scandal had resulted in the grisly revenge murder of two dirty vice squad detectives on the premises in the summer of 1959.

Now the place was crowded with stevedores, day laborers, commercial fishermen, charter boat skippers, the occasional hooker who'd forsaken all pretense of hope, and the simple, straightforward, clear, sweet, and blue-sky alcoholics.

The Mark, yeah, that's what the local rum-dums called it now. The place had a nautical thing going on, "atmosphere," as the hoi polloi liked to call it. Each and every battered table had a solid brass ship's lantern in the center, either red or green glass, port or starboard, take your pick, Cap.

The conditioned air inside the Mark was choked with reefer and cigarette smoke; from the rear wafted the pungent aroma of fried fish and the stink of stale beer and powerful bathroom disinfectant. A colorful old Wurlitzer jukebox in the corner was deafening: Neil Diamond crooning "Love on the Rocks," Elvis, the Ramones, whatever. The sharks shooting nine-ball at the threadbare table made a point of hammering balls into the corner pockets and then slamming the rack down on the slate as hard as they possibly could.

That kind of place. Go on TripAdvisor for Miami? Definitely wouldn't recommend a romantic evening for two with a view at Marker 9.

Stokely and his business partner, Luis Gonzales-Gonzales, were not regular customers. Not that anyone in the place was sober enough or cared enough to take any notice of the two of them. Even if they did, they wouldn't say anything. Blind drunk or bored stiff, the Mark's clientele had seen it all, or imagined they had, anyway. That's why Stoke liked the old Mark. Under the radar. Way, way under the radar.

"Una mesa para dos, con ocho cervezas muy frías," Luis had said to the guy on the door when they first walked in.

The Cuban waiter guy laughed and Stoke said to Luis, "Did you just say, 'A table for two and eight cold beers?' "

"It's a joke, okay," Sharkey said to Stoke. "Don't worry, he gets it."

"Oh, it's a joke," Stoke said, a smile tugging at the corners of his mouth. He loved the little guy.

Sharkey reached up and put his hand on Stoke's shoulder. It felt like a chunk of concrete.

Sharkey, as Luis was popularly known, was pretty tough for a one-armed little hombre. Cuban. Stringy. But a guy who looked like he'd need only one arm to take you out. People naturally stepped out of his way as they made their way back to the table at the rear. Luis and his compadre, a handsome African-American gentleman named Stokely Jones Jr. Stoke was one of the larger individuals on the planet. The man was a freelance counterterrorist who sometimes liked to go by the name of Sheldon Levy when the tactical situation called for it.

Like tonight: Lieutenant Sheldon Levy, United States Coast Guard. Stoke had used the Levy nom de guerre many times before. Its absurdity, he believed, made it all the more plausible. Yeah, he knew he "really didn't look all that Jewish" was what he would say to people whom he wished to mislead. And they laughed to show they got the joke and believed him.

Stokely Jones was an American warrior in his late middle age or early-onset maturity, depending on who you asked. He was a former Navy SEAL, former New York Jet (one season), and ex–NYPD cop. Pretty impressive résumé. He was a man of whom it was often said, by his closest friend, Alex Hawke, that he was "about the size of your average armoire."

Whatever.

He was black. He was big. He was bad.

Deal with it.

Stoke's life story was that he had gotten himself caught dealing product on a Harlem street corner at age seventeen. Judge gave him a choice, Rikers Island or the U.S. Navy. Stoke manned his ass up and took a Greyhound bus out to Coronado in California, blew through the SEAL training program, then did two combat tours as a bona fide Navy SEAL. Back home, he played one season at right tackle with the Jets, got injured in the season opener, and joined the NYPD, rising to the rank of detective, working goodfellas all the hell over Brooklyn.

One day he'd saved the life of a kidnap victim, pulling a beat-to-shit Brit from a burning warehouse in Bed-Stuy where some Jersey mob punks had left him handcuffed to a steam pipe to die. The man he saved that day just happened to be the sixth-richest man in England. A fellow descended from pirates, as it turned out, who went by the name of Lord Alexander Hawke.

The sky outside the bar was black, and hard rain thumped down on the tin roof and rapped its knuckles against the windowpanes.

The Christmas-like glow of all the red and green lamps inside the joint lent the place a nautical air that seemed superfluous in light of its location fifty yards from one of the world's busiest and, from a criminal standpoint, most notorious harbors. Not to even mention a hard-core clientele that literally reeked of the oil-slick sea and assorted finny denizens of the deep.

It was almost midnight.

Outside, a tropical squall was passing through, pissing rain inside the wind, the leading edge of a cold front moving up over Biscayne Bay from the northern Florida Keys. Key Largo rain moving over Miami battered the corrugated tin roof overhead so loudly Stoke had to shout to be heard by his buddy three feet across the table.

Luis Gonzales-Gonzales had lost his arm to a bull shark who'd decided he needed it more than the Sharkman did. Better known around the Boca Chica docks ever since as Sharkey, he pulled his fish-gut-stained yellow slicker tighter around his bony shoulders, shivering so bad you could see it.

"Damn, they got the AC in here freezing my ass off, boss."

This skinny little one-armed Cuban had become something of a dandy lately, a man who chain-smoked yellow, purple, and crimson cigarettes with gold bands at the business end. He was acquiring a lot of Miami and South Beach style notes since moving up from his bonefishing gig in the Dry Tortugas. No socks with his two-tone shoes, like this was Palm Beach or something, rolling up the sleeves of his white linen blazer and drinking Gran Patrón Platinum instead of Bacardi, that kind of thing.

His frame appeared strung together with gristle and long, ropy ligaments. To look at his outside, you'd never guess at the layers of strength and sheer guts deep inside him. So what if a shark had ripped his right arm off? You dealt with it, that's all. You are the shark. You never stop swimming. Because if you stop, you die. That's what he told everybody who asked, anyway.

Tonight he wore his signature yellow porkpie hat, strategically dipped below his bushy black left eyebrow. Beneath the brim, he had darting, shiny black eyes that didn't miss much. Beneath the straight nose, a neatly trimmed little black mustache. His skin was weathered a nutty copper color from decades spent as a bonefishing guide out of Cheeca Lodge down in Islamorada.

The Atlantic Bar at Cheeca, that was where he'd met his employer and companion for this evening, the huge man mountain that Sharkey revered if not loved with all his great big Latin heart.

The giant sipping a tall Diet Coke across the table was the nearest thing he had to a friend in this world. Stoke was his boss at Tactics International in Miami. They had a little office over in the Grove, but most of the government work they did was outside, underwater, or undercover. They operated mainly in South Florida, the Bahamas, the Caribbean, and Latin America, but they went anywhere in the world their services were needed. Always sailing under a black flag, as Hawke would put it.

Tactics did frequent errands and odd jobs for the U.S. government—hostage rescue, regime changes, running traces—all of them one hundred percent off-the-grid black ops, and near seventy percent were courtesy of a CIA field agent named Harry Brock.

Shark thought Brock was frequently an obnoxious dick, and he knew Stoke did, too. But they all tolerated him because, A, he was their number one client and, B, he was a former marine and a battle-hardened CIA warrior who had personally killed more bad guys than most battalions.

Stoke had once told Sharkey something he never forgot. That God was on the side of the big battalions. And he was right. For Luis, that meant God was on Harry's side. And any friend of God's was for damn sure a friend of el señor himself, Luis Gonzales-Gonzales, the dude so nice they named him twice.

Sharkey looked at the Navy SEAL watch the boss had given him and frowned. Harry was late. Very late. Typical. He looked at the boss man and shook his head. "Harry's late," Shark said.

"Tell me about it."

"Ain't like him, boss, is it? Man is usually always so prompt. And courteous. Surprised he hasn't texted or called to say, 'Sorry, running a little late.' "

"What can I tell you, Shark? Harry was born with his ass on upside down, that's all. Ain't always his fault."

"Official Mayor of Crazy Town, is all I'm sayin'."

Stoke smiled and looked over at the pool table, watching a snark in cutoff Levi's rack 'em up. Luis felt a shimmer of relief. Shit just didn't get to Stoke like it did to Sharkey himself. Or even if it did, man never showed nothing. Man absorbed the blows, all the bad stuff, owned it, stowed it in the bilge, somewhere deep, and kept moving, a human quicker-picker-upper if there ever was one.

"So tell me. How's life in the newlywed fast lane, Shark?" Stoke said, his voice a rumble to challenge the thunder above. "Second honeymoon down in Key West? Little Palm Island, right? That pretty little bride of yours treating you okay, taking care of business?"

"Oh, yeah, boss," Luis said. "I spent at least a couple of hours defrosting the fridge last night, or 'foreplay,' as my lady likes to call it."

"Sharkman," Stoke said, his white-toothed grin producing a deep rumble of laughter, "that's funny."

"Hilarious, right? So then the other night Maria she ask me, say, 'Luis, how many women you sleep with? Tell me the truth, Luis.' Know what I told her?"

"I can't even guess."

"I tell her, 'Only you, baby. All the others? They kept me awake all night long.' "

Stoke laughed out loud again and slapped the table with his ham-sized palm, hard enough to levitate the glasses and china plates a couple of inches off the table.

"What are you, Shark, like filling in for Jay Leno, now? Guest-hosting *Saturday Night Live*?" he said to the snappily dressed little guy in the porkpie hat. No matter what Shark said, marriage obviously agreed with him. He was one happy cat.

"You know what I discover, Señor Stokely? All those years down in the Keys, a poor Marielito, a Cubano boy finding bonefish for rich white people? Even President Bush at Cheeca that one time I tole you? Man. I never knew nothing about the real world back then, you know, how to be a real man in it. You know what I mean? But now? Working for you all these many years?"

"Tell me."

"I discover that maybe I only got one arm? But, baby, let me tell you something. I got two balls. And, you know what, they both solid brass."

Chapter 20

S tokely was about to laugh when Harry Brock with a full head of steam, head lowered, chin resting on his collarbone, barreled through Marker 9's front door like a raging bull entering a phone booth.

Harry had something in his right hand and, as he barged ahead through the sliding pools of light in the smoky darkness, Stoke and Luis saw that it was, in fact, a small human being.

The fact that Brock had another guy with him bothered Stoke only because it wasn't part of the plan. A plan that started wrong usually ended wrong was his experience both on the football field and in and out of combat in the navy. Now, working a lot with Harry Brock? You had to learn to anticipate a problem before it happened. Brock was a badass with baggage, basically.

Harry was one of the legendary misfits in the intelligence community. How he'd survived so long as a CIA field officer was a mystery. But as Stoke would often say, "What can you expect? How can you ever really trust somebody who grew up in some gated community in Southern California? Who grows up like that?"

Stoke saw Harry had one arm cinched around the little guy, the other one stuck up against him hard, like Brock maybe had his snub-nosed .38 in the man's ribs. The guy was cuffed under his ratty raincoat, you could see that.

"Whiskey Tango Foxtrot, Harry?" Stoke said, smiling up at Brock.

"Huh?"

"Never mind."

Sharkey smiled, knowing Brock wouldn't get the lame Facebook lingo: WTF, what the fuck.

"Evening, gents," Harry said with his big shit-eating grin.

Luis jumped up and pulled two more chairs round the table. Harry smashed his tiny prisoner down into one seat and then took the other for himself. Flipped the chair around and rested his forearms on the backrest. Harry wore his mostly bald head shaved military style and was handsome in that granite-faced hard-ass way. You want a picture of Harry? Think Bruce Willis. Most people do.

"Sorry I'm late," Brock said. "I had to bail this diminutive gentleman here outta slam. Over at the courthouse? All of a sudden, he decides he has a last-minute appointment. In the men's room at the Shell station on the other side of the fuckin' turnpike. Made a run for it and of course I had to outrun him across eight lanes of oncoming traffic in order to haul his ass back here."

"Who the hell is this character?" Stoke said, staring at the fidgety little guy. He had wild crazy hair, frizzy to the point of looking fried, and a long nose between wide dreamy eyes. Imagine a tiny Oriental Gene Wilder and you've pretty much got the picture.

"Oh, him? Nobody. A scumbag junk mule from Shanghai named Hi Lo. I've forgotten his real name. Hunan Hiram, maybe Peking Ducks. Who the fuck cares? Coast Guard cutter *Vigorous* nailed his skinny ass moving high-end crystal meth and shit up from Cuba. Picked him up on sonar two miles outside of Cienfuegos Harbor. Ready for this? The Coast Guard tracks him all the way to Miami and the cutter hoists him to the surface, right? A crane? And up comes a two-man submarine, believe it or not. You believe that shit? This little numbnuts here driving a minisub packed with China white and Cuban crack? Running submerged that far and that long under the deep blue and actually surviving?"

"He doesn't look like a submariner," Stoke observed.

"How'd they nail him?" Sharkey said.

"They tracked him, Luis, like I just told you. He finally ran aground just outside Government Cut. Some weekend scuba club from Coral Gables found him by sheer accident. I mean, fuck me all to hell. Raise the *Titanic*, right? Jesus H. I mean, cheaper to lower the Atlantic; never know what you'll find down there."

"This guy, your friend Hi Lo, you say he is from my country, from Cuba, Señor Brock?" Shark said.

"Oh, excuse me, Sharkey, didn't see you over there in the dark. Lighting in here sucks, right? Sharkey, my brother, this here is Hi Lo. Hi Lo, you little fuckwad, say hello to the Sharkbait here. Baddest one-armed hombre north of Ramrod Key."

This wasn't Harry's idea of good manners or common courtesy, and Sharkey understood that. He knew the man. Just Harry's idea of trying to be funny, showing off, riffing his shit for Stokely and a good-looking waitress serving at the next table.

"Hi, Hi," Sharkey said to the Chinese guy, being funny himself.

"What he say me? Hi? Hi?" Hi Lo said.

"Just saying hello to you," Brock said to him. "Get it? Hi, Hi. That's funny. In our country, I mean. Shark, seriously, man. Since when did you get funny?"

"Since I got married."

Brock laughed.

"Now he's married, he's a stand-up comedian, huh, this guy?" Harry said, looking over at Stoke, shaking his head in disbelief. "Right?"

Stoke said, "Harry, shut up."

"Why?"

"We don't have time, for one thing. How far south is that damn gunrunner's yacht? Gotta be moving up into lower Biscayne Bay by now."

Harry pulled out his cell and tapped a couple of keys.

"Thirty, thirty-five nautical miles out, moving at seven knots, north-northeast up Biscayne Bay from Ocean Reef Club at Key Largo. I got a sat track app on my iPhone. GPS, see? Key West radar blimp is tracking them, too. So is the USCG cutter *Vigorous*. The CG skipper and I have been yakking on our cells all day. He's going to give me a shout when it's time for us to motor out there for a meet and greet, okay? But of course you know that."

"What I know is you could have given me a shout to say you'd be an hour late."

"Stoke, cut me some slack here, man. I spent all afternoon chasing this little prick through the Everglades. Didn't really have time to chat, okay? And by the way? He's a biter, for fuck's sake. He bit me! Look at my hand. Broke the skin! Little dude would bite a sick bat if he thought he could get his hands on one. Look at the little shithead's teeth, man, he files them down. They're like Ginsu knives!"

"Calm down, Harry," Stoke said.

"Reason I'm late? Had to stop by Miami Dade ER for a rabies shot."

"Harry. No. Stop."

Harry couldn't stop. "But wait! Order now and he'll shove a complete set of serrated shivs up your ass. Okay? This is what I've been dealing with all day. Seriously."

Stoke sat back in his chair, watched the lazy ceiling fan whirl a moment, quiet, within himself, just sort of exuding cool for a minute.

Then he said, "Is there any particular reason you thought it was wise, or even vaguely appropriate, to bring this Oriental gentleman to a private party?"

Harry leaned forward, his elbows sliding across the beer-slick table.

"Yeah, Stoke. Uh-huh. There is a reason, as a matter of fact. A great reason. This megayacht we're taking down tonight, *Jade*? The one we're intercepting on behalf of the agency? My agency? Your client? Well, as it turns out, whoever painted the hailing port on her transom is a very shitty speller. Instead of C-A-R-A-C-A-S? He should have spelled it S-H-A-N-G-H-A-I."

"What?" Stoke said, lasered in.

"You heard me. *Jade*? Ain't a Venezuelan vessel after all, Stoke. No. What it is, it's a goddamn private Chinese megayacht out of Shanghai! So, call me crazy, but it follows that the Sharkman here, much as I love him, would make a very shitty translator tonight. You know, when it comes down to nut-cutting time communicating with the Chinese crew on board that gun-running gutbucket? Okay? Get my point much? Jesus Christ, Stoke, gimme a little credit here."

Stoke was nodding his head.

"You're absolutely right, Harry. Shark's Chinese sucks. I'm sorry, man. My bad."

"Forget it. Hi Lo will handle it. I made him some monetary promises, okay. Let's move on. Want another ice-cold Cherry Coke, Stoke? How 'bout you, Sharker? Beer? Bacardi? Tequila Mockingbird? Name it."

Shark shook his head no. The little guy was wound up pretty tight tonight. He actually did want a Gran Patrón badly, but he didn't drink on the job. Even when the boss wasn't looking.

Stoke said, "We're good. Have a beer, Harry; we won't tell the brass at Langley. Promise."

"Brass can kiss my ass," Harry said, and meant it.

Brock whistled and flagged a waitress, a cute little redheaded home wrecker who seemed to recognize him. "Hell-o, J-Lo," he said.

She flinched when Harry put his hand on her beauteous J-Lo ass before Stoke reached over and chivalrously removed it for her.

Harry glared at Stoke and said, "I will have one double-XL order of extra jalapeño, extra hot wings, extra spicy. And one long tall Sally, an ice-cold draft Bud, little darlin'."

"Coming up," she said, showing a little extra cleavage.

Harry said, "J-Lo, say hello to Hi Lo. Maybe you two are related."

"Harry, for God's sake," Stoke said.

"What? We got ourselves a little Lo family reunion right here! Hi Lo, speak up, name your poison, podner. Sake martini? No, no, wait, sake, that's Japan, isn't it? That whole warm sake thing. Wrong country entirely. Man, I'm sorry, little guy. No offense intended."

"I no talk to you," the little guy said. He crossed his arms, pursed his lips out, and stared up at the ceiling fan.

"Is that it?" J-Lo asked.

"You ever married?" Stoke asked the cute waitress. "I only ask because my friend Harry here is currently out shopping for a new wife."

"Sorry. Married," she said, cocking a hip.

"What?" Harry said, his head swiveling around. "You never said you were married, baby."

"Right. Married. But not now. I was married. Just once," she said, cocking the other hip for action and taking a quick swig of somebody else's frosty from her tray.

"You were married? What happened?" Brock said.

"Oh, that. Well, see, we were both suffering from depression for a while. Got pretty bad there. My husband and I were going to commit suicide on our first anniversary. Made a pact. But strangely enough, once Gordon, I think that was his name, killed himself, I started to feel a little better. A whole lot better. So I thought, 'You know what? Fuck it; soldier on, girl!'"

She spun on her broken heel and marched away.

"Attagirl!" Stoke said, all three of them transfixed by that mesmerizing booty, boom-shocka-booming itself on back to the bar like a live animal suddenly uncaged.

"Damn," Harry said wistfully, and there was really nothing else to say.

"Bathroom," the interpreter suddenly interjected.

Harry spun on him. "See? Okay. Here we go again with the bathroom. It never ends. No way, pal. Not happening."

"Yes! Shit pants!"

"I said, no. Hold it. Sit your ass back down! I ain't letting you out of my sight again, kemosabe. And I sure as hell ain't going anywhere near that filthy shit-box back there with you. Everywhere this guy goes is crazy-town, I swear to God."

"Got to go! I sick."

"Yeah, yeah, sick, I know," Harry said, "the Diarrhea Kid rides again. Sick, he says."

"Don't be such a hard-ass, Harry," Stoke said. "Man's gotta go, he's gotta go. There's no windows in that head back there. He isn't going anywhere on us."

Sharkey stood up and said, "I'll watch the door while he's in there, boss. I don't think he's kidding. Look at his face, man. He looks green."

Brock said, "Right, Sharkey. He does look green. Know why? That's because this light on the table? Green."

"Harry," Stoke said. "Stop. Don't even start." He clenched Brock's forearm with one of the juice extractors he called his fists and squeezed.

"Awright," Brock said. "Stick his ass in there and stay right by the door, Shark. He's got five minutes and then we're out of here. Got a late date with a Shanghai lady named *Jade*."

Luis took the guy's arm, lifted him up, and walked him back down the short dark hall to the men's john. It had "Buoys" in faded red paint on the door. "Gulls" on the door right next to it. What passed for humor around here.

Harry called out, "Hey, Shark, don't you dare go in there with that lit cigarette. Gas explosion will blow us all sky-high. Take out half downtown Miami Beach."

Shark threw the butt on the floor and stamped it out.

"I was only kidding," Harry said to Stoke, "but better safe than sorry. Guy is lethal."

His hot wings came and he dug right in. Harry always ate like he was in an eating contest, trying to shave minutes and seconds off the Wing-Eaters World Record.

Stoke leaned across the table toward him and said quietly, "Harry. Any idea what the agency expects us to find on board this damn yacht? *Jade*?"

"Weapons out of China and North Korea by way of Venezuela, that's all I know. Guns, missiles, nukes, who knows? You thought the late, unlamented Venezuelan presidente Señor Hugo Chávez was a bad actor? The new guy down there makes Stalin look like a fascist. CIA station in Caracas set this up. They have this whole intercept op locked down. Anything China related is politically sensitive at the White House. You can't even say the word 'firecracker' around there out loud, less somebody chews your ass."

"Thanks for the heads-up."

"Then there's the whole North Korean threat. Babyface Kim says he's going to nuke Seoul, Hawaii, Guam, D.C., Austin, Texas? That whole incident, those dead U.S. Navy kids on a CIA surveillance vessel in the East China Sea and all that? Well. There you go."

"The North Koreans are way the hell out of control right now, Harry. Why is that?"

"All about the real deal between China and the NKs, brother. With the Pac-Man."

"Pac-Man?"

"That's what we call the new North Korean Dear Leader. Little Kim Jr., I mean. You ever seen this cat in action? Chomp-chomp, wokka-wokka-wokka. Pac-Man, right, spitting image. Seriously. Anyway, China? They're just using that chubby little Pyongyang dipshit and his crayon-shaped nukes as a distraction. Keep us focused on something else while they do their real dirty work somewhere else in the world."

"Like what? Like where?"

"Here? L.A.? D.C.? Lots of Internet chat lately about hijacked high-tech U.S. weapons systems. Weird shit, some of it. Star Wars shit. Then you got some big

Asia conference coming up in Hong Kong. A whole lot of shit going down now between the White House and the Forbidden City boys in the run-up to that little picnic. A delicate moment in history, Stoke. That's why we're boarding *Jade* instead of the Coasties from *Vigorous*. If we're wrong about what she's got aboard? Bad intel, and the Coasties have to take the rap? This would be a real bad week for another international incident, apparently."

"Weapons headed where?"

"Here, amigo. The good old U.S. of A. Some fuckin' terrorist group based in a mosque near Princeton, New Jersey, of all places is on the receiving end. The imam there is a guy named Zawahiri. We been watching this cat like forever. First time he's made a dumb move. Last time he'll make any moves at all, believe me. This is good, Stoke. Real good stuff, if we can nail it down tonight."

"Yeah. But why the hell is China selling weapons to al-Qaeda? They got a dog in that fight, too?"

"Beats the crap out of me. But they'll sell shit to anyone, especially enemies of Uncle Sam. You don't think Beijing and Tehran are in bed together, brother? Think again. Beijing's going down a long bad road, man, I'll tell ya. They are screwing with the wrong president. Beijing thinks Rosow is just a pale copy of his predecessor? Wrong. I hear that Rosow's lying low in the weeds to lull them to sleep. That he is a badass at heart just itching for a good global excuse to kick China's butts back to pre-nineteenth-century reality. You watch him when it heats up."

"He's been in there five minutes," Stoke said. "Go get him outta there."

"Sharkey!" Harry called out. "Go get his sorry ass off the john. We gotta go. Now."

Luis rapped on the door.

"Time's up," he said.

"On toilet!"

"Tell him shit or get off the pot," Harry barked. "Seriously. We're leaving. Right now."

"No! Sick!"

Harry stood up. "Go in there and grab his ass, Shark. Fuck him. I'm sick of his shit. Literally."

"Locked," Luis said, twisting the knob. "He's locked the door, Señor Brock."

"Unbelievable. Sonofabitch, I knew it! Kick it in, Shark. Locks are crap in this dump."

Sharkey kicked hard and the door splintered inward out of the jamb and off the hinges.

The first thing Luis noticed about the room was that there was no lethal stink at all. The second thing was that the Chinese interpreter was not in the stall where he was supposed to be. No. He was crouched in a shooter's squat facing the door with his back against the filthy tiled wall.

He had his manacled hands extended straight out in front of him, gripping a small nickel-plated automatic pistol. Little dude was smiling up at him, like, *Hey, it's a joke. Get it?*

Luis had taken one step backward when Hi Lo fired, a popping noise reverberating off the tiled walls and floor, sparks coming out of the barrel. Sharkey's eyes went wide with surprise as the round caught him high and hard in the chest. His knees gave out as he stumbled back and collapsed, his hands covering the hole in his slicker, back of his head hitting the hardwood floor with a loud crack.

Harry, his features contorted in fury, was first through the door. He hurdled over Sharkey's bloodied and twitching body, his Glock 9 out front held in both hands. Stoke was only a half-step behind him when he heard Brock's nine fire once, twice, three times, more, and then Harry crying out in rage and in pain as he emptied his weapon, screaming at the guy who'd shot Sharkey.

"You wasted our friend, you little scumball, now it's your turn to die, motherfucker."

Stoke knelt down and took Shark's hand. "Stay with it," he said. "Stay with it."

Chapter 21

At Sea

Lieutenant Moose Taylor was first to scramble up the rope ladder and onto the acres of steel deck. And so it was that he was first to make the earliest of many startling discoveries his men would find aboard this "rocket ship" (as the captain was now calling it) that had come from beneath the sea.

Nobody, not the captain up on the bridge or anyone else on board *Dauntless* had even gotten a glimpse of the entire structure of the sub due to the thick fog.

But from where Moose was standing, all alone amidships on this vast black steel plain, Taylor made his first amazing discovery.

There was no damn conning tower on this thing!

Really? A submarine with no conning tower? What the hell was going on here? He could see all the way to the stern . . . and there was nothing. There wasn't even a damn periscope, communications aerials, nothing . . . which raised a question: How the hell did you *steer* the damn thing?

He adjusted his headset lip-mike to raise Stubbs down in the patrol boat. "Turtle, this is Joyboy, you copy?"

"Copy."

"You are not going to believe this shit, brother."

"Talk to me, papa."

"There's nothing up here to see. A clean deck. I mean, a vessel three football fields long with no conning tower? No abovedeck superstructure whatsoever. No nav systems, radar, or comms aerials. Nothing! Just one giant long-ass empty deck stretching for miles in both directions. It's nuts! How the hell do they see to navigate this mother?"

"Port lights in the bow? Below the waterline? Like that *Nautilus* James Mason skippered in *20,000 Leagues Under the Sea?*"

"Locate the conn in the bow? You know what, Ensign Stubbs? That's not the stupidest idea you've ever had. But, still . . . okay, I'm stamping my boots on the hull. See if I get a reaction inside. . . . It's all clear up here, Stubbie, send the first guy up the rope."

A few minutes later, Taylor stood on the wet deck in the thick fog, helping his men scramble up onto the broad foredeck. The entire deck, far broader than any sub deck he'd ever seen, was covered with a strange, spongy black rubber grid. Like a honeycomb. It was obviously meant to be slip-proof and it felt good underfoot. Whoever had designed this crazy monster may have forgotten to give it a conning tower, but he sure as hell knew what he was doing otherwise.

"You're not going to believe this," he'd say as each man mounted the final step of the ladder. "Look down there. No conning tower. No periscope. No nothing."

"Holy shit, Lieutenant," Stubbs said, gaining the top and looking from stem to stern at the wide featureless deck. "I had to see it with my own eyes to believe you. Kinda creeps me out, Skipper. *It Came from Beneath the Sea* kinda thing, you know?"

"Boo!" Taylor said, and Stubbs jumped back but only a little and a couple of guys snickered. Taylor was the kind of young officer who could get away with stuff like that because you could do it right back to him and he didn't get all ranky about it.

"Okay, rescue team on me," Taylor said, and the mystified team from *Dauntless* hurried back from wandering around in awe to huddle up with their commanding officer.

With the entire team gathered round him on deck, Taylor barked out orders. Check sidearms and weapons. Be alert for any sound of survivors. He would take five men forward to inspect the vessel. Locate the hatches and listen for signs of life. Stubbs and his five-man squad would go aft and do the same.

They would meet back here amidships in ten minutes.

Taylor fanned his men out and they all walked six abreast toward the bow, eyes down, scouring the decks. He searched in vain for nonexistent hatches and found not one. But that was far from the most troublesome thing.

The really bad thing was a seemingly endless number of long-range missile silos. There were silos arrayed to port and starboard. In fact, the entire forward section of the submarine deck was an ICBM launch pad. He counted the hatch covers. Twenty to port. And twenty to starboard. Not just your everyday submarine missile launch tubes, either. Monsters.

These hatches were six feet in diameter, the covers twice as big as New York City manhole covers.

Forty giant nuclear warheads.

Forty?

On one behemoth of a sub? With no freaking conning tower and not a solitary sign of life aboard?

Whatever this goddamn thing was, it was not good news.

"You found what, sir? Lieutenant?" Stubbs asked Taylor when they regrouped amidships. The temperature was dropping rapidly, and another storm front was moving in from the west, winds topping forty knots riffling the surface, sweeping across the seas and plowing up huge, heaving waves in endless ranks toward the horizon.

Taylor told him about the forty launch tubes he'd seen forward. "What about you guys? Anything?"

"Nothing," Stubbs said. "Nothing nearly as interesting as what you found."

"Nothing," Taylor repeated.

"A whole lot of nothing, sir, that's what we found. I don't know exactly how to tell you this but . . . there are no hatches on this boat, Lieutenant. Not a one."

"Yeah, I know. Did you hear anything? Anything human, I mean. Banging a coffee cup on the overhead like the old WWII movies?"

"Nada, sir."

"There's got to be a way inside this damn thing."

"You'd think."

"Well, we can always go back and tell the skipper, sorry, we couldn't find the crew, sir."

"That would be a very bad idea, sir."

"So we'll torch our way in. There's a broad section of bare deck just aft of the missile silos. We'll use acetylene and go in there. Cut a hole in her and see what we see."

"I've got two men with torches, sir."

"Good. Let's get moving."

It was the work of about twenty minutes to cut a three-foot-diameter hole in the center of the hull. Taylor dropped to his knees on the rim and peered down inside. It was dark, but he could make out a fairly wide companionway going fore and aft. Oblong shaped. No visible lighting. No sign of life at all.

And eerily quiet.

"We are a boarding party from the USS *Dauntless*," he called out through his loud-hailer. "Do you require assistance?"

He got only a hollow echo in reply.

He repeated the message twice more to no effect; as he got to his feet, he heard his radio squawk in his headset. It was the captain.

"Lieutenant Taylor, what the hell is going on over there? Any survivors?"

"No exterior hatches, sir; we had to cut our way in. They're not answering our hails, sir."

"For crissakes, Lieutenant."

"They're either all dead or they're trapped in a different watertight hull section from the one we penetrated. If I had to guess, sir, I'd say any survivors would have ended up in the stern sections after that insane high-speed ascent straight up."

"Agree, Lieutenant. Go find 'em and report back when you do."

"Aye-aye, Captain," Taylor said and signed off.

"Wait. Look at that!" Ensign Stubbs said. He dropped to one knee and peered inside.

"What have you got?"

"Some kind of a hazy red light. Just started blinking. Seems to be in the companionway, way forward of our entry point."

Moose said: "Same drill below as topside. Two details, one goes forward, one aft. My detail goes aft. I want to find survivors. And I want to get a look at the reactors. Stubbs detail goes forward. Find out what kind of missiles this ghost ship is packing. Weapons at the ready. No LED lamps unless it's an emergency. Use your night vision. Clear every goddamn room and call it. Got it? And watch your asses. This thing spooks me. It feels like a colossal goatfuck just waiting to happen."

Five minutes later, they were all belowdecks and gathered inside the belly of the beast.

Standing in the grey and misty sunlight directly below the gaping hole they'd cut in the hull, Taylor said a silent prayer for the safety of his men. Then he lowered his NV goggles and led them aft toward the stern. They moved in single file, slowly along the length of the dark tube, ready for anything. The ship had clearly powered down after the furious ascent.

It may have been dead in the water.

But it was a killing machine. And it exuded a kind of dark kinetic energy they could feel in the marrow of their bones.

Chapter 22

Cambridge

There was a small hamlet in the rather flat country-side situated about thirty miles from Cambridge Town called Haversham. It was not a picture postcard village by any stretch, just a rather drear little place, forlorn, really, with a couple of dingy pubs, a sad, ill-lit curry house, fish and chips, and a petrol station.

One of its few notable distinctions was that the Greenwich prime meridian line passed directly beneath the eighteenth-century Anglican church at the heart of town.

The only other thing of any real note could be found in a heavily wooded forest at the end of a long dirt cart path, a seldom used road winding between fenced sheep pastures and farmland. Hidden deeply from sight within the folds of a vast stand of great birch was an epic structure dating to the fifteenth century.

That's when it was known as the Palace of the Bishop of Ely.

The palace, now a less holy structure, had definitely seen better days. The mere fact that the towers, domes, and crenellated walls were still standing defied physics, but the new owner had no misgivings about her purchase of it. Decay was one of her private fetishes.

The palace was remote, private, and removed from the public eye, the fact that it was overgrown with climbing *Hedera helix,* or ivy, vines, had more than a few windows missing, and was in a fairly advanced state of decomposition did not trouble her in the slightest.

Tiny veins of moss had grown into the cavities of the stones until, viewed near at hand, the entire edifice seemed shaggy with vegetation. The slender and corroded mullions of the windows had old panes, the glass flecked with oblong bubbles and tinged with lavender. The foreboding entrance in the forecourt boasted two massive stone ravens to either side of the doorway.

"Well, then, what do you think of my find?" Professor Moon said, hands on her hips, leaning back to admire her newly acquired dream house.

"My God, Chyna, it looks like something out of a 1930s horror film," her young friend Lorelei Li had said as they'd gotten out of the backseat of Moon's silver 1930s vintage Rolls-Royce.

"I knew you'd like it, Lorelei," Chyna Moon said with a smile that couldn't mask her condescension. "It's perfect, right? Look, it's even got a moat!"

"You mean an algae pond. And, please, look at those old walls," Lorelei said. "Even those are covered with slime! Sorry, but it's gross."

"It is not slime, darling," Chyna said, "it is moss. *Barbula unguiculata*. Bird's claw, look it up. C'mon, girl, let's have a look inside."

"Tell me it doesn't have a dungeon."

"Oh, no, darling, I think it actually does. And acres of gardens full of poisonous plants once used for, as they say, medicinal purposes."

Lorelei had wandered off into the overgrown gardens, stumbling upon a bizarre edifice.

"A poison garden? Oh my God, you've really lost it. Hello, look here. What is this, pray tell?"

Chyna peered around a bush.

"Why, it's a Victorian aviary! How absolutely divine. Imagine the birds!"

"An aviary? Whatever on earth are we to do with an aviary?"

"Oh, I'll think of something, darling, don't worry your pretty head about that."

She'd written a cashier's check for the property that very day.

Chyna Moon grinned as her vintage Vincent Black Shadow motorcycle skidded to a stop near the secret entrance to her drive. The roads were sheer black ice in this part of the countryside, but she was a crack rider and had barely reduced her speed on the way home.

She checked her rearview mirrors quickly before reaching for the toggle switch mounted on the shiny black fuel tank. The radio signal would part the overgrown hedgerow and admit entrance to her property. The clouds of snow had settled, and the path behind her was clear. She thought she'd seen a car, a black Audi A7, pick her up on the M14 roundabout just outside of Cambridge. But she was fairly certain she'd lost the bugger on the narrow and twisty roads leading to Haversham.

There was a normal gated entrance to the estate, of course, but she seldom used it. The massive wrought-iron gates were guarded round the clock and Chyna liked to come and go as she pleased. And she came and went at all hours, being one of those ultra-beings whose need for sleep seemed nonexistent.

She depressed her left boot, geared down, and accelerated rapidly and noisily up the gravel drive. The road to the palace wound through the dense, dark wood, and she arrived at the back entrance of her home five minutes later.

A houseman, a young kitchen boy she was rather keen on, was waiting to take her helmet, goggles, and briefcase full of papers. She'd given an important university lecture that morning on the deteriorating state of Asian political affairs. The BBC had been there with a film crew, hence the tight black Chanel skirt riding dangerously high on her thighs despite the cold.

She gave the kid a deliberate flash of palest pink panties while dismounting the bike and was happy to see him blush scarlet as he took her things with shaky hands.

"Welcome back, Dr. Moon," he said, waiting for her to shrug her way out of her tight-fitting vintage leather racing jacket.

"Is Miss Lorelei at home?"

"No, Madame. She's out riding with the new trainer. Over to Huntingdon or St. Ives, they went. She said to tell you she left something important for you with the mail on the front hall table. Courier brought it up from London, midday. Important, she said."

"Did she really say all that? What is your name again?" She was standing with her hand on her cocked left hip, a small very expensive black purse dangling from her wrist, clearly impatient.

"Well? Answer me."

"Tommy's me name, ma'am. Tom."

"Ah, yes. Tommy, how quickly one forgets. Well, Tommy, why don't you run inside and get whatever she left inside for the pretty boss lady before she slaps you silly for incompetence and impertinence? Hmmm?"

The boy bolted like a scalded cat, and she laughed at the sight.

Foolish little towheaded creature. But he was a pretty blond and she liked pretty boys around. Lorelei, the most brilliant of her graduate students, still didn't appreciate their youthful charms. But she was learning. Not only was Lorelei a very fast learner, she was deathly afraid of her older friend and mentor. Which was smart.

Chyna Moon, on the other hand, knew exactly who and what she was. She wasn't a monster. But perhaps there was a monster living inside of her.

She spied a sealed folder on top of the stack of mail piled on the sideboard beside the front doors. She grabbed a sterling stiletto, sliced open the manila envelope, and fished out an envelope. She knew who it was from without even thinking. Her father.

It was marked RAVEN: EYES ONLY! In the bold red letters favored by the man she worked for.

Raven. Her MSS secret police code name. She'd rather fancied it and her father had given it to her. It fit. Perfectly. Ravens had been a hobby of hers since her days at the Te-Wu Academy in China. She adored them.

She carried the envelope into the paneled library and collapsed into her favorite chair. There, beyond the soaring leaded-glass windows, wintry afternoon light was fleeing the skies. Solid grey shafts of light filtered down upon the faded Aubusson rugs and the priceless Queen Anne desk that dominated the library. It was her favorite room. It was where she did her reading, her thinking, and her frightful dreaming.

Still, there was light sufficient to read by without turning on one of the gas lamps used for illumination throughout the house. There was electricity, of course, but Chyna Moon detested artificial lighting. She detested artificial anything.

Glad to be home again after an exhausting day of conferences and advising doctoral thesis candidates at her private office at Cambridge, she sighed and got down to the real business at hand.

Her other life. Her *secret* life.

There were several typed sheets stapled together and a small vellum envelope addressed to her, which she opened first. It was, after all, from her father. General Sun-Yat Moon. The letterhead was from his office as Headmaster, Te-Wu Academy, on Xinbu Island, China.

As head of the Chinese secret police, her father, General Moon, was considered the second most powerful man in China. General Moon knew where the bodies were buried, primarily because he'd personally put most of them there. There were in Beijing those who thought he held more power than even his bitter rival, President Xi Jinping. The two men had been classmates at Tsinghua University, and both began their ascent to power there.

There was indeed a power struggle going on inside China, she knew, only her father's enemies didn't know it yet.

The letter was headed "From the Office of the Directorate, Chinese Ministry of State Security." The MSS. And, below, "Attention: Colonel Chyna Moon. Memorize the contents of the material in the enclosed report and destroy it. Be prepared to discuss it with the director on your CODEX phone at 0200 hours, GMT."

Her father's infamous one letter "M" signature was scrawled in bright red ink below.

Her eyes skimmed rapidly over the flash communication text, impatiently searching for the gist.

"Shit," she said aloud. Flinging the documents to the floor, she then pressed a hidden call button that would bring her manservant running. The button rang in the butler's pantry. Still bone cold from her motorcycle journey, she needed a scotch badly. She'd really have to rethink the Chanel skirt in this kind of bitter weather, especially riding her bike. Too often she found fashion dictating terms to reality.

In less than two minutes, Optimus would appear with the desired potion. Optimus Prime was a passable butler but an extraordinary personal bodyguard. He was, she had to admit, better on offense than on defense and he was superb on defense.

The fact that he was an ex-convict, TV wrestler, and psychopathic sadist hadn't appeared on his CV, but she'd seen it in his stone-dead eyes. She liked his dark, brooding aspect. He'd been hired on the spot.

"Trouble, Madame?" he said as she plucked the heavy Baccarat tumbler from the silver tray. He instantly dropped to one knee and gathered the scattered pages of the document she'd flung across the floor.

"Yes, dear Optimus, trouble. A love letter from my father. The fucking Japanese again. Everywhere I look."

"What has transpired, Madame?"

"It would seem that our aged Japanese friend, Professor Watanabe, is a double. An MI6 field agent, so my father tells me. For the last ten years! How could I have been so stupid! I treated him as a colleague. As a friend. He's dined under this roof! He has betrayed me, the old bastard. He will pay for his own stupidity. And his treachery."

"May I be of service, Madame?"

"Yes. Find Watanabe and bring him to me. Not now. This weekend. He's got a small cottage down on the Fens. He usually spends his weekends out there. Alone. Go get him, Optimus. Next Saturday night. Get him and bring him here. I think we'll introduce him to a few of our fine-feathered friends. That usually gets them chattering like monkeys. He'll talk. He'll give me names. And then he'll die from something worse than the Death of a Thousand Cuts. My father has just ordered his execution. You are invited, of course. I intend to use the Shining Basket."

"Yes, Madame."

"These Japanese are playing a very dangerous game, Optimus. In addition to spying on my father through me, now it seems the Japanese admiral Yamato has elected to send a small naval vessel to one of the disputed Diaoyu Islands in the South China

Sea. Despite numerous warnings not to undermine China's territorial sovereignty by the foreign ministry spokesman Qin Gang. Fourteen Chinese pioneers were arrested. Tokyo plans to parade them before the CNN cameras sometime in the next twenty-four hours."

"Outrageous."

"Yes. But, like Watanabe-san, Japan will pay, Optimus. Dearly."

"I've no doubt, Madame."

"Indeed. We'll soon see what their much-vaunted National Defense Force is capable of, shall we not?"

Optimus bowed deferentially.

She drained her whiskey and put the empty glass back on the tray. She gazed out the window before turning to her manservant.

"Optimus, I understand from kitchen staff the little bitch has been out riding on horseback with her trainer."

"Indeed she has."

"What time did she go out?"

"I'm not exactly sure. But sometime in the forenoon, Madame."

"How long is it, horseback over to St. Ives?"

"I've not done it myself, of course, but I would hazard a guess of . . . over there and back in roughly two hours."

"You've not seen her since?"

"I have not, Madame."

"Where the hell is she, then?"

"It is my understanding that she remained down at the stables. With one of the groomsmen. Rodney, I believe his name is."

"Did she now? Fascinating. Whatever do you suppose they're doing down there? Mucking out the stalls? Mucking or fucking would be my guess. Or maybe both."

"Shall I send someone down to retrieve her?"

Chyna got to her feet. "No. I shall do that myself. But first another whiskey. Make it a double."

"Indeed, Madame. Will that be all?"

"No, Optimus," she said, smiling at the bomb-scarred face of her butler. "It will never be all."

He smiled as he walked back to his pantry.

The old dragon was a piece of work, all right.

They didn't hear her.

But they heard the oily click of her gun.

And then the low cold of her voice.

"What the f—?" Lorelei said, eyes wide. The stableboy was on top of her, thrusting himself into her like he had a stallion fixation. Lorelei stared over his glistening shoulder at her friend. "How dare you! Get out of here now!"

"Shut up, slut. This . . . this . . . ? You decide this peasant is worthy of stealing your virtue?"

Lorelei Li laughed and pushed the boy's face away.

"My virtue?" she said. "You stole that long ago."

"You, stableboy. Get your venereal dick out of my little friend before I blow your pathetic brains out."

The strapping youth withdrew from the naked girl lying spread-eagled in the straw and turned to face his employer. Chyna saw fear, her favorite emotion, in his face, but her eyes were drawn to his formidable erection. For an instant she thought she just might fuck the boy herself. She was tempted, but she realized that it would send distinctly the wrong signal to her protégée, not to mention the only son of her head groomsman.

"I am so s-sorry, Madame Moon," the boy stammered. "She told me that if I didn't . . . uh . . . didn't comply—"

"Liar!" Lorelei hissed, raking his flushed cheek with her nails. "How dare you?" she screamed.

"Silence! You! Pull the little slut to her feet. Good. Now, lover boy, put your jeans on and get the hell out of my sight. Now!"

The boy didn't need to be told twice.

"All right, Lorelei, get dressed. We're going home now. Try to act like a lady. On the way up to the house

I want you to think about something. You ever do anything like this again? Embarrass me in this way in front of staff? You're house-hunting. But. You play by the rules? My house, my rules. We'll see."

"My, my, aren't we strict?"

"You've no idea, honey."

Chapter 23

The old man knew what was coming next.

The birds.

Earlier, down in the dungeon, he'd been beaten and battered about the head so much it was easy to feign unconsciousness now and then. He'd heard the two women whispering to each other, pausing in their torture when they thought he'd passed out on the stone floor. They'd used a phrase that was wholly alien to him then; the words had no meaning. But there was no mistaking its meaning now:

The hunger birds.

The first bird missed; the second plucked his right eye out. It landed on his cheek, the organ dangling only by a viscous thread of tissue and muscle.

A bolt of red pain seared the interior of the now empty socket. A gelatinous substance ran down his cheek. The old man whirled about. He could no longer see the hazy pale moon high above the thin and drifting clouds.

No, the hunger birds filled his vision: a great mass of beating black wings that filled the air now. Terror-struck, in shock and disoriented, the man stumbled through the tangled undergrowth that covered the frozen ground inside the cage of the ornate black wrought-iron aviary.

The shrieking black monsters were everywhere, all beaks and talons, fueled with bloodlust now, diving straight down and stabbing at their carrion feast viciously, striking with long serrating blows using their razor-sharp beaks, raking his bald head with their steel-encased talons until his blood flowed down in sheets.

He shouted, half blind, flailing at the screeching ravens with his balled fists, tripping over his own feet as he ran. He couldn't beat the swarming birds away, could not tear the masses of them from his body.

They alit upon both his shoulders, three stubborn blackbirds to each side. He slammed through the trees, trying to shake them off. He could not.

The birds' steel claw spurs were embedded in the soft flesh of his naked shoulders and they could not be flung or pried away. They began fighting one another over his ears, stabbing at each one with their sharp little beaks, tearing away small morsels of tender tissue before retreating a moment to let the others feast.

His knees weak, he clung to a tree and cried out, insane with pain.

"Stop them! Please! What more do you want to know? I've told you everything! For God's sake, have mercy upon me! Let me out! I beg you!"

He paused, threw back his head, and roared at his shrieking tormentors. The cruelest of all birds.

The hunger birds.

"The ravens," he cried to the heavens.

These demonic creatures would surely peck him to death within minutes. His would be the slowest of deaths. It was a hideous end to a life spent in the service of the mind, a quiet life, working in the shadows of the library stacks, sometimes in light, sometimes, yes, even in secrecy. Like every man, he was not quite what he appeared.

It could all have ended so differently. He could have died in bed, in his beloved cottage upon the Fens, surrounded by his books, his pictures, the warmth of his sleeping dog wrapping him in comfort.

But he'd been caught out. Oh, yes. He'd slipped up somewhere along the way. And his silent enemies had come for him. He'd always known it all might end this way. He'd been playing the great game for many, many long years. Since the war in the Pacific had ended. He was very old for a spy. Many did not live nearly so long. But he didn't want to die, not yet, not like this.

This was hell.

And that was not even the worst of it.

He knew what lay in wait for him if he survived this terrible trial. He'd seen it with his own eyes; they'd shown the dungeon to him before they began the interrogation. Shown him the ancient death device. And a death more horrible than any conceivable. Worse, yes, worse even than the birds.

Better to die here? Die now? End it?

Yes.

Surrender.

Let the loathsome feathered fiends have their way, then. Let it end here. Now.

He considered the end of his life. It was time.

Come, ravens, flock all to me, and satisfy your hunger.

It was the middle of the night. The wind was up, rattling the bare branches. A change in the weather. The nearest farm was six miles distant. No one could hear the victim's cries for mercy. No one had ever heard anything. It was a place of secrets. A place where the secrets had secrets. Where secrets flourished like hot-house orchids.

It was a place where evil felt at home.

Two women, both exotically beautiful, but one a decade older, stood outside the two-story Victorian aviary and watched the horror unfolding within. The complex iron lacework structure was beautiful, finely wrought in the shape of a cathedral dome, designed by the Bishop of Ely, who had built this place nearly two hundred years earlier.

The women were bathed in the cold blue artificial moonlight pouring down from the floodlights mounted high up inside the cage. Six large round lamps mounted inside the dome of the aviary and illuminating the nightmare below. A cold, dry wind blew hard from out of the east. Dark, snow-laden clouds scudded past the moon, touching the fields and barren black forests below.

"What do you think?" Chyna Moon, the elder of the two said.

"He's had enough, I should think. Let him out, poor sod."

"No. He has not. He'll talk if it kills him. He's betrayed us! The professor here's been working the other side for years. My father sent me a shot of him sitting on a goddamn bench with some Six agent, a man in Berkeley Square. Doing a pass. My father demands the bloody name of that agent, and I will have it from his mouth or seal it forever."

"God, stop the birds then, Chyna. Look! They're going for his tongue now . . . there's one trying to get inside his mouth!"

"Christ, you're right, he's down . . . giving up," she said, unbolting the ornately carved cast iron door and darting inside. She knew she'd extracted just about every syllable of information she was going to get from the old traitor. But he had one more name, she knew it. And she wanted to hear it before he died.

She carried a thick canvas tarp, stiff with blood, with a weighted edge like a fishing net. She shooed the birds away, then flung the tarp out in a perfect arc. It landed atop of the victim, covering his body completely.

The birds were not done. One of the nightmares dove at the tarp, letting out a piercing scream of ravenous appetite and furious frustration.

The older woman stepped between the bird and covered victim. She wore a sterling whistle hung round her neck. Now she put it to her lips and blew. The pitch was well above the range of human hearing, but it was certainly effective enough for her pets. Miraculously, all the whirling birds seemed to halt in midair, retreating in an instant, darting above, finding perches high in the leafless arms of the great trees that grew inside.

The ravens became perfectly still.

Their black eyes glinted malevolently. They were only waiting for a signal. A second sound from the whistle meant resume attack.

"Ravens, vultures, and crows," Lorelei Li whispered as if mesmerized. "Ravens, vultures, and crows . . . ravens, vultures, and crows . . ."

"Stop chanting! Come and help me, girl, will you!" the older woman cried. She had one arm around the old man, trying to drag him out with the cover still protecting him. He wasn't helping, too weak from loss of blood. "He's too bloody heavy, damn you. Get in here!"

The younger, arguably the prettier, one slipped inside. Together they dragged him outside and laid him down. The older one knelt on the frozen ground near his head, bent over him, caressing him gently.

"Tell me," she whispered. "Tell me who you met with on that bench in Berkeley Square. Give me his name! All these years, asking me your innocent questions about my family in China. About my father. All about my father! Why? For money? Silly old fool, look what it's cost you. You've got me to deal with now . . . and I know you'll believe me when I say I can be vastly more unpleasant than your little friends at MI6."

"Kill me," the old soul whispered in a ragged croak.

"Not just yet . . ."

The two women struggled with the old man going down the steep, twisting stone staircase that led to the cellars. When they reached the bottom, they lit some of the torches that stretched off into the darkness, bolted to the stone walls with ancient iron brackets. The old man was unconscious again, sagging between them. His feet bumped along on the cobbled stone as they took him to meet his fate.

It was a large stone room and the site of many evils over the centuries. Tears of water seeped from the stone above and fell upon their heads. At the far end stood a heavy wooden structure. It had served as a gibbet at one time, a guillotine later on. It now served as something far worse.

Steps led up to a wide square platform of white tile with stainless steel gutters on all four sides. It was those awful gutters, actually, that made the trembling, half-blind, half-mad victim's skin crawl.

Where once a noose had waited, there now waited the current executioner's recently installed machine of death. A gleaming, razor-meshed contraption in the shape of a large bag hung from an overhead beam.

Dating to the Tang dynasty, the hideous device was called Qian Dao, the "Shining Basket."

It was a torture even more terrible than the Death of a Thousand Cuts.

Outside in the forecourt, it had begun to snow.

Really snow.

"I got the name I wanted," Chyna said. "The man photographed in Berkeley Square. He whispered it to me just before I let the bag drop."

"Who is it? What name did he say?"

"Hawke. Alex Hawke. That bastard."

"You know him?"

"Oh, yes. I know him, all right. Lord Alexander Hawke. Ex–Royal Navy, now MI6 intelligence officer. He's been a thorn in our side for as long as I can remember. Years ago, my father had had enough and sent my older sister Jet to Cannes to kill him. She fucked him instead."

"Why?"

"Simple. Because he's the most attractive man you'll ever meet. And charming. And rich as the gods. He treated Jet like a common whore and disposed of her like a soiled tissue. And, later, he got my other sister killed for her troubles. My father and my sister Jet loathe this man. Wait till I give them this little piece of information."

"I'd like the chance to meet this Alex Hawke before you do anything drastic, Chyna. Okay? Just once. I promise."

Chyna frowned. "You little slut."

"What of it? You ought to know me by now. I'm the kind of woman who can fuck a man *and* kill him."

The two women loaded the almost weightless corpse into the boot of the old silver Rolls-Royce, slammed the lid, and climbed inside. There was little blood spatter in the boot. The victim had bled out suspended above a rain barrel in the Shining Basket. Now he was wrapped inside the canvas tarp.

"Where do we take him?" the younger one asked.

"Cambridge."

"Cambridge? You're bloody joking."

"On the contrary. I know a spot. A secret place, actually. No one has set foot inside its walls in a decade or more. It's perfect. Besides, look out there. It looks like quite a snowstorm. And snow covers any number of dreadful sins."

Chapter 24

At Sea

The central companionway was wide and mostly featureless save for the miles of tubing and conduit. At least forty feet in diameter, it seemed to be little more than an oval stainless steel tube with a flat, honeycombed deck that ran the length of the vessel. Missiles forward, reactors aft, he knew that. But, Taylor wondered with mounting curiosity, where the hell were the crew quarters?

A sub this size would carry a complement of at least 150 souls. So where was the damn head? The wardrooms? Where was the galley? Where were the pots, the pans, the dishes, and the damned garbage? And, most curious of all, where in God's name was the sub's control room?

"Skipper, hold up," a young crewman said in his earphones. "It's Sparky, sir. I got something back here. Almost missed it."

"What have you got, Sparky?" Taylor called back.

"Recessed panel in the bulkhead, sir. Large enough to be a hatch."

"Open it," Taylor said, making his way back.

"Can't, sir. Look. No handle, nothing."

"Gotta be a way . . . wait, a keypad."

Taylor looked at the thin outline carved into the bulkhead. About seven feet high by four feet wide. Definitely a hatch into a room of some kind. He leaned forward and peered closely at the keypad. There was something else above it. In the low NVG light, he'd almost missed it.

"Okay, here we go, gentlemen. Small brass construction nameplate screwed into the bulkhead. And with some kind of writing below . . . looks . . . yeah, it's Chinese . . ."

"A giant Chinese sub with almost forty nuclear warheads just outside U.S. territorial waters?" Sparky said. "Holy shit, where's Wolf Blitzer when you need him?"

"Yeah. This vessel is Chinese, all right. Wouldn't you just know it? Seaman Ka-Ching, get up here now, I need a translator."

An athletic young seaman in heavy black glasses came forward, stood on tiptoes, and peered at the small steel plate for a second or two.

"Bingo," the sailor said.

"What's it say, Ka-Ching?"

"Here at the top it says 'Gaius Augustus' . . . gotta be the name of the vessel. Weird, right? A Roman name? I think, anyway. Well, and then, right below that, 'First Centurion of Rome.' "

"What's this bit at the bottom?" Taylor asked.

"Down here at the bottom it says, 'Control Room/ Sonar. No entry.' "

"No entry? A control room you can't enter?"

"That's what it says, Skipper."

"Well, guess what. We're entering it. Ordnance, gimme a thin line of C-4 around the edges. Blow it. Rest of you guys come with me out of harm's way."

They moved along the corridor to get away from the blast and Taylor got on the radio to Stubbs, whose detail was doing the bow recon. "We got a control room back here, Stubbs, but we have to blow the door. Just a heads-up so you don't shit your Jockeys, Ensign. Stand by . . . okay . . . thirty seconds . . . fuse lit . . . Count it off . . ."

BOOM!

The noise was deafening inside the length of the closed tube. But the door was gone, blown inward.

Taylor entered first, sweeping his automatic weapon side to side. Not a soul. He flicked on his helmet LED light as did the others. Shafts of pure white light now crossed and crisscrossed the darkened space.

"Control room, clear!" he said, motioning his detail inside.

It looked like a control room, all right. Extraordinarily high-tech but still recognizable. But the first thing they noticed was that it was a control room with no god-damn place for the captain to sit. Or, they saw looking around, anybody else for that matter. Weird. You spend all day staring at an instrument panel, you need a place to sit!

But there was at least a periscope!

It emerged up out of a well and disappeared through an opening in the overhead. Clearly, there was a deck hatch directly overhead for when the periscope was deployed, but they'd missed it somehow. There were no eyepieces. Clearly, whatever the lens saw was projected directly onto digital displays. But how the hell did you control the thing? How did you steer the *boat*, for God's sake? Another mystery.

The control room was nothing but an austere space packed to the gunwales with twenty-first-century technology. Racks upon racks of servers obviously capable of feeding data throughout the sub via wired and wireless networks. Large digital monitors, imaging technologies including what looked to be IR camera feeds for night vision, sonar screens for acoustic data, laser-ranger finders, huge bundles of fiber-optic cables snaking across the deck (really odd!) they couldn't help tripping over.

To port were all the combat and situational awareness systems, hundreds of terabytes of processing power to crunch data during combat and arrive at the most complete picture of the wartime environment. And next to that, a grid showing all forty long-range missiles in their silos, their current status, "Armed," and the myriad of systems' readouts that accompanied any complex launch platform.

"I feel like I'm in the middle of a *Matrix* movie," Sparky said, "just walking around the set looking for my Xbox joystick."

"Yeah. Not exactly a user-friendly workplace environment, is it, gentlemen?" Taylor said. "All right. We've seen it. The weather topside's not getting any better. We'll go aft for a quick recon of the stern compartments, verify whether or not there are survivors. And then get the hell off this ghost ship."

All Lieutenant Taylor and his men found in the stern were the sub's nuclear reactors. There were no sealed watertight compartments. No crew quarters, no heads, no messrooms. There were no survivors aboard because there was no place, no room, for survivors to be!

When they'd completed searching every square inch of the vessel, Taylor radioed Stubbs and told him to get his men headed back to the amidships section where they'd entered the sub. On the double. He wanted to get back aboard the motor launch and back to *Dauntless* to inform the captain about everything he'd seen.

He already knew what he was going to say, and he could already hear what the captain would reply. He got the old man on the radio:

"Captain, there are no survivors. Because that vessel out there is the world's first USV."

"The first what?" the skipper would say. "No survivors?"

"There is no crew. No provisions for one. She wasn't built for that."

"What the hell was she built for?"

"It's a submersible launch platform, sir. Just massive reactors and forty huge long-range nukes being driven around the world's oceans by some sub driver-controller in an underground bunker in Beijing."

"Are you out of your mind, son? What did you call this fat bastard?"

"A USV. I made it up."

"What's it stand for?"

"Unmanned submersible vessel."

"Are you out of your effing mind, son?"

"No, sir."

"Get your ass back here for debriefing. Now!"

Taylor froze. The goddamn sub had started to *move*!

First he knew in his gut the sub's silent reactors had come back up online. Then he heard the powerful roar and whir of the massive props at the stern. He felt the ship shudder . . . She was moving forward, gaining momentum . . . and then the unmistakable roar of seawater flooding into the three-foot hole they'd cut in the hull. Mother of God, the dead boat had somehow come back to life; he could feel it, hear it, all around him.

And she was submerging.

The giant USV nosed over into a steep dive.

"Stubbs!" Taylor shouted. "Evacuate immediately! She's diving!"

"Aye, sir! We're on our way. We see the water now, sir! A goddamn flood of green water sloshing right for us! It's ankle . . . no, it's knee-high already, Skipper!"

"How far are you from the breach we cut in the hull?"

"I'd say four hundred yards . . . but . . . there's no way to tell, Moose. We're going to be swimming in a second or two here. . . ."

The roar of the flooding breach amidships in the hull was deafening. "Move faster! Whatever it takes, man. I'll meet you amidships, Stubby. Move your ass! Count your guys off as they go out the hole. I'll do the same. Go, go, go!"

With no handholds or overheads inside the steeply down-angled companionway, Taylor and his five-man stern detail practically tumbled forward toward the bow. Taylor knew Moose and the men now struggling back from the bow had the opposite problem. They'd be scrambling up a slippery slope into an onrushing flood tide.

Death had been the last thing on his mind on the bridge this morning. But now . . . he knew a couple of things:

There was no crew.

That's why wherever sat the asshole who was driving this boat, he had brought her up vertically. With no men aboard, it simply didn't matter—the angle, the speed, nothing.

And now . . . with all that water weight accumulating in the bow . . .

She was going into a vertical dive.

Taylor could now see the dark green water pouring in. He could see men from Stubbs's detail fighting uphill against the invading seawater, grinding through thigh-high water in a last-ditch effort to reach the escape hole.

One young sailor, whose blue shirt was drenched with salt water and blood, had gotten there first. He had a one-handed death grip on the perimeter of the hole, water pouring down over his head. He was reaching down to his guys with his free hand in a desperate attempt to haul them up and out.

Taylor saw one bow guy get out, then another, then a third, all kicking frantically and clinging to the heroic sailor risking his life for his comrades. The guy was literally fighting the sea. He was obviously in excruciating pain, his arm muscles surely giving way, and Taylor could see in his eyes that he was done.

He reached him and grabbed his straining forearm.

"Go! Go! Go!" Taylor screamed in his ear, prying the guy's fingers from the rim. "I've got this! You are relieved, sailor! Swim for it!"

Another of Stubbs's guys instantly appeared and Taylor got him out fast. That was five, he'd counted. Taylor waited, holding on, knowing the whole bow detail had to get out first. There was one to be accounted

for. He'd give Stubbs a minute and then he'd have to
. . . a cry above the frothing seawater.

"Sir!"

It was Ka-Ching. His normal smile was replaced by
a mask of terror, his right hand raised toward Taylor in
what looked like a plea.

Taylor took his hand and pulled him up into the
roaring funnel that was the hole.

As Ka-Ching kicked up and away toward the surface, Taylor saw the rest of his own guys clawing their
way toward him as the speed of descent increased every
second.

Where the hell was Stubbs?

He grabbed the nearest hand and yanked with all
his strength.

They were all seconds away from plunging to the
bottom of the ocean—taking with them the knowledge
of a watery grave and certain doom.

Chapter 25

Miami

The rain had let up. The high white moon sailed on through black strips of cirrus cloud. The ambulance carrying Luis Gonzales-Gonzales to Dade Memorial ER had just left the lot on two wheels with a police escort clearing the way on the crowded causeway. The dead Chinese interpreter was still dead in the filthy toilet. Sprawled on the foul floor of the lavatory where the ME guys worked on him and other officers worked the scene, took statements, the entire enchilada.

Harry, looking at his watch in exasperation, had finally flashed his Langley credentials at the ranking Miami Dade officer, took him aside and explained the situation. The CSI guys immediately deferred any further questioning of either him or Stokely until sometime later tomorrow morning.

Stoke, meanwhile, had stepped outside, gotten on his cell, and called Mrs. Gonzales-Gonzales and told her what had happened to her husband. She dropped her phone, already on her way to Miami Dade ER. She'd wanted to know how bad it was. Stoke told her it was bad. He didn't say how bad.

Sharkey, as had been prearranged earlier that day, had left his pale blue Contender 34 moored just outside the entrance to Marker 9. The boat was tied at the dock, ready to rumble offshore. She was Sharkey's pride and joy. She had a tuna tower, state-of-the-art GPS and electronics, bow and stern thrusters, and triple Yamaha 300s. Basically, one kick-ass 900-horsepower sportfishing boat. Harry Brock had helped Sharkey acquire it at a DEA auction in Hialeah two months earlier.

The *Miss Maria*, Shark had called her, after his new wife.

This is a debt I never repay, Señor Brock, Luis had told him at the time, the day he took proud possession of her. *What you did for me and my wife today, Mr. Brock.*

Yeah, well, you're paid up now, Harry thought, thinking about Shark's wife and what she was going through right now. He'd tried to comfort her when he'd called standing behind the ambulance. Told her how brave Sharkey had been. Too brave to know when he was supposed to be afraid. And far too good a man to understand he was incapable of ever doing bad.

Now Brock and Stoke jumped down in the boat. Stoke cranked it while Harry cast off the bow, springs, and stern lines. He shoved them bow out away from the dock and into the channel toward open water. Stoke leaned on the twin throttles. Nine hundred angry horses lifted the bow almost straight up, and *Miss Maria* shot the hole and roared out into Government Cut, headed southwest to Biscayne Bay.

Stoke flicked on the big new LED spotlight Luis had mounted forward on the bow only this morning. He'd also mounted a siren and a "headache" flasher bar atop the windshield. At night, at high speed, the target would take the blue flashers for Coast Guard.

Stoke used the spot to pick out the channel markers ahead, now flashing by to either side in a blur. At this speed, they were coming up fast and he was correcting his course at the last second as each one flared up in his peripheral vision. It was a tricky business, but no one was better at it than the old swift boat vet. *Miss Maria* was doing forty-five knots on a black windless night, but only because they were late.

"Tell me some more about Hi Lo," Stoke said, eyes dead ahead, concentrating. He didn't even glance at Harry standing beside him at the helm station.

"Like what, Cap?"

Now Stoke looked at him.

"Like how the hell he had a goddamn weapon, Harry. For God's sake! Like how you didn't know about it. Start with that."

"He didn't, Stoke. I swear. I patted him down. He was clean."

"You're sure."

"I wouldn't lie about something like that. Cut me a little slack here. Jesus. Shark's my friend, too."

"My partner's down. Maybe dead. Make that probably. Because of a guy you brought along without even talking to me first, seeing if I was okay with it. I'm not in a slack-cutting mood."

Harry was silent.

A few minutes later, Brock said, "Aw, shit."

"Aw, shit, what?" Stoke said.

"I didn't pat him down."

"What?"

"I didn't frisk him. I mean, after the Shell station thing."

"What?"

"He could have had a prearranged piece stashed there, waiting for him inside that goddamn gas station restroom. Somebody on the outside left it waiting for him in the toilet tank. Or inside the paper towel dispenser. Wherever. The station's just across the road from the county lockup. Would explain why he bolted across the turnpike like he did. All that crap about being sick."

"Yeah. That would explain it, all right," Stoke said.

He leaned on the throttles and *Miss Maria* jumped up a little higher on the plane. Harry watched him a minute. Stoke had that thousand-yard stare. The one he'd picked up in the jungle.

Stokely Jones looked out into the blackness. No boat showed a light. *Jade* was out there to the south somewhere, steaming north to Biscayne Bay. The plan was to board her down south, near the Keys, where they wouldn't attract much attention. This was a black op, off the radar intercept, and they didn't need civilians shooting video with their iPhones.

But what he was really thinking about was Sharkey.

"Harry, go below and set up the equipment. Get your gear on. Weapons check. We're closing fast. We'll be on top of them in twenty minutes or less at this rate. I have her lit up on radar now."

There was a small cuddy cabin forward and Harry went below. All the weapons he'd had delivered to Sharkey at the dock that afternoon were laid out just the way he'd ordered. In addition, there was Tactic's full complement of assault gear: FN SCAR short-barreled assault rifles with FN40 grenade launchers mounted on the lower rails, Sig P226 navy pistols, web belts with smoke and flash-bang grenades, balaclavas to hide their faces, the whole nine yards plus a couple more.

He got his rig on, zipped up his ceramic-tile-plated assault jumpsuit and got Stoke's equipment ready. He'd relieve Stoke at the helm in ten minutes; then Stoke would come below and get his shit together.

Three miles out from the rendezvous zone, Stoke would throttle back to dead idle and they'd go through the whole thing one more time. Weapons check, timing, signals. They had the element of surprise going, and whoever was on that boat had no idea anyone suspected a damn thing. But Harry'd learned the hard way that if a black op can go south, it will go south in a heartbeat.

It's already gone south, Harry, he said to himself and then banished that unhealthy thought from his brain.

"Ready?" Stoke said to Harry. He was still pissed, but they had a job to do. You didn't carry emotions into battle.

They could see *Jade*'s running lights approaching them in the blackness. Harry flicked the switch and put the powerful LED spotlight on her. She was big, all right, hundred and forty, hundred and fifty feet maybe.

"Born ready," Harry shot back.

"Standing up and talking back?"

"Kicking ass and taking names."

"Awright. Game on."

Stoke snatched up the VHF radio mike and depressed the send button.

He said: "Vessel located position 38 degrees, 26 north, 129 degrees 131 west, steering course bearing two-eight-zero, speed seven knots, this is United States Coast Guard vessel *Vigorous,* approximately five nautical miles off your port beam, standing by on channel 16, over."

"We read you loud and clear, Coast Guard. This is *Jade,* over."

"Roger, *Jade,* this is Coast Guard, request you switch to channel 22, over."

"Going to 22, over."

"*Jade,* Coast Guard, standing by on channel 22, over."

"Go ahead, Coast Guard . . ."

"*Jade,* I am going to send over a boarding team. Maintain your current course and speed, over."

"Roger that, Coast Guard, maintain course and speed, *Jade* standing by on 22 . . ."

Stoke smiled.

"You think he bought it?"

"Think? Hook, line, and sinker. Let's go see what they're hiding aboard that floating pussy palace."

Brock said, "The *Jade* guy on the radio. Sounds like some old redneck from Podunk to me. Didn't sound hostile."

"They never do, Harry. On the radio, anyway."

"Right. I knew that."

Stoke just looked at him and shook his head.

In his own small way, Harry Brock was the price America had to pay for freedom.

Chapter 26

Cambridge University, United Kingdom

Pip Trimble trudged along snowbound Sidney Street, his large pointed ears glowing red with the cold. The old fellow was shivering badly, even though the sun was well up now, doing business at its old stand. Pip was astounded. He'd never seen a snowfall like this one, this late in the spring.

Pip was bound for the Porters' Lodge at Sidney Sussex College. This was no mean feat on a snowy morning like this. The elderly gardener was trying to shield his face from the wind-driven sleet, not-so-artfully dodging the sheets of ice periodically sliding from the rooftops above, sharp ice particles glimmering in the air as they came crashing down.

Sidney, as his beloved college was commonly known, was the place he'd called home for all but ten of his seventy-five years. His kingdom was the college gardens, large and small, public and private . . . and some, even secret. Pip had spent the majority of his allotted hours on this earth inside walled gardens, with all the pleasures and limitations that implies.

Last night's heavy snowfall had brought the ancient market town to a standstill. In the narrow streets, the white stuff was knee-deep, crusty on top, and bloody hard sledding for a man his age. Pip stuffed the oily paper bag containing bacon sandwiches and crisps inside his mac and slogged forward.

Taking daily breakfast to the boss, the college's head porter, was perhaps a small tradition in a town so chockablock with them as Cambridge, but render unto Caesar, as they say. Old Bill Woolsey was a hard man but a fair one, and Pip had long ago come to consider Bill a friend rather than a superior.

"Morning, Pip," the fellow said cheerfully to him as he pushed through the heavy wooden door and into the warmth. Dark warrens of old rooms, the traditional Porters' Lodge at Cambridge is usually a beehive of noisy students milling about, crowding around freshly posted test scores, plucking their mail from the slots, or parking their bicycles at the door. Not this morning however.

Just Bill, alone, squatting before the crackling fire, throwing on another log.

Woolsey was burly, gruff, and ex-army like most of the head porters here at the university. He'd held sway over the Sidney lodge for nigh on thirty years now. The head porter at any college was a man traditionally held in high esteem, treated with great respect and even deference.

Pip placed the sodden bag on the deeply scarred wooden countertop and Woolsey, face alight, stood plucking out his breakfast, devouring it in two or three voracious bites.

"Morning yourself," Pip said, chewing his own sandwich thoughtfully, his old bones grateful for the warmth of the fire. Bill eyed him sidewise, going over the day's schedule of events, a list that included the Olympic torch relay along Sidney Street, pausing at Magdalene Bridge before lighting out for St. Ives, Huntingdon, and the Cambridgeshire countryside beyond.

"You remember when they shot that film here, Pip? *Chariots of Fire*? Well, they're running another torch relay today. Street will be mobbed, all right."

"Remember it? I was in it, by Jove! Sitting up on top of the garden wall, waving at the lads running by. My moment of bloody stardom, wasn't it?"

Bill put the schedule down and stared at the old boy.

"Hell you doing out and about on such a bitter day, you old fool? Y'er a gardener, for God's sake. Planning to pluck a few daisies and mow some grass, are you now, Pipper?"

"My favorite tree come down in the night, it did, sir. In the Master's private garden. That lovely old cherry, she just couldn't bear up under all that heavy wet snow, Bill. Saw the whole thing from me own window at dawn this morning. Broke me heart, it did. Unsightly, too."

"Should have stayed in bed, Pip. Master's eyes ain't what they used to be, are they? Rheumy. I doubt he can even see that far from up in his rooms anymore. Besides, he ain't set foot in that garden since the last century."

"Well, I can see just fine and it's my garden and it's a bloody eyesore, that's what it is, thank you very much, indeed."

Pip secured an axe, a spade, and a hacksaw from his shed. Then he made his way through the labyrinth of twisting high-walled pathways until he reached his destination. The Master's Garden. A weathered gothic arch set deep in an ancient dun-colored wall was mostly hidden behind thick black ivy. The door, too, was black with age. Removing a large brass key ring from his side pocket, he fumbled with ice-numb fingers for the proper key. His hands were shaking badly and he had a hard time getting the heavy bronze key into the lock.

He twisted the key and felt the tumblers tumble.

It was a very small garden, this one, perhaps thirty by forty feet. In summer it was a lovely green sanctuary and Pip frequently took his lunch there, enjoying the fruits of his labor, his back against the old cherry that stood no longer. He leaned his spade against the wall and slogged to the far corner where the tree had come down. He was just ten feet from his cherry when he stopped dead in his tracks. He had spied something protruding from the crusted top of the snow.

It was dead white and he'd almost missed it but for the first stroke of light to find the garden just then. He knelt down, wincing at the pain in his stiff joints, and peered at the thing sticking up about two inches above the snow. A fishy white thing, crisscrossed with faint pinkish depressions. What on earth? Thinking he'd pluck it from the snow for closer examination, he pinched it twixt two fingers and pulled, lightly at first, then with more effort.

It was frozen stiff and wouldn't budge.

He bent forward and peered at the thing more closely, his curiosity growing by the second. When he realized what he was looking at, he gagged on the gorge rising in his throat and toppled over backward. Some long moments later, he blinked his watery eyes and realized he was staring up at the clear blue sky. Must have fainted dead away, he thought, turning his head so he could see the horrid, mutilated thing again.

It was a human thumb.

"Good God, man," Woolsey said five minutes later.

He was prone on his stomach in the snow beside a kneeling Pip, breathing heavily, having come all the way from the lodge on the run when he got Pip's call.

"It's a bloody thumb!" said Bill.

"Right. A thumb. Like I said."

"Show me the mortal man who could believe it, Pip? A thumb? In the Master's Garden? Had to see it with my own eyes before I ring the Cambridge police, didn't I?"

"Call 'em, now," Pip said, unable to take his eyes off the offending frozen digit. He wanted it removed from his garden. Now.

Woolsey grunted, rolled over on his side, and pulled his mobile from his trouser pocket. "Cambridge," was all the officer at the other end had to say.

After giving this underling a lengthy explanation of the extraordinary circumstances, Bill was finally put through to a Detective Inspector Cummings and was saying, "You heard me right, sir. A human thumb. Sticking out of the snow in the Master's Garden here at Sidney. Frozen stiff and it's not going anywhere, but I'd get your team over here on the double. Medical examiner, whoever. There is some . . . uh . . . mutilation involved."

He rang off and looked at Pip. "On their way. Sounded excited to have reports on something besides some rowdy frosh pissed out of their gourds, actually. A human thumb, he says to me, you're joking."

"Think there's a body attached to it?"

"You pulled on it, right? What happened?

"Stuck fast. To . . . whatever."

"When was the last time you were here? In this garden, I mean."

"Yesterday morning, raking. Nothing out of the ordinary."

"So sometime between then and the snowfall last night. They'll ask us that."

"Right. Best keep our stories straight."

"What?"

"Everyone's a suspect, Bill."

"You're bloody joking, right?"

"Got you." Pip laughed. He seldom got the drop on the boss.

"Bugger off, Trimble. They'll find an empty bottle of Russian tap water with that body, I'll wager."

Pip hadn't thought of that. A drunk? A man who had stumbled upon the garden by accident? No. But it was a good thought. Bill had been a military policeman in the British army. How his mind worked still, was Pip's experience, a good bit of the copper still in him after all these years.

Detective Inspector Cummings had interviewed the two men separately in the small back room at the lodge. All business, polite but efficient he was, with a pair of unblinking, wide-set brown eyes behind steel-rimmed glasses, ramrod straight, proper copper posture. Pip and Woolsey told him everything they knew, which didn't take long at all.

Now, back at scene of the crime, if that's what it was, Pip and Woolsey were standing around stamping their frozen boots, watching the pathologist and his team lay out a grid of string surrounding the offending thumb. A police photographer had taken countless photos from every angle.

"Just like CSI," Woolsey had muttered to him. Pip had no idea what CSI was, had never owned a telly, but he'd nodded affirmation. He found the whole police process fascinating. They were delicately inserting probes into the snow, fishing around for a corpse, he supposed.

Half an hour later they started digging in earnest.

Pip strained this way and that, trying to see. He couldn't make out very much, as there were so many official people standing around the site. His bones ached with cold and he was longing for the warmth of the Porters' Lodge but he stood fast. He wanted to see who had violated his garden for himself. Woolsey finally excused himself and lumbered off, claiming a full bladder but wanting the warmth of a shot of whiskey most likely.

Somewhere beyond the walls a cheer erupted for the lone runner with the torch.

Pip waited for an eternity.

"Christ Jesus."

It was Cummings who'd said it.

The circle of men leaned forward and peered down at whatever it was beneath their feet. Three or four of them turned away and were sick in the snow.

"Mr. Trimble?" Cummings said, turning to catch his eye. "You'd better come take a look at this."

There was a body, all right, and the sight of the dead man made Pip want to puke, too.

He was naked, faceup, and his entire torso, arms, legs, hands, and feet were crisscrossed with thin pink lines, tiny indentations in the flesh that made the dead man look like a large frozen ham bound up in a string mesh wrapper. Every square inch of skin was raised in fat goose bumps. His face was the worst, a mask of bone and black blood. His nose, lips, and eyelids were gone, as well as his ears. Like they'd been sliced off by whatever had made all the thin marks on the thin, albino white body, cutting into the skin—Pip felt his legs give way and collapsed down to his knees, his eyes never leaving the corpse.

All ten fingertips had been removed. Clean cuts, as if they been sliced off with a heavy pair of garden shears. Had he been alive for that?

Through the shroud of shock, Pip gradually became aware that someone was speaking in a dull monotone.

"Male. Asian. Bald. Age approximately seventy-five to eighty. Frozen before decomposition could occur. Cause and time of death unknown. Some lividity around the buttocks and shoulders. No gunshot wounds. Soft facial tissue missing due to mutilation—"

Pip sat back on his heels.

How could one human being wreak such horrors upon another?

He slowly got to his feet and walked back to his position beside the downed tree, shaking his head and muttering quietly to himself.

"This garden will never be mine again. No, no, it will be a bloody tourist attraction now, that's what it will be, all right. The garden that sprouted a thumb, or some such nonsense. World famous. Like Downton Abbey."

Chapter 27

The White House

"The president will see you now."

"Thank you."

"Right this way."

Lieutenant Moose Taylor saluted the two ramrod-stiff marine sentries outside the Oval as he entered the world's most famous room. He'd met the man who occupied it before on a visit to the Hill. He'd been a young cadet at Annapolis. He'd met Rosow only because he'd been in the company of his father, an admiral, and an old classmate of the new president's at Annapolis. David Rosow had been the up-and-coming senator from Connecticut in those days.

"Mr. President," the young lieutenant said, saluting the commander in chief, who stood up to shake his hand.

Rosow wore the mantle well, he thought. He had the POTUS uniform (navy blue suit, starched white shirt, red-and-blue tie) down pat, and he looked healthy and very fit. He had thick wavy hair, still chestnut brown tinged with grey, and strong blue eyes. He also had a deepwater tan. He spent a lot of his limited free time out on the Potomac or on the Chesapeake Bay sailing his beloved gaff-rigged cutter, the *Jeanne*.

"Lieutenant Taylor," Rosow said with a broad grin. "Still the spitting image of the old man, minus a few years, of course."

"Yes," Taylor said, laughing. "Yes, sir. And proud of it."

"You should be, you should be," the president said. "The look of eagles, your old man used to call it. Please, let's have a seat over there, shall we? Would you care for some coffee, tea? Grog?"

Moose smiled. "No thanks, Mr. President. I'm good."

They sat opposite each other on the two pale blue sofas. Rosow gave the sole remaining marine sentry a nod, clearly a signal to everyone else in the room that he wished to be alone with present company. They all filed out discreetly.

"Your father was a fine man, Lieutenant," the president said. "A great warrior. A great American. I miss him to this day."

"Thank you, sir. He always said the same of you."

"I always wondered: Why in hell did he nickname you 'Moose'?"

"I couldn't rightly say, sir. Brain size?"

Rosow laughed and said, "You got his humor. Thank God someone did. "

"He had plenty to spare, Mr. President."

"Pass that on to a son someday, will you?"

"I will, sir."

"Well. You know why you're here, of course. I've seen all the *Dauntless* reports and photographs of that sub that your skipper filed. All highly classified as you can imagine. Before I take any further action, I thought I'd ask you here to tell me firsthand precisely what you saw and, second, what you think about what happened out there."

"I understand, sir."

"First of all, I'm sorry for the loss of your crewman aboard that thing. A good friend, I understand."

"Yes, sir. Will Pullman. A fine sailor."

"Upon learning of his death I yesterday ordered the secretary of the navy to award a posthumous Navy Cross for valor to Ensign Pullman."

"Thank you, Mr. President. I can't possibly tell you how much that will mean to his family down in Texas. I just returned from visiting with them, sir.

His mom's taking it pretty hard. The whole town is, to be honest, sir."

"I plan to invite his family and friends here to the White House for the ceremony. I'd like you to be here as well."

"Thank you, Mr. President."

Rosow paused and looked at the framed portrait of John Paul Jones hanging on the wall beside his desk for a long moment. Whatever he was thinking, he shook it off.

"You went down and took a look at it? What remained? After SS *Devilfish* torpedoed it?"

"I did."

"Anything left?"

"Nothing much bigger than a teacup. Massive debris field. All forty of those missiles blew, sir. Created a sizable tsunami, but nothing reached landfall."

"Right. We had NOAA put out an undersea earthquake alert. One more thing. Why the hell do you think it surfaced? Within sight of one of our destroyers?"

"I think it was a control systems malfunction. Or possibly human error. The controller back in Beijing or wherever screwed up. Blew her ballast tanks by mistake and she rocketed vertically to the surface. Nothing else makes much sense."

"You think that controller half a world away had any way of knowing a U.S. Navy vessel was in the vicinity?

Had personnel aboard at the time? Did you guys trigger any alarms?"

"None, sir. I think what happened is he lost her, finally regained control while we were aboard, and was simply taking her deep, down to her hidey-hole on the bottom. Zero knowledge that U.S. Navy personnel were on board when he initiated that crash dive."

"You saw no evidence of security cameras aboard?"

"Not one, sir. What would be the point? These things are designed to sit on the bottom for a lifetime without being observed."

"Good. Let's start with the vessel itself, Moose. Tell me the—what did you name that thing again? They tell me you came up with it yourself."

"USV, sir. Unmanned submersible vessel."

"Right. USV. Good for you. Your own personal acronym. You found a manufacturer's plate screwed into a bulkhead in the control room. Had it translated from the Chinese by one of your detail. Is that correct?"

"I did."

"*Gaius Augustus*. Quite an odd name for a Chinese naval vessel, wouldn't you agree, son?"

"Yes, sir. We all thought it was strange."

"You know I'm a bit of a history buff, like your dad. He was Civil War. I'm Ancient Rome."

"Yes, sir."

"Gaius Augustus was a centurion of Rome. Some time during the reign of Caesar, 44 B.C. to A.D. 19. Gaius Julius Caesar chose his legion commanders, the centurions, for their intelligence but primarily for bravery in battle. First over the wall, first through the breach was the centurion credo. Safe to say those guys were what your generation commonly refers to these days as 'badass.' Caesar's SEALs, to coin a phrase."

Taylor had to laugh. "Right, Caesar's SEALs, good one, sir."

"So. I've been thinking about that, Moose. A lot. Even got out my dog-eared Plutarch and did a little research. Interesting. I'll tell you about that in a minute. Let me ask you, how the hell do you think that sea monster came by her name? Something just a little out of focus there, right?"

"I've pondered that myself. I can honestly tell you that I have no earthly idea. It just doesn't jibe with anything I know about the Chinese naval tradition, sir."

"Right. It doesn't. But somebody named it. In our own navy, as you well know, the chief of naval operations suggests names based on various traditions, for carriers, destroyers, submarines. Then the secretary of the navy makes the final call. That's how we do it. But how does the People's Liberation Army Navy do it? Call themselves the Chinese Navy now, but I still like the old name. Like to think about their annual Army-Navy game, y'know. I guess they play themselves?"

Taylor smiled. "Yes, sir, I suppose they do. Go, Army Navy! Beat Army Navy!"

The president laughed out loud and looked at the young lieutenant fondly, seeing his old friend at that tender age.

"Well, I can tell you this much, Moose. The Chinese have got a new guided missile destroyer they named the *Luyang I.* And a frigate called the *Jiangkai II.* Now that's what I think the name of a CN ship ought to sound like. But *Gaius Augustus*? Tell me. How weird is that, son?"

"*Twilight Zone* weird, Dad would call it. Sir, one thing I think was missed in the reports—"

"Yes? What?"

"Once we cut our way inside I went aft. I sent Ensign Pullman forward to inspect the missile silos I'd seen topside . . ."

"Forty of them."

"No, sir. One of Pullman's detail contacted me after I filed my report. Just recently in fact, here in Washington. He said something had been bothering him . . . finally put his finger on it. He said there were twenty tubes to starboard but . . . only nineteen to port."

"Meaning?"

"The forward-most starboard tube was different. The sailor, Ensign Rick Hynson, told me there was no hatch cover over it. Whatever weapon was inside that tube was never meant to leave the boat."

"What do you make of that?"

"I think it was a fail-safe system."

"Destroy the sub in the event of a malfunction. Or if one fell into enemy hands."

"That was my thought, sir."

"I'll pass that along to the secretary. Good information."

"Yes, sir."

"Listen. I've got an assignment for you. Highest sensitivity, obviously, so I'm giving you top-secret clearance. I've screwed this entire episode down as tight as I can. Since only you, I, and a very small number of our people know anything about this new weapon, I'm asking you to look into something for me. Director Brick Kelly at CIA will provide you with a temporary office at Langley. On his floor. Look at the Chinese Navy's central command structure. Get bios on anyone high ranking enough to suggest names for newly constructed vessels. Find out their naming process. Maybe fleet admirals suggest names. Get bios on them, too. Or maybe it's political; look at President Xi Jinping

and then down the totem pole from there. You're looking for someone in their system with a thing for Roman
history. Understand?"

"Yes, sir. Consider it done."

"This remains strictly between you and me. If news
of this goddamn death machine leaked? Catastrophic.
Panic. You know what I mean? These things are being
constructed in a secret location. I need to identify that
location so I can take it out."

"Yes, I certainly do understand, Mr. President."

"Well. Good. See what you come up with. Anything
even remotely smells promising, you call my private
number. You still have it? The one your dad used?"

"Yes, sir."

"Before you go. I mentioned Plutarch earlier. Well,
here's the thing, Lieutenant. Caesar created only a
handful of his officers centurion during his lifetime.
Six, to be exact."

"Yes, sir."

"Gaius Augustus? He was the fifth centurion Caesar
named. You draw any conclusions from that fact? As it
relates to the sub you found?"

"Yes, sir, I do. Five is not a random number. There
may be more than one of those things still out there.
Unmanned missile platforms. Lying inert on the
bottom in the deepest parts of the world's oceans.

Each one with forty live ICBMs ready to launch. No thermal signatures. No screw signatures, no radio activity. Incommunicado. Utterly and completely undetectable."

"Exactly. We don't have a whole lot of time to figure this all out, Moose. Hell, it may already be too late."

"I hope not, Mr. President. I pray not."

"Here's my problem, son. Boys in the Pentagon? The Joint Chiefs? Langley? NSA? They all sit right where you're sitting and tell me we don't even have to even start worrying about the Chinese military capability until well into the next decade. That's the mindset here in Washington. The White House, on the Hill, wherever. Hear that garbled sound? That's our best current military thinking talking through their hats you hear."

"Yes, sir. I understand."

"We need to find out who built that USV monstrosity, Moose. And we need to find out how many they built. And we need to find out where the hell the rest of them are. When I say 'we,' I'm referring, of course, to you. I appreciate your help. Now get to work, sailor. Dismissed."

"Aye-aye, sir!"

Chapter 28

The Cotswolds

Chief Inspector Ambrose Congreve of Scotland Yard had a recurring dream. Had had the reverie since early childhood; since St. Albans, as a matter of fact, when he was but a timid, mildly overweight day boy who never seemed to fit in with the lads. Of course, this was in those dark playground days when he'd not yet learned to use his size to his advantage.

When he did that, he was a holy terror.

Ambrose never did quite grasp the significance of this recurring dream of his, but since it was such an obvious founding pillar of his psyche, he never relegated it to the mere piffle drifting about in some of the more remote and convoluted corners in the formidable chambers of his brain . . .

In the dream, he would fall sound asleep. Dead to the world, the bedside windows of his mind opened onto some frosty midwinter's night. And then . . . whammo! Abruptly . . . white gave way to green . . . and it became full summer! The last wintry gale had finally blown itself inside out!

It was if someone (was it him?) had come creeping along his winding lane that night, inflated all the trees and bushes like so many green balloons, scattered bulbs, blossoms, and shrubs about like confetti, opened up a cage full of plump red-breasted robins, and, then, after a quick look round, signaled up the curtain upon a brand-new backdrop of liquid blue summer sky.

That, at any rate, was his dream, his favorite dream. Some kind of awakening, he imagined.

And such were his thoughts as he fired up his stalwart motorcar. Because at the moment he was, to put it delicately, freezing his bloody arse off. It was chilly. It was a crisp cold morning with spiny frost shooting along the grasses in every which way.

Snow?

In May? *Ah, right. Global warming,* Ambrose thought, wrapping his muffler more tightly round his neck. That was the answer. The more the globe warmed, the more the center of England cooled. Q.E.D., and all that stuff. To hell with it. The Morgan's long yellow louvered bonnet stretched out ahead of the windscreen and, save for the inclement icy climes of England in springtime, all was right with his world.

He depressed the starter button . . . wait for it . . .

Glorious.

He took a deep breath of the bracing air, engaged first, then shifted up to second for the upcoming right-hander, and steered the old girl through the turn with what he felt was a good deal of finesse considering the ice and snow on the roadways.

How he did love motoring about the countryside, even in this iffish weather. Besides, it wasn't as if he hadn't bothered to dress for the occasion, was it? No. He was wearing, beneath his heavy grey woolen overcoat and purple cashmere scarf, a three-piece suit from Gieves & Hawkes, bespoke tailors in Savile Row. The suit had been done up for him in a rather sprightly young check rendered in shades of green, brown, and tan.

His feet were shod in cable-stitched purple socks inside an old and much-loved pair of spit-polished leather wing-tipped loafers courtesy of Lobb & Co., St. James. He had three identical pairs in his closet. His friend Hawke had teased him about it. Why on earth would a man want four pairs of the same shoe?

"Because," he replied in a huff, "to do otherwise simply isn't fair to the shoe."

Bidding adieu to her fiancé in the forecourt that morning, Lady Diana Mars had observed that he "looked like some character from a bygone, vanished era."

"Really?"

"Really."

"More's the pity," he sniffed, and roared off. His views on fashion were as immutable as the phases of the moon, the very tides, the . . . whatever.

The Taplow Common Road was empty, and he gave the old girl the juice. He wished he'd remembered his bloody gloves, he thought, barely holding the flat cap down on his head with one frozen hand, the other on the frozen wheel.

As usual, he was driving "alfresco," and the frigid air was biting and snapping at him like some arctic hurricane. He glanced at the speedo. He was going like sixty, as the old expression had it. A bit quick for the icy country roads, but then he was running a bit late after that postbreakfast spat with his fiancée. Something or other about his memory, he thought, but wasn't quite sure. Couldn't remember, really. Maybe it was that he "didn't listen." That was it.

His ancient Morgan roadster had been dubbed the "Yellow Peril" by his oldest and closest friend, Alex

Hawke. This moniker didn't sit at all well with the former chief inspector of Scotland Yard. No, not at all. True, the splendid conveyance was a lovely, buttery shade of yellow. But it was not, by any stretch, even remotely perilous.

He was new to this magical world of automobiles, having only bought and learned to drive his beloved forty-year-old wheezer a scant five years earlier. But he'd been smitten from the start. He now drove it any-where and everywhere, rain or shine, snow or—bloody hell!

He swung the wheel hard to port, then swerved wildly to the right to avoid the looming and unseen snowbank that had loomed up on the far side of a sweeping curve and now barreled straight at him.

The Morgan's rear end suddenly swapped places with the nose, more than a few times, and he found himself spinning and skidding with a carnival-like air, a gay and colorful carousel whirling about along the icy lane. He was progressing thus down a gently curving slope until at long last he plowed into another snowbank some hundred meters or so on, finally bringing the entire matter to a gentle, if ignominious conclusion.

Dizzy, he peered through his snow-spattered wind-screen. The long-louvered bonnet he so dearly loved was partially hidden in the fluffy white stuff. He extricated himself from the chariot and walked round the vehicle, inspecting the working bits, tyres, et cetera, for damage. None. None that he could see, at any rate. The innermost workings of the thing were a secret he'd rather not learn.

Still, it irked.

What the devil were these motorway crews doing if not keeping the roads safe for sporting motorists such as himself?

He jumped back into the old girl, grabbed reverse, and gave her just enough throttle to back out of the embankment without spinning her wheels. Pointing her at last in the right direction, taking control of the curves with gentle downshifts and cautious braking, he resumed his onward journey.

Ambrose was en route to Hawkesmoor, the family seat of Lord Alexander Hawke and his ancestors since the early seventeenth century.

Alex had rung up first thing and summoned him. Said it was rather important. Something or other to do with Cambridge, apparently. There was a steely urgency in Hawke's voice Congreve had heard many times over the years. It could mean only one thing. It meant, as his hero the incandescent Sherlock Holmes was wont to say, "The game is afoot."

Afoot it certainly was. Arriving red-cheeked with an inch or so of permafrost coating his entire body, his face flushed with cold, Congreve stood on the wide doorstep at the south portico of Hawkesmoor. He was soon greeted by Pelham Grenville, Hawke's octogenarian gentleman's gentleman and general factotum. He of the snowy white hair, pale blue eyes lit by an inner twinkle, and the utterly unflappable demeanor.

Pelham had, as he liked to say, been through it all: the thick, the thin, and the unthinkable with their young charge, Lord Alexander Hawke.

After the horror, when Hawke's parents had been brutally murdered by drug pirates aboard their yacht in the Caribbean, Pelham and Congreve had assumed responsibility for raising the devastated seven-year-old boy. The child had been strong-willed from the outset. A boy, as his father had remarked, born with a heart for any fate.

At the age of nine, for example, young Alex had insisted on moving from his great rooms high in Hawkesmoor's west wing to take up permanent residence in the stables down the hill. Moved all his books, toy soldiers, stamps, coins, whatever he could carry. There, in a tiny room above the stalls among the rowdy stableboys, he'd installed himself. And there he'd remained until he'd been sent off to his boarding school, Fettes, in Edinburgh.

To his credit, he'd lived the life of the boys. He'd mucked out the boxes with the best of them, cared for a sick foal long after the other boys had given in to sleep, and earned the respect and love of all and sundry. He was an odd boy, full of an ingrained fighting spirit; but he was the soul of kindness when it came to the less fortunate, the weak, the downhearted or downtrodden.

For the two doting caretakers, Congreve and Pelham, intent on raising a young gentleman, it was all uphill from there.

It had been a challenge, certainly, but, safe to say, the pair of them had been more than up to it. From Pelham, Hawke had learned civility, gracious manners, and the nobility of service to others, the kindliness bestowed on the less fortunate, the organizational skills required to run a complex enterprise, and the power of humility over arrogance. From Congreve came a love of military history, literature, and language as well as the nature of deductive reasoning and the ability to see clearly limned trees where others saw only forests. He had learned to shoot, mastered weaponry of every description, and learned how to use his bare hands to defend himself against any who would do him harm.

It wasn't until later in his life that he made a profound discovery: the murder of his parents had not killed him; no, it had made him strong.

Lord Alexander Hawke, the man, had emerged as a surprisingly formidable bulwark against the forces of anarchy and evil around the world. And two men, Ambrose and Pelham, had formed an unbreakable bond with each other as a result of their shared experiences during little Alex's upbringing.

Congreve reached out to press the bell and heard the familiar toll of the deep gong echo from within.

"Morning, Chief Inspector," Pelham said moments later.

He eyed the new arrival's high-volume motoring attire without comment. Pelham well knew his comrade in arms was somewhat of a dandy, but it was a lifelong trait he found endearing rather than annoying. Taking the visitor's ice-stiff woolen tartan cap and equally stiff overcoat (a subtle grey check), he said, "Please come in and defrost. They're chatting in the library. I assume you'll want your tea rather than the coffee?"

"I would, please. I'm sorry. Did you say 'they' are in the library?"

"I did use that word, sir. Another gentleman, you see. Arrived last evening barely in time for supper. Down from Cambridge, his lordship says. Delivering an update into the drone attack on President McCloskey's funeral. I fear the news is not good, judging by the mood in the room."

"Ah. And does this mysterious stranger have a name, by chance?"

"Indeed."

"Anyone I know?"

"That I couldn't really say, sir."

"Oh, please, Pelham, you irascible old party. Do not even begin to attempt this soul-of-discretion charade with me. It's not in the least becoming, if you must know."

"His lordship gave strict instructions, sir. The visiting gentleman's name is to be kept under a strict cone of silence. Those were his exact words. 'Cone of silence.'"

"You refuse to divulge his identity? To me? Don't be absurd. For heaven's sake, man, I'm going in there now!"

"That would be most injudicious of you."

"To go in there?"

"I don't advise it."

"Pelham, get out of my way."

"As you say, sir."

"I'm going in."

"Then all will be revealed. Right this way, sir," the tall but stooped old soul said and led the way from the entrance hall down a long corridor to an ornate set of tall doors on the left.

He rapped twice, opened one door a wide crack, and announced, "Chief Inspector Ambrose Congreve to see you, m'lord."

"Ambrose!" he heard Hawke bellow from deep within. "Where the bloody hell have you been?"

Pelham turned to Congreve and smiled as he swung the door inward for admittance.

"He would seem to be expecting you, sir."

"He doesn't *seem* to be expecting me, you old relic, he is expecting me," Congreve sniffed, and, buttoning his tweed jacket, pushed inside.

"Oh, bugger off," Ambrose thought he heard his old friend mutter as he pottered off toward his pantry.

Chapter 29

Miami

S toke caught the crest of a wave and shoved the heavy-duty chromed outboard throttles in opposite directions. The Contender 34 spun off the top of the curl in a perfect . . . pirouette. He cranked the wheel over hard to port, dipping her into the trough, and, finally, nudged the helm and swung his bow up; *Miss Maria* nestled up alongside *Jade*'s nearly vertical emerald green hull. The big yacht was riding dead in the water, her powerful engines at a deep idle. But the wind out of the south had freshened, and when Stoke felt a shudder, he saw he was banging his starboard rail against *Jade*'s beautifully awl-gripped green hull pretty hard.

High above the *Miss Maria,* two burly, bald-headed crewmen were leaning out over the rail, peering down at them. Stoke stepped aft, raised the Zeiss lenses to his eyes, and scoped them out. They didn't appear to be armed. Which meant absolutely nothing, of course. At least they weren't giving him the finger.

Boardings were always tricky business. Sometimes, when the inspected vessel had nothing to hide, they were routine. You did a thorough search, thanked the skipper, and got out of Dodge. Routine. Other times, they were anything but. You just never knew, was Stoke's experience.

Until, of course, you knew.

Stoke radioed the CG cutter his position and situation, stepped once more out from under the Contender's custom Kevlar-mesh escape T-top, and signaled up to the two at the rail. Immediately, they lowered a ladder and dropped two mooring lines, one fore and one aft. Harry, standing next to the .50 caliber he'd mounted on the bow as they'd left the dock, grabbed one line, cleated off the bow, and started upward on the dangling ladder.

Stoke kept the binocs and the spotlight trained on him all the way up the steep side. He didn't relax until he saw Brock over the gunwales and safely aboard, assisted by the two crew.

Then Stoke rigged fenders on the boarding side and secured the stern line to an aft cleat. *Miss Maria* wasn't going anywhere now. He remained standing with his legs apart in the center of the cockpit, swiveling his head back and forth continuously. He kept his eye on the crew above, his weapon at the ready, on full auto. Waiting for Harry's sit rep, he had a clear field of fire from stem to stern.

He wasn't going by the book and he knew it.

Normally, the standard Coast Guard boarding team of two never separates during an op like this. But Stoke didn't want his team to present a single target up there tonight. Not just yet, anyway. Just didn't feel right. He liked having his weapon trained on any *Jade* crew up topside for the moment.

They didn't look hostile, but then, they never did until the real shit hit the fan. If CIA and Brock were right, and the Chinese were running guns illegally, things wouldn't get spicy until he'd actually located the alleged smuggled weapons cache somewhere deep in the hull. That's what he figured anyway.

Brock finally leaned over the rail and looked down at him, adjusting his radio's lip-mike in front of his mouth.

"Looks clear, Skipper."

"How many?"

"Only the two we saw on the main deck so far. Unarmed. Cooperative."

"Stand by."

Stoke went to the helm and shut the three big outboards down. He tuned the VHF radio to monitor 22 on cockpit speakers. This was the channel the Coast Guard cutter *Vigorous* was standing by on. The Coasties were sitting out there just out of visual contact, OTH, over the horizon, but they had a heavily armed helicopter with a spec-ops team aboard that could be hovering over this scene in two minutes if it all went to shit in a hurry.

Stoke slung his weapon on his back and began his ascent up the side of the emerald hull. He swung up and over the rail like a goddamn gymnast and planted his boots on the pristine teak decks.

"Good evening. I'm Lieutenant Sheldon Levy, United States Coast Guard," Stoke said to the two crewmen. "This is USCG Ensign Brock. We'd like to speak to your captain. I believe we're expected."

The two guys seemed all right, deepwater suntanned, bleached-blond crew-cut boys in starched white uniforms. Unless they were wearing ankle-biter holsters, Harry was right, they didn't appear armed. Or, for the moment, dangerous.

One false move and Harry would have them both facedown on the deck, hands cuffed behind with plastic ligatures.

"Yes, sir, Lieutenant," the older one said. "Captain's expecting you. Please follow me up to the bridge, gentlemen."

They climbed three sets of exterior steps, the second crewman bringing up the rear. This was a vulnerable moment, and Stoke was glad when it was over.

A solid wall of frigid air greeted them as a hidden door in the stainless steel bulkhead slid back to reveal every wannabe megayachtsman's wet dream. The yacht's darkened bridge looked like the control room of the damn *Starship Enterprise*. A huge crescent-shaped console beneath the wraparound windows, cutting-edge electronics up the wazoo, all of it lit up like rows of Vegas slots in a personal home theater.

They stepped up and inside, Stoke already freezing his ass off in the frigid AC air.

"Captain?" the mate said, almost loud enough to be heard anywhere aboard.

No answer.

"Cap'n," the mate said it again, ushering them forward, "I have Lieutenant Sheldon Levy from the U.S. Coast Guard cutter *Vigorous* aboard, sir."

No response.

Stoke registered alarm, and his finger found the inside of the trigger guard. He didn't see anyone in the room looking or acting remotely like the skipper. Nor did anyone at the controls say anything. The crew, all Chinese from what he could make out in the smoky red darkness, were staring at the two of them like they'd just landed from Mars. The whole thing? Starting to look like a first-class goatfuck.

"Whiskey Tango Foxtrot," Stoke said quietly into his helmet mike.

"What. The. Fuck," Harry agreed.

A giant captain's chair in black leather was mounted on a gleaming steel hydraulic piston. Higher than all the other seats at the console by a few feet. The chair was so damn big you couldn't tell whether or not there was anybody sitting in it. Suddenly, it began descending slowly toward the deck.

A disembodied voice from out of the deepest heart of the southland came from the chair.

"Hey! How y'all doing, Lieutenant . . . Levy, is it?"

"Correct," Stoke said to no one. "Sheldon Levy."

"Captain Randy Wade Wong, Lieutenant Levy, how can we help y'all?"

The powered chair swiveled on its axis. And Stoke and Harry got their first good look at this modern-day

Ahab. He was wider than he was tall. *A hybrid,* Stoke thought. Half Chinese, half American. The combo didn't really work. A wide flat jigsaw of a face, where the individual pieces didn't seem to have come from the same box. He was wearing huge gold Elvis Presley mirrored sunglasses, which didn't help his look.

Captain Wong said, "Damn, Lieutenant, I gotta say, you don't look like any Sheldon Levy I've ever seen."

"Yeah, funny, right? But then, like I always say, look at Sammy Davis Jr."

Wong laughed out loud.

"You, sir, I will vouchsafe, are the largest man I have ever seen," Wong said.

"And the thing is, Cap? What you see here? Man, this is just the facade," Stoke said, edging ever closer to him.

What a piece of work was this Randy Wong character. A short, stocky guy, all gussied up in crisp whites, who managed to fill the big black chair. His small lace-up white shoes still quite didn't reach the deck, and he was swinging his feet back and forth like a toddler.

Wong said, "If the man mountain won't come to Muhammad, Muhammad comes to the man mountain," he said, still swinging his legs back and forth as he neared the deck.

Harry whispered in Stoke's earpiece, "Seriously, Skipper, this ship of fools is deranged."

The captain's feet touched the deck, where he pushed out of his chair and said, "Well, well, well, and what can we do for y'all on this whole lovely South Florida evening?"

He had his tiny fists on his hips like a miniature dictator might do.

"We have orders to search your vessel, Captain Wong," Stoke said.

"Is that right?"

"Is the owner aboard?"

"She is not."

"She?"

"The owner is a woman."

"Interesting. And who exactly is the owner of this vessel?"

"That would be my employer."

"Her name?"

"Moon."

"First name?"

"Madame."

"Madame?"

"Madame Moon?"

"Yep."

"Aboard?"

"No, Lieutenant. As it happens, she's in England. We were proceeding there to pick her up. Until you interrupted our voyage."

"Miami is not your final port of call?"

"No, Lieutenant Levy. Philadelphia, New York, and then Southampton. The one in England."

"That's it?"

"No. We are taking the owner aboard at Southampton. A sybaritic cruise in the Greek isles, as she describes it."

"Your last port of origin was?"

"Caracas."

"Right, Caracas. My paperwork says something else. Are you bringing anything into the United States that you now wish to declare?"

"You mean like diseased fruits and vegetables? Like exotic and endangered birds of the rain forest? Rotten avocados?"

"No. I mean like drugs. Or weapons."

"Ah. No, Lieutenant. In that case, nothing to declare."

"How many crew aboard?"

"Seven altogether, not counting me."

"I want you to muster them all here on the bridge. Not now, but right now."

"Well now, I don't know if I can do—"

"That's an order, Captain. I am authorized by my government to search this vessel. If you resist, or cause me and Ensign Brock here even a hint of trouble, we can handle this in a different way. The USCG cutter *Vigorous* is standing by. Would you like me to radio her skipper now and tell them that you are not cooperating?"

"Hell, no, Lieutenant Levy. I ain't got nothing to hide here, son. You search this old barge all night long, you want to. Ain't nothing worth spit aboard this vessel but a Rolls-Royce automobile."

"Make the muster announcement over the PA system, Captain. Get 'em up here on the double. All of them."

He did, but he wasn't happy about it.

Once all seven crew members were accounted for, and had been patted down and searched for weapons by Harry Brock, Stoke said to the guy, "Where you from, Cap?"

"Me? Lower Bottom, Kentucky. Know where that is?"

"No. Where is it?"

"Down in the holler. Just below Upper Bottom. My beloved mother was a coal miner's daughter. My father from Shanghai was another story altogether. Crazy little dude, seriously. Hazardous."

Stoke nodded and said, "Ensign Brock, guard these men while I initiate the search. I'll be back in twenty minutes. Anybody gives you any trouble, you order in the chopper from the *Vig*. Got it?"

"Aye, sir."

Stoke started in the forward hold.

There were only two objects of any note, covered in canvas drop cloths, which Stoke ripped away. A brand-new Rolls-Royce Ghost in the same emerald green shade as the yacht. And a thirty-foot Aquariva speed-boat, an old one, a beauty. Madame Moon apparently knew how to live.

Next, having come up empty in the largest hold, the one located amidships, he headed for the stern. "Nothing forward or amidships," he said to Harry on the radio. "Going aft."

He stepped silently through an open door in the after bulkhead and found himself at the top of a steep flight of steel steps leading below, the bottom steps lost in the semidarkness.

Voices.

He took a breath and held it.

Two men down below, talking quietly, unaware that someone was listening. He could smell the cigarette smoke wafting up, could sense them, waiting for him.

The captain had said there were seven crew members, but with these two unaccounted for, he'd apparently meant nine. Big mistake.

If he went down the steps, they'd see his boots before he saw them. Silently, he removed two of the four grenades hanging from his web belt—a flash-bang for disorientation and a smoker to blind them.

He pulled the pins and threw them downward hard enough to bounce off the iron deck below. In the movies you always see the grenades being rolled across the deck. Which gives the bad (or good) guys the opportunity to pick them up and toss them back where they came from. No. Like an onside kick, you bounced those bad apples as hard and fast as you could off the deck.

First, the loud *CRACK* and blinding light of the flash-bang, then the muffled *WHOOMPH* of the smoker. Stoke grabbed the rails on either side of the stairs, raised his feet, and slid rapidly to the now-smoke-filled bottom of the hold.

One of the two guys began firing wildly into the smoke hoping to get lucky. Didn't work out for him. Stoke saw his muzzle flash and instantly dropped him with his nine-millimeter H&K automatic pistol.

"Your buddy's dead. Drop your weapon!" he shouted to the other guard, taking a knee and swinging his weapon through an arc. "I want to hear that bad boy hit the deck."

Silence. He could feel the guy moving to his left inside the smoke, trying to get behind some cover or come up next to him.

"Really? That's how you want to do this? Last chance."

The guy was getting closer; Stokely could sense more than hear his rubber-soled advance across the oil-slick deck. Enough. Stoke flicked his assault rifle to full auto and sprayed lead from left to right, the full 180 degrees. He heard the guy scream once and drop heavily to the deck.

"Two tangos down," he told Harry.

"Motherf—"

"Don't say it."

They'd been guarding a hidden door.

Thick and heavy, it was locked, but Stoke molded a handful of plastic explosive around the latch and blew it. He switched on his powerful LED torch and peered inside the darkened hold.

Crates.

Stacks of them all the way to the ceiling. Wooden, about twelve feet long by four feet wide, secured by heavy steel bands. Identical Chinese markings in red on each box. He counted them, five stacks of six, thirty. He reached into his pocket and pulled out his iPhone, got the Camera Genius app running and snapped a bunch of pictures he could e-mail to Harry, who could e-mail them to the brass at Langley. Now. Tonight. Technology.

"Bingo," he said into his mike.

"What?" Harry said.

"Don't know yet. But something and a lot of it down here. Everybody behaving up there?"

"Restless. Wong's getting itchy."

"Lice or crabs probably. Look. I'm going to open a crate. I'll be back in ten. These are bad guys. He had two extra crew down here in the aft hold guarding a stockpile of something. Shot at me without warning. Not alive anymore. Somebody messes with you up there, you mess right back, Harry."

"Roger that, Stoke. I'm cool."

The crates were heavy as hell, but he managed to manhandle one of the ones on top down to the deck. They all had the same big red symbol on the lid. Stoke grabbed a shot of it with his iPhone, then started on the steel band with his heavy shears.

Two minutes later he lifted the lid and peered inside the crate.

Five minutes after that he was racing back up three decks to the bridge, on the radio to the CG cutter, describing what he'd found and asking for immediate assistance. The CG skipper said the *Vig* was on her way to arrest the crew and take the vessel in tow, but he was launching the chopper with an assault team now for their immediate safety.

He said the helo would be hovering over the yacht in four minutes max and the team would fast-rope to the deck.

When Stoke stepped inside the bridge, he could tell the captain was surprised to see him still alive. Not part of the game plan.

"You lied to me, Randy," Stoke said. "A big no-no."

"I just drive the bus, pal."

"Yeah. Now I'm going to throw you under it, pal. You're toast. And your boys waiting for me in the aft hold? They're not alive anymore. That send you a signal? Asshole."

"What'd you find?" Brock asked.

"Drones," Stoke said. "Attack drones, twelve feet long. Painted with this weird matte-black coating. Every one of them has this symbol on each wing."

He held up his iPhone so Harry could see the shot he'd taken of the stubby-winged UAV in its crate.

"Jesus. That thing looks seriously badass. Nose cannon. Missile mounts on the wings and shit. What's that symbol?"

"Hell if I know."

"Where's my funky little Chinese interpreter when I need him?"

"Dead. We could use him. But it would be messy."

"Yeah. I guess."

Stoke looked hard at the *Jade*'s skipper. "Listen up, sideshow, get one your homeboys over there to tell me what this symbol means. Send him over here with his hands up. Now."

A young Chinese officer came forward, and Stoke held up his cell so the kid could see the picture he'd snapped below.

"What's that symbol mean, son?" Stoke asked him. "That thing on the wings of the drones."

"Rheaven," the guy said, "rhymes with 'heaven.'"

"In English, please."

"Raven."

"Like the bird?" Stoke said.

The guy lowered his eyes and giggled like a girl.

In that moment, Stoke finally understood the meaning of the word *inscrutable*.

Chapter 30

Hawkesmoor

Lord Hawke was dressed casually for the week-end. Badly faded jeans ripped at one knee and a black turtleneck jersey. He was reclining in his favorite leather chair, one long leg hooked over the armrest, his foot idly swinging to some imaginary rhythm.

Hawke was smiling at something his guest had just said, but he owned the room; tall, lean, well muscled, still boyish in his midthirties, the startling ice-blue eyes, the thick head of unruly black hair, and the strongly chiseled face that had launched a thousand female daydreams, serving to remind one as always of the late film actor Errol Flynn.

He's always seemed to me a boy born with a heart for any fate, his father had said of little Alex the night of his sixth birthday here in the library at Hawkesmoor.

Flynn, the legendary Hollywood actor, had gone to seed, but not Hawke. He was in better shape than men ten years younger, not an ounce of fat on him. Royal Navy regimen. Six miles a day in open ocean whenever he could manage it. He worked at it. Every day. Hard.

Always such an irony, Ambrose thought. The sixth-richest man in England, a courteous, well-mannered peer of the realm, yet he knew thirty ways to kill you before you knew it with his bare hands.

And always reading. A book to shield him against the world and its terrors.

There was a well-worn volume in his hands right now; Congreve could see the tattered cover of the first edition. Hemingway's *A Farewell to Arms* for the umpteenth time. God. He'd once asked Hawke what on earth he'd ever learned from Hemingway, a writer he himself had little patience for.

"I don't rightly know. Not to blow my head off with a shotgun?" Hawke had replied, not even bothering to look up from the pages.

Ambrose turned his attention to the other visitor.

A great bear of a man, he was, and staring down into the blazing fire, warming his hands. He, at least, was well dressed in pale grey flannels and a double-breasted black cashmere blazer. He may have had his back to the door but Congreve was pretty certain as to his identity. It was a man whose very presence indicated trouble ahead. A man whose knowledge and skills at the tradecraft of espionage bordered on the supernatural. Professor Stefan Halter.

He heard a tiny laugh coming from the windows and searched the room.

And then he saw the child.

Hawke's beloved son, the four-year-old Alexei, was seated cross-legged on the bare floor beneath a window seat. He was wearing white flannel trousers and a fire-engine red sweater over a white turtleneck jumper. He was currently engaged with a battered tin hook-and-ladder fire engine that Ambrose recognized as having once belonged to his father. The boy, his face a mask of concentration, was trying to extend the tiny ladder from the tufted cushion up to the window's broad sill. His puppy, Harry, asleep in a nearby leather armchair, was blissfully unaware of all their excitement.

Hawke looked up, fired a flash of blue across the room, and laughed at the sight of his old and dearest friend in the world.

"Don't tell me! These old eyes don't deceive me, it can only be that Demon of Deduction, that august

repository of wisdom and scientific criminalist learning, come to darken my door once more!"

"Good morning, Alex," Congreve said, smiling.

At the sight of his old friend entering the room,
Hawke jumped to his feet, strode across the room.
Hawke had a lifelong habit. He left charm trailing in
his wake, like it was something incidental to his being,
something to be cast off . . . left behind.

He embraced his closest friend, clapping him rather
too soundly on the back. Then he placed his hands on
Congreve's shoulders and smiled broadly.

"Ah, yes, Constable, my God, but it's good to see
you! Thanks for coming all the way out here in that
bloody blizzard out there. You remember Professor
Stefan Halter from Cambridge, of course? Stef, come
say hello to former chief inspector Ambrose Congreve.
Of Scotland Yard."

Congreve smiled at the heavyset man who now turned
round to face him. He was ruggedly handsome, with
bushy black eyebrows and a deceptively warm smile.

"Chief Inspector. How lovely to see you again."

"Yes, yes, of course, the good Dr. Halter," Ambrose
said. "Delighted you're here at Hawkesmoor. Your
esteemed presence always bodes well for whatever dev-
iltry the future holds. And ill for the devils who perpe-
trate it."

Halter laughed and came over to pump the famous criminalist's hand warmly.

"True enough, sir. I fear I am seldom the bearer of glad tidings, as you well know," Halter said, his trademark Cheshire grin making a welcome appearance.

"Then I trust you won't disappoint me this time, Professor."

"I'm afraid I won't. It was I who asked Alex to invite you out. We could use your help, sir."

Hawke smiled. "He told me to remind you to bring your formidable brain along. Did you?"

"Like a certain credit card, one never leaves home without it."

"Excellent!" Halter said. "The joyful outcome of this nasty business is all but certain."

Professor Stefan Halter was a life Fellow at Magdalene College, Cambridge. He was also a rather large cheese at POLIS, the university's own spy command, the Department of Politics and International Studies. Most of the senior officers at MI6, MI5, the CIA and NSA, and other assorted acronyms did their top-level recruiting at Cambridge.

Many postdoctoral candidates at Cambridge under Halter's tutelage at POLIS returned to their home countries as counsel to prime ministers, presidents, and the like. To say that this prestigious Cambridge

department was highly regarded in international diplomatic and espionage circles would be putting it rather
mildly.

After they were comfortably seated before the roaring hearth, and Pelham had shimmered in with a
tray of tea and more coffee, they quickly got down to
chases.

"There's been a murder at Cambridge," Halter said,
turning his strong brown eyes on Congreve, who registered mild shock at the words.

"Murder at Cambridge? Really? Anyone I know?"
Ambrose said, leaning forward, his keen interest in
this matter already fully engaged. He had close, long-
standing ties to the university. He'd taken his doctorate in languages there many years ago, but still had
colleagues and close friends among the faculties at the
various colleges.

"The victim has not yet been identified, I'm afraid,"
Halter said. "However, a professor at King's has simultaneously gone missing."

"Which one?" Congreve asked the two men. "The
man at King's, I mean."

"A Dr. Watanabe. Know him?" Hawke asked.

He saw Congreve's face fall.

"Know him? I do, indeed. A lifelong friend and
mentor. Watanabe's a brilliant chap. Good man, too.

Watanabe-san, we called him then. Japanese by birth, but raised in China by his Chinese mother after the death of his father. Proud of his heritage, of course, but never drank from Beijing's Communist Kool-Aid pitcher. And he was a perpetual thorn in the side of those at Cambridge who had imbibed."

Halter laughed. "Good Lord, Alex, he's already picked up the scent!"

"Our own master Sherlockian," Hawke said.

"Has the local constabulary gotten anywhere with this?" Congreve asked. "You say there's been no positive identification."

"Afraid not," Halter said. "Nor is there likely to be one soon. The victim was tortured and then mutilated postmortem. Fingertips and facial features removed. Also, the teeth, I'm afraid. Nasty business."

"Good God," Congreve said. "Doesn't sound like the Cambridge I knew, does it."

"It isn't," Halter said. "Believe me. The place is a political tinderbox."

"Tell him what's going on, Stef," Hawke said.

"You're familiar, no doubt, with the Te-Wu, Chief Inspector?"

"I am indeed. Assassins. Chinese secret police. Societies, sworn brotherhoods, whatever, first to recognize the PRC and first to fly the Communist Party flag. Very active in the States and here in Britain to some extent. There was certainly some Te-Wu activity at Cambridge back in the day. Nasty lot. Capable of anything."

"Still is, perhaps still are, capable," Halter said, lighting a Russian unfiltered cigarette. He looked at Congreve as if deciding how much to reveal.

Halter, Congreve well knew, was sitting on not a few secrets of his own. He was the longest-serving MI6 mole inside the Kremlin, in the living history of the Secret Service. Dr. Stefan Halter, Hawke's go-to in events dealing with the West in general and the United Kingdom in particular. The idea that he was still alive after all these years was a never-ending source of amazement to both Hawke, Congreve, and everyone with a need to know at MI6.

The man was a magician, a fact he'd proved once saving Hawke's life on an island in the Stockholm archipelago some years back.

"A resurgent Te-Wu gang at Cambridge? Really?" Congreve said, getting his pipe going. "I suppose that's a viable path of investigation. But I thought we'd rid ourselves of that curse upon society decades ago."

At that precise moment, Pelham slipped in and announced that luncheon was served.

"Didn't we all, Chief Inspector?" Halter said, shifting his gaze toward the window. "Didn't we all? Do either of you know a man at Cambridge by the name of Sir Lucian Hobdale? I seem to recall that you both do, although I can't for the life of me recall why."

"He helped us identify and run down that rogue Iranian scientist, remember?" Hawke said. "The mad inventor of Perseus, the Singularity machine."

"Mmm," Halter said, but his eyes were far away. "I was thinking Hobdale might help us identify the corpse . . ."

The wintry day outside was pressing against the cold glass. And the snow was still coming down, much harder.

Chapter 31

The Cotswolds

Hawke never slept very well in an empty bed, and currently he had the problem of sleeplessness to cope with. He couldn't turn his brain off. It was always thus, he thought, whenever the possibility of a new case or mission would spring full-blown into existence.

Having said good night to little Alexei and his guardian, Scotland Yard's detective sergeant Nell Spooner, Hawke had wearily climbed into bed and fallen asleep. It had been a long day at Cambridge and he'd arrived home late, expecting Nell's welcoming arms in his bed.

Normally, except when they had quarreled, Nell shared his bed. But on this night she'd chosen to sleep alone. Her room was on the same floor as his but situated at the distant end of the hallway, right next door to the nursery. She'd been wearing an odd expression when she'd kissed him good night. Something was bothering her. He'd asked if she was all right and she'd brushed it off, rising on tiptoes to peck his cheek before vanishing, a rustle of silk gliding into the darkness of the long corridor.

It was raining, and he listened to the rain and to the rain turning to ice and to the thunder. Rain always sounded like darkness somehow, darkness and night storms—and, perhaps, youth, he supposed, since it always struck him as a pleasant sound. He'd always preferred bad weather to good, the moody and electric drama of a looming cold front; he liked imagining the abiding solace of a strong roof over his head, hatches battened down, anchor to leeward, his better angels keeping the black dogs at bay.

Imagining because the black dogs were always out there, always snarling at the door. No matter how fast you ran, how far, their red eyes gleaming in the pitch-black night.

Usually the sound of a storm had the power to distract him and he'd sleep again. Not tonight. No, on this wintry night nothing at all worked, and at 3:00 A.M. he rolled over in bed and switched on the bedside lamp.

He picked up the book he was reading, plumped up his pillows, and settled in, soon lost in the story.

A wave of happiness settled over him. A good book on a stormy night, the drafty silence of the big house, the soft glow of dying embers in the hearth, shadows climbing the walls around him. He was reading a slim volume Ambrose had bought for him when they stopped in a bookstore in Cambridge. On Chesil Beach. It was the tale of a doomed marriage, of lost hope and dashed dreams. It wasn't the stuff of his favorite author, P.G. Wodehouse, plainly—no *Right Ho, Jeeves!* or *Pigs Have Wings* tonight—but the author wrote beautifully and Hawke found himself growing sleepy again.

He must have drifted off because now everything was quiet again, the storm having moved out over the Evesham Valley. Only the dim sound of a farm dog barking somewhere in the distance. He had that overwhelmingly pleasant sensation of the full weight of his body upon the bed, heavy and somnolent. He didn't want to open his eyes yet; he wanted to feel the steady rise of consciousness leaving the dream state and pushing up through the grey clouds of—

Then he heard, very close to him, a footstep and a cough.

He felt that terrible hardening of the flesh that always accompanied the absolute surety that you were being watched. Footsteps in the fog . . .

"Daddy! Wake up! It's snowing!"

"Is it, darling?" he mumbled sleepily. He rolled over and saw that precious face hovering in the grey light filling the high-ceilinged room.

Alexei laughed.

And in that fleeting moment Hawke thought: *we're all going to be all right here. . .*

"It is, it is, Papa!" Alexei cried. "Come to the window and see. Treasure Mountain is all covered with snow. We can go sledding, Spooner says so. Isn't that exciting?"

"Yes, it certainly is snowing, all right," he said, gazing toward his windows.

Hawke sat up in bed and reached down to lift the boy up onto his wide four-poster bed. Alexei was dressed in his bright red snowsuit and was wearing a matching woolen cap and mittens. The intensity of the love Hawke felt threatened to overpower his ability to speak.

"Have you had your breakfast yet, son?"

"Oh, yes. Spooner and I have been up for hours, Papa. I've been waiting and waiting to wake you up."

"And you say that our very own Treasure Mountain is covered with snow?"

"Yes!"

"Hmm. That presents yet another mystery. Do you know where pirates go in the snow, Alexei?"

"No . . . but . . . to their rooms?"

Hawke smiled at this.

"Maybe. As good a guess as any. But, Alexei, you do know that if we do see a pirate, no matter how big or how fearsome that blackguard looks, we are going right up to him and demand to know if they've buried any more secret treasure on that mountain lately."

"Oh, Papa," Alexei said, his shining eyes conveying his shivering pleasure in the direction his morning was taking. Pirates. Snow. Sled. Treasure. He wanted to put his arms round his father's neck and squeeze so tight . . .

Since October Hawke had been reading *Treasure Island* to Alexei before bedtime in the nursery, a new chapter every night. Like all boys, his son was captivated by the story, and even insisted that his favorite, meaning terrifying, passages about Long John Silver and his dastardly crew be read over and over again.

Pirates had appeared on the little boy's horizon and his world was a far better place for it.

One morning, Hawke had risen at dawn. He'd found the old wooden lockbox he'd had hidden away in his closet since childhood, the one where he'd kept the priceless treasures of youth: a crow feather, a clear marble, the shriveled rose he'd worn in his lapel the day of his parents' funeral, a skate key, a lock of his mother's hair, many old coins he'd collected, some of them even gold, tickets to a country fair, a faded black-and-white snapshot of his mom and dad aboard their ill-fated yawl, *Seahawke*.

That morning, Hawke, holding a candle, had added a few new gold and silver coins from his collection inside the battered box, then tucked it under his arm and made his way through the darkness outside, through the parterre and up the long incline beyond, a narrow mown field that rose to the river's edge. There was a stand of birch near the end with a pathway leading into the woods. The narrow dirt path led to the sizable hill of earth then and ever after officially known as Treasure Mountain by his family.

He climbed to the summit and looked around for a location suitable to his purposes.

He carefully paced off the chosen spot by triangulating three trees twenty paces distant. There he drove the sharp end of a broken branch into the hard ground and began to dig. *Not too deep,* he reminded himself. Alexei's patience with his little shovel was limited.

Returning to his library, he'd scrawled a map of the buried treasure in charcoal and left it that night under Alexei's pillow. A heavy black X marked the spot. Later that morning, the sun high, the two of them had climbed the hill. It had been a clear blue winter's day and Alexei had returned home in the evening clutching the little box that had once belonged to his father, pledging never, ever to lose it. He'd fallen asleep counting his treasure and dreaming of pirates digging in the moonlight on the hilltop he could see from the nursery window.

Chapter 32

Now Hawke sat beside Nell on that very same hilltop, holding hands on the wooden garden bench as Alexei went speeding down the slope again and again, crying out gleefully for the love of speed and the sheer beauty of this bright shining morning, knowing that the two people he loved most were watching over him.

"I remember that feeling, Nell," Hawke said. "Sledding, I mean. Speed, for a boy, maybe for a girl, too, is so powerfully felt at that age. It's one of my earliest memories of— What's the matter, Nell? Why are you crying?"

"Oh, Alex. I am just so very, very sad."

"You are? Please tell me why, darling. I don't want you to be sad. Ever."

"I am sad . . . I'm sad because all this . . . all this is over. And it's been the very best time of my life, Alex. I will always love you and . . . Alexei, too. More than I can ever say. But—but—"

She put her head on his shoulder and clung to him, sobbing, tears streaming down her pink cheeks.

He put his arm around her, pulling her closer, dreaded what might be coming, shocked, of course, but somehow not surprised.

"Nell, please don't do this. This is your home. We are your family. If you, if there is something, anything, that I can do to make it more—"

"Just let me cry, okay? Let me get it all out. You know how I am."

"I'm sorry. Are you cold?"

"No, I'm fine."

Hawke was silent, his eyes on Alexei trudging up the hill pulling his bright blue sled behind him. The boy's face was glowing with excitement and joy, and at that moment Hawke feared for him. Nell was leaving. It would break his own heart. But, even worse, it would break the boy's heart. She had been a mother to him, a wise, strong, and caring mother. She had saved Alexei's life, twice, and she was always there, making sure he was safe from harm, especially when his father was away on business . . .

Nell squeezed Hawke's hand and pulled away, creating a space between them on the bench. Creating a space in his heart.

Hawke looked at her, tried to smile, and handed her one of the white linen handkerchiefs he always carried in the breast pocket of his jacket. When she had wiped away her glistening tears, she turned to him.

"I never wanted it to end," she said.

"I still don't. I'm in love with you."

"Oh, God, darling! If only there were any other way. If I could change the world, I would do it. I would! I promise you this is the hardest thing I've ever done. You came into my life and it all made sense finally. You . . . and Alexei . . . were . . . are . . . everything to me. The family I never had. The man I didn't think existed. The child I'd dreamed of. It was so . . . perfect."

She looked up at him, her eyes brimming with fresh tears, and saw that his own beautiful blue eyes were spilling over.

"I do love you, Nell. You know that."

"I know you do, Alex. Believe me, I know love when I see it. But I never really felt that we were forever. I hoped that we were, prayed that we were, but I never felt that—"

"You don't have to say it, Nell. I know what's in your heart. We both know the problem is mine, not yours.

It's my inability to let go of Alexei's mother that's killing us. And even though she refused to leave Russia and come home with my son and me . . . I can't seem to . . . I can't let go of—"

He buried his face in his hands, his shoulders heaving with sorrow.

"Alex, please don't. We've been through this all a thousand times. It doesn't change. And that's the problem between us. We both knew this moment might come, even if we kept lying to ourselves that it wouldn't."

He looked up, getting himself under control.

"Yes, yes, I suppose you're right. Tell me, dear Nell. Tell me where are you going, darling? Back to London?"

"No. To America. Washington. I've been offered a position with the British ambassador there. You know him. Sir Richard Champion. He thinks the world of you. All his staff does. I had a hard time convincing them that you would be all right and—"

He managed a smile. "I'll be all right. We . . . will be all right."

"God, I hope so. Otherwise I could never forgive myself for—"

"Is there someone else? You don't have to tell me."

"Yes, Alex, there is. A man I went with in college at St. Andrews. He works for MI6 now, but he's posted as a second secretary at the British embassy."

"What's his name?"

"Fielding. Fielding Lawrence. We've been corresponding these last six months. I saw him again when I went on holiday in Madeira some months ago. On the last night, he asked me to marry him and come to America. I refused, but he wouldn't give up. He wants to have children, Alex. So do I. And he does love me."

"He's very lucky, darling."

"Is he, Alex?"

"You are the most wonderful woman. The smartest, bravest, most beautiful woman, Nell. When I think of all you've done for Alexei . . . for us . . . We simply could not have survived, literally, without you."

Nell dabbed at her eyes once more, and he could see her willing herself to go on.

"I—I took the liberty of trying to find someone for Alexei. Only if you wish it, of course. I'm not leaving until you've found someone you trust for Alexei. I can't. Her name is Sabrina, Sabrina Churchill. Distant relation. She works for Royal Protection, Scotland Yard. She's lovely, Alex. One of the very best the Yard has at what she does. You've actually met her. She worked for the Prince of Wales a few years ago, back when the two boys were in their early twenties and frankly a handful."

"A trial by fire. I'd say she's been tested." Hawke smiled.

"Yes. You can talk to Prince Charles about her. She's fairly young, not quite thirty, a little younger than me, but she has a sterling reputation and has earned the respect and trust of the Royal Family over the years . . . what do you think?"

"I'd like to meet her, Nell. Introduce her to Alexei. And I appreciate your doing that for us. Finding her, I mean."

Nell looked away.

"Oh, Alex. Oh my God, it's all just so very sad, isn't it?"

"Sad doesn't begin to cover it, Nell."

"Look. I want you to know something. If ever there comes a time, a time when you think you need me, or Alexei needs me, I will be there for you both. Always. I mean it."

"I'll always remember."

"I will, too."

Hawke looked away, gathering himself, and said, "I think one of us should tell Alexei soon, don't you? He must know something's not right . . ."

"I can do it."

"No. His father should do it."

"I suppose that's right. I'll go down to the house then . . . unless . . . Would you rather I do it, Alex? Shall I tell him? Would that be easier for you?"

"It should come from me, I think."

"I pray God he'll be all right."

"Yes. He'll be all right."

She rose, squeezed his hand one last time, and turned away.

After she'd disappeared down the hill and into the woods, he watched Alexei and his sled for a long, long time before he got up to take his hand and lead him home.

A bleakness swept over him then, not wholly unexpected. A bitter, sick feeling in his gut, the knowledge that he was losing yet another person he cared deeply for. He had always pretended to himself that he didn't love Nell as much as he'd loved Anastasia; it was a cheap, even dishonest way of keeping a certain distance. He'd reassured himself that his heart was already fully booked, that the woman he truly loved most was his son's mother. Anastasia. Married to another man, but still as in love with him as he was with her. So what the hell was he supposed to do?

He'd tell his son about Nell tonight, when he was tucked safely into his bed.

And then he'd pour himself a good stiff Irish whiskey and sit before the fire, think about Nell and his own shortcomings as a man and, perhaps, what a fool he'd been to let her go.

When he was sufficiently anesthetized, he'd go to bed.

He had a tough day ahead of him come Monday. He was having lunch with C, the ornery old salt.

"Nell," he whispered as he finally fell asleep that night, "Nell . . . don't go . . ."

Chapter 33

Alex Hawke could count on one hand the number of times he'd been summoned to Sir David Trulove's home, Quarterdeck, for lunch. Sir David Trulove, traditionally known within the MI6 spy mecca as C, was not a particularly social animal. He would join Hawke for lunch, cards, certainly drinks, or the occasional supper at Alex's club in town, Black's, but only occasionally. Those brief and spotty encounters were the extent of the two men's relationship outside the confines of Six's headquarters at Vauxhall on the South Bank of the Thames.

Sir David, a crusty former admiral in the Royal Navy, was one of the great heroes of the Falklands War. Beneath that rough exterior lay, as Hawke liked to say, an even rougher interior. C was in fact a hard man but a fair one, as salty as they come, and there was a lot of real but steadfastly unacknowledged affection between the two men.

Hawke was not operating under any illusions. Especially any faint notion that there was to be anything social about this occasion. Something was up.

Odds were it had to be something fairly serious, too. If the old man wasn't comfortable discussing it within the soundproof confines of his sanctum santorum, namely his triple-secure office at MI6 HQ, then it had to be serious all right, deadly serious. Perhaps the old man had finally run down the bastards behind the attack on his friend McCloskey's funeral at Arlington. That would be welcome news. The Americans seemed besieged in the Pacific, and it wasn't at all a healthy state of affairs.

Ah well, things had been a bit slow at home ever since Hawke had returned from the hospital after the South China Sea business. He'd spent weeks at both RAF HQ in London and, in Washington, at the Pentagon in top-secret meetings. He was endlessly debriefed about his China experiences. The SAM that had brought him down, the new Chinese carrier itself, the F-35C Lightning the Chinese had duplicated and somehow surpassed. And, of course, the huge black, bat-winged stealth drone he found hiding in the carrier deck hangar, now believed to be a prototype of the one destroyed over Arlington.

He decided not to worry about his upcoming meeting, whatever it was about, and just enjoy the ride. He relished the deep rumble of the finely tuned Jaguar racing engine as he geared down for a tight right-hander. The view of countryside over the swooping British racing green bonnet of the vintage C-type race car gave the whole world a better aspect.

Hawke noticed something immediately upon arrival. At the guarded entrance to Quarterdeck, it was obvious that security on the heavily wooded estate had been dramatically enhanced. Once he'd been waved through, he noticed that not a few operatives in mufti were visible, and surely many more in full camo who were not. Hardly surprising, Hawke thought, considering recent events.

One month earlier, in the wee hours of a Sunday morning, four intruders wearing ceramic-bead bomb vests inside their anoraks had managed to gain access to the property. Three had been shot dead after scaling a wall by two very alert members of household security dressed as scrub brush on the perimeter.

When killed, the fourth was crouching with a serrated knife on a small balcony outside Sir David's second-story bedroom. Britain's head of Secret Intelligence lay sleeping not fifteen feet away.

That man, the leader, was later determined to be a highly sought Chinese Te-Wu (secret police) assassin named Ku Lin. The leader of a UK-based terrorist cell, Ku Lin had been linked to the Chinese intelligence agency in the past. And involved in the assault on the British ambassador just prior to the brutal murder of the American ambassador Christopher Stevenson and three other Americans at the U.S. embassy in Tokyo.

The drive wound upward and so to a clearing where the classic Georgian house stood in its glory, four-square to the wind. Rumbling to a stop under the porte cochere, Hawke switched off the snarling engine and saw Sir David standing by the opened front door.

"So. I invite Lord Alex Hawke for lunch and I get Sir Stirling Moss, do I?" Trulove said as Hawke bounded up the broad steps to the formal entrance, snatching the vintage racing goggles off his head. The car had only the tiny twin racing windscreens, and eye protection was necessary at speed.

"Sir Stirling doesn't get trapped behind a broken-down removals lorry for twenty minutes like I just did. Sorry I'm late."

"Well. Come inside and have a drink before lunch. This way, please."

C had a roaring fire going in his book-lined library. Through the tall ice-frosted windows a thin watery sun was trying to make its way through the clouds. A white-jacketed Royal Navy steward was decanting a bottle of claret at the drinks table. When he saw the two men enter, he finished his task and discreetly disappeared without a sound.

"Do you want wine or rum?" C said, or rather barked. "Do sit down."

Hawke sat in the deep leather chair, crossed his long legs, and smiled at the boss's lifelong habit of making even the slightest suggestion sound like an order from on high.

"Rum, please. Neat. Gosling's Black Seal if you have it."

"Of course we have it. You're the only one in this corner of England who drinks the damn stuff and there's always some left over from the last soiree." He handed Hawke a glass. He took his own whiskey to the chair opposite and collapsed into it.

"*Slange var*," Trulove said, raising his glass and sipping. It was the Gaelic toast meaning "Get it to the hole!"

"Cheers. You really should try the damn stuff, sir. You might enjoy it."

"You like it, Alex, that's what matters, I suppose. How are you? How's the bum leg? Still using the swagger stick, I see. Holding up all right?"

"As well as can be expected I suppose. Still a bit stiff. Oh. And Nell Spooner has flown the coop, I'm sad to say."

"Yes, yes. Know all about it. Dumped you for one of our very own Six lads at the British embassy in Washington. A step up for her, in my opinion. And he'll make an honest woman of her, I daresay. We all knew you had no intention of marrying the dear girl."

Hawke stiffened. He didn't at all like his personal life being scrutinized in this way and was very tempted to say so. He had to bite his tongue to remain silent.

"Sorry," C said, sensing his offense. "I was trying to be jovial. No bloody good at it, I suppose. Your private life is none of my affair. But only to a certain extent. The fact is, Alex, I'm seriously concerned for little Alexei's safety."

"As am I, sir." Hawke said, sipping his rum. "But Nell's promised to find someone to step in for her. A woman named Sabrina Churchill has been mentioned. Formerly Royal Protection at the Yard. Quite a formidable woman, from what I've heard."

"Never heard of her. But I'll have her vetted immediately. Meanwhile, what's the security status at Hawkesmoor? The grounds, et cetera."

"The perimeter is as impenetrable as can be done. The usual motion, audio, and heat sensors all over the grounds. More than a few of the groundspeople, gardeners, and maintenance staff are security. If there's a way inside all that, I don't know what it is. And it will remain that way until I have a new bodyguard."

"Still. If someone wants to get at him, they can and will. As you well know."

"I do. I worry about it all the time."

"You let me know if you need anything more during this transition period, won't you? Until Miss Churchill arrives?"

"Thank you, sir."

"No need to thank me, Alex. We're all family here. Are we not?"

"Well, if you put it that way, sir, yes, I suppose we are."

"Lunch?"

"Sounds delightful."

Chapter 34

"Operation Lightstorm," C said. He replaced his soupspoon, sat back, and got his pipe going. "Heard of it?"

"No, sir. Can't say that I have."

"Good. I still have a precious few secrets from you."

"Need-to-know is not what it used to be."

"Hmm. You will remember that some years ago, back in 2009, actually, a brilliant American scientist and inventor vanished. Puff of smoke. The whole family, gone. Urban myth was he had gotten rather tired of the game and moved his whole family to Borneo. A genius protection plan, some wag said at the time."

"William Chase?"

"That's his name, yes."

"I do recall that. Chase. The fellow who founded Lightstorm Advanced Weapons Systems. America's pre-eminent twenty-first-century genius. My understanding is that he is gravely ill, sir. Although he hasn't been seen in public in years, he's apparently on life support holed up in one of his grand estates in the western United States. Utah, I believe, or the Front Range of the Rockies."

Trulove nodded absentmindedly. Hawke was not at all sure he'd been listening.

"Cover story. Chase and his family—wife, Kathleen, and their two children—were all abducted from a street corner in Georgetown one foggy night and disappeared without a trace. They were on their way home from a birthday dinner for Chase's wife at a local restaurant three or four blocks from their home. According to the live-in housekeeper, they never made it home."

"Vanished into thin air? No witnesses?"

"Indeed. Imagine, Alex. A man and his entire family. A wife and two small children. Gone. My God. For reasons apparent only to themselves, the CIA and the White House immediately suspected the Chinese of the abduction. Although no mention of this incident was ever made public, of course. For delicate political reasons at the time, Washington could not go public with the administration's suspicions."

"And now?"

"Well. The Americans' investigation is still ongoing, unofficially of course. The Chinese admit nothing, offended at the mere suggestion, et cetera, et cetera. But now, Alex, here's the nub of it. The fighter you flew home to England has now been torn apart and examined from nut to bolt."

C paused to refire his cigar.

"Yes, sir?"

"And what we found belies Washington's nonsensical illness cover story. Chase holed up somewhere dying and all that bollocks."

"Hmm."

"Have a look at this."

C pulled a shiny steel object from his pocket and handed it to Hawke.

"What's this?"

"Part from your stolen jet engine. That bit was removed from the nozzle and delivered to me by courier this morning."

"Why?"

"Have a look at it through this magnifying glass, Alex."

Hawke took the glass and studied the object, turning it over in his hand.

"Ah. I see something . . . W . . . L . . . C . . . Carved by hand into the steel."

"His initials. William Lincoln Chase."

"My God. Proud of his work?"

"No. He was trying to get a message out. We knew instantly that only one man on earth was capable of designing that fighter you managed to nick from a carrier deck, Alex. Chase's fingerprints are all over that bloody airplane. As the Yanks will find, I'm sure, all over that high-altitude drone you discovered in the hangar."

"That fighter of theirs is an almost exact replica of our Euro F-35C Lightning. Only vastly more advanced avionics and weapons, defensive and offensive. That damn fighter can fly circles around anything we've got. I think I see where you're going with this, sir."

"Listen carefully. It could be argued that a single Chinese carrier, its battle group, and its fighter wing of stolen F-35s, with their attendant advanced weaponry and technology is, all by itself, more powerful than most nations. And there is another . . . threat."

"I don't like the way you said that."

"I have no direct knowledge. But the Americans have uncovered evidence of something very, very troublesome. CIA has its lips sewn shut. No one is talking. But it's bad."

"How bad?"

"Some new undersea weapon capable of shifting the balance of power in the Pacific. Immediately.

Hell, capable of shifting the balance of power around the world. Chinese money, but built in some secret location in North Korea, perhaps."

"The NKs are involved in all this?"

"Up to their bloody eyeballs. As you well know, North Korea is officially China's bitch. If China is the Dragon of the twenty-first century, which it clearly is, then North Korea? They are the Teeth of the Dragon. As you well know from your past visits to Pyongyang."

"Vastly sharper teeth, it would appear, sir, since my last midnight dental examination in Kim's workers' paradise prison."

Chapter 35

"Very busy boys lately, our friends the North Koreans," C said. "A high-level leak inside the White House claims it was a North Korean–built drone used in the horrific attack at McCloskey's funeral at Arlington National Cemetery. Most likely a variant of the one you saw aboard the carrier."

"We've been running down the Chinese for that one, night and day. Haven't gotten any bloody where, I'll grant you. But it smacks of China, sir, I must tell you. The sheer brutal arrogance of that attack has knocked us all back on our heels, Sir David. I don't know how the White House manages to keep a lid on that simmering pot. I can tell you the Pentagon is not at all happy about the lack of progress. That's why I'm bringing you aboard."

"North Korean origin, Alex, trust me. Who knows who designed it? China? Bill Chase? Forget it. You never heard about this. President Rosow also has this one screwed down so tight it only squeaks. But North Korea is only part of this Chinese checkers puzzle. Just get yourself up to speed on the Sino-Korean alliance with all the alacrity you are capable of. I'll have the head of section provide you with all relevant dossiers. Understood?"

"Aye, sir. You really think the Pacific balance of power is in jeopardy? The Yanks alone have ten carrier battle groups. Not to mention what the Aussies and the Royal Navy bring to the party."

"Alex, from what I've been able to piece together, we are talking about enemy war-fighting technology taken to an entirely new level, pure and simple. Immense advances, giant leaps forward by the Chinese. A heretofore unthinkable weapons system. Some damn thing barely even germinating on the books here in the West. And the technology? Stolen from under our damn noses."

"Ah. The infamous Chinese hackers. Pentagon, Whitehall."

"No, no, no, Alex. I wish it were that simple. But no, no hackers involved, not the Pentagon, not Whitehall, not Number 10 Downing, not the NSA, CIA, and not MI6, either."

"Where on earth was the intel stolen from, sir?"

"It appears they have hacked a human brain, Alex."

"Sorry, sir?"

"You heard me. They've hacked the brain of Dr. William Lincoln Chase. According to the CIA, his is the only mind on the planet capable of these near miraculous quantum leaps forward in military technology. It's now crystal clear, Alex. Bill Chase is China's latest secret weapon."

"So Chase is somewhere in China?"

"Yes. And they've obviously got some kind of hold over him. Threatening the captive family members, torture, that sort of thing, unless he performs. Dr. William Lincoln Chase is the brain trust behind the new and vastly improved Chinese war machine."

"Good God. So that's it."

"And, thus, Operation Lightstorm. A joint CIA/ MI6 op. CIA wants to find and neutralize Chase. Now. Before the poor chap can do further damage to the West. Before this Centurion Project, whatever the hell it is, gives China an irreparable war-fighting lead over the West in the next confrontation. Before, may I say, China acquires the ability to win the next world war."

"You think they want war, sir? I mean, today?"

"Perhaps. Until recently, I would have said, hell, no. They're vastly outnuked by the Yanks and the Russkies . . ."

"But?"

"This weapon our CIA friends are so closemouthed about. The so-called Centurion Project apparently changes all the dynamics. Look. All China wants is the world. And Beijing is smart enough to know that these days you don't have to actually go to war to get it."

"That's certainly food for thought, sir."

"Win their kind of war. And, thus, the world, Alex. That is China's sole objective. I am deadly serious about this. Everything hangs in the balance."

"But neutralize Chase, sir? Surely we don't have to do that."

"We don't?"

"No, sir. We do not. We take him out of there. Hostage rescue."

"Can't be done."

"Why not?"

"That's a five-hour conversation. Trust me. It cannot humanly be done. We don't even know where the hell they're keeping him, for God's sake. Or his family for that matter."

"Let me try, Sir David. I know I can do it. I know China. And I've certainly got a personal score to settle with them after what they did to me aboard that carrier."

"We don't settle personal scores at MI6, Alex."

"Figure of speech. In addition to my treatment aboard that carrier, I've a good deal of unpleasant prior experience with the Mandarins in Beijing and other scenic spots. Hard lessons. But I know how they think versus how they act. I want to go back inside China. I'll find him for you, sir. And his family. And I will bring every last one of them out of there alive."

"Good. Well said. The precise words I was hoping I'd hear you utter."

"It's what I do. I'll need a team. I'll need resources."

"Goes without saying. You'll have whoever and whatever you require. This will not be one of your traditional snatch-and-grab ops, Alex. Chase is at this moment perhaps China's greatest natural resource. They will hide him well and protect him to the death."

"Remarkable statement."

"And no overstatement. They know what we know. Thanks in part, no doubt, to the deep infiltration of Chinese spies at Cambridge. Knowledge that we know all about their new aircraft carrier. Their new fighter's performance parameters. Perhaps even the existence of a new generation of high-altitude attack drones.

God help us, they may even know we're aware of the Centurion Project."

"In which case, they may be thinking preemptive strikes?"

"Who knows, Alex? That may be why the Yanks are so desperate to neutralize Chase. I'll have a chat with Langley, make your case. But it's a new world. You need to lock on to this, Alex. I anticipate diligent preparation and keen focus on your part this time. None of your occasional lapses. No shooting from the hip this time. Clear?"

"Clear."

"I'm going to run this op personally, keeping the director at Langley in the loop. I alone will decide when and if you're ready to go. And you'll be reporting directly to me throughout this operation."

"Yes, sir."

"You tell me who and what you need to get this hostage rescue done and they will be yours. Logistics, infil, exfil, weapons, air and sea, all the services, any and all personnel will be placed at your disposal. Understood?"

"Understood. There is one chap I would like to have along for the ride."

"Name him."

"Stokely Jones. American spec-ops veteran. Navy SEAL, three combat tours, highly decorated. And a very good friend. I was best man at his wedding a couple of years ago. But I don't think you've ever met him."

"No. He's the fellow, I believe, that went into Balmoral Castle with you, correct? Operation 'God Save the Queen'? Possibly your finest hour, Lord Hawke."

"Could not possibly have done it without him, sir. Believe me."

"I do believe you. Team effort. I understand he's being honored here in England in some fashion?"

"Yes, sir. Arriving Heathrow via BA 147 tomorrow from his home in Miami. With your permission, I'll approach him with this mission."

"Consider it done. Like to meet this superhuman fellow someday, actually."

"You should. I'll arrange it, sir. About time you two met. A lunch at my club in St. James? Say, noon at Black's, perhaps? Day after tomorrow?"

"I've something on, but I'll move it. I look forward to it. Rather a large chap, from what I've been told."

"Roughly the size of your average armoire."

"I'm glad you recognize the enormity of this mission, Alex."

"Thank you, sir."

"And now you know precisely why they say that there is no free lunch, don't you, Lord Hawke?"

Chapter 36

Cambridge

When Hawke, Halter, and Congreve had arrived at Cambridge four days earlier, after their meeting at Hawkesmoor, they crossed the narrow bridge spanning the river Cam and parked in Halter's reserved space at Magdalene College. Space for automobiles was severely limited in narrow lanes of the old market town and only the highest of the high rated such a perk as Halter had. Ambrose was suitably impressed and said so.

Congreve and Hawke bade good-bye to the good professor and made their way across a snowy Jesus Green, and so to the labyrinthine maze of gardens, dead ends, and circuitous alleyways leading to the nineteenth-century building that housed the Cambridge morgue. Congreve, who had had reason to visit on numerous occasions, led the way.

The mortuary was to be found in the basement of an old military hospital built in 1879. It had been erected as part of the initiative of Florence Nightingale after the Crimean War to improve medical facilities for the army, Ambrose informed Hawke as they made their way.

"Really?" Hawke said. "Fascinating."

"Listen and learn," Congreve replied, not willing to rise to the flick of sarcasm he knew so well. "Look, there it is. Quite fabulous, isn't it?"

Hawke lifted his eyes from the gravel path and saw a somber black van drawn up in the building's courtyard. The place was massive and foreboding, dominated by a large clock tower. He didn't care much for hospitals, and morgues even less. But he was intensely curious about the corpse waiting for them in the basement. One is naturally beset with morbid feelings upon visiting such places, but Congreve seemed to relish the whole idea.

"Impressive," Hawke said as they entered the dingy grey foyer, and meant it.

The hospital had been built on a grand, traditionally solid Victorian scale, with malevolent green corridors that seemed to go on for a quarter of a mile if not longer. Hawke began to think they would never arrive at their destination. Finally, they entered a creaky musty old lift and began their descent. Hawke felt ever more uneasy in the grim confines.

Hawke, seeing the detective who'd agreed to meet them emerge from a swinging door, strode forward to meet him.

"I'm Detective Inspector Cummings, how do you do, sir?" the fellow said, extending his hand first to Hawke and then to the world-famous criminalist Ambrose Congreve.

"Thank you for taking the time," Hawke said, shaking the man's hand. "You've met Chief Inspector Congreve, I believe?"

"Indeed. We worked a difficult chase together some years ago. Nice to see you again, Chief Inspector."

"And you as well, Archie. I understand we're in for a treat this evening."

"Not sure I'd call it that. One of the worst I've seen, actually. Right this way, gentlemen."

They followed him down an oppressive green-tiled corridor made hideous by fluorescent lighting and entered the morgue proper. It was precisely as dismal as Hawke had imagined a mortuary of the Victorian era might appear, but an unexpected feeling swept over him just before the detective inspector pulled out the stainless steel drawer and revealed the victim.

Sadness, prompted by the presence of ghosts of all the young lads from Verdun, the Argonne, the Battle of Britain, Dunkirk, and countless dead and youthful souls who had resided for a time in this building. Only the monstrous sight of the mutilated corpse stretched out before him interrupted his fleeting reverie.

"Not a pretty sight, I'm afraid," Cummings said.

"What the hell?" Hawke said, stifling his revulsion at the sight. "I've never seen anything like this."

Congreve moved around the slab, bending down and peering carefully at various areas of the body before quickly moving on. He had brought a small digital camera and was photographing the corpse from head to toe. There were toes, Hawke noticed, just no fingers and no face. Ambrose took a sequence of shots of what little was left of the visage from every conceivable angle.

"What's your take, Ambrose?"

"Well. My first thought is *lingchi*, obviously, known as the 'death of a thousand cuts' used in China from roughly A.D. 900 until its abolition around 1905. The term derives from a classical description of ascending a mountain slowly. The executioner grasps handfuls of the fleshy parts of the body such as the thighs and breasts, slicing them away . . . the limbs are cut off piecemeal at the wrists and the ankles, the elbows and the knees, shoulders and hips. And then . . ." He paused.

"And then what?" Hawke said.

"After hours of unspeakable agony, the condemned is stabbed to the heart and his head is cut off."

"And?"

"This is obviously not *lingchi*, is it? No penetration, no decapitation. And the cuts are utterly uniform in their diamond-shaped pattern, as opposed to random slicing."

"Well, what then, Chief Inspector?" Cummings said. "It's got us baffled, frankly."

"I think this poor fellow suffered a far worse fate than *lingchi*. Far more insidious and long-lasting. I think he was suspended inside a collapsible mesh cage made of razor-sharp steel wire. The sheer weight of his body would cause the cage to slowly contract, slicing his flesh in the precise geometry of these diamondlike incisions. What was left of the soft facial tissue was removed postmortem. As were the fingertips."

"Do you recognize the methodology?" Hawke asked him.

"Yes. The Shining Basket, as it's called. The historian George Ryley Scott claims that many unfortunates were executed precisely this way by the Chinese Communist insurgents. He cites various claims made by the Nanking government in 1927 in his 1940 volume *History of Torture*. Also, Sir Henry Norman, a writer and photographer whose collection is now owned by the University of Cambridge, gives an eye-witness account of just such an atrocity as this one. A rather lengthy volume published in 1895 entitled *The People and Politics of the Far East*."

Hawke was suddenly aware of the stifling heat and the stench of chemicals, decay, and death. He needed air and he needed it badly.

"Thank you so much for your time, Detective Inspector Cummings. I think we're done for the day here. If you think of anything not in your crime scene report, you can reach me on my mobile at this number." Hawke handed him his card and made for the exit, because he desperately needed to get out of this house of horrors.

Congreve lingered near the corpse, studying his photographs on the camera's tiny screen, discussing them with his former colleague. *He likes it here,* Hawke thought. *He's comfortable.*

He's home.

Chapter 37

Cambridge

Early that evening, after the grisly visit to the morgue, Hawke and Congreve checked into the ever-so-trendy Hotel du Vin in central Cambridge. The magnificent Fitzwilliam Museum stood just across the road and cast its long violet shadow over the lamplit hotel entrance.

Once registered, the two men climbed the steps to their rooms and showered and changed, having agreed to meet for dinner in the lobby at seven. Ambrose had suggested one of his old haunts, a cozy candlelit wine bar in the cellar of the hotel.

Hawke could see that his oldest and closest friend, despite his nonchalance that afternoon, had been deeply disturbed by the gruesome events at the morgue. He decided to avoid that train of thought entirely and keep his tone and manner light.

"Well, you can't keep it from me any longer, Constable. The rumors are rampant all over London."

"Rumors? What bloody rumors?"

"I have this upon the full authority of the lads at the Men's Bar at Black's. I'm told that you and the lovely Lady Mars have finally set the date."

"Date for what? Oh, yes. That. Well, I suppose we have."

"Out with it, then. When is the blessed day?"

"Christmas Day. At Brixden House, of course."

"How charming. A lovely setting. I hope it snows. Were you planning to invite me? Or restricting the guest list to include only blood relatives and perhaps a smattering of your closest friends?"

"Don't be ridiculous, Alex. You're to be best man."

"Am I?"

"Of course you are. Who else would I ask? My hideous cousin Rupert from Swinburne?"

"I've no idea. You haven't asked me. That insufferable chum of yours, Sir Percy Squires, rather inferred that it was he and he alone who had the best shot at the title. He was quite sure you were going to anoint him, in fact."

"He said that?"

"He did."

"Hmm. Quite right. I haven't asked you, have I?"

"No."

"Well?" Hawke said, smiling.

"Well, what?"

"Will you?"

"Will I what?" Congreve said, exasperated. "Damn it, man, you know what I'm saying."

"Then say it."

"Do I have to go down on one knee? I am asking you if you would do me the very great honor of being the best man at my impending wedding to Lady Diana Mars on Christmas Day next at Brixden House. Will you or won't you?"

"Hmm. I shall take it under advisement."

"Under—"

"Calm down. Of course I'll do it. And I am honored. And very happy for you both. She's too good for you, of course, but then you knew that."

"She is indeed. I know I'm no prize in the great feminine sweepstakes. But she loves me. There you have it. And I absolutely adore her."

"I see an endless sea of bliss awaiting you both. This calls for champagne, don't you think?"

"Of course I do."

"Wine steward, a bottle of your best vintage Taittinger, if you please. Well chilled. My friend here is to be married on Christmas Day!"

After the champagne was gone, the two old friends enjoyed a good filet steak and an even better bottle of the best claret.

Congreve wanted a pipe after supper, and they stepped outside onto the bricked terrace. The night was clear and cold, pinprick stars in the blue-black sky above.

"Where are you on this bloody Master's Garden murder? Surely you have some preliminary findings in that supercharged cerebellum of yours," Hawke said as they sipped a brandy. They'd found two chairs on the small brick terrace and settled into a comfortably ruminative silence, smoking and drinking.

"Puzzles, bits and bobs, nothing more substantive," Congreve said.

"Such as?"

"Oh, the obvious political ramifications. We've a friend in Japan and an enemy in China. This murder has something to do with that. Politics. The murderer, we know, was clearly Chinese. No one else on earth is capable of executing a variation of *lingchi* in that specific fashion. Not sure about the victim, of course. We'll see what we see after we've met with Hobdale. One thing is troubling me."

"Do tell."

"Idle speculation, and nothing more. Not worthy of discussion at this point, Alex. Yes. I'm afraid we're really at the mercy of Sir Lucian Hobdale before we take the next leap. More cognac?"

"Why the hell not?" Alex said.

"Why the hell not, indeed? Who's to tell me I can't have more cognac?"

"The feminine leash is short and getting shorter? Christmas nuptials are right around the corner?"

"Precisely."

"Chief Inspector?" A young woman said as she emerged into the moonlight.

"Who's there?" Ambrose said.

"It's Lorelei. Lorelei Li."

"So it is! How are you, my dear? Come say hello to my very good friend Alex Hawke."

Hawke stood up and extended his hand. Hers was cool and warm at the same time, soft to the touch.

"Won't you join us for a brandy, Lorelei?" Hawke said. "It's a lovely night for it. Ambrose, move over."

"Oh, no, I can't. My editor's waiting for me inside. I just stepped out to sneak one of these. Do you mind?"

Hawke's gunmetal Zippo appeared out of nowhere and he held it to the tip of her cigarette. She took a puff and expelled a thin blue stream that missed Hawke's right cheek by inches. Her eyes were flashing as she said to Ambrose, "Perhaps I'll see you both in the morning. I'm down from London, covering the press conference for the *Times* tomorrow."

"Press conference?" Congreve said.

"Yes. The Cambridge police are issuing a statement on the murder at Sidney Sussex College."

"You don't say?" Congreve said. "Murder? Here at Cambridge? Really?"

"Really." She smiled. "And I suppose you two don't know anything at all about it?"

"Shocking," Hawke said. "Is it not? We're just here for the punting. Have you been out on the river today? Smashing."

She was not amused.

"Well. So awfully good to see you, Chief Inspector Congreve. And you as well, Mister—?"

"Hawke. Alex Hawke."

She held his eyes for a moment too long; then she was gone.

"Who the hell is that?" Hawke said.

"Old student of mine. One of a number of Chinese postdocs in my seminars, back when I lectured in international criminology here ten years ago. Why do you ask?"

"Why?"

"Yes, why?"

Hawke sat back down and looked at Congreve a moment before speaking.

"Is she a good guy? Or a bad guy?"

"Hard to say, really. Lads at Six weren't really keen on digging into the Chinese students' backgrounds here at Cambridge back then. Smart as a whip, that one. After Cambridge she took two more doctorates. History at Oxford and economics at LSE."

"Now she's a reporter?"

"No, an occasional stringer. Freelance. Odd bits and bobs of stuff for the *Times, Daily Mail.* Covers current events with a political perspective. Why are you so curious about her? Aside from the fact that she's outlandishly stunning to look at, of course."

"She was flirting with me."

"Don't take it personally. She flirts with everybody."

"We'll see about that," Hawke said. Opening his gunmetal cigarette case, he extracted a stick and stuck it in the corner of his mouth.

"I suppose," Congreve said with a sigh. "She is fabulous looking, isn't she? A very well-proportioned female. If one likes them, as the French put it so nicely, '*Il y a du monde au balcon.*'"

"Meaning?"

"Everyone's sitting in the balcony."

"Ah."

"Bosoms, Alex. The balcony?"

"I got it, for heaven's sake! You stay away from her, Constable. You're getting married, remember? Christmas Day?"

"God save me, you're serious."

"Deadly serious. One more thing. Should I ever see that goddess again? She's mine."

Hawke lit his cigarette and took a drag.

He'd seen that gorgeous creature somewhere once before. But damned if he could remember when or where.

Behind the wheel of a speeding automobile, perhaps?

Chapter 38

Hotel du Vin

The bedside phone jangled. Alex opened his eyes, sighed, and looked at his watch. Two o'clock in the bloody morning. Who the hell?

"I can hear you snore," a vaguely familiar female voice said when he picked up.

"Ah. So sorry."

"I like it."

"Really? So few women do."

"I'm not like most women."

"How very fortunate."

"Try not to be a rude, sexist pig if you can possibly avoid it."

"Sorry. How is that you can hear me snore?"

"You're loud."

"But still."

"I'm right next door."

"Ah."

"I hear everything."

"Surely not everything."

"Unfortunately, yes."

"Is there no privacy at all in this damned hotel?"

"Apparently not. You'd best behave."

"Behave, is it? And if I don't?"

"I'm not sure. Is your door locked?"

"Of course."

"Unlock it."

"Yes, dear."

Click.

She'd rung off.

He replaced the receiver, yawned, and swung his long legs over the side of the bed. Feeling the cold against his naked skin, he grabbed his navy silk robe. The scant remains of his nightcap stood beside the phone, and he snatched up the glass and downed the dregs.

"Bottoms up," he said, laughing softly to himself, while he idly scratched his bare stomach inside his robe. "Or at least one certainly hopes so."

There came a tapping at his chamber door.

"Miss Li, I presume?" he said, opening it a crack.

She bowed her dark head, bent from the waist, and pressed her palms together.

"At your service, Lord Hawke."

"I do like the sound of that. Won't you please come in?"

"Come into my parlor, said the fly to the spider."

He thought about that a moment and laughed. "Quite a good one, that. So you're the infamous Spider Woman I've heard so much about."

She smiled and stepped inside. She was wearing a sheer black peignoir thing that barely covered her bum. Black silk stockings held up by intricate lacy suspenders with small red ribbons at the fasteners. Black high-heeled Jimmy Choos and nothing else. Her quivering breasts were a bulging miracle encased in transparent silk. She smiled, the tip of her tongue darting out for the briefest moment before she spoke.

"My room is much nicer."

"Pity you had to leave it."

"We'll see, I suppose."

"Drink?" he said, picking up the bottle of Gosling's by the bed.

"No. But you go right ahead. Do you need it?"

"I don't know yet. But I think not."

"Good boy. Look at you. You are like a little boy. So full of hope and expectation."

"Hmm."

"What are you hoping for, Lord Hawke?"

"At the moment? I'm hoping you're not a lesbian."

"I'm not, I assure you," she said.

"Good. That's settled, then. Thank you. Have we met before?"

"Don't you think you'd remember these?" she said, freeing her breasts from captivity.

"Yes, I suppose I would, wouldn't I?"

"You appear to have an erection."

"Do I?"

"Don't be shy. It's flattering. The much-loved compliment left unsaid."

"You had me at 'Lorelei.' Down there on the moonlit terrace."

"I noticed. Shall we fuck, Lord Hawke? Or not?"

"I can't think of any good reason not to."

"I like to be on top."

"Surprise, surprise."

"Lie down, Lord Hawke."

"Bossy, bossy."

"I said, lie down!"

He did, smiling up at her, and said, "Tell me, dear. Did you leave your riding crop at home?"

She laughed and stroked his cheek.

"So sorry to disappoint you, darling. Yes, I did."

"It wasn't me I was concerned about. Darling."

"What do you like, your lordship?" she said, climbing onto the bed and arranging herself astride him. Leaning toward him, she dipped the tops of her breasts creamily into the soft light of the bedside lamp.

He sighed involuntarily at the sight of her.

She smiled and took him gently in her hand, guided him slowly inside her. With another, deeper sigh of pleasure, he yanked the thin straps of the peignoir completely off her shoulders and cupped her heavy breasts in his hands, caressing her erect nipples with infinite tenderness.

"Let's see. What do I like? Oh, yes. Sex," Hawke said. "I do like sex. Always have."

"Vanilla, one would suppose, m'lord. How mundane and haute bourgeois of you."

"I beg your pardon?"

"You know what I mean. Tell me what you want."

"I aim only to please, darling. Besides, you're my guest of honor. I'll follow your lead. Where are we going with this magical sexual mystery tour?"

"I would say a bit of kink, ordinarily. It's where my oh-so-deviant tastes lie. The sting of the crop and all that. Delicious. But it's so bloody hard to lug around all that kinky paraphernalia when one goes out for an evening of romance. Don't you agree?"

"Hmm. Cumbersome. Awkward, too, arriving for a passionate fling in one's spiffy black Range Rover towing a U-Haul for all one's erotic bondage appliances."

"You're funny. I knew you would be."

"Thanks. Now shut up and fuck."

"Say that again."

"Shut up and fuck."

"Yes. Do that some more. Deeper. Yes. Like that. A little harder. And slower. Oh, yes. Yes . . . like that. Right there. On my clit."

Harder. Slower. Harder.

"Good?" he said.

"Good. Yes."

"You're very beautiful, Lorelei."

"So are you. But I'm only after your money, m'lord. You are rich, I suppose . . . oh, yes, please, don't talk now, just fuck me."

"I will."

"Don't stop that. Come. Now. I want to feel it inside me. And then if you're a very good boy, I'll let you make me come."

His back arched involuntarily and a cry escaped his lips.

Exhausted, they lay side by side in the dark. Two glowing orange coals hovered above their faces as they inhaled their cigarettes.

"That was good," she said.

Hawke said, "Last time? The woman I was with said 'Was it good for you?' "

"Really? What did you say?"

"I said, 'Weren't you there?' "

"Good one."

"Do you always smoke after sex?" he asked her.

"I've no idea. I've never looked."

When Hawke awoke the next morning, the girl was gone. She'd written her mobile number in red lipstick on his bathroom mirror. A bit theatrical, he thought.

He picked up the phone to order a pot of black coffee.

A bit odd, that one. Too cute by half, perhaps. Some kind of an agenda?

He considered a moment, and then rubbed her lipstick number out with the cuff of his terry bathrobe sleeve. Uninvited trouble already came his way with sufficient regularity. The very last thing he needed was to invite more.

Little did he know that he already had.

Chapter 39

Trinity College, Cambridge

Professor Sir Lucian Hobdale, Nobel laureate, was a fixture at Cambridge. He was a university senior lecturer in machine learning and an advanced research Fellow and director of studies. The windows of his tumble-jumble of a corner office at Trinity College overlooked the ice-filled river Cam flowing stolidly, always reassuring somehow.

Hobdale had that leonine cast of character so frequently aspired to by not a few aging professors who affect to have no such aspirations. Thick white hair, somewhat watery gin-blue eyes, and a strongly sculpted face and jawline. Beautiful skin. His tweed suit had seen better days decades ago. But he managed to outweigh his tatty wardrobe with wit, brilliance, and a decidedly patrician air.

"Chief Inspector Congreve," Hobdale said, swiveling round in his chair, "How marvelous to see my illustrious colleague again. I must tell you, I was thrilled with the results of our last . . . mission . . . together. The Singularity Affair, as it's now known around here. Splendid show, that. We jolly well sent that Persian madman packing, did we not? What was his name?"

Congreve smiled. "Darius Saffari. Indeed we did, sir. And we've Alex Hawke here to thank for a good bit of that. You remember Alex Hawke, of course?"

Hobdale's great head swiveled.

"Lord Hawke. Of course. An honor as always."

Hawke strode forward with his hand extended and said, "Professor Hobdale, how kind of you to see us on such short notice."

"Not at all, not at all. I've already fired up the quantum supercomputer at the U.K. Machine Intelligence Research Center in Leeds in light of your visit. Something to do with facial reconstruction and recognition this time. That poor chap found in the Sidney Master's Garden, missing most of his face and all his fingers and teeth, according to rumor. Ghastly, just ghastly."

Ambrose finished firing up his pipe and said, "No human being should ever be made to suffer like that,

Sir Lucian. It pains me to say this, but Lord Hawke and I fear a rather fiendish type, politically motivated, is on the loose in Cambridge. A ghoul of the old-school Chinese Te-Wu persuasion. He must be stopped."

"We'll certainly do our best to identify the victim, Chief Inspector, I can assure you. Do sit down, both of you. I'd offer tea, but I sense you'd prefer to get down to cases. My assistant informs me you've brought morgue photos of the victim, yes?"

Congreve nodded and pulled a manila envelope from his tatty leather briefcase. "Here they are," Congreve said, handing the older man the folder. "Prepare yourself, sir."

"I've been doing precisely that for sixty-some years, Chief Inspector."

Hobdale, who'd dabbled in forensic anthropology, thus waved the notion away and slit the envelope, spilling the eight-by-ten glossies across his cluttered desktop. He picked up the nearest one, studied it a moment, and then reached for his antique glass. He hovered over each section of the mutilated face, peering through the magnifier, tsk-tsking cheerily at the unmitigated horror he'd been presented with.

"Chinese torture," he said, putting down the glass. "Fifteenth century."

"Yes," Congreve said, arranging his corpus in the comfortable armchair. "Most definitely Chinese handiwork."

"*Lingchi*? That would appear to be the method."

"My first thought as well, Professor Hobdale. But no, no knives were used during torture. The victim was suspended in a razor-sharp mesh bag called the Shining Basket that slowly collapsed and constricted under his weight. Almost every square inch of facial epidermis was removed, as you can see. Meaning he was suspended facedown. We're hoping the quantum computer can build on the bone structure and rebuild it. Is there any hope of that, Sir Lucian?"

"Indeed there is, indeed there is, sir. Take a look at this."

Hobdale clicked on his computer, and a geometric modeling of George Washington's face appeared.

"It's a program called PRISM," the professor said, "developed in concert with Arizona State University. We brought together forensic anthropologists, digital artists, and computer scientists to effect the 3-D digital reconstruction of Washington's face that you see here. Remarkable, isn't it? This is exactly what the man looked like at nineteen years old! A century prior to the invention of photography! Give us the proper tools and we can literally bring the dead back to life."

"Extraordinary," Hawke said, peering at the eerily lifelike image on the screen.

"Would that you could," Congreve mused, puffing seriously. "Would that you could."

"You're afraid the victim may have been a colleague, I take it?"

"Yes, Professor Watanabe. He's still missing."

"Oh, Lord. I had the pleasure of attending one of his lectures on the Rape of Nanking. Brilliant man."

"Yes, he was. Watanabe-san was a friend, really. Changed the course of my entire life. He was—"

Congreve looked away, stricken.

"If this victim proves to be your friend, I shall help you find out who did this, Chief Inspector. Upon my word, I shall."

Hawke put out his hand and said, "You'll let us know as soon as you have something, Professor?"

"I shall, indeed, Lord Hawke. I bid you both good day, gentlemen. You'll hear from me soon, I assure you. We shall get right on it. Our methods are foolproof."

They both shook his hand and left, crossing the square and the river to Magdalene College, where their car was waiting to take them back to London.

"It's Watanabe, isn't it?" Congreve said, his head down, slogging through the snow.

"Yeah," Hawke said. "I'm afraid so, Constable."

Chapter 40

London

Stokely Jones Jr., a battle-hardened American warrior in his late middle age, was a large man.
Whatever.
He was big.
He was black.
Deal with it.
Stoke made his way down the long, long la-di-da hotel corridor to the elevator bank on his floor. Fanciest damn place he'd ever hung his hat in London Town, by far. Gold everywhere, huge columns in the lobby, gold-plated crystal chandeliers as big as small battleships. Mirrors everywhere, just in case you forgot who you were, you know, just walking by.

Claridge's, they called this joint. Sounded like the name of some beachside condo in Palm Beach to him.

But just walking into the lobby of Claridge's Hotel the first time, he felt like he oughta be wearing diamonds on the soles of his shoes. Like the old Paul Simon song. He hit the down button and stood there cracking his big knuckles, staring at the gilded angels on the ceiling, and shaking his head.

He should have known better. It was so damn predictable. What he should have done? Checking in? Gone over to Martin, the head honcho, and said, "Hey, Martin, listen up, I haven't even seen my room and I know it ain't good enough. All right? Help me out here."

Handed him fifty pounds on the spot or something. But no, he hadn't done that. And now look.

Fancha, it seems, didn't like their room, excuse me, suite.

But.

And here's the problem. Mama ain't happy, ain't nobody happy. Wasn't that the truth? Wasn't that the single most important God's honest truth all married men eventually come to learn for themselves sooner or later? And learn it the hard way, brother? Seriously?

The thing about it was, Stokely had been in London many times, but never once in the company of his fairly new bride, a semifamous and totally beauteous torch singer from the Cape Verde Islands named Fancha. Girl came from nothing, grew up in some ghetto, in one of the island's tar-paper palaces where the rats ate the dogs.

But she had faith. Just like he'd had. All his life. Belief in one's self. Yes. Said she always knew from the time she was a little girl she wouldn't die there, not in that slum anyway. Not in that particular hell.

He knew all about that feeling.

One-name kind of entertainer now. Big time. Cher-style. The winner of the championship title match in a first-round TKO, the new Mrs. Stokely Jones Jr., she was now a woman long accustomed to the deluxe lives of the rich and famous.

All this was, of course, courtesy of her first husband, a deceased Miami nightclub impresario and gentleman of dubious distinction named Joey Mancuso.

People loved the old guy. Called the wide but vertically challenged Mr. Mancuso everything from the King of Biscayne Bay to the Mayor of Miami Beach, you know, back in the day. The Rat Pack ring-a-ding-ding days when Old Blue Eyes had really ruled the roost at the Fontainebleau on Miami Beach, knowing in his heart of hearts that Dino had the better set of pipes. Those were Joey's salad days, baby.

Now, to be honest, Joey had departed this earth under suspicious circumstances. Leave it at that. Speaking of leaving, Mancuso had left the grieving widow, Fancha, a huge Spanish-style estate overlooking Miami's Biscayne Bay. Not to mention butlers, Bentleys, a garage full of metallic-painted Rolls-Royces, offshore accounts up the wazoo, and a whole shitload of cold hard cash. That was Joey for you. Praise the Lord and pass the buck, baby.

His reputation predeceased him.

But most people Stoke had met here and there, in Miami Beach and Vegas, people who knew the late, great Joey Mancuso, all said pretty much the same thing about the dead cat:

"Joey reminded you a whole lot of Jackie Gleason, only he wasn't funny." Couple months ago, when Stokely had received a very fancy engraved invitation to come to England for a special award, he'd told Fancha he was going to reserve them a room at his favorite hotel, the Hilton on Hyde Park. Fancha gave him a look and he knew he'd once more inadvertently tiptoed into the social minefield that constituted his new life with a rich wife. The heavy-lidded look told him immediately that the Hilton was a nonstarter and that he'd better rethink his notions of what did and did not make for an acceptable hotel in London.

"Claridge's, Stokely Jones," she'd said, and sighed. "It's the only decent hotel in London."

Decent? It was a damn palace.

Long as you got the right suite.

It was funny. When Fancha wasn't sighing, she pretty much held her lips tightly together, which told you a lot about the woman and how she felt about Stoke's lack of worldly sophistication when they were out jet-setting. At home she pretty much let him do his thing, what he wanted to do—work out, wash his GTO convertible, watch golf and football on TV. And the good news in all this was, he loved her and she loved him.

Bottom line, they were still busy acclimating themselves to each other, the way he saw it. Only a matter of time.

He pressed the down button again and waited. Damn. He figured a hotel that stuck you with a nightly room rate of over two grand per would have faster elevators. Think again.

When the door finally slid open, it revealed a woman, a lady who looked a hell of a lot like an angry supersize version of that *Murder, She Wrote* TV dame. And maybe even was. He entered the lift, as Fancha called it, nodded, said "Good morning," and stepped inside as the door slid shut.

Woman tried hard to smile, but it just didn't come natural.

"Nice lift," he said, just trying to be friendly.

"What?"

She looked at him like he was insane. He noticed she was smoking a cigarette even though there were signs everywhere saying NO SMOKING.

"Filthy out," she said, taking a puff and giving him the eye. Angela Lansbury, yeah, that was it. Female detective in that cute little town on the coast of California supposed to be Maine or something.

"Filthy?" Stoke said, thinking about it.

Garbage strike? he wondered.

"Freezing, for this time of year. Spitting rain."

Spitting rain? He didn't have a clue how to answer that one, so he just started humming and singing a little bit, pass the time.

" 'Foggy Day in London Town, had me blue, had me down . . .' " he warbled.

He instinctively knew all Brits loved to talk about the weather. Which seemed weird to him, considering they didn't have much. No hurricanes, for instance, no tornadoes, no twisters, no nor'easters, nothing at all that qualified as real weather, in his view. But you never met anyone over here, anyone anywhere, who didn't bring up the weather right off the bat.

"We just got here," he said to Angela or simply a woman separated at birth from the former TV star. "Checked in last night. Nice place. Claridge's, right? That how you say it?"

"American. I knew it." She sighed.

Stoke watched the numbers descending.

"You ever stay at the Hilton?" he asked her.

"Never."

"You ought to try it sometime. You meet a more relaxed class of people. Lot of salesmen, for instance. Beauticians."

"Really?" she said, like she was spitting rain. "Salesmen? How utterly charming it all sounds."

"You're a smoker, I see. I used to smoke. You like it?"

"No. I just like to cough."

Chapter 41

The door slid open and he stepped aside and let the old biddy sidle on out ahead of him. Gave her a wide berth. It was an old habit of his, letting ladies out first. Most times, they said thank you. Angela, no surprise, did not utter a peep.

He walked out and took a right, headed for the lobby. He was looking for a guy named Martin who was the head porter and a guy he'd given fifty bucks to last night, hoping he'd help them get a room Fancha would approve of.

Martin was a funny little guy, a real character. He was dressed up like a palace guard for the Wicked Witch of the West, the one in the *Wizard of Oz* movie, but he didn't act like it was anything all that unusual. He acted like it was perfectly normal for a hotel employee to be wearing a striped vest, a cutaway coat with long tails below his knees, white silk kneesocks, and big brass buttons all down his front. Plus, a shiny black top hat. Perfectly normal outfit, right?

Martin had a sense of humor, though, and Stoke sort of instinctively liked him. In his own way, Martin was street. If there was such a thing as street in London Town. Hard to tell.

"Ah, Mr. Jones," Martin said, touching the brim of his fancy lid, "did you have a good night, sir? How is the suite? Does Madame approve?"

"The suite? Not so good, Martin. She doesn't like it. Too dark, too small, bad pillows, on and on, yadda-yadda. You gotta help me out here. Seriously."

"Really? How odd. Which suite did they give you?"

"Seven seventy-two."

"You're joking."

"No. Here's the thing, Martin, I'll be honest. She hates it. But I like it. It's kinda funky, all those red plaid carpets and all. Plus, I actually like the smell of cigar smoke."

"I'll say it's funky, Mr. Jones. No one has stayed in that suite since Truman Capote died." He pronounced it "Ka-po-tay," but Stoke knew who he was talking about. The funny little lispy writer guy who wrote one of Stoke's all-time favorites, *In Cold Blood*.

He had stayed in Stoke's suite? Wow. Made him like it even more.

Stoke discreetly peeled off another fifty-pound note and slid it into Martin's palm. It disappeared instantly, so fast Stoke didn't even see where the cat had stowed it. Martin was all smiles suddenly.

"Thank you, sir. I'll see what I can do. Shall I call you a cab?"

"Depends. Do I look like a cab?" Stoke clapped him on the shoulder maybe a teensy bit too hard.

"Beg pardon, sir?"

"A joke, Martin. How far away is this place, Black's, I think they call it?"

"Black's, sir?"

"Yeah. Black's. That's where I'm going."

"And you're talking about Black's? The gentleman's club?"

"That's what I said. Black's."

"Ah. I see. Well, I must tell you, Mr. Jones, the thing about Black's is that it is a very private club. Perhaps the most exclusive gentleman's club in all London. Members only, I'm afraid. Very posh."

"Don't be afraid. I won't hurt you. Just tell me how to get there."

"Ah. Well, I uh . . ."

"Martin. Listen up, sporting life. I'm meeting a friend of mine there for lunch, okay? At Black's. The club. He's the member. Not me. Alex Hawke's his name. Heard of him?"

"Not Lord Alexander Hawke?"

"Yeah, that would be him."

"Mr. Jones, I had no idea he was your . . . friend. Why, his lordship is one of our very own here at Claridge's. His mother brought him here for afternoon tea once a week when he was but a toddler. He still comes in to afternoon tea occasionally. With his son, little Alexei."

"Yeah, well, there you go, that's him all right. One place you don't want to be is in between Alex Hawke and a pot of hot tea. Now, you going to tell me how to get to Black's?"

Martin told him. Too far to walk in the rain, he said, so he signaled one of the other costumed doormen to hail Stoke a taxi. Martin grabbed a big black umbrella, and they made their way out to the sidewalk and waited in the spitting rain.

"One other thing, Martin. Where exactly is Buckingham Palace? I mean, from here? Can I walk it?"

"You can. But I must warn you, you've just missed the Changing of the Guard, I'm afraid."

"Damn. Love to see that, watch 'em changing and all that. But I'm going over there for something else. After lunch at Black's, I mean. To the palace."

"Ah. The tour, is it, then? I can give you a schedule, guv'nor." *Shed-yule* was how he said it.

"No tour. I'm invited to Buckingham Palace, too. Funny, huh?"

"Invited, sir? To the palace? By whom?"

"Well, you see, the Queen herself sorta gave me the nod, so . . . I don't want to let her down."

"The *Queen*?"

"Uh-huh. You know her? Great woman."

"You don't mean to say you actually know the Queen, Mr. Jones? The Queen of England?"

"Sure, I mean to say it. Why not? Met her once in Scotland up at Balmoral Castle. Oh, this was, what, a couple of years ago? Incredibly brave woman. Poise? Forget about it. Never saw anything like it, Martin, believe me. And you know what else, Martin?"

"No, sir. I'm a bit . . . taken aback is all, sir."

"That woman, the Queen I mean, there's no other way to say this. She has a lot of class."

Martin looked as if he was about to faint dead away. His high-pitched response sounded like a dehydrated bird trying to screech out a single peep.

"Class?"

"Damn straight. One of the classiest damn women you ever want to meet, Martin. Seriously."

"Wait. You say you visited at Balmoral, Mr. Jones?"

"Yeah. But not really a visit. Sort of dropped in kind of thing. On the roof of her castle. From a helicopter.

Thing was, some Iranian terrorist assholes were threatening to kill the whole damn Royal Family up there and me and Alex Hawke had to go in and extreme prejudice their asses straight to Paradise, pardon my French. That's why I'm going to Buckingham Palace. I think she likes me . . . We're tight, in a way, if you know what I mean."

"Here's your taxi, sir . . . and . . . I'm sorry, why did you say you were going to Buckingham Palace?"

"Oh, yeah. I'm invited to some kind of ceremony or other. I guess they do it every year. You know, a whole lot of hoop-dee-doo over nothing. I'm being knighted."

"I'm sorry?"

"Yeah, knighted, I think they call it. I dub thee, and all that sword-on-the-shoulder thing. Sir Lancelot was one, remember? The Round Table? I don't know if they still have that."

"Knighted, sir?" Martin said, barely able to get the word out, holding the door wide open for this massive coal-skinned gentleman who seemed to have charmed his hotel, the staff, the entire clientele.

Stoke climbed into the rear of the shiny black London cab, paused, looked back over his shoulder, leaned out the window, and flashed his big white teeth at the drop-jawed head porter.

"Yeah, that's it. I'm getting dubbed, brother. Knighted, Martin. My uncle Sonny, up in Harlem, he says it's pretty cool. Says Sir Laurence Olivier and Sir Richard Branson are in the house. So, we cool? Say hello to 'Sir Stokely Jones,' brother! Oh, and one more thing?"

"Yes, Mr. Jones?"

"Cheerios, old Chapstick!" Stoke laughed.

A dumbstruck Martin, with one foot planted squarely in the street, turned to the next guests in the hotel queue. "Cheerios, did he say? Breakfast cereal, isn't it? In America, I mean?"

"Oh, we wouldn't know, now, would we? We're not Americans. We're from Ipswich, you see, aren't we?"

"Did he say, I mean, did he call me, 'Chapstick'?"

"I believe he did," the wife said. "Didn't he, Harry?"

"Black's," Stokely said, leaning forward to speak through the small plexiglass partition to the hunched-over cabbie with the tweed flat cap.

The white-haired man up front craned his head around and took a long, disbelieving look at his passenger. Always full of surprises, these bloody Yanks were.

"Black's, sir? On St. James?"

"Black's it is!" Stoke smiled. "And don't spare the horses, either. I mean, step on it!"

"Right you are, guv'nor," he said, engaging first gear and pulling out into the steady traffic on Brook Street en route to Piccadilly and St. James Street.

Chapter 42

London

The Men's Grill at Black's, Alex Hawke's gentleman's club on St. James, was filled to overflowing with ebullient gentry and other hearty, somewhat florid members of the well-to-do. Congenial, well-turned-out gentlemen of every size and shape were standing shoulder to shoulder at the bar. This was the prime hour of midday, and they were all tippling, quibbling, chattering like mad.

Luncheon was being served soon, and if you were to have that second whiskey neat or vodka rocks, best have it now, before being seated.

This upper-crust bastion of London male society was abuzz with the usual happy social hubbub and gay repartee of men at drink. As some waggish clubman had once remarked, "It's always happy hour at Black's, somehow or other, I find." Happy, as well it had been, since the club's inauspicious founding, in 1693, as a popular chocolate shop. Later, in the early eighteenth century, it was notorious as a gambling house, so much so that no less a personage than Jonathan Swift had once referred to Black's as "the bane of half the English nobility."

Beau Brummell himself had been a member here then, followed close on the heels by various dukes, earls, assorted Princes of Wales, as well as luminaries David Niven, Evelyn Waugh, Randolph Churchill, and other cads and men of that ilk who would come later.

Lord Alexander Hawke was a direct descendant of the notorious pirate John Black Hawke, known on the Spanish Main as the fearless "Blackhawke." There was no disputing the fact that he himself was of that ilk. Hawke had, as he liked to remind friend and foe alike, "pirate blood in his veins."

It was a great, grand, high-ceilinged, and wood-paneled room, with towering leaded glass windows. In every season, sunlight streamed down in splendid shafts, slanted columns of gold in the smoky, dusty air. The shifting light revolved with the day, sliding across worn Persian carpets, making an observer feel as if he were in the cabin of a great ship on a curving course.

There was always a certain lighthearted jocularity in the air, especially here in the third-floor Grill. A palpable bonhomie born of old school ties, old familial bonds, and simmering rivalries forged on the playing fields of Eton or Harrow; and shared time spent in the kindred trenches of war, of love, and of mere commerce.

Lord Alexander Hawke, Sir David Trulove, and Chief Inspector Ambrose Congreve, a formidable trio if ever there was one, sat at Hawke's customary reserved table. It was a quiet, tufted leather banquette situated beneath a window at the farther reaches of the large room. The hubbub was reduced to a dull roar back here, and one could speak easily of private, even secret, matters with scant fear of being overheard.

C always preferred this reserved table of Hawke's for any rendezvous that was in the least bit sensitive. And there was no more sensitive a subject within the corridors of MI6 these days than Operation Lightstorm.

They'd ordered cocktails and just begun to get down to cases when a white-gloved steward approached the table, appearing to glide across the carpet.

"M'lord," he said to Hawke, "so sorry to disturb, but there's a gentleman arrived downstairs."

"Yes? Who is it?"

"A Mr. Stokely Jones, he says his name is, your lordship. He says, I mean to say, I believe he's expected?"

"Ah, good; he's a bit early, in fact. Sir Stokely Jones! Indeed, he is expected," Hawke said, glancing at his wristwatch. "Please show him right up, will you, Edward?"

"Indeed, your lordship," the fellow said, withdrawing silently into the gloom and with seemingly little or no effort required.

Sir Stokely Jones? Congreve had just taken a deep draft of his spicy Bloody Mary. Upon hearing the name, he suddenly found the concoction inconveniently regurgitating. He quickly put his napkin to his lips and tried to contain his surprise.

"Are you quite all right, Ambrose?" C asked, patting him soundly on the shoulder.

"Constable," Hawke said, "what's the matter?"

"'Sir Stokely Jones'?" Ambrose finally managed, coughing, his eyes red and tearing up. "Is that what you said, Alex? Sir Stokely Jones?"

Hawke laughed and said, "Hmm. I suppose I forgot to mention it, Constable. Stokely is to be knighted. Tomorrow, in fact."

"Knighted?" Congreve said. "We are speaking of your dear old American friend? Are we not? Chap from Miami?"

"I am. He is."

"Bloody well deserved, if you ask me," the chief of MI6 said. "The man's a hero of the very first rank."

"Well, no one said a word to me," Congreve said somewhat sulkily. "What's this knighthood all about?"

"Sorry, Constable, my fault that you're not quite up to speed. You'll remember the Balmoral affair, when Stokely Jones almost single-handedly saved the life of the Queen? Not to mention most of the Royal Family? A few years ago, as I recall."

"Ah, yes."

"It was in all the papers? Telly as well."

"So sorry, Alex, of course I bloody well remember. It was a day of national celebration. A singular result to an iffy gambit at best. You played no small part in that business yourself. But then, I had no idea. A knighthood, you say?"

Hawke looked up, alerted by a definite volume rise over the general roar at the bar beyond.

"Here he comes now. Look impressed."

"I am, believe me," Congreve said, glancing up and smiling in appreciation of the sight he beheld.

The sight of a giant black gentleman, splendidly bedecked in an exquisitely tailored and bespoke Savile Row three-piece suit, a worsted navy chalk-stripe, striding through the Men's Grill at Black's with a huge white grin on his face, was bound to cause a bit of notice, even in this most cosmopolitan milieu, home to some of the most poised, the most unflappable gathering of well-bred gentlemen in all London.

Stoke, of course, loved all the attention thrown his way. He suddenly remembered he was still wearing his newly purchased hat, a perfect dove grey fedora he'd snagged that very morning at Lock & Co., the famous hatters of St. James Street.

Stokely smiled and waved his new hat at everyone as he passed along the great length of the bar, saying, "Hey, how's everybody doin'? Good? All right. That's great!"

"How do you do, my good sir," a diminutive but rather large-waisted, mutton-chopped blond fellow said, sticking out his pink, ham-fisted hand as Stoke passed him by.

"I'm good, I'm good," Stoke said, pausing for the moment to address the man. "How do you do, yourself? You look good, brother. Real good. Love the tie."

"I am very well, indeed. Lord Cork is my name. I say, will you perhaps join us for a quick sip of something formidable and expensive? A fortifier before luncheon is served?"

"Need a rain check on that one, but thank you. I'm joining my friends back there for lunch."

"Whom are you lunching with, may I ask?"

"Fellow over there by the window? That's him. Waving his arm, all giddy with excitement over my arrival."

"You don't mean to say our Lord Hawke?"

"That's the one."

"Ah, splendid chap indeed, young Hawke. Old college chums, you see, we were at Dartmouth together. Our naval college, here in Britain. Yes, and a chap much beloved by my family as well. Welcome to Black's, sir. Honored by your presence."

"Honor is all mine, Lord Cork," Stoke said with a smile, and pushed on toward his friend's table at the rear.

Chapter 43

"Sir Stokely Jones," Hawke said, getting to his feet and shaking his old friend's hand. "Quite an entrance, I must say, and I would expect no less!"

"All the world's a stage," Stoke said, bowing slightly from the waist. "As Shakespeare or somebody like that said, I believe."

"Shakespeare, indeed!" Hawke said with a grin and then embraced him warmly, pounding him on his vast shoulder with a closed fist. "Let me be the first to offer you my heartiest congratulations, Stoke. God knows you deserve it."

"Second," Congreve said, standing and offering his hand. "Well done, sir!"

"Last, but certainly not least," Sir David said, also rising and pumping Stoke's hand vigorously.

"Sit down, everybody, sit down," Stoke said, taking his seat at the table. "Sorry I'm so early. Guy at the hotel, Martin? He told me it was a twenty-minute cab ride over here. But the traffic? Nada."

Waitstaff appeared promptly and Stoke said, "Diet Coke, or Coke Light, as you folks say over here."

"Certainly, sir."

"With ice, please. I love ice."

"Indeed, sir."

They all placed their luncheon orders as well, Stoke settling for a large chopped salad. When the waiter had departed, Stoke spoke up.

"Let me guess. Something has come up. This feels like a business lunch to me. What's up? Who are the bad guys and how many of them?"

"I'll let Sir David fill you in."

Trulove then proceeded to tell Stokely, in great detail, about the disappearance of the American scientific genius Bill Chase, the hostage rescue code-named Operation Lightstorm, the top-secret Centurion Project, and the rest. When he finished, everyone was quiet, waiting for Stoke's reaction.

"So lemme get it straight. This guy Chase, the world-famous weapons designer. He and his entire family were abducted one night off the street in

Georgetown almost five years ago. And they're not dead?"

"Apparently they're not," Sir David said.

"We don't know where they are now, do we, Sir David?"

"An extremely rough idea. I would suspect a remote country safe house in the Chinese countryside. However, there's another possibility. CIA informs me that a twenty-nine-year-old man, ex–South Korean army officer, a Colonel Cho, miraculously escaped from a North Korean death camp last week. Guards were firing at him as he swam across the Yalu River. As you may know, Kim Jong-un gave orders to shoot anyone attempting to escape. The escapee, Colonel Cho, sought asylum at a Swiss consulate. In his debrief, he told the Swiss consul he believed at one time there had been Americans held in the camp. But that they may have been killed."

Hawke said, "Have any other Americans recently gone missing over there, Sir David?"

"Not to my knowledge. And certainly nothing to that effect from CIA."

"Then maybe we should start with that camp, Alex?" Stoke said.

"Yes. I think we should. Sir David?"

"Don't rule anything out. It's been years. They could be anywhere."

"And Chase himself?" Hawke asked.

"We've been on his trail via satellite and ground personnel ever since Alex landed that Chinese fighter at Lakenheath RAF. Chase was seen one week ago today by one of our MI6 chaps leaving the Chinese Ministry of State Security in Shanghai in the company of two thugs. Here's the photograph. The tall thin fellow in the middle wearing sunglasses."

"Was he tailed?"

"He was hustled into the back of a Mercedes 600 with blacked-out windows and whisked off in the direction of Shanghai Pudong Airport. We followed but lost him in severe traffic."

"And exactly how long ago was the Chase family abducted?"

"Going on five years," Trulove said. "Bill Chase is single-handedly altering the balance of power in the Pacific. He's obviously been coerced into working for the Chinese military, creating weapons that weren't even on the drawing board when he was working for the Pentagon."

Stoke said, "But nothing else popped up all these years until this Shanghai shot was taken? No word from him or his family?"

"No. Listen, Stoke," Hawke said, lowering his voice. "This is a joint op with CIA. And CIA would like Bill Chase taken out. Extreme prejudice."

"You're kidding. We're supposed to waste the smartest guy on the planet? Guy who's kept us on top for two decades? The guy who, if rescued, would provide the intelligence mother lode of Chinese military inner workings of all time? Insane."

"Sorry," Hawke said. "C and I have a major difference of opinion here. CIA wants extreme prejudice. I think this is a straight HR play. A hostage rescue, in my opinion, is both feasible and the way to go."

"The prime minister and the U.S. president both support the CIA position that termination is the only way, Alex," the chief of MI6 intoned solemnly. "I've told you all the reasons why."

"Excuse me, Sir David," Stoke said. "I know it won't be easy, never is. But this is what we do. We go in there, stealth mode, find his family first. Wherever they are, doesn't matter. We'll find the wife and children. That's number one. Make sure they're all safely out and off the table before we go after the man himself. When the NKs lose that leverage over Chase, and the victim has got nothing else to lose, that's when we locate him. We go in strong. We get Bill Chase out and we get him out alive and we bring him and his family home."

"Sounds so simple," Congreve said, smiling at Stokely, "when you put it like that."

"It is. Hostage rescue. Hell. You do it enough times, it's like riding a bicycle," Stoke said.

"All right, all right," Sir David said, smiling in admiration at this American giant's utter and fearless nonchalance. "The two of you have convinced me. The prime minister and President Rosow will just have to take deep breaths and convince the Yanks to trust you two on this one. When I tell them the man who saved the Queen, Sir Stokely Jones himself, is on the case, I'm sure they'll relent."

"It'll take more than two of us, sir," Stoke said.

"What do you think, Stoke?" Hawke said. "Who do we need for this?"

"Much as I hate to say it, Brock. As in Harry."

"Oh, God, here we go again. That chap drives me starkers. But we will need a CIA liaison, and he's the best there is. And the rest of the team?"

"You remember my friends from Martinique, Alex?"

"Of course. Thunder and Lightning. Counterterrorist mercenaries. Worked with them in Cuba, didn't we? I thought they'd split up after that botched Syrian affair, vanished to the four winds."

"Thunder? Lightning? What the hell are you two talking about?" C said, leaning forward and relighting his pipe.

Stoke said, "Two of my old Team Six platoon leaders back in my navy days, sir. Soldiers of fortune, now. We always called one of them 'Thunder' because he was so good at blowing stuff up. Best underwater demolition tech in UDT history. And the other 'Lightning,' because you were dead and gone before you knew he'd hit you. FitzHugh McCoy is Lightning's real name, Medal of Honor winner. Thunder is Chief Charlie Rainwater, a full-blooded Apache Indian. Navy Cross, two presidential citations for valor. Always call their base camp, wherever it's located, 'Fort Whupass.' "

C smiled at that. "I must say, they do sound rather colorful. Mercenaries, I take it, Sir Stokely?"

"Indeed. These boys parachute into enemy-held islands or infiltrate by sea in the stormy darkness of a rain-filled night on a fairly regular basis. Operate all around the world with big-time success and an almost miraculous ability to avoid capture and bullets. Colorful, I guess you might say, sir."

Hawke added, "A more ragtag collection of soldiers of fortune, ex–Foreign Legionnaires, ex-SEALs, retired U.S. Army spec-ops guys, SAS boys from our side, Nung and Montagnard mercenaries from Vietnam, Gurkha fighters from Nepal, chaps like that."

"How big a force does this Thunder and Lightning outfit maintain, Stokely?" C asked.

"Size varies from time to time. But they're organized just like a SEAL platoon. Two squads, seven guys each, plus Fitz and Rainwater as squad commanders. Sixteen guys altogether."

"Big team. How do they move around?" C said.

"Got *Dumbo*. It's their own patched-up but heavily armored C-130 Hercules. Vietnam era. Fly in, snatch and grab, hop and pop, blow stuff up, kill bad guys anywhere on the planet."

"Still in Martinique, Stoke?" Hawke said.

"Nope. I met Froggy at a bar in Miami Beach two weeks ago. The Frogman says they've completely reinvented themselves in the wake of Syria. More . . . what's the word . . . elite. Yeah, more elite. Not just a bunch of hotheaded badasses on a tropical island getting shit-faced on rum all day."

"No?"

"No. Straight hard-ass now."

"New and improved. Good. Where are they based now?" Hawke asked.

"A private island down in the Keys," Stoke said. "I've been there before. So have you. I'm the one told Froggy about it couple of years ago. Called No Name Island. You remember, boss?"

"Where you ran down the man who killed my first wife? The quicksand pit."

"That's the place, all right. Scissorhands. He needed killing in a bad way."

"How fast can they be ready?"

"How long do we have?"

"How long do we ever have, Stoke?"

"Yeah. I figured as much."

"Where are you headed next, Sir Stokely?

"After the thing with the Queen? Fancha and I are going home to the shores of Biscayne Bay."

"Get Froggy on a secure line as soon as you arrive in Miami. Tell him you, Brock, and I will pay him a visit down in the Keys. One week from today."

"Done," Stoke said. "Game on."

C smiled.

"God go with you boys," the old man said almost wistfully. "I only wish I could go too."

Chapter 44

The Cotswolds

"Going down to Cambridge?" Congreve's fiancée, Lady Diana Mars, exclaimed, yawning extravagantly. "Are you really? Have you finally and at long last gone full barking mad, darling?"

She cracked a solitary eye. It was still dark beyond the tall windows, just a faint rosy glow on the charcoal hilltops stretching to the horizon. "Cambridge? Is that what you said?"

"Yes, dear," Ambrose replied. "Back to Cambridge, I'm afraid."

"But you've only just come back from London. And you were just there in Cambridge a few days ago, darling. Did Professor Hobdale call with news of Dr. Watanabe after I went to bed? Have they been able to identify the wretched body found in the Master's Garden?"

"I'm afraid so, yes, they have. Professor Hobdale was able to re-create the victim's face. Modeling, you know. All this three-dimensional computer imaging or something like that. He e-mailed me the resulting photographic portrait."

"And?"

"Professor Watanabe was the victim, just as I had feared."

"I'm so very sorry. I know how much you loved him."

"Thank you. So sorry am I that I don't know quite what to do. Go down there and search his little cottage on the Fens. See what I can find."

"What's that in your hand?"

"This? Just my murder bag. Tools of the trade, my dear, nothing more."

"So. You're off, then?"

"Indeed. Someone's got to do it. Might as well be a hardened and canny professional, don't you think? The Yard's very own much-vaunted Demon of Deduction?"

"Is Alex Hawke going with you?"

"No. No need to disturb Alex. He's got enough on his plate right now. I'm perfectly capable of taking care of this little matter on my own, I assure you, Diana."

"Taking care of what, precisely? I simply do not for the life of me understand why on earth you feel the need to—"

"May I quote Holmes, my dear?"

"If you can't stop yourself, I suppose."

"Sherlock Holmes said, 'Genius is an infinite capacity for taking pains. . . . It's a very bad definition, but it does apply to detective work.' From *A Study in Scarlet*, as you'll recall."

"I don't recall, and frankly I don't care!"

"Please, please, my darling, don't worry yourself over nothing. There is no need to fret for my safety, I promise you. I'm simply going out to the professor's cottage and see if I can find anything the Cambridge Police may have overlooked. The local constabulary sometimes has a habit of leaving more than a few highly suspicious stones left unturned."

"I suppose there's nothing I can say, is there?"

"You can promise your future husband love everlasting."

"Oh, Lord, come over here, you big old bear, and give us a kiss."

He went to her bedside and bent to embrace her. The warm scent rising from her neck and deep bosom was very nearly overpowering. Most wet mornings like this he would have crawled in with her; on this particular morning, his blood was up.

"Good-bye, my dearest love. Back for cocktails and supper, don't worry."

"The weather's awfully dirty. Don't forget Mary Poppins."

"Brilliant notion!"

"Mary Poppins" was what he called his fiftieth birthday present from Alex Hawke. A sturdy and fairly standard-looking British black umbrella, but with a plethora of fiendish bells and whistles the lads at MI6's tech squad had come up with. You couldn't fly with it or anything, but it was pouring out and it was a perfectly serviceable brolly in any event—he snatched it from the stand.

"Good," Diana said. "And, do listen, why don't you take my Range Rover, darling? Four-wheel drive. The roads are like black ice out there, I'm sure."

"Thank you, but the Yellow Peril stands in need of a bit of exercise. Stretch her legs. Besides, nothing beats the old girl in the twisty bits on the icy back roads, even in the wet."

He looked at those sleepy brown eyes, gazing up at him with their heartful of concern. And realized once more just how deeply he loved her.

He was off.

Cold grey dawn. The weather had changed again overnight. A backing wind had brought forth a granite sky and a drizzling rain with it. The pallor of late winter had closed upon the hills, cloaking them in mist. The air was clammy cold as Congreve climbed behind the wheel and pushed the starter button.

The leather seats felt damp to the touch. The cold drafts, for all the tightly closed windows, had penetrated the interior of the small sports car. There must have been a perforation or two in the top because now and again little drips of rain fell softly through, smudging the leather of the passenger seat, leaving a stain like a splotch of ink.

Congreve, muffled in a greatcoat to his ears, waved a gloved hand of farewell at the estate's gatekeeper as he rumbled through the great wrought-iron gates of Brixden House. He engaged second gear and accelerated out onto the Taplow Common Road, bound for the Fens in the countryside just beyond Cambridge.

He had roughly a two-hour journey ahead of him and he tried to get comfortable, as much as the little yellow Morgan would allow at any rate.

The Morgan's minuscule wiper blades were such that whatever view there might have been of the countryside was hopelessly obscured. Not that it mattered. He was far too preoccupied with the chase at hand. He had long ago trained his agile brain to do his bidding. He turned to it now, feeding it facts, inferences, deductions, and suppositions, pausing sensibly now and then to allow digestion to take place.

He found driving a good place to work. One could rejoice in the solitude of it, the joy of a fine machine at one's fingertips, the whizzing hum of the tyres, the pleasure of keeping one's course arrow straight and true. If only the heater worked.

And so the hours passed.

He'd lost track of time and space. He was surprised to find himself arrived in such a bleak and barren landscape. The country on either side of the high road had somehow grown rough and untilled. Trees were sparse, hedges were nonexistent, and still the wind blew and the rain came down with the wind. He pressed on, occasionally glancing at his road map, looking for the turning.

There were no trees at all here, save one or two that thrust bare branches to the four winds, bent and twisted from centuries of storm, so blackened by time and tempest, he thought, that even if spring should ever breathe upon this place, no buds would dare come to leaf for fear a late frost might kill them.

It was a scrubby, Martian land. He saw a hillside town off to his right, many roofs and spires; its broad cobbled streets, glowing streetlamps, and warm tea shops beckoned, but he pushed on. The wind tore at his poor roof and the showers of rain, increasing in violence now that there was no shelter from the hills, spat against his windscreen with renewed venom.

He topped the breast of a hill at a furious gallop, saw the shiny black road snaking up yet another incline, while on either side of the road was rough moorland, looming up ink black in the mist and rain. Ahead of him and to the left, at the end of a long and twisting causeway through the moorland, was the silhouette of a thatched-roof cottage with tall chimneys at either end. It stood on another crest quite far back from the primary road. He braked, geared down, and took the first turning he came to. A narrow dirt causeway that led through the Fens to the cottage.

Professor Watanabe had always lived on a desolate island in the midst of this forlorn and lonely bog. He said once that the terrain out here spoke to something in his soul. But it was an overwhelming desire for solitude that drew him here; his soul was neither barren nor bleak. All men are islands, however, and Watanabe was no exception.

There was a jumble of deep tire tracks rutted into the raised mound of the causeway. Odd, but he supposed there'd been no end of police traffic to and fro out here in recent days. Police, the press, and even morbid curiosity seekers. The disappearance of one of Cambridge's preeminent scholars had not gone unnoticed on the local telly live at five or the papers either, for that matter. An ongoing murder or disappearance investigation always drew the attention of a concerned local citizenry.

It was the thatched cottage that had drawn the old Japanese scholar out here. His was a lovely little seventeenth-century abode, with a warren of tiny rooms on the ground floor and two or three cramped rooms upstairs, one for his bed and the other for his work desk and bookcases. In the spring, multiflora roses would surmount the rooftops of a house desperate for off-season charm.

But now it looked foreboding and even, he hated to admit it, malevolent. One winter evening over a quiet supper in the cottage, this was years ago, Congreve recalled, Watanabe-san had actually referred to this domicile as his own "Bleak House."

Bleak enough at the moment, certainly, Congreve thought, slowing the Yellow Peril to a crawl. Something nagged at him, told him it wouldn't do to simply drive across the winding causeway up into the muddy yard that lay at the far end. One never really knew in a murder investigation, but one could never be too cautious.

He doused his headlamps and coasted another few yards before coming to a halt just shy of a rise in the road.

He switched off the engine, grabbed his tightly wound umbrella, and got out, closing the car door silently. He gazed at the lowering skies, deciding there was no necessity in raising his umbrella; for the moment he had to contend only with the fine mist. Besides, his tweeds were already damp to the point of wetness.

He made the balance of the ten-minute journey on foot, his head lowered against the cold wind, peeking up occasionally for a flash of light in a window, a wisp of chimney smoke, or any sign at all of life from within the cottage. None. He stepped very carefully here. To either side of him lay the marsh, black and sodden from the heavy rains, a good four feet below the path he trod.

He entered the muddy cottage yard feeling confident he was alone. The cottage and two small outbuildings formed three sides of the little square that was the yard. In the center was a drinking trough, the water cold and peaty when he tasted it. He turned and looked behind him, taking a deep breath.

The air was strong and sweet-smelling, cold as mountain air and strangely pure. His automobile was blotted by the incline, the black hills lay beyond, sinister and obscure. But no one had followed him, of that he was certain.

Large puddles of standing water now lay between him and the front door in the shadow of the eaves. He walked as quickly as he dared, but the mud was sucking deep out here and he despaired of not thinking to wear his Wellies. A good pair of Lobb walking shoes would die this day, but there was nothing for it. Duty, as it so often did, called.

As he started across the soupy terrain, an odd sight caught his eye. Perched atop the pitch line of the sodden thatched roof was a very large black raven. Odd, because birds instinctively took cover during foul weather. And also odd because the bird's beady black eyes seemed to be tracking him as he slogged forward toward the house. For reasons he could not fathom, the raven gave him a distinctly uneasy feeling. But he shrugged it off, pulled his tweed cap lower on his brow, and continued on.

The front door, surprisingly, was unlocked.

There was evidence of tattered crime scene tape, of course, but it had all been ripped away.

He pushed and the weathered and seamed oak door swung inward with a loud creak. He stepped inside, ducking to avoid banging his head as he crossed the threshold.

He smiled upon gaining entry. There was and always had been a demon of curiosity inside Ambrose that could not be stilled.

It was dark and bitterly cold inside as well, what with the vaporous and invasive air intruding. The famous detective shivered, pulling his great woolen coat tighter around his girth. He turned his flash on, beaming the torch up the narrow staircase. The pale green stair carpet climbing up into the darkness was worn and stained and gave off an unpleasant odor of age and dirt.

He was about to climb it, then paused as finer instincts took over. His pupils dilated in the dim light, and his nostrils flared as he processed the myriad odors inhabiting the place. It was tobacco, primarily, for Watanabe had been a lifelong pipe smoker like himself.

And there was, too, the smell of dusty furniture and draperies, of boiled beef and cabbage and pungent brussels sprouts from the rear of the cottage, where the kitchen would be; a trace of peat smoke came from the rear as well. Yes, and what else? There'd been a cat or two at one point, perhaps more, and even a canary if the moldy scent of soggy Hartz Mountain seed was any indication.

The detective found none of this surprising or troublesome, really. No coppery scent of blood, at any rate. Nothing to indicate odd gases or poisonous chemicals.

No obvious death or decay, nothing evident but the remains of the day.

He bent and stepped carefully through to the low-ceilinged front parlor.

Here was oak paneling and hideous Victorian sconces on all four walls, the balance presenting an inappropriate, tortured, Gothic decor despite Watanabe's best attempts at style. Congreve found a switch plate and flipped all three brass toggles. Nothing. The electricity had surely been turned off by the police, as well as the gas. He turned his attention to the hearth, to a smattering of half-burned pages in the grate and—

There was something else in the air.

He put his murder bag on the floor beside his feet, closed his eyes, and inhaled deeply once more.

Yes.

A scent now came to him, one most startling to his highly developed and attuned olfactory systems.

A very faint trace of very expensive perfume. How very odd, indeed, but there it was. A female visitor? One sophisticated and of sufficient means to afford . . . yes, he had it now . . . Les Parfums de Saint Laurent? A memorably musky scent. Diana had dabbed it on her wrist for him a month or so ago at Harrods. Not the one perfume he adored, the Chanel No. 5, but something unfamiliar called . . . Shalimar. A portrait of the wearer gradually formed in his mind. She was a somewhat younger, rather than older, woman, a fashionable young thirties perhaps. And well heeled to boot.

He tried to imagine just such a woman traveling out to the back of beyond to visit an elderly, brooding loner like Watanabe-san. A man for whom books and Brahms were life's sole companions. He couldn't do it. He'd be more than surprised if Watanabe had ever had a visitor out here in all those decades. He'd had a woman look in once or twice a week to make sure he was still breathing and had something in the larder to eat, but—

A noise.

A slight scraping sound from the floor above.

And then the squeak of a door hinge.

Chapter 45

The Cotswolds

Hawke heard a soft rapping at his library door.

He almost missed it. Having returned to his country home again on that same Saturday night after the lunch meeting at Black's, he'd just concluded a troubling conversation with Lady Mars. She was deeply worried about Ambrose, off on some wild-goose chase again, driving that damnable car on icy roads . . .

"He's an old hand, Diana, you know that," Hawke tried to reassure her.

"Too old, in my view, to be chasing around the countryside in weather like this."

"It's what he does, dear. It's what he does. He'll be all right. After all these years, he knows how to take care of himself, I assure you."

"If anything ever happened to that man, Alex, I just don't think I could . . . you know . . ."

"I do know."

He'd calmed her as best he could before he rung off. Then put his head back on his chair and closed his eyes. Times like this, knowing a battle was coming, that an enemy masthead would soon peek over the horizon, he forced himself to take time to gather himself. It was said he was good at war. Maybe it was because he was so inordinately fond of peace.

He listened to the sounds of the great house. The low crackle of the dying embers. The ticktock of the bracket clock on the shelf. The wind . . .

A massive horse chestnut stood sentinel outside, beyond the tall windows; her barren winter branches, blowing in the winds off the hills, scratched and scraped against his windows.

"Going back to China," he whispered to himself, subconsciously rubbing his wounded leg. A place where he was extremely unpopular. Had been for years.

Ah, well.

He looked at his watch and yawned. Nearly ten o'clock. He'd been hard at it since noon, plowing through the boxes of CIA intelligence briefings and Lightstorm dossiers that had begun arriving daily from

C. *Must have lost track of the time,* he said to himself, stifling another lengthy yawn. Another knock, more insistent.

"Yes?"

Who could it be? It wasn't Pelham's familiar knock, so . . .

The door opened a crack.

"So sorry to disturb you, sir."

"Not at all, Miss Churchill. Please come in. I'm just catching up on my reading. Nothing that can't wait, I assure you. Come in, do come in."

He closed one of the bright red MI6 "Eyes Only" DPRK folders he'd been studying, placed it on the table beside his chair, covering it carelessly with the as-yet-unread *Financial Times.* He couldn't wait to return to the dossiers. He'd always known things were godawful inside North Korea under Kim Jong-il. He'd had no inkling till now just how bad they had become under his son, Supreme Leader Kim Jong-un. It was an inhuman and almost incomprehensible situation. Intolerable, if you overlooked the depressing fact that the entire world tolerated it.

And now, according to this dossier, the North Koreans had nuclear-tipped intercontinental missiles capable of—

"Ah, there you are," he said.

Sabrina came into the room, commented on the abysmal weather, paused before the lovely crackling fire, and finally found his eyes.

"Good evening, sir," she said quietly, hands clasped behind her back, peering up from beneath long lashes. What was the word? Demure.

"Good evening, Sabrina. Alexei asleep yet?"

"Yes, sir. We read *Wind in the Willows* until eight. Fast asleep now. Such a lovely little boy. So very sweet."

Hawke smiled.

Sabrina Churchill was a very pretty girl. A bit on the pleasing side of plump, as Congreve would say, and he could well imagine why legions of men would be wildly attracted to her. She had lovely skin, a creamy English rose complexion, and an abundance of honey blond hair. And her face was lovely, too. Pretty china blue eyes, upturned nose, dewy red lips . . . an ample bosom . . . Yes. A gracious, lovely young woman indeed.

And tough as hell in a pinch, apparently, according to Nell Spooner. Never afraid to put her life on the line in the course of duty.

Hawke, watching her enter his favorite room, decided it was all going to work out for the best. He had been bereft, heartbroken, really, at Nell's decision to leave him. He understood it and could not lay a hint of blame at her doorstep. But, apart from his romantic feelings, he had thought she was irreplaceable, and so far Miss Churchill had proven him wrong.

Still, he sometimes wondered what must be going through her mind.

Did she know about his passionate relationship with her predecessor? Of course she did. The two career women were very close friends, had shared a small bedsit at the Lygon Arms in the historic Cotswolds town of Broadway once upon a time. The pub life for young people back then was thriving; perhaps it still was. Surely they'd shared everything, every intimate secret, over a pint or two on a Saturday night, including, no doubt, the nitty-gritty details of his relationship with Nell.

One thing was obvious in Sabrina's eyes. Love and life had perhaps treated her somewhat harshly. Sadly, she seemed to have been searching in vain for love or some approximation of it for a very long time. And had never found it. Her unfulfilled needs and desires were well managed and she kept all well hidden beneath her exterior. Camouflage. But not quite enough of it.

He'd heard a good deal about her torturous love life from Nell in the days before she'd left for Washington, a new man, and a new life. Not by way of gossip; Nell was never that. But by way of relevant information.

Ms. Churchill was, after all, inheriting a very sensitive and demanding position. Somewhat high profile, you might say.

Here was a precocious young charge, a boy whose life had already been seriously threatened three times. All attempts had been foiled, of course, one by Hawke on a Siberian railway and the other two by Nell herself in the Florida Everglades and in London's Hyde Park two short years ago.

So. The story of Sabrina Churchill. Perhaps not an entirely happy tale, he was sorry to say. But it was none of his affair. She was here to protect his son from harm, and her credentials in that department were impeccable. At the Yard, she'd been responsible for the well-being of two headstrong young men belonging to the Royals and she'd done a magnificent job of it.

So here she was, a young woman with both Charles's and Andrew's blessing, as well as the Yard's, now in the employ of Lord Alexander Hawke.

She placed her fist before her mouth and coughed to gain his attention. He'd apparently been staring into the fire, rather rudely lost in thought, for quite some time, it appeared.

"Oh. Sorry," he said. "Mind was elsewhere."

"I understand you wished to see me, sir? Pelham mentioned something this evening. I hope this is not an inconvenient time, m'lord."

"Not at all. Please, do sit down. Yes, right there is fine, just fine. Bit drafty in here tonight, closer to the hearth the better. Good, good."

She settled into the wing-backed chair beside the crackling fire and smoothed her dress. *Prim, too,* he thought.

"Thank you, sir."

"How are you finding it here, Sabrina?"

"Wonderful, your lordship. Delightful. Alexei is the dearest child imaginable. I can see why Nell was so heartbroken. To leave you. Leave him, I mean. Of course."

"Yes."

"Sorry. I didn't mean to—"

"No. Of course you didn't. Tell me, Sabrina. How are your rooms? Finding everything to your liking? Pelham and I had them freshened up a bit for you. Bit of paint and putty, and all that."

"Yes, sir. Very nice, indeed. The view of the south gardens and the hills is sublime. Pelham has fresh flowers placed there in my room every day."

"Good. Very good."

"Lovely man, Pelham. So kind. And generous to a fault . . ."

She'd apparently run out of dialogue.

"Well, then. We haven't really spoken much since your arrival. I just wanted to tell you that I think you're doing a fine job, Sabrina. I was of course a bit worried about my child when Nell announced her resignation. But you've stepped right in and picked up the reins where she left off. Alexei seems very comfortable with you. Happy, in fact."

"Thank you, sir. I thought . . . I thought . . ."

"Thought what, Sabrina?"

"I was afraid that you were . . . that you weren't pleased. With my job performance. That I'd disappointed you."

"Not at all, Sabrina. On the contrary, I'm very pleased with how you've accommodated yourself to our rather odd situation. We are, truth be told, a bit eccentric around here. We dance not only to a different drummer, but to an entirely different orchestra. Always have, I'm afraid."

She sat forward in the chair, awash with relief.

"Oh. Good. I'm so glad you're pleased, sir. Thank you very, very much."

"Sabrina, listen. The real reason I asked to see you was not to shower you with well-deserved praise. It is because I will be going away shortly. I have to leave England for a few weeks. Business, you know. I wanted to make sure everything was all right before I left. Both for your comfort and my own peace of mind."

"I appreciate that, sir."

"I'm leaving first thing Monday. It occurred to me that you haven't taken a day, much less an hour, off since you arrived. I'm well aware how exhausting caring for an energetic four-year-old boy can be. I think you should take a day or two off this coming weekend before my trip. And I do think you could use a break from all of us. No?"

"Well, m'lord, I don't know what to say. I—"

"Sabrina, please. Go into town. Have some fun. Perhaps go over to Broadway for a couple of days. That charming inn there, the Lygon Arms. Do whatever you'd like. A minivacation. How does that sound?"

"Are you sure that would be all right?"

"Of course. It's my idea."

"Well, I suppose I will have to arrange for another Royal Protection officer to cover me in my absence."

"That won't be necessary. I'll be here with him."

"I'm afraid it's a very strict policy, your lordship. Besides, my dearest friend, Lauren Powell, is one of the Royal Protection officers they usually send out to cover. Lauren is a delight, sir. But all business. An extraordinarily capable woman."

"Even better."

"Well, then. Thank you. I should be delighted to take you up on your very kind offer, sir."

"Good. It's settled, then."

"I do appreciate your kindness."

"Not at all, Sabrina."

She stood and straightened her dress.

"Good night, sir."

"Good night, Sabrina. Sleep well."

After Sabrina had gone, Hawke picked up his China and North Korea files and cracked them open. He read two or three paragraphs about the atrocities perpetrated on these poor people by a corrupt, immoral government and couldn't decide who was worse. The North Koreans for their appalling abuse of human rights. Or the Chinese for looking the other way just to keep this bloody buffer zone on their border.

There was a disc in a paper slip chase marked "NK Propaganda Film, 60 secs."

He popped it in. He found himself watching the most bizarre snippet of film imaginable. A North Korean man falls asleep to dream of an NK missile being launched. His face remains superimposed as the missile circles the globe, finally descending through the clouds toward a city that looks like New York. An American flag shields the city but the missile pierces it and explodes, turning the city to fire and ash. The man smiles in his sleep and turns over. All this to the music of Michael Jackson's "We Are the World."

Insanity.

He made a note to show the damn thing to C. These people were not only murderous thugs, bellicose and getting worse . . . he was now convinced that they were utterly and completely insane. For the first time, he was absolutely convinced the rest of the world was dealing with a nuclear power with zero sense of right and wrong, without even a scintilla of respect for human life. How long, he wondered, would civilized societies continue to put up with this?

He sighed. He was sick of reading about brutal torture, starvation, and summary executions. But he was damn well going to find out if there were any Americans imprisoned there and, if so, get them the hell out. And, by God, he'd make sure these lunatics knew his name before this was all over. Knew it, and would never forget it.

His father, an old navy bastard himself, had a saying he had liked to repeat whenever someone irked or threatened him . . .

You fuck with a truck, you get run over.

He'd have to remember to mention that to the North Koreans as soon as he arrived.

Chapter 46

The Fens

Ambrose froze momentarily at the sound from above, then calmly hung his tightly rolled umbrella on the back of the nearest chair and switched off his torch. He next bent down and unclasped his leather murder bag. Among the many disorganized vials, pairs of thin latex gloves, glassine evidence bags, black lights, and Luminol . . .

Was his loaded .38 snub-nosed revolver.

He got it firmly seated in his right hand and moved swiftly and silently into the shadows of the hallway leading back to the kitchen. Anyone entering the parlor would have to show himself. Odd, he'd seen no evidence of another vehicle on the property. But of course he'd neglected to double-check by walking around to the rear of the house, hadn't he?

At first he could hear nothing but the beating of his own heart. And the faint ticking of a clock somewhere.

And then he heard the sound of footsteps on the stairs.

Careful, deliberate steps, as if someone was testing his weight on different areas of each step, trying to avoid making a sound. Too heavy for the elegant and perfumed woman whose scent still lingered. A man, no question, heavyset with labored, husky breathing. A man descending with one hand on the banister and the other against the wall to lighten his weight. A man who'd seen and heard his Morgan motorcar turn off the high road and rumble-rumble along the causeway, heard the piercing creak of the front door, and yet for all that, a man had chosen to remain hidden and silent, undiscovered. A man who—

The fifth step from the top creaked . . . and so did the last.

The hall was dark as a pit. But Ambrose saw a dim glint of light . . . the twin barrels of the side-by-side shotgun slowly protruding into the parlor gloom. This before he could see who was carrying the weapon. It was as if the fellow were probing the air with the gun, unsure of his next move.

"Police!" Congreve said sharply. "Scotland Yard. Drop the weapon now. Throw it down where I can see it. Come out with your hands where I can see them. Do it now."

No reply.

Suddenly, and with a wild animal howl, a squat, heavy figure clad all in black leaped into view, aiming his double-barreled shotgun directly into Congreve's face.

"Drop it, now!" Ambrose said calmly.

"Aieee!" the man screamed, then lunged forward and fired one barrel.

Congreve was in the process of dropping to one knee and raising his own gun. The pattern of shot tore into the ceiling above his head. A shower of plaster and fine dust filled the air around him and Ambrose squinted desperately to see what he—

The man lowered the shotgun to fire the other barrel.

Congreve shot him before he could pull the second trigger.

The shotgun thudded to the floor, and the man pitched backward, landing faceup, his head and torso twitching in the foyer, his thick legs spread-eagled in the parlor.

Ambrose rose and went to him, kneeling to check his vital signs. The bullet, because of the angle, had entered his chest, struck a rib, bounced around, and severed something major. A sucking wound. He was very dead, he just didn't know it yet. His eyelids were fluttering and Ambrose knew he didn't have much time.

Congreve leaned over and spoke slowly and clearly to the dying man.

"Can you talk?" Ambrose said.

"Wh-what?"

"What's your name?"

"G'fook yerself," he said in a death rattle rasp.

"Beats dying. Did you kill Professor Watanabe?"

"Why? They gonna hang me for it? I didn't kill him."

His eyes were rolling back in his head, eyeballs turning to marble already.

"Who did?"

"Fookin' hunger birds killed him."

"Birds?"

"You heard me . . . get a doctor . . . it hurts . . ."

"I will. Why'd you come back here tonight?"

"Lookin' . . . the . . . For the bloody . . ."

"Never mind that. Tell me now. Who killed Watanabe?"

"Ch-Chyna . . ." he managed to croak. "Chyna . . ."

"China? A Chinese assassin? The Te-Wu? Talk!"

"Aw, sod all, it hurts . . . it's all about . . . I'm . . ."

"Hurry up, for God's sake, man, save yourself . . ."

"Moon," he said, and his dead eyes rolled back.

"Moon?" Congreve said, looking beyond the dying man to the window. There was a fingernail moon, barely visible through the heavy cloud cover. He placed two fingers on the carotid artery of the dying man.

He was already gone.

Congreve noted the blood spatter on the wall and surmised that the forensic police would have a perfect picture of whence the fatal shot had been fired. He assumed he would not find himself in the inconvenient position of having to prove self-defense. It was self-evident. Good.

China, the fellow had said. This man had worked for the Chinese. A Te-Wu assassin, most likely, from the look of him.

The dead man had a flat Asian face. Thick black brows that joined in the middle above his nose, red-rimmed eyes now vacant.

Adult acne scars on his cheeks and neck. He was powerfully built, massive biceps beneath his tight-fitting black turtleneck and . . . his hands. They were gnarled and bruised as if he had lived a life of hard labor. Long, powerful fingers, hideous in their strength and brutality. Fingernails chewed to the quick. And look. The tip of his right index finger was missing. Neatly snipped off, as it were.

Something about the maimed digit rang a distant bell. He couldn't be sure, but somewhere along life's highway, he heard mention of such a mutilation. It wasn't any form of punishment. It was some kind of reward. Yes, that was it.

A reward for services rendered.

In the world of the Chinese secret society.

The bloody Te-Wu.

Congreve got to his feet and strode to the grimy window, all his senses on alert now. He extracted his mobile from the pocket of his tweeds and rang the Cambridge Police. He asked for Detective Inspector Cummings. When the man came on the line, Ambrose told him precisely and in great detail what had happened. Precisely who did what to whom. He listened for a moment. He said, no, he wasn't hurt and that he would wait for Cummings and his medical examiner to arrive at the scene.

Cummings countered that it would take at minimum a couple of hours to gather up his team and drive all the way to the professor's cottage from the station in central Cambridge. He asked the legendary Scotland

Yard man for all his telephonic contact information, told him (he ignored the faux pas in the spirit of the moment) to do nothing at all to disturb the evidence, and go home and get a good night's sleep; they would contact him the following morning.

That sounded good. Happy to be alive and unhurt, Congreve desperately wanted to be at home with his feet up, whiskey to hand, basting by a roaring fire and listening to the offshore shipping forecast weather on Radio BBC 4. That was his preferred soothing ritual, and God knows he needed to cleave to it now.

There was, Ambrose fervently believed, a tender spot in all great men. Achilles had his heel. For one Ambrose Congreve, it was the shipping forecast. Couldn't possibly exist without it. None of the broadcast information was of the slightest use to him, of course, nor for that matter the millions of nonseafarers who listened to it religiously, mesmerized by the calm, cadenced recitation of names of sea areas followed by a sonorous recitation of winds, weather, and visibility . . . names like Fisher, Dogger, German Bight . . . ah, bliss, for a man to be comforted and strangely uplifted by what someone or other had called "that cold poetry of information."

He rang off with Cummings and called Alex Hawke, repeating word for word what he'd told the Cambridge copper. Then he added a wee bit more.

"He was still alive, Alex. I got two words out of him. Asked him who he worked for."

"Yes?"

"China."

"China. As in the country?"

"I hardly imagine he was referring to tableware, Alex."

"Well. Good work. I should hang up right now, call Sir David and tell him the Chinese are definitely involved in the murder of your friend . . ."

"But, Alex, wait—"

"You said two words. What was the second?"

"Moon."

"How odd. Was the moon out? In all that messy moorish weather?"

"You could barely see your hand in front of your face. But, yes, a sliver of moon above. So what?"

"Agreed. So, China, at least . . . That's something, I suppose."

"Well. That's all I got out of him. Oh, and Alex?"

"Yes?"

"No trace of a car. Anywhere. So how the hell did he get here?"

"Someone dropped him? Sometime before you arrived."

"Hmm. My thought exactly."

"He was waiting for you. Watched your approach from an upstairs window. Remained hidden after you'd entered the house."

"It would seem that way."

"Who else knew you were going out there?"

"Diana, of course. Inspector Cummings in Cambridge. I alerted him in case he felt the trip might be unwise . . ."

"That's it?"

"Yes."

"Well, not Cummings, that's for sure. Someone else in the Cambridge constabulary, possibly. Someone on the pad for our friends?"

"The Cambridge Te-Wu."

Hawke told him to stop talking about the Te-Wu. Despite Congreve's infatuation with the notion of renascent gangs, they had not a shred of evidence pointing in that direction.

He said get the hell out of there and hurry home to Diana. She had rung up Hawkesmoor three times. Worried sick about him. Besides, Hawke needed to get on to Sir David immediately. Tell him what they had.

"What have you got, Alex? Death rattles, nothing more."

"One dead assassin. One dead professor. Two words from a dying man's lips. Moon. And China. Maybe together they actually mean something. Find out who dropped him off and we've found Watanabe's killer."

"One would hope."

"Hang up, would you, Constable? You've caused quite enough trouble for one evening, I should think."

Ambrose rang off and looked once more around the shadowy scene of the crime, knowing he'd probably not return. He memorized the important spatial relations of objects, doors, windows. Then he turned to the corpse and began methodically going through the dead man's clothing and effects, looking for any possible clues to his identity.

Perhaps this corpse would actually lead him to Watanabe's killer.

And perhaps, of course, it would not.

His fingertips brushed something in the dead man's pocket and he withdrew it.

A shiny black feather. A bird's feather.

Something the dead man had said stuck with him. A phrase he'd used. Something nonsensical he'd entirely forgotten to mention to Hawke.

Hunger birds.

Chapter 47

Congreve stepped through the doorway and out into the rank and bitter air.

A stiff wind blew across the tufted, tempting grass to either side of the narrow ribbon of earth winding back to his automobile. Despite its benign, meadowlike appearance, it was not grass at all, he knew, but a vast soggy marsh. When the wind blew upon the distant hills, it whistled mournfully in the crevices of granite, and sometimes it shuddered like a man in pain.

He winced at the thought.

The encounter inside the cottage had shaken him, he suddenly realized. Here he was, anthropomorphizing nature, giving it human qualities. This was the stuff of romantics and poets, he laughed to himself, not bloody policemen.

These people, whoever they were, were not to be taken lightly. They were stone killers. And he had to find out who they were. And why they killed. He tightened his woolen greatcoat around him, pulled down his cap, and set off, glad to be escaping this execrable place.

As he walked, he repeatedly glanced back over his shoulder, looking at the dark cottage and trying to draw information from it and the very ground it stood upon. He was perhaps a quarter of a mile away from it when the oddest thing happened.

A solitary bird began to bother him.

Or perhaps a bat. Diving on him and swooping out of the darkness to brush the top of his head. He felt repeated soft bumps through the woolen cap. He tried to bat it away and quickened his pace, even though the footing was sketchy at best.

But he couldn't escape the shrieking bird!

It returned again and again to beleaguer him, and now its aggression was sharply defined. It had its claws out, and with each pass it was raking the top of his head and slashing at his frozen ears painfully. It would be humorous were it not so terribly disturbing, a wild creature harassing a lone man in the middle of nowhere and—

Blood was pouring down his face.

He tried to swipe it out of his eyes so he could see where he was going, but there must have been a large gash on his forehead. He slapped at the air and paused to think a moment, gather himself, and curse softly.

Then the creature attacked again, its most vicious stabbing yet. It staggered him and he plunged forward, desperate for the safety of his car. He hadn't taken five steps when he felt the ground sag under his feet and he plunged down the rocky muddy slope and into the mist. He got to his feet, still blinded and now disoriented. He managed to keep his legs under him and headed in the direction of the causeway that was somewhere above.

He stumbled and fell again. And suddenly he was up above his knees in weed and slime. He reached out for a tuft of grass and pulled. It sank beneath his weight. He kicked out with his feet, and they would not answer him. He kicked again and one foot sucked itself free, but as he plunged ahead, reckless and panic-stricken, he trod deeper water still.

Now he floundered helplessly, beating the weed with his fist and rolled umbrella. He heard a scream rise from his throat. He was sinking into the muck. He knew how this ended. Alex Hawke's friend Stokely Jones had nearly suffered a similar fate once in the Florida Keys. Quicksand. Stoke had been breathing through his nose when the cavalry arrived. But Congreve's cavalry was a good two hours away, and he didn't have that long.

A curlew startled him. It rose from the marsh directly in front of him, flapping its wings and whistling its mournful cry. His tormentor chased it across the moorland and disappeared.

His face was covered in muck and blood, and it came to him to cup his free hand and scoop up bog water, splashing it against his face. The bog waters were now chest high, and he could no longer even feel his feet. The tempting tufts of grass were useless, and many had died learning that lesson.

He blinked, trying to see.

Somehow he'd gotten closer to the bank he'd fallen from. And there he saw his salvation. A heavy root protruded from the mucky dirt about halfway to the top. He stretched a trembling hand toward it and fell miserably short. No way. He could never reach it with his hands. Haul himself up that steep embankment by sheer force of will and survival instinct.

But.

He still had Mary Poppins, didn't he, and by Jove, he used her now, whispering a solemn and heartfelt prayer of gratitude to his beloved Diana as he hooked onto the root and clawed his way up the muddy bank.

It was odd, wasn't it? You went down one road looking for one thing and found something else entirely. "Yes!" he exclaimed, having reached the summit at last. He got to his feet, inhaled a bite of boggy air, and straightened himself up. This was one of those moments he lived for. The very reason he'd chosen to be a copper in the first place.

Live to tell the tale and you're halfway home. Have a few precious clues in your pocket? You're an ace detective!

The murder plot, like the swirling fog, was thickening.

The Yellow Peril fired right up, spitting smoke and making joyful popping sounds. He managed to get her turned around and proceeded carefully along the muddy ridge until he reached the main thoroughfare. *Hello, what's this?* he thought, peering through the rain-spattered windscreen.

Two wavering wafers of light were approaching on the roadway from the north, rounding a wide curve. A large car, slowing, as if looking for the proper turning . . . He reached for the switch to cut his own headlamps, but it was too late. The car—he could make it out now—was an old Rolls-Royce saloon. Silver in color. A vintage Roller from the 1930s, he'd guess, the Phantom II, most likely.

It sped up immediately, disappearing into the fog before he could make out the number tag. But he'd caught a glimpse of two people up front in the glow of the dash lights. Small. Women, most likely, as one had longish dark hair and the other a short bob.

That was interesting.

He flipped on his headlamps and fog lamps, deciding to follow the Phantom II. He felt good. Never happy about taking a human life, of course, but mostly satisfied with the evening's adventure.

He turned over events of the case in his mind all the way home. He was able to follow the silver Rolls along the twisting road for perhaps an hour before it dissolved into the fog. Never was able to make out the number plate on her, sadly enough.

Chapter 48

Buckingham Palace

"Stokely Jones Jr., I swear, if you had told me on the day we got married, I'm talking about that hot sticky day down there in the Everglades, that one day soon you'd be taking me to London to meet the Queen? At Buckingham Palace? Hell. I'd have left you standing right there at the altar on the grounds of insanity. And now look at you. Look at your bad self. Just look around you, honey!"

"Buckingham Palace, baby," Stoke said, not quite believing it himself.

The long procession of the anointed on the grand staircase moved up two more steps. He knew he was getting close now. His moment was near.

"Don't stand still too long, sugar," he said. "Else you get gold-plated, red-velveted, or crystallized. Just like that crystal chandelier up there? Big as a damn Volkswagen!"

He pulled at one wing of his white tie. Damn thing was way too tight, but it was too late to retie it now. Rearranging one's wardrobe right now, couple of hundred yards shy of meeting Her Royal Majesty, well, would be a serious breach of palace protocol.

"Don't be nervous," Fancha said.

"I'm not nervous. Do I look nervous? Because I'm not."

"Yes, you do."

"Really?"

"Really. You're fidgety; look at you. Quit messing with your tie. Only four more knights ahead of you now. You ready? You remember what they told you?"

"How could I forget?"

They'd had a preliminary run-through at Buckingham Palace yesterday to make people more comfortable with the ceremony. Apparently Her Majesty's folks were sticklers for protocol around here. But he'd taken the whole thing seriously, even memorized the damn rules and gone over them with Fancha during dinner at the Ivy in the West End last night.

He recited for her, very quietly.

"DON'T speak unless spoken to. 'She doesn't want to hear your prattle. Even if you're Prince Philip,' the guy joked. DO follow the dress code. Only woman in the world with the constitutional power to force people to wear hats. DON'T touch the Queen. It's illegal. And DON'T pat her corgis, either, much as you may be tempted. DO use the right form of address. First time you meet her, you say, 'Your Majesty.' After that, 'Ma'am.' Rhymes with jam. DON'T offer a handshake. Wait for her. DO keep handshakes short. 'Don't pump the Royal hand,' the head protocol guy said. 'In fact, try not to pump anything.' DO curtsy when meeting the Queen. This does not apply, of course, if you're a man—even Liberace, apparently."

"Okay, okay, that's good," his wife said.

Stoke laughed just thinking about it. The rehearsal guy was actually pretty funny, believe it or not.

Way the whole thing would go down today, according to the funny protocol guy, each person would get to spend a few private moments with Her Majesty alone before moving on. So he was going to get to talk to her, tell her how much he admired her. Best part of this whole thing, seeing her again.

The procession of those being honored continued to make its way slowly up the winding marble staircase to where the Queen was receiving honorees. They were all dressed to the nines, some of them to the tens, twenties, and even the thirties in his humble opinion. Medals, diamonds, swords, all kinds of shiny accessories hanging all over everybody. Hell, all he had were the small ruby cuff links his daddy'd left him. But to him they were shining as bright as all the jewels in the palace.

Last minute, he'd removed all his ribbons, Navy Cross, decorations, and medals he had from his war experiences, leaving them back in a drawer at Claridge's. Fancha pitched a fit, said he should wear them. He'd earned the right, she said. He couldn't say why he didn't want to. Decided they were too personal, maybe. Not anybody's business but his own. And, anyway, there was just too much blood on those things that belonged not to him, but to his band of brothers.

They moved up more two steps, and the world's fanciest conga line paused again.

"Oh, baby, I am so damn proud of you," Fancha said, her bright brown eyes gleaming as she squeezed his hand hard. "You are something else, Mr. Jones."

He looked at her, so damn proud of her, too. Man. All royal blue silk and satin bows and little white pearls down the front of her dress. She really looked like a queen herself, surrounded by all this finery and gold and all that glitters, his Queen for a Day, anyway.

The long, long line moved up two steps again, each knight-elect holding on to the gilded banister for dear life. People, not just him, seemed nervous. Hell, who wouldn't be? The Queen of England is going to lay a sword on your shoulder and make you a knight of the realm? Serious shit. No matter who you are.

Knighted. Whoa, baby. How badass is that? Arise, Sir Stokely!

Fancha popped his balloon. "And don't you forget to call her 'Ma'am' like 'jam,' now, you hear me, Stokely Jones? That's the rule. Because you already met her once before up in Scotland. So don't you go embarrassing me by calling her 'Your Majesty,' understand?"

"I won't."

But I probably will.

"And you remember now, don't you turn your back on her. Ever. You back up a few steps. Keep facing her before you walk away."

"I'll remember."

"And straighten up your tie before it's your turn. It looks funny. Crooked."

"I will."

"And stop smiling."

"I can't."

She laughed.

The procession moved up two more steps.

It was funny. The nearer he got to the Queen, the more relaxed he felt. He could see her face now. And he remembered how much he had admired her that night when she was standing there in that dark cellar at Balmoral Castle, surrounded by her family and a lot of her friends, with people being randomly shot point-blank dead by the terrorists. Thinking her son or one of her grandsons would surely be next. But not thinking about herself.

No.

When he and Hawke and the hostage rescue team had finally made it down to the castle's cellar, Stoke had seen why the Brits revered her—hell, loved the whole family. These people, this whole nation, sometimes behaved in a way you could associate only with 1940s war movies, or Edward R. Murrow radio news broadcasts during the blitz. These folks had been bombed all right, night after night, endlessly. They had suffered total and prolonged war. And they had endured.

What did Churchill say?

"Never give in, never give in, never give in."

Damn straight, Winston.

And they hadn't, either. Give in? Hell. Just the look on the Queen's face that night—her eyes shining with righteous courage in that dark cellar at Balmoral

Castle—that alone had made the whole ragtaggy, scraggly-headed terrorist bunch holding her family captive look like the pitiful cowardly lowlifes they truly were. Lower than low. Punk-ass murderers hiding behind religion.

As his investiture drew near, he let go of Fancha's hand and moved forward alone. Not at all nervous now. No, sir. He was not even slightly—

"Stokely Jones Junior!" the equerry said loudly, his name reverberating throughout the great hall.

Stoke took a deep breath and approached the Queen.

She caught his eye as he drew near. He thought he saw a little smile of recognition on her face (hell, who wouldn't recognize him in this crowd?), and he smiled right back.

"Mr. Jones," she said as he knelt on the investiture stool.

"Ma'am."

Rhymes with jam.

He'd remembered!

The Queen offered her white-gloved hand.

"Stokely Jones Junior, is it not?"

"Yes, ma'am."

"I wish to tell you how deeply my family appreciate what you did at Balmoral, Mr. Jones. Your valiant efforts did not go unnoticed. My grandsons, William and Harry, told me that night that there would have been no happy ending without you."

"I can only say it was my great honor to meet you and your family that night, Your Majesty. All the men involved in the rescue felt that way, ma'am. Your bravery inspired us."

"You're a warrior, Mr. Jones. I saw, and see, in you a strong, brave heart. England is honored to count you among her friends. Please remember that."

"I thank you, ma'am; I always will."

"And this, now, our small tribute to your act of valor."

She placed the sword, first on his right shoulder, then on his left.

He was so stunned, he couldn't move.

The Queen smiled and whispered in his ear, "We are running a bit late, please arise, Sir Stokely Jones."

He found Fancha. Somehow, after all that, he found his wife amid the crowd in all the excitement following the ceremony.

"Sir Stokely," she said looking up at his beaming face, both of their eyes shining with tears. He embraced her, hugged her to him.

"Let's go home, Mrs. Jones," Stoke said, hugging her more tightly to him. "Let's go home."

Chapter 49

Hawkesmoor

S abrina bade farewell to her young charge next morning, kissing him twice and giving him a hug. She'd taken her employer's advice and, on a whim, she'd booked a small single room for one night at the Lygon Arms. It was a dreamy spot and only a stone's throw from Hawkesmoor in the event of an emergency.

Suddenly she was excited about her weekend prospects. Over the years she'd made friends with many of the pub staff at the lovely old inn, as well as not a few of the regular patrons. Happy memories, for the most part. Many other young single women had, like herself, frequented the pub on weekends, hoping to meet attractive, well-bred, available men. In her time there, some had, some had not. So it goes.

Her favorite female chum during that period of her young life, someone with whom she'd lost touch when she'd moved to London, had been the beautiful Lorelei Li. A free spirit and a brilliant student of political science at Cambridge back in those days, she was always up for anything.

She'd texted Lorelei from London when she'd learned she'd be taking on a new position in the country and had immediately heard back from her. Still down in Cambridge, Lorelei said, a part-time newspaper job in London but also still frequenting their old haunts on weekends and holidays, especially the Lygon Arms.

Sabrina had had the silly fantasy she might actually see Lorelei sitting at the bar when she arrived. Such fun that would be! Before she put Alexei to bed and turned in herself, she checked to see if she'd had any messages. She found one and it was from Lorelei! Was she psychic or what? She dialed back, and Lorelei said she wanted to get together. She was in the neighborhood and wanted to meet her for lunch the next day. Where would be fun? Sabrina reminded her about the Lygon Arms and it was a done deal!

Another good thing had happened. She remembered that the bartender in those halcyon days was a handsome young man named Jeremy—she wondered if he still remembered her. And whether or not she might catch sight of him, too.

Sabrina stopped by the butler's pantry to say good-bye to dear old Pelham. He assured her for the tenth time that Alexei would be safe and sound while she was away. In the event of an emergency, he had her mobile number. She was taking her iPad as an e-mail backup. She made sure he had Alexei's meal schedule and cough medicine on hand, then carried her bulging needlepoint Union Jack bag out to the former stables, now Lord Hawke's row of garages. His lordship had an amazing collection of vintage race cars and other exotic automobiles behind those doors—including the particularly smashing bright red "le Ferrari" roadster.

She blushed to remember how he'd picked her up in the sports car at the rail station one afternoon, tossing her bag behind the soft leather seats. She'd been in Hawke's employ for only a short time and had been to London to visit her doctor in Baker Street. She was feeling full of confidence and hope for the future. She'd pretended the dashing Lord Hawke was her beau all the way home!

And what a home it was, too. Hawkesmoor. It was all so lovely, enchanted like a young girl's dream. Sabrina had felt a stirring in her heart and knew it for what it was, her life beginning at last.

Her own car was waiting for her, fueled up and freshly washed by the very handsome Young Ian, Hawke's cheerful Irish mechanic and occasional chauffeur. Her little racing green MINI Cooper was sparkling in the morning sun, positively gleaming atop the wet bricks. The blond-haired Irishman had even lowered the top for her in deference to the sunny warmth and promise of the day.

"Thanks so much," she said as he handed her the keys.

"Not at all, Miss Churchill," he said, smiling. "It's my pleasure."

Had he winked at her?

She was suddenly suffused with happiness. One must always count one's blessings. She'd promised Pelham she'd be home on Sunday evening to feed Alexei his supper around six o'clock, which meant she had a whole day and a half all to herself to do exactly as she pleased.

How lovely!

So now a delicious lunch with an old friend would kick things off. She waved good-bye to the smiling Irishman and began Hawkesmoor's long winding drive down to the small two-lane country road. She soon came to the main gates. Her heart quickened as she accelerated steadily out of the drive and began the long climb through the forests to the top of the hill and her destination. She loved these quaint little Cotswolds villages with their omnipresent pubs.

The quaint hamlet of Broadway is one of the most popular tourist destinations in the Cotswolds. After the Norman conquest, Sabrina recalled, six new market towns were founded, including Broadway, Chipping Campden, Moreton-in-Marsh, and Stow-on-the-Wold. Farms had sprung up everywhere, and, as farms became larger, employing more laborers, new gentry arrived. Their gabled stone houses became an important legacy in these hills.

The Lygon Arms, formerly known as the White Hart, was steeped in history, dating to 1532. King Charles I conferred with his confidants there and Oliver Cromwell actually slept beneath the eaves the night before the decisive civil war Battle of Worcester in 1651.

Sabrina saw the familiar LYGON ARMS sign and turned into the drive. The old inn stood on three acres of parklike grounds that included lawns, flower gardens, and croquet. There was still a whiff of pre-Victorian elegance and luxury about the place that she loved.

She turned into the car park, found a spot, and locked her car. It was lovely out, and she decided to have a quick look round. Checking her watch, she saw that she had a good twenty minutes.

Sabrina wandered around the various public rooms, and from there stepped out into the sunlight of the beautifully manicured gardens. She found herself remembering all the good times spent within these garden walls. Strolling about, she simply lost track of time.

Hurrying back inside, she realized she'd have to postpone checking into her room before her lunch with Lorelei.

Nothing had changed inside the old Duck & Grouse, despite the passage of the years. It still felt good and cozy.

She was all smiles as she entered the familiar room. An abundance of padded wine-red leather with brass studs and mahogany. Framed hunting prints. And the sign above the low-hanging ceiling leading to the loo still read MIND YOUR HEAD! just as it had in the days when she, Lorelei, and Nell Spooner had enjoyed so many happy times.

She looked around the crowded tables for Lorelei, didn't see her, and paused for a moment at the bar. The barman, a lean, jovial sort, ambled over, wiping down a glass.

"Hullo. I beg your pardon. I wonder if you could tell me . . . does Jeremy Somersham still work here?"

"Jeremy! He does indeed, if you want to call it work!" the old fellow said. "Doesn't work Saturdays, I'm afraid. But he'll be here for luncheon tomorrow, that's a dead cert. Shall I tell him you asked, miss?"

"No . . . no, it's not necessary. Thanks so much. Perhaps I'll stop by again and—"

"Sabrina! Sabrina, over here!" She turned, saw her old friend waving from a table beneath the frosted window, and rushed over.

"Why, Lorelei Li!" Sabrina cried happily. "How dear of you to call."

Lorelei reached up, held her arms out, and the two women embraced warmly, kissing each other's cheeks before breaking the clench, then just staring at each other through happy eyes.

"How wonderful to see you again!" Sabrina said. And it was, too. Lorelei was pretty, clever, and rich. She was part of an ancient and powerful Chinese family with connections at the very highest levels at her home in Beijing. She'd attended boarding schools in Switzerland before coming to Cambridge and her French, German, and English were pitch-perfect.

Lorelei always did just as she pleased, highly esteeming the judgments of those older and wiser, but directed chiefly by her own. If there was a bad side to Sabrina's friend, it was the innate power of having rather too much her own way. And a disposition toward thinking a little too well of herself. But for all that, you could put the word *fun* all in caps in her plus column.

"And you as well, darling! Now, let's have a look at you," Lorelei said, "and then have some lunch as

I'm starving. My treat. I don't really care who invited whom, so sit down and I'll go grab us each a pint of the best. The waitstaff had a private party here last night and they're all too hungover to work, apparently."

"Just tea for me," Sabrina said.

"You're not on duty, darling. Have some fun."

"In the Royal Protection Service, one is always on duty, darling."

Sabrina watched Lorelei weave her way expertly through the crowded bar, her hips swaying beneath the very short silk print skirt. A moment later, Sabrina saw the barman pulling a fresh pint of frothy Guinness for her friend and serving up a steaming cuppa for herself. And then Lorelei was back, her face alight, with the sloshing schooner of lager and the tea.

Lorelei raised the mug and laughed. In a perfect parody of a German accent, she said, "Zo, if I only had zose big pink German bosoms like you und a very small dirndl, I could put my hair up und look like zose pretty barmaids at Oktoberfest biergartens in Munich! Ja? Nein? Noch ein bier, bitte!"

She sat down and took a sip.

Sabrina joined her, beaming at her good fortune. Old friends were best friends, her mother'd always said.

Two hours later, they were still at the table, chatting like mad. Lunch had come and gone, and they were just getting warmed up. Discussing men, of course, but also some of their youthful adventures beneath this very roof. Sabrina was having so much fun she hardly noticed when Lorelei suddenly laughed and said, "I have the most marvelous idea!"

"What's new?"

"Precisely my sentiments, Sabrina."

"I'm sure it's marvelous, but is it a good idea, this idea of yours, or a bad idea, that is the obvious question."

"This one's a corker. I believe you said you haven't checked in yet, have you? Your room upstairs, I mean?"

"Definitely did not. I was running late. Here's my overnight bag. So. What's the idea?"

"You've got two whole days of holiday, right?"

"Right."

"Cannot afford to waste them."

"Cannot."

"So, drumroll, you and I, are driving down to Cornwall."

"Cornwall."

"Yes. To an exquisitely beautiful cottage on a stony bluff overlooking the sea. Too picture-perfectly lovely to be imagined. We'll walk along the shore. We'll picnic, we'll ride horses, stroll the beaches, troll the pubs . . . all too marvelous for words, darling."

"I'm in."

"Damn right, you're in. Let's go. Frightfully noisy in here now, have you noticed?"

"What about my car?"

"We're leaving it here in the hotel car park. It will be fine overnight, don't worry. We'll tip the attendant a quid to mind it."

"If you say so."

"I say so."

"I don't know about this, Lorelei."

"Trust me, Sabrina. We'll have a swell time. Have I ever led you astray?"

"I won't answer that, thank you."

Sabrina pulled her mobile out of her purse and punched in a number.

"Just give me a minute. I'm going to call my friend Pelham and let him know my plans have changed. It's ringing now. Oh, by the way. What's the name of the cottage in Cornwall?"

"Nevermore," Lorelei said. "Like the raven quoth in the poem."

"Did you say 'quoth'?" Sabrina said, laughing, and after she'd told Pelham her plans, they were off to the races.

Chapter 50

Key West, Florida

An hour earlier, a gleaming midnight blue Gulfstream IV, having spent a long starry night streaking a high arc across the broad Atlantic, touched down in brilliant sunshine at Key West International Airport. Aboard were the three men chosen by their respective governments to lead the rescue of William Lincoln Chase and his family.

Hawke had stopped briefly in Miami and picked up Stokely Jones and Harry Brock, who were waiting at Galaxy Aviation, Miami International. Both men were in high spirits, excited about the possibility of yet another high-stakes mission together with Alex Hawke.

After a taxi to a remote part of the field at Key West, Hawke's pilot and copilot helped offload the pallets of spec-ops tactical assault weapons and gear he'd ferried from England. Everything was neatly loaded into the rear of the black Escalade Hawke had arranged to have waiting.

Stoke, meanwhile, had prearranged to have Sharkey's boat, the *Miss Maria,* delivered to the Conch Island Marina on Key West. *Miss Maria* was the ideal boat for getting around in the Keys, what with all that speed and firepower. Not that Stoke thought they'd need heavy ammo down here, but you never knew, did you? The three of them had enemies just about everywhere on the planet.

Since Stoke knew the way to the marina, he climbed behind the wheel of the big SUV and they headed off to the marina.

Late last week, Sharkey, from his hospital bed at Dade Memorial, had given his personal permission for the use of the Contender 34, *Miss Maria.*

It was a miracle. But the little guy had survived.

And only God knew how he'd overcome a point-blank shooting at the low-life gin joint in Miami. Luis always been a tough little character. The doctors all said it was nothing but a sheer will to live that had pulled him through. One even called it *un milagro,* a miracle.

One of the happiest days of Stoke's life? That would be when he had picked up Mrs. Gonzales-Gonzales and driven the GTO over the causeway to Dade Memorial to pick Sharkey up and take him home. Maria and Stoke had helped him inside the house and got him into his own bed.

"How you doing, little buddy?" Stoke said, fluffing his pillows. "You happy to be home, little brother? Got your *amorcito* waiting on your ass hand and foot?"

"I'm happy to be anywhere, man."

"You just stay here and do whatever Maria tells you do. You got that? Doc said you're going to need at least a month's worth of bed recuperation before you get back on your feet. I got you that new flatscreen over there; *Oprah* and *Jeopardy!* will keep your sorry butt occupied."

"I appreciate that, boss, I really do."

"You take care of yourself, okay?"

"I'll be back on the job, boss," Sharkey said, safely back in the little two-bedroom stucco bungalow on Calle Ocho in Miami's Little Havana. "Don't you worry about that, man."

"You better be," Stoke said. "I've got a little mess to clean up over in China. Shouldn't be gone more than a few weeks or so. Soon as the doctors say it's okay, you get yourself back to the office and hold down the fort, all right? I'll feel a whole lot better if you're there."

"You bet. You know you can count on me."

"I sure do," Stoke said, giving his friend's one good arm a squeeze. "I sure do, partner."

Ten minutes later, when they pulled into the marina parking lot, it was baking hot in the tropical sun. Conch Island Marina was a typical South Florida boat haven. Beer, bait, boats, slips for rent, charter service, guides, the whole nine yards.

Stoke had a rough idea of which dock, but he was not entirely sure, so he drove around to the harbormaster's office, a cement block structure, to ask for directions to the slip.

Conch Island Marina was typical, but with that special Key West flavor the world knows and loves. Conchs, as the residents called themselves, had their own way of doing things. The marina was filled with colorful boats as well as colorful characters. Who, by the way, for the most part, all got along.

The temperature inside the air-conditioned office had to be below freezing, but it was cleaner and brighter than Stoke had expected. There were floor racks of fish-oriented merchandise, a display case of reels, a wall rack of rods, a couple of coolers, and along one wall a line of bait bins with a constant flow of running water, home to a lot of vaguely apprehensive shrimp.

A heavy man in a stained canvas apron was skimming off some of the dead baitfish floating on top of the water in one of the middle bins, using a small dip net and dumping them in a plastic bucket.

"Make pretty good chum," Stoke said. So obvious the guy gave him a look.

"What they gen'rally used for. What can I do for you?"

"Looking for a Contender 34, the *Miss Maria*? Down from Miami?"

"Slip B-25, right out chonder. You a gummint man? DEA? Lotta damn far powr on that thang. Fifty cal? Shee-it."

"Just a movie prop, don't worry. Shooting a sequel of *Miami Vice* for Warner Brothers. I play the black guy," Stoke said, and winked at the guy in an overtly fey way. Just messing with the cat.

When he climbed back in the car, he told Harry about what he'd said to the harbormaster, knowing it was Brock's kind of humor.

Harry laughed.

There was a large gay population in the Conch Republic, as everyone knows, and leave it to Harry Brock to have something to say about it. He piped up from the way backseat where Hawke had stuck him with the equipment, while he rode up front with Stoke.

Brock said, "So I'm on the phone with the police chief of Key West last week, right? Giving him a heads-up that I'm going to be down here on a matter of national security, right? And that a very special government-equipped Contender 34 is going to be showing up here at the marina, right, not to get his tighty-whiteys all in an uproar about it."

"Yeah?" Stoke said, not wanting to encourage him.

"Yeah. And the chief says to me, 'Agent Brock, I don't want to alarm you, but the crime rate down here on Key West has skyrocketed.' So I say, 'Really, Chief, I didn't know you had a lot of crime down there.'"

"And then what, Harry?"

"Well, then, the chief he waits a beat and then he says, 'Oh, yeah. It's brutal. Last six months alone, the number of drive-by spankings has gone through the roof.'"

Harry laughed. He always laughed at his own jokes.

Neither Stoke nor Hawke laughed, Stoke because he'd heard Harry tell that one so many times before, and Hawke because, in truth, he didn't really get it, but didn't want to admit it.

"What?" Harry said. "That's not funny? Guys? Really? C'mon."

"Shut up, Harry," Stoke said, beating Hawke to the punch. "Look, there she is. Sharkey's boat."

Stoke said, "I told the guy I hired to deliver her to load her up with fuel, ice, and Cuban sandwiches. SmartWater and Diet Coke for me; Kalik, the Bahamas' finest beer, for you two. It's only about three hours to No Name Key from here. We should get there by five, if the weather holds."

NOAA weather radio was reporting a low-pressure front moving up from Cuba. The leading edge wasn't supposed to hit the Keys until around midnight, but tropical forecasts were often iffy. Navigating in an area known as the Ragged Keys was something Stoke knew a lot about, though. During his SEAL days, his squad had trained around here for a few months. "Heat 'n' Skeet," his knucklebusters had called the bug-infested swamps back in the day.

They hauled all their crap aboard and stowed it below. Harry cast off the lines while Stoke cranked her up and backed out of the slip. Harry felt the chilly vibe and knew enough to keep his mouth shut. He went below to properly organize and stow the equipment.

A couple of hours later, Stoke was gunning the *Miss Maria* across the shallow saw grass flats, grabbing a hard northeasterly angle toward No Name Key.

Hawke had taken his shirt off and was sitting on the stern in a pair of baggy khaki shorts, sipping an ice-cold bottle of Kalik and soaking up the warm Florida rays. He seemed happy to be out of cold and rainy Olde England for a while and Stoke didn't blame him. He was glad to be back in sunny South Florida himself.

"There it is," Stoke said, pointing over at the little bump that was No Name Key in the distance. "Scene of the crime."

Hawke stood up and came forward to stand beside Stoke at the helm console. He remembered this place, all of it. He stared at the island, then looked at Stoke for a long moment before he spoke.

"Yeah. We saw it once before when I was down here in Islamorada, recuperating with a beautiful woman who, like that island over there, shall remain nameless."

"I remember that. I took you to see it, remember? Little skiff I rented. You wanted to see where the man who killed your wife on the steps of the church had died."

"Yeah. Quicksand."

"Straight to hell, boss."

Stoke eased the throttles back, and the bow settled down. The high-powered boat slipped through the razor-sharp saw grass and into the outskirts of the mangrove swamps that guarded the island. The swamps were full of twisty-turny channels, snaking this way and that, with no rhyme or reason, some leading to open water, some dead ends. Nothing on the charts, either. If a person didn't know exactly where he was headed? He didn't get there.

"Hang on, boss, here we go!" Stoke said with a smile.

Suddenly Stoke leaned on the throttles as they broke through into open water again, a broad patch, sparkling in the sunshine. Stoke remembered the little bay and hung a tight right and blasted through a fairly wide opening in the mangroves on the far side of the bay, where there was still plenty of deep water. The bow came up, and a very narrow channel loomed ahead. Stoke, full throttle. Hawke looked at the skipper with alarm.

"Do you have any idea where we're headed?"

"Hell yeah. You choose the wrong channel back in here? You never find your way out. I'm serious. Find your bones, that's all, picked clean by buzzards."

"Why don't you just use the GPS?"

"I am a GPS," Stoke said with a laugh.

Chapter 51

By-the-Sea, Cornwall

Nevermore was a rather large, rambling cottage, Sabrina saw. In the middle of nowhere, it was precariously perched out at the far end of the meandering wooden boardwalk rambling across a rocky promontory, the outcropping of rock a jutting sheaf of granite dominating the crashing sea far below.

Two stories high, the house had great gabled windows, immensely thick grey stone walls, with a dark-tiled roof surmounting weathered black shutters and doors. Chimneys jutted up everywhere. Adjacent and beyond were sheer rock cliffs, a tangle of fields, and a stand of hazels. Brambles and briar roses on the back side of the house were flanked by a flint lane that wound its way into the distance, bordering a barley field on the left. The flints were knobbly and bonelike.

Snow-white seabirds tumbled and dove from the skies everywhere one looked.

Lorelei had not exaggerated the charm or the pictorial grandeur of the seaside setting. *Breathtaking, actually,* Sabrina thought. There was a biting tingle in her nostrils, the invigorating whiff of sea brine on the air. Invigorating. Restorative. Life itself.

She was suddenly glad she'd come. She paused for a moment, extricated herself from her friend's sky blue Morris Minor, and studied the oddly named Nevermore.

It was, she considered, a lonely house. Yes, she thought with a cold shiver, but perhaps a good lonely, not a sad one. She was happy to be here near the sea, glad she'd let her old friend talk her into suddenly changing her plans for the holiday weekend. This was far more adventure than a tiny single-cot room under the eaves of the Lygon Arms.

She inhaled, letting the brisk air fill her lungs. Grabbing her Union Jack overnight bag from the Morris's rear seat, she said, "Thanks awfully for inviting me. It is rather lovely here, isn't it? It looks like a David Lean film, actually."

"It's too divine for words. So. Let's change into something warm and go for a long walk down on the beach. Quite bracing in this weather."

"Lead on, Lady Lorelei, I'm right behind you."

They traversed the narrow wooden cliff walk along the rocks, the sea crashing directly, far below, and to either side. It was more than a little frightening, but at last they came to the cottage. Lorelei mounted the wide stone steps and pushed through the heavy wooden door, waving her inside. They entered a dim foyer with only a pair of candles, flickering yellow in sconces high on the dark-paneled walls. There was a smell of wax furniture polish and old wood and something left too long on the stove.

It was unexpectedly eerie inside the cottage, and Sabrina shivered, pulling her wrap close round her shoulders.

At that moment a figure stepped forward out of the shadows, tall and imperious. It was a woman, a woman with wide dark eyes, heavily made-up, and a gleaming black helmet of hair done up with ivory combs. For some unknown reason, the woman's sudden movement caused Sabrina to take an involuntary intake of breath and a step backward.

"You startled me," Sabrina said.

The woman in the shadows was silent.

Lorelei saw her perplexed expression, grabbed her hand, and pulled her forward, saying, "Oh! Look who's here!"

"Who?" Sabrina managed.

"This, dear Sabrina, is my very good friend Chyna Moon. Proprietress and owner of this little bungalow by the sea. Chyna, won't you say hello to one of my oldest and dearest friends in all the world? May I present Miss Sabrina Churchill."

"Hullo," the Oriental woman said, in a deep, yet very fluty, upper-crusty British accent. "Welcome to Nevermore."

"Nevermore. What a lovely name for a cottage." Sabrina tried for a smile.

"Yes. Isn't it, dear? Poetic."

"So lovely to meet you," Sabrina said, taking another deep breath. She was feeling a bit dizzy. She thought the tall woman was smiling at her, amused at something she'd said or done . . . but . . .

"You must be quite exhausted after such a long drive, dear. Won't you come into my library?" she said smoothly.

"Said the spider to the fly," Lorelei whispered to Sabrina.

"I heard that!"

There was a very brief flash of red anger in the older woman's eyes. She wasn't used to being the object of sarcasm, obviously.

"Behave yourself, Lorelei," she said, softening her tone. "Now. Come along, Sabrina, dear, I've a lovely fire going. Take the chill off, I should think. Lorelei, do be a good girl and fetch us something to drink, won't you? A nice chilled wine, perhaps. Yes. The Krug Rosé would be nice. We'll be in the library. Follow me, Sabrina."

Sabrina hung back a second and caught Lorelei's sleeve. "What was that all about?"

"It's all an act. She wants to be the dragon lady. Silly, I know."

"Weird."

"Mmm."

"Are you coming?" Chyna said from the doorway.

Lorelei laughed for no apparent reason and said, "Okay. You two chat. I'm going down to the cellar, but I'll be right back. Don't you dare talk about me while I'm gone! Either of you!"

Lorelei was laughing gaily, sailing off down a long, dark, and vaulted hallway.

The elegant Asian woman extended her long, slender hand once more, the golden charms on her bracelets tinkling as she did.

"Come, my dear. Follow me."

Chapter 52

The lead mullioned windows in the Nevermore library were shot through with a gauzy light from the sea, and a faint blush of roses quavered beyond the windowpanes. The watery sunshine fell softly into the high-vaulted room, painting the faded rugs and raised wooden panels of the walls, highlighting the Old Master artworks, picking out the silver framed photographs, and lightly touching the darkly exotic face of the mistress of the house.

Chyna Moon.

Sabrina found her hostess posed regally beside the hearth. Her luxuriant body was sheathed in a tight silk brocade dress of jade green. Her long bare arm was draped along the marble mantel, and from her hand dangled a jeweled black cigarette holder with a cigarette wreathed in smoke. The heavy choker of black pearls encircling a long sculpted neck above a thrusting white bosom set off her jet-black hair and extraordinarily dark and shining eyes.

She was herself a fascinating picture. Alluring, even, with her lipstick such a vibrant red, her eyes so luminous. Sabrina watched in something approaching awe as Chyna reached forward, beckoning, as if trying to gather the younger woman into her orbit, a stray planet to her sun.

"What an exquisite room," Sabrina said.

"Isn't it. Feel free to have a look round," Chyna said, delicately sliding onto a pale yellow brocade chaise facing the fire. She lit the cigarette in her long ebony holder and expelled a thin stream of bluish smoke, watching her pretty young guest with undisguised fascination.

Sabrina moved about the room, looking at everything, the art, the marble figures of birds everywhere, the delicate objets d'art that seemed to have been flung about everywhere. *Deliberately casual,* she thought. So as to give the appearance of nonchalance. A film set.

"Well, well, well. Aren't you the charming little creature," Chyna Moon whispered with a wry smile.

She huffs and puffs like a dragon, Sabrina thought, *and where there's smoke . . .*

"Oh," she said, pausing at a round table near a window. "This is quite the loveliest thing I've ever seen . . ."

"What is, dear?"

It was a delicate gilded Victorian birdcage. It stood on a piecrust table covered with stacks of faded copies of *Country Life* magazine. The golden cage had been artfully designed to replicate the soaring structure of a great Chinese pagoda. And there was a bird inside!

She bent down and peered inside. A gleaming blackbird, it was, keenly intelligent eyes darting this way and that.

"It's positively enchanting. I've never seen anything quite like it. What kind of bird is it?"

"A raven."

"A raven," she said, and bent down to study it. "Wherever does one find birds like this?"

"One doesn't. One trains them."

"Must be very rare, I suppose."

"Not quite so rare as a red canary, perhaps, but still unusual. You see, Sabrina, I do love birds, all birds, but most especially black ones. Ravens. I breed them. And I train them, you see. To do all sorts of marvelous things. They are my children. My flock, as it were, and I am their shepherd."

"How do you train them?"

She pulled a slender silver object suspended from a thin chain dangling deep within her perfumed bosom. *Shalimar*, Sabrina thought. The same scent favored by the Duchess of Kent.

"I use this little silver whistle, for one thing. They learn to obey any order at all on command."

"Oh. How wonderful. Is that your hobby? Trained birds?"

"One of them."

"Oh."

"Would you like to have it?"

"Sorry?"

"The pretty little raven. Would you like to have it?"

"Oh, no. I could never . . ."

"Don't be a silly girl. I'd love for you to take it. The bird is yours. A memento of your visit here. Now, don't be rude. Just be a good girl and say thank you."

"Oh. Well. Thank you. So awfully kind of you."

"You're quite welcome, Sabrina dear."

Sabrina studied the bird in its cage, finding some magic in it, the notion that it could be trained to perform on command. That any bird could learn to behave like that.

"I'm awfully grateful. I suppose it would make a lovely addition to the nursery of the child I care for. Just imagine that exquisitely trained creature radiating its brilliance throughout his room every morning."

"Exactly my thought. I do love it when my birds bring added joy into this world. I'm delighted for you to have it now, Sabrina."

"Thank you. I don't know quite what to say."

She felt the weight of the woman's dark eyes upon her and smiled.

"So charming here," she said, looking around aimlessly, as if she had nothing better to say. "The light, you know. And the architecture."

No reply. And then, "Tell me, Sabrina. You and Lorelei would appear to be very well acquainted. Yes-s-s?"

The woman positively purred.

She actually did sound a bit like a cat, possessing a timbre of voice that reminded Sabrina of that feline American songstress Eartha Kitt. And it wasn't a purr, really. No. Lorelei's friend actually growled when she spoke.

Sabrina laughed. "Oh, well acquainted. Well, we're all that. We've logged more hours than either Lorelei or I would care to admit . . . at that pub where we met today. And others, I'm afraid . . . Miss . . . uh . . ."

"It's Dr. Moon. But let us be friends. And do call me Chyna, dear. Ah, here's our mutual friend now. Back so soon? Why, we hardly had time to find anything naughty to say about you . . ."

Lorelei laughed and handed Sabrina and Chyna each a stem of rose-tinted champagne before being seated next to Sabrina on the sofa.

Putting her glass on the side table, Sabrina said, "I don't drink. I'm sorry."

"Oh, I know that, darling. I just thought you might like a taste of the stuff. It is delicious. She is pretty, isn't she, Chyna?" Lorelei said then, winking at Sabrina.

"Oh, please," Sabrina said, leaning forward. "Stop it, Lorelei. Now you're both embarrassing me."

Lorelei said, "Don't be ridiculous. It's only a compliment. You do look bloody marvelous! Prettier than ever, I daresay, the quintessential English rose. And I must add that this nanny business clearly agrees with you. Or someone agrees with you."

Chyna smiled at that.

"Well, I'm not exactly a nanny, Lorelei."

"No? I thought that's what you said in your e-mail from London. You'd taken a position in the country. As a nanny."

"Well. The Yard prefers that I use the term 'nanny' when discussing what I do in public. But I'm more of a . . . bodyguard . . . actually."

Chyna Moon leaned forward, her sharp eyes full of keen interest. "A bodyguard. How fascinating of you.

And so adventurous. Lorelei was telling me you work for Scotland Yard. So that's right?"

"I do. Been there ever since university. Recruited, actually. It's a marvelous place to work. So many challenges, so many interesting people one meets."

"And what exactly do you do there?" she said. Sabrina could almost see her twisting and stretching like a feline animal, warming her voluptuous backside by the fire.

"I am a Royal Protection officer."

Chyna, leaning farther forward and speaking in her lowest register, said, "Royal Protection officer! Most impressive! Well, I can imagine that would be most interesting. Quite exciting, I should think. Tell us more. Do you carry a gun? Are you an expert shot?"

"Well . . . yes. I do. I am. Why do you ask?"

Too many questions. She looked away, hoping to find understanding in Lorelei's eyes.

"Oh, Chyna, don't be so rude to our guest!" Lorelei said. "Honestly, Sabrina, don't take anything she says seriously. Give her a glass or two of good champagne and she goes all giddy."

Sabrina smiled and forced herself to relax, concentrating on her breathing. For some reason, she found she was becoming less and less intimidated by the older woman. Chyna Moon was . . . what was the word?

. . . The woman was a character. A true exotic . . . A what . . . what was the phrase?

A rare bird.

That was it.

"Lorelei tells me this man you work for is divine," Chyna said.

"Really?" Sabrina said, looking at her friend. "How on earth would you know that?"

"Well, his picture's everywhere, isn't it?" Lorelei said. "Besides, he's quite famous, isn't he? In the society rags, I mean."

"Oh. I suppose I see what you mean."

Chyna said, "What's his name, again? I too have seen his picture before, I'm sure. *Tatler, London Society,* or *Country Life* or somewhere like that. Lord Alexander Hawke. That's it, isn't it? A widower, I believe. Is he as smashing in real life?"

Sabrina paused before answering. It was odd. The two of them had been talking about her? And her employer? Well, obviously. The idea that she might come down here for an overnight visit must have been discussed the previous evening. As if this visit had been Lorelei's plan all along. She'd have a word with her about that when she got the chance.

And why in the world had Lorelei never bothered mentioning that she knew who her current employer was?

Troubled, she plowed on.

"My current assignment is to Lord Hawke's family, actually. He's the most wonderful man. And a great father as well. But . . . tell me about you, Chyna, and Lorelei. What are you two doing at Cambridge?"

"I'll let Lorelei take that one," Chyna said, extracting another gold-tipped cigarette from a slim piano-black chase embossed with jade floral designs.

Lorelei frowned. "Oh, my dear. What am I not doing, Sabrina? I'm trying to get another doctoral dissertation done, for one thing. God! It is a massive undertaking, I won't lie. I feel like I've been on it for a decade. I've been editing the damn thing all year."

"What's your thesis?"

"Asia's growing global role in the twenty-first century. Focus specifically on China."

"Fascinating. But it sounds rather heavy sledding. How do you do all the research? Google?" Sabrina could hear herself chatting away and wondered what she must have sounded like to these two erudite academics. Lorelei had always been the great intellect of their set. And her friend Chyna Moon was clearly an extremely bright and accomplished scholar herself.

Lorelei laughed. "Hardly. That slave driver over there makes me read endlessly. And we travel, of course. Beijing. Tokyo."

Sabrina smiled at Chyna. "Are you helping her with her studies?"

"No!" she exclaimed.

Lorelei laughed at the outburst, finished her wine, and headed to the drinks table for the Krug bottle. "She can't help me at all. Conflict of interest. She's the head of my department. Chyna, give me your glass and I'll pour you a splash more."

"You're at Cambridge, too, then?" Sabrina said to Chyna.

"I am. I'm a Fellow at St. John's College. It works out quite well for us. Lorelei boards at my home in the country, you see. She likes horses, and I have yards, paddocks, and stables."

"Don't forget the stableboys," Lorelei said.

"Hush up. She pays me rent but hardly enough to keep the lights on, I assure you."

"How wonderful. Where is your house?"

"Oh, God. The back of beyond, really. Little village called Haversham. I doubt you've ever heard of it. About thirty miles or so from my college in town. You must come visit us some weekend. We have more room than God."

"Fifty bathrooms," Lorelei said dryly. "Can you believe it?"

"Do you ride at all?" Chyna asked her.

"I do, a bit, yes. Part of my equestrian training at the Yard. Nowhere nearly as beautiful a rider as Lorelei, I'm afraid."

"Perhaps not as beautiful a rider. But certainly as beautiful. You are a picture, my dear."

Sabrina could feel the color mounting in her cheeks once more.

"Oh!" she said almost involuntarily, adding a slight hiccup.

Chyna laughed, seeming to enjoy her embarrassment. "Don't be shocked. I do have a terrible tendency to say whatever pops into my mind. And perhaps two glasses of wine is my limit. I'm so sorry. Have I offended you?"

"No. Not at all. It's just that—"

"What, Sabrina?"

"I feel . . . so . . . tired. Might I lie down for a bit? I'm so sorry. I just . . ."

"It was a long drive down, actually. The traffic and everything. A nap before dinner is in order," Lorelei said. "And if you don't want to come down, a tray will be left outside your door. Get a good night's sleep, and we'll set out for a hike first thing in the morning."

"Of course you may rest, dear," Chyna said, concern clouding her perfectly sculpted features. "How rude of me. Lorelei, show your friend upstairs to her room. She's in the Blue Room. Her overnight things are already laid out for her there."

"The Blue Room?"

"Yes."

"Right next to you?"

"I'm sorry. Did I not say the Blue Room clearly enough for you, Lorelei?"

Lorelei grabbed Sabrina's hand and quickly led her from the room and along the flickering candlelit hall leading to the stairs. It was quite dark outside now, and someone had lit all the sconces in the hall. Was there someone else in the house? She'd heard no one. Odd.

"I'm so sorry," Sabrina said as the two women made their way up the steep staircase. She just felt overwhelmingly tired. Not herself at all. Truth be told, she missed the comfort and solidity of Hawkesmoor. The cozy late-night chats with Pelham in the pantry while he did his needlepoint, the gossipy mood of the kitchen staff at the end of the day.

And she missed . . . Dear God, how she missed Alexei.

"I'm just not myself, I'm afraid. I've not been off on my own very much at all, you see."

"Don't be silly, darling. Everything's going to be fine. Don't let the dragon lady get to you, darling. It's all an act, a show, her idea of drama. Get a good night's sleep. You'll wake up tomorrow, a brand-new girl to a brand-new world."

Lorelei was kind and helped her unpack and put her few things in the dresser. She went round the room drawing the heavy drapes and turning out lights, pulling back the bedcovers. Once Sabrina had her flannel nightgown on and had brushed her teeth, Lorelei even tucked her into the boggy soft bed and held her hand for a few moments.

She must have dozed off for a moment.

"Drink this," Lorelei said, offering her a small snifter of amber liquid. "Brandy. And a sleeping pill. It will help you nod off."

"Oh, no, I never—"

"Sabrina, please, just do as I say, won't you? I promise. You'll feel right as rain come morning, won't you, now? You're tired, darling. You need your sleep."

"Oh, all right. What the hell. I have had trouble sleeping, you know. I lie awake, listening for Alexei's breathing all night long."

She popped the sleeping pill and swallowed it with the brandy.

"Yes-yes, dear. Sleep tight and don't let the bugs bite," Lorelei said, crossing the room and closing the door behind her.

The room was black as coal, black as night.

Black, she thought, staring up in to the darkness, black as a raven's wing.

Chapter 53

When she awoke next morning, things were some-how rather different at Nevermore Cottage.

The room was dim. Full of dark shadows. The heavy velvet drapes cloaking the seaside windows were still tightly drawn. The only specter of light seeped in through a half-opened door to the upstairs hallway. So hard to push sleep away. Her mouth was so dry. What she really wanted was a deep drink of water and then simply to close her eyes and return to slumber.

A noise—a whisper.

Lorelei. Sitting by her bedside holding her hand and gazing into her eyes. The lamp beside her bed was not lit, which was strange. Why would she come to her in the middle of the night? Was she ill? Had she cried out?

"Lorelei?" she said, not trusting her own eyes. Maybe this was a dream, too.

"You're awake, Sabrina dear. How are you feeling?"

"Like I've been kicked in the head," she said, trying unsuccessfully both to sit up and to stifle a massive yawn. "What was in that pill?"

"Lorazepam. A mild sedative. You've been asleep for a long time."

"Feel like I could have slept a millennium."

"You almost did."

"What?"

"You've been asleep all day, darling. You must have really needed it."

"You're joking, right?" she said, sitting straight up and looking at her watch. "I never sleep all day!"

For some reason, her watch had stopped. It was a Timex she'd had for decades. Odd. It had never stopped once. Takes a licking and keeps on ticking.

"Listen," she said. "Someone's playing. How beautiful."

She could hear the faint sound of a piano somewhere in the house. Lovely. Someone was playing Bach. *The Well-Tempered Clavier.* Prelude no. 1 in C Major. It was her favorite piece of music on earth. She often played it herself when she was feeling low and no one was about.

"What time is it?" she asked.

"Almost five."

"In the morning?"

"No, darling. In the evening."

"I slept all day? No. That's not possible. I never do that."

She sat straight up in bed, rubbing her eyes.

"Oh! What happened to my nightgown?"

"What do you mean?"

"The buttons. Down the front. Look, they're all ripped."

"How very odd. You must have done it in your sleep, darling. A nightmare perhaps. I shouldn't worry too much about it . . ."

Sabrina stretched her arms above her head and yawned loudly. "I never sleep all day, I tell you. Ever."

"Well, you did this time. We've been checking on you every hour all day long. Each time we found you sleeping peacefully, even snoring a wee bit. I wanted to wake you; it was a lovely morning to go for our walk along the sea."

"Oh! That was our plan. Why didn't you?"

"Chyna insisted I just let you sleep. She thought you'd looked exhausted when you arrived and that what you needed most was a good rest. It's not wise to argue with her when she's in that mood."

"I had a bad dream. She was . . . in it . . . I think. In the dream she was—she was—well, it wasn't really a dream now that I think about it. More of a nightmare, to be honest, now that I think about it."

"Tell me about it. I love dreams, the stories they tell."

"Well, it was one of the those childhood dreams, the kind where something or someone is after you? You know what I mean? And you want desperately to get away but you can't run? You're frozen in place. Can't even move. It was like my feet were bound and my hands, too. I tried to move, to get away from—but I couldn't! I was terrified. I remember crying out for help. Calling your name, Lorelei. It was all so real . . . so . . . horrible. Chyna . . ."

"What about her?"

"She was . . . in my dream."

"Don't fret over it. Only a silly dream. Chyna told me she found you absolutely enchanting. Oh, poor baby . . . Don't fret over a dream. Everything's fine! Just a dream, that's all."

"Oh, never mind. I'm okay. It doesn't matter. Just a silly dream, that's all. Like you said. Let's go find Chyna so I can apologize for being such a frightfully boring guest." She swung her legs over the edge of the bed and sat fiddling with her torn buttons.

"Oh, but she left, darling. Earlier this afternoon."

"But then, who is here now? Who is playing that piano downstairs?"

"Oh, that's just Optimus."

"Who? I'm sorry, did I meet him?"

"No. He drove down late last night. One of her men-servants. Optimus is her butler, I suppose, but he does just about anything. He's the caretaker here on week-ends. She had to be back at Cambridge for a black-tie dinner at her college. She—"

"Dinner?" She looked at her watch. "Gosh! We have to go! Right this second! Come on, help me pack."

"What's wrong, Sabrina?"

"I have to get back! That's what. I have a job, you know, and I need to get back to Hawkesmoor. I prom-ised Pelham I'd be home for supper with Alexei tonight. Put him to bed. And now it's . . . how long will it take us? The drive?"

"If I push it, you can be home by seven."

"Push it."

Ten minutes later they were loading up the Morris Minor. The evening skies along the coast were violet, shot through with the dying rays of sunlight. It was cold and blustery up on the cliff, a strong wind com-ing off the sea below. Sabrina tightened her coat against the chill.

"Nevermore," she told herself, flicking off her flashlight and gazing one last time at the darkened cottage above the heaving black sea.

"All right, that's all my stuff," Sabrina said, slamming the boot and seeing Lorelei across the roof of the car, hurrying along the walkway, something cradled in her arms. She rushed across the rocky ground, slightly out of breath.

"Not quite all your stuff, darling. Look what you forgot!"

Lorelei strode toward her, carrying an object draped with a black velvet cloth.

"What is it?" Sabrina said.

"Lift the cover off, silly."

She did.

"Oh! You cannot be serious."

"Chyna said you'd admired it, and she'd given it to you as a gift, a memento of the weekend. She absolutely insisted you have it. She said it would make a charming nursery companion for your little charge. Keep Alexei entertained whenever you're not with him . . . Go on, take it."

As she held delicate cage in her hands, Lorelei placed a silver whistle on a chain round her neck. It was how you controlled it, Chyna Moon had said, the brilliant blackbird perched inside the golden pagoda.

A small black raven with bright, beady eyes and a razor-sharp beak.

After they'd been driving for an hour or so, Sabrina looked over at Lorelei and said, "So. I've been wondering."

"Wondering what?"

"Wondering why you never mentioned the fact that you actually knew my employer. Lord Hawke. I find that distinctly odd."

"Really? I don't. I didn't mention it because I thought it was so insignificant."

"Why would you think that?"

"Because I don't know him, darling, not really. It was just to say hello. No more than a minute."

"Oh. And where was this?"

"In Cambridge, actually. At the Hotel du Vin."

"That's where you met him? A hotel?"

"Yes. The garden patio after dinner. He was having a drink with someone I sort of know and I stopped to say hello. We were introduced and that was it."

"Really. That's interesting."

"Not really, Sabrina. It's not like I went to bed with him or anything. Christ. Get over it."

"Really? Get over it?"

"What's wrong with you?"

"Funny, isn't it? I was just wondering the very same thing. What is wrong with me, Lorelei? Any idea?"

They drove on in silence for a few minutes more before Sabrina spoke.

"I believe I was drugged and abused by someone last night. I cannot prove it, but I do believe it."

Silence.

Chapter 54

No Name Island, Florida Keys

A sun-blasted dock, encrusted with broken crab shells and spattered with white guano, emerged from the dark thicket of mangrove and protruded like a beckoning finger into the bright and shining bay. Gulls, in flocks like low white clouds, screamed and rippled over the heaps of small waves, looking for garbage that was dumped, often in no particular area. "Mine, mine, mine," they shrieked, wheeling and diving as if their very lives depended on it.

Stoke put the helm hard over, hooked a tight right, and *Miss Maria* sped over the silvered riffle toward the beckoning dock across the bay.

When first he saw that familiar dock, Stoke smiled. This was it. He knew he'd finally arrived at the true back door to the back of beyond. The island with no name.

The home of Fort Whupass.

Hawke was more than deeply struck by the familiar sight of the island. It was not green, as he'd remembered it; somewhat miraculously, it was snow white. Huge clouds of white herons had descended upon the swampy key. More birds alighted into mangrove thickets, already so thickly covered with them that the whole island seemed magically coated with a heavy layer of animated snowfall.

He had no idea how Stoke had ever found this place.

This small island was set so deeply back among countless thousands of tiny islands scattered about the dank, humid swamp, that if you didn't know that this little sunlit bay and something called No Name Island existed, you'd not find them by chance in ten million years.

Both men saw a shortish nut-brown man emerge from the shadows and run out to the end of the dock. He was pumping his legs and waving his arms, drawn by the sound of the rapidly approaching sportfishing boat. He had a coiled line in one hand ready to heave. The small tank of a fellow was as wide as he was tall. Even from a distance, he was all muscle, his bulging forearms like lodgepoles.

Stoke throttled back for his approach to the dock, maintaining the lowest speed that would keep her on plane, white wake hissing behind her. A minute later, he lugged down as *Miss Maria*'s hull settled into the brackish brown water. He saluted and gave a smile of recognition to the man on the dock. It was him, all right. Short but wide, the man had the approximate proportions of a municipal Dumpster. It was the infamous Frogman, an ex-Legionnaire better known in certain circles as "Froggy."

His head was clean shaven, gleaming with perspiration and frosted with sunblock. His faintly piratical and long black beard looked like it hadn't been trimmed since the last century. He even had a French Foreign Legionnaire's white kepi on his bald head, an exotic machine gun slung over his shoulder, and his trademark smoldering Gauloise cigarette jammed in one corner of his parched mouth.

It was Froggy, all right, and he was wearing his standard faded grey T-shirt with the bloodred T&L logo and the famous legend:

YOU CAN RUN,

BUT YOU'LL ONLY

DIE TIRED

"Ahoy, Frogman!" Stoke shouted over the triple-threat burbling V-6 four-stroke offshore engines burbling at his stern. He put the helm dead ahead and eased up to the dock, using only an occasional burst of reverse to swing her stern against the swirling currents and nestle against the pilings.

"Bienvenue, mes amis, au paradis!" Froggy said, heaving the line and smiling at Stoke with a deep bow. "Welcome to Paradise, Skippair! Is that my old friend Hawke aboard with you? Eh bien, Monsieur Hawke, it is you?"

"Froggy," Hawke said, smiling broadly as he lightly stepped up onto the bow to secure the ex-Legionnaire's bow line. "Comment ça va, mon ami? Been too long a time."

"Way too long; it's good to see you, old friend. Ça va bien!"

Froggy looked down at the very aggressive-looking black-hulled *Miss Maria* and whistled.

"Sonofabeetch, eet's one sweet ride, mais non? Fifty cal on the bow? You must cause quite a stir when you dock her at the Pier 66 up in Lauderdale."

Hawke laughed.

"When was our last encounter, Frogman?" Hawke said, climbing the ladder up to the dock. Stoke was busy shutting the engines down and locking up the boat. Harry was still down below, gathering gear, weapons, and tactical equipment.

"You don't remember? You don't remember that fooking day in Green Hell, Hawke? Eet was zat murderous gig in the Amazon River jungle, mon ami. Merde! The day the jungle skies rained fire and lead! How could anyone forget zat day? We snagged that Scotland Yard inspector friend of yours from the top of a hundred-foot-high rain tree cell block about twenty seconds before they killed him! What was his name?"

"Ambrose Congreve," Hawke said, reaching down and giving Brock a hand up the ladder, his arms full. "My oldest friend. Only your team could have saved him, Froggy. All of you. So here's the deal. That's exactly why we're back here today. We need you."

"Merci, m'lord."

"You're quite welcome. Now," Hawke said, smiling at Harry Brock emerging from below. "You remember this big ugly character, Froggy?"

Harry stuck his free hand out.

Froggy said, "Of course I remember this big ugly character! D'accord! C'est le tres fameux Monsieur Ned Scrotum, d'accord?"

"Scrotum?" Harry said, withdrawing his hand and looking at Hawke for confirmation. "Is that what he called me?"

Harry frowned. He'd slept through a whole lot of high school Frog classes, but he knew just enough to be pretty damn sure what this Frenchman had called him.

"Frogman, did you just call Harry a scrotum?" Stoke laughed.

"C'est une blague! A joke, Monsieur Harry Block! But of course I remember you. The baddest of the bad! How are you, Harry?" He stuck out his meaty hand, and Harry, much relieved, shook it warmly.

"Frog, you old bastard. It's good to see you, too, man."

"And you as well. We shall go ourselves and kick some more ass, eh? Thunder and Lightning to the rescue, eh? Hop and pop, snatch and shoot, boom and doom? Death from above, death from below, and sometimes death from sideways?"

"Damn right we will. My trigger finger's so itchy I dab Preparation H on it every damn day."

Froggy laughed.

"Then you have arrived at the right place, my friend. And, believe me, you will find us in far better fighting shape than you last saw us, old warrior. No less an authority than *Soldier of Fortune* magazine has declared it. FitzHugh McCoy and Chief Rainwater? All of us here at Fort Whupass, we are now ranked the number one counterterrorist and hostage rescue mercenary force in the world."

"Holy shit," Brock said, genuinely impressed. "Congratulations, Froggy."

"Yes," Stoke said, finally making it up the ladder and scrambling up onto the dock, "but what the Frogman here does not tell you is that he and the editor in chief of that particular magazine were in North Africa together under rather difficult circumstances. And that those two dudes are therefore tighter than two ticks in heat. Right, Frog? Two bugs in a rug, you two guys?"

"He is shitting you," Froggy said. "We're not that close. He is now married to my younger sister from Marseilles, that's all. Now. May I help you with your . . . luggage? I have zee Jeep"—he called it "Jip"—"and an ATV wagon for the weapons and tactical equipment waiting right at the other end of this dock."

"You know what I always wondered about you, Frogman?" Harry Brock said. "No offense."

"It is beyond my imagination."

"That fuckin' cigarette. Always lit and always stuck in your piehole but you never smoke it. What is up with that, man?"

"Ah. Zee Gauloise! An old trick of the trade, n'est-ce pas, Harry? The cigarette I keep it lit and keep it handy, that's all."

"What kind of a trick?"

"Lighting bomb fuses, of course; it is what I do for zee living, you know?"

Stoke sat up front jawboning, swapping old lies and old war stories with the Frogman. Hawke and Brock sat right behind them on a hard bench seat, holding on as Froggy's battered "Jip" tore along the deeply rutted sand road through the scrub and jungly undergrowth at a helter-skelter pace.

Hawke's face, turned up to the sun, was a picture of bliss. He'd just done one of his favorite things: arrive on an island by boat. The whole day was shot through with blue. He was breathing hot, humid air, tinged with the sharp tang of salt on a tropical breeze. The brilliant sunshine of the Ragged Keys was glorious.

He could feel a huge surge of energy within him. It meant the game, his special game, was afoot once more.

And he was ready.

He'd always remembered an old black-and-white backstage interview with Frank Sinatra he'd seen on the BBC late one night. The famous singer sipped whiskey, smoked endless cigarettes, talked about why he loved what he did. He said, "When I walk out onto that stage, man, in front of all those thousands of people, you see, for once, I'm all alone. The spotlight is on me. No security, no voice coaches, no agents, composers, or arrangers, no nobody, see? It's just me. And you people waiting out there. And that . . . that's when I get to sing."

The Jeep suddenly broke free of the dense mangroves and emerged into the broad light and Hawke could see the road narrow to a sandy lane traversing the island's coastline. As the open Jeep ping-ponged along beside the turquoise waters lapping at the white sand, Hawke could make out a strange moundlike structure off to his left. He reached forward and tapped Stoke's shoulder.

"What the hell is that thing over there?" he said, pointing. "All covered with vines and vegetation. Looks like a bloody Mayan ruin."

Stoke turned his head, cupped his mouth, and shouted, "That's the hangar. Where the boys keep the chief's C-130 airplane. Big black mother they call *Dumbo.* Fly that thing all over the world. It's how they cut down on airfare for business travel. Got a five-thousand-foot airstrip just over there, cut right into the mangroves."

A minute later, the Jeep was just passing under a huge gumbo-limbo tree when Hawke heard a sound above. He looked up to see two men hanging in the branches, in full jungle camo and greasepaint faces, smiling down at him over the barrels of their MP6 submachine guns. Hawke waved, impressed with the improved security.

In the old Martinique days, those two boys would have been snoozing at the base of the gumbo-limbo.

A moment later, the caravan entered a sizable clearing of soft white sand. In the middle stood an amazing four- or five-story structure that looked remarkably familiar.

It was, Hawke saw, a perfect emerald cube, perhaps forty by forty and gleaming in the sunlight. From where he stood, the solid glass building made entirely of clear green glass building blocks seemed to be lit by a green fire glowing deep from within.

"I remember this building," Hawke said. "Back in Martinique, at the old fort, they called it the Emerald City, right, Stoke?"

"Right. It was built as a museum for the spoils of war back then, a place to display all the things the boys would pick up off the ground after the shooting died down. It was half this size then."

Froggy waved an arm, encompassing the entire bizarre structure.

"Is much better, now, no? We had the old one shipped over block by block. Then, we make it even bigger, adding new blocks. This is the new HQ for Fort Whupass! Zo beautiful, no? An architectural jewel, FitzHugh McCoy calls it. He and Chief Charlie Rainwater are waiting for you inside. Allons-nous, mes amis! Let's go, let's go!"

Harry Brock, sweat soaked and with his arms full of weapons, looked askance at the green cube glinting in the sun and said, "Okay, somebody tell me this crazy-ass glass sweatbox is air-conditioned, okay? Seriously. I was born at night, but not last night."

"It's air-conditioned," Stoke said.

"Not," Frog said.

"Wait," Brock said, "you mean it's not? No AC?"

"Harry!" Stoke said.

"What?"

"Shut it."

Chapter 55

Hawkesmoor

Pelham Grenville, the octogenarian butler in service to the Hawke family for six decades, a fellow
much beloved by Alexander Hawke since early childhood, was working late into the night. He was alone in
his dim pantry. The house around him was dead still.
In the muffled distance, the tall George III clock standing sentinel in the great hall rumbled as if getting its
courage up and then struck a resounding twelve times
in slow, stately procession.

The butler looked up in the direction of some unseen
noises beyond the windowpanes. He saw the fat raindrops beating against the tall leaded windows, heard
the sigh of a breeze in the barren early spring trees,

and returned to the work at hand. Normally this was his favorite hour. The massive old house, portions of which were some six centuries old, was sound asleep and would remain so for perhaps another eight hours. He had time to do what needed doing, what he loved to do. All the time in the world.

And yet.

The master of the house had gone off to war yet again. Every time he left, it was left unsaid but always understood that there was a very good chance he might not return. And Hawkesmoor felt such a different place in his absence! It was just ancient stone, brick and mortar, empty rooms and galleries without his presence, without his laughter and great good spirit. Lord Alexander Hawke, as Ambrose Congreve had once remarked, was the true "engine" of this house. And it was he and he alone who made it hum with life.

Pelham was perched comfortably on his three-legged stool, his snow-white head bent with solemn concentration. Admiring his work, he smiled. He was nearing completion of a lovely needlepoint gentleman's waistcoat. The garment featured playfully twisting garlands of green ivy on a scarlet background. It was to be a surprise wedding and Christmas gift for his dear friend Congreve. A man who loved style above all else save his true love, Lady Diana Mars.

Ambrose was the man with whom Pelham had shared the difficult task of raising little Alexander Hawke after the murder of his parents when the boy was only seven years old. When discussing Hawke, meaning the man himself, as they frequently did, they reminded each other that, even in his thirties, he was still very much "a work in progress."

In Pelham's practiced fingers the needles flew. In the stillness of the hallways beyond, he heard only the faint *tick-tock, tick-tock* echo of the grandfather clock at the foot of the wide staircase. And then—

A scream.

A woman's animal howl of such piercing anguish, he could scarcely credit it as being human. He felt like he'd been struck dumb. Had he fallen asleep? Was he dreaming, or—

And then another desperate wail of terror, far louder than the first, and this one shook him to his marrow. This was no dream, but what in heaven's holy name was it?

He dropped his work to the floor and raced through darkened rooms to the Great Hall. He could hear it clearly now, at once deafening and terrifying and—

The screaming was coming from above.

It was coming from . . . dear God . . . the nursery!

It was Sabrina! The boy must be hurt or—

"I'm coming, I'm coming!" he shouted as he dashed through many darkened rooms and raced up the first broad flight, across the landing and then on to the second and third flights. His old legs weren't as good as they used to be, but they served now. No man of any age could have reached the top floor more quickly than he.

The hall was, for some strange reason, dark. But he could see the slender bar of yellow light beneath the nursery door at the far end of the hall. He sprinted for the door, reaching for the handle . . . twisted . . .

"Help me! Oh God, help me!" Sabrina cried out, terror in every syllable. "Stop! Get away from him! Get away . . ."

The solid oak door was locked.

And there was another voice inside the child's room, a woman's voice, a voice he did not recognize. An intruder . . .

"OPEN THIS DOOR!" Pelham shouted, banging his fist repeatedly on the solid panel. "OPEN IT NOW! I'M CALLING THE POLICE!"

Sabrina's screams and the sounds of a struggle had stopped. Now there was only a racking sob . . . a moan of pain. And the tearful sobbing of Alexei.

He frantically wrenched the lock once more, knowing he had only seconds to get inside the room. There was a utility closet at the other end of the hall. Inside it lay the only possibility of rescue.

He ripped the closet door open and yanked down on the dangling lamp cord. To his right was a large brass fire extinguisher and beside that, a fire axe. He grabbed the axe, whirled, and raced back to the nursery.

Alexei was screaming now, screams of pure terror, crying out, "Get away! Get away from me! Bad bird! Bad bird!"

Pelham swung and swung, again and again, horror fueling his muscles and determination as great slivers of wood flew, giving him hope.

He took a step back and swung with every ounce of strength he still possessed.

The panel gave in at last, splintered inward just above the doorknob.

He reached inside and twisted the lock open, yanking at the door in the same instant.

The first thing he saw was the horror of blood-spattered nursery walls. He heard a grunt. Through the opened French doors to the third-floor balcony, a dark-haired young woman, who seemed to be wounded, was escaping into the night. Howling wind and rain tore at the curtains and whipped the shades as she disappeared. He looked aghast at the chaos around him, then raced to the window to see a large sedan careening away.

His heart broke. Huddled on the floor near the banging doors, he saw the inert form of Sabrina in her torn nightgown. She was bloodied from head to toe and unmoving. Her eyes were gone, empty black holes. She was dead. Where was Alexei?

"Bad bird!" the boy shouted, shrinking back, covering his face with his small hands.

He whirled in a rage to see little Alexei, hidden by the half-closed closet door, huddled half inside the closet where he'd fled, his head down, now using his hands to try and defend himself from . . . the raven. Blood trickled down his forehead, from his ears, his hands, his eyes . . .

The bird was not just attacking. This bird was trying to kill Alex Hawke's son. Whirling and diving, pecking at his head, his face, his poor bare shoulders . . .

"Get away from that child!"

His face contorted with fury, Pelham swung the axe at the swooping bird. He missed, of course, the axe too heavy and the bird too quick and cunning. He dropped the axe and started moving after it, swatting at it with his bare hands. Swiping at it, screaming at it, all the while getting in between Alexei and this bloodthirsty demon . . . it worked. The bird was now after him, diving and raking its claws across the top of his crown, trying to peck his eyes . . .

And then, spying the silver whistle clutched in a death grip in Sabrina's bloody hand, he remembered.

"This is how you get him to come to you or fly back to his cage," Sabrina had told him that first morning the bird had arrived in its golden pagoda cage. She had opened the cage door and the bird flew to the windowsill. "Now, just watch this," she said, placing the whistle between her lips and blowing a note beyond human hearing.

And the bird had flown to the cage.

Pelham snatched up the whistle from Sabrina's cool dead hand, certain she was beyond all help now, and put it to his lips.

He blew it.

The bird instantly ceased its attack.

God bless you, Sabrina.

The raven now flew up near the coffered ceiling, winging once around the room and then returned to the opened door of the cage. It paused a long second or two on the sill, then hopped inside and up onto its perch.

Pelham took several deep breaths, calming himself with each exhalation. Without taking his eyes off the raven, he took slow, small steps backward toward the foot of the child's bed. He bent to a crouch and got his arms under and around Alexei, holding him to his chest as he got back to his feet.

"Sshh," he whispered to the boy. "We have to be very still now. Can you do that, Alexei?"

"Y-yes, I guess so . . ."

"Are you all right?"

"Sabrina, she tried to—"

"Tried to save you, I know. We have to be quiet now, Alexei, just for a minute."

"Where's my dog? Where's poor Harry? Harry? Where are you?"

Pelham's heart sank. Had Alexei lost his much-loved little puppy as well?

The dog had heard his name and peeked his nose out from under the boy's bed. He growled once at the raven and withdrew to relative safety.

Pelham shifted his eyes to the bird, almost daring it to move. With the whistle clenched in his teeth, Alexei secure in his left arm, he advanced slowly toward the raven, the bird watching him warily from inside the still-open cage.

His steps were slow and deliberate, his movements minimal, without even a hint of threat, his pale blue eyes locked onto the raven's, the bird's sharp black eyes watching his every step closer toward the golden pagoda standing atop the little boy's dresser.

Pelham's long black shadow accompanied him, moving alongside him across the circus-papered walls of the softly lit child's room. His young charge whimpered in his arms. Alexei's wounds all appeared superficial, thank heaven, but he was in pain and shock.

The aged man's soft footfalls echoed on the hardwood floor.

Each measured step he took toward the bird he counted as a minute victory.

He came to a stop two feet before the dresser. Alexei buried his head against Pelham's chest. The poor child was shuddering with fear.

"Almost done," he whispered. "Almost over . . ."

The fire axe was leaning against the wall, just where he'd left it.

With his one free hand, he reached forward, to close the small golden door of the cage . . .

The raven suddenly stiffened, squawked loudly, and flared its wings.

Chapter 56

Fort Whupass

"Hail to the chief, my brother!" Stoke said, striding over to the long conference table to embrace Chief Charlie Rainwater. Rainwater was a tall, good-looking full-blooded Comanche warrior. He wore his long blue-black hair in a heavy ponytail that fell to his waist. To hold his hair back, he wore a solid gold napkin ring, a little souvenir he'd picked up in one of the late Mr. Gadhafi's many palaces.

The chief had blazing black eyes beneath thick black brows, and his long nose was sharp as an arrow above somewhat cruel lips and white teeth. He wore a great deal of southwestern silver jewelry on his wrists and around his neck for a stone-cold warrior. Bare chested as always, Rainwater was wearing a pair of worn skintight buckskin breeches that Hawke recognized immediately.

"The baddest of the bad," Rainwater said, pointing at Stoke and smiling broadly.

"And the largest of the large," Stoke said, smiling back at his old comrade.

Hawke called out to the big ex–Navy SEAL. "You are indeed a sight for sore eyes, Chief!"

"And you as well, Hawke," Rainwater said, his big teeth bone white in his copper-colored face.

There was a good deal of back-pounding going on when Hawke and Brock mounted the final set of steps and entered the War Room at the new and improved Fort Whupass.

A big, strapping Irishman with close-cropped red-gold hair entered the room with Froggy in tow and went directly to Hawke. He was ruddy complected and weather burned from years spent out of doors, but his clear green eyes still shone brightly through sun-wrinkled flesh. And his close-clipped matinee-idol moustache was always animated above his smile.

"FitzHugh McCoy, Commander," Fitz said, reintroducing himself in his thick Irish brogue. "Aye, we've been counting the hours. How are you, sir? And how do you like our new digs?"

Hawke saluted the Congressional Medal of Honor winner, as was his due under U.S. military code.

"Magnificent, Fitz, on both counts. Things must be going well."

McCoy laughed out loud, leaning back, hands on his hips.

"Things are going to shit, m'lord! That's why we're doing so well."

"Extraordinary times call for extraordinary measures, Fitz. Not to mention, men."

"Good Christ, is that right," he said. "Whoever is steering the ship of state needs a few strongly worded lessons in fookin' navigation, eh?"

"Bloody hell," Hawke said, "I'm not sure anyone's even at the helm these days, Fitz."

"And so we find ourselves with yet another little mess to tidy up, don't we?" the chief said. "North Korea? Never been. Cannot wait."

"Shall we roll up our sleeves, then?" Hawke said, and then, eyeing Rainwater's bare chest and arms, "You're excused, of course. From rolling up your sleeves, I mean."

Rainwater laughed. "Still the Hawke I remember from the Cuban incursion. I am happy we are all comrades in arms once more. Please. Everyone gather around the table. We have gamed a few scenarios to discuss."

Hawke looked over at the table. It was a large round plate of thick clear glass, perhaps twelve feet across. Above it, a digital projector had been suspended from the ceiling. This table was apparently used for multiple displays of maps, satellite imagery, infrared thermal imaging, live on-site weather, et cetera, on the tabletop. There were state-of-the-art systems like this inside the Pentagon, the White House, and NSA in Washington, he knew, but surely nowhere else in private hands.

These modern soldiers of fortune were impressive, to say the least. T&L was taking twenty-first-century counterterrorism straight to the future. The team gathered round the display table as the first 3-D holographic images appeared.

Hawke said, "Gentlemen, we thank you for agreeing to be part of this hostage rescue operation. Our success is hugely important from Washington's point of view as well as our own as America's closest ally. It is, as you well know, a joint op using combined resources from both CIA and MI6. Mr. Brock here is our CIA coordinator for the duration of the mission. I, as mission commander, represent my team at Six HQ in London. Understood?"

"Aye-aye," they all said in unison.

"All well and good, then," FitzHugh McCoy said, and swiped a finger across the glass. This action pulled up a satellite photo of the coast of North Korea.

"Commander Hawke," Fitz said, "you will recognize this as a CIA shot you forwarded to us from MI6 in London. It was taken six weeks ago by an American spy satellite at 0200 hours. It shows the relevant geography of the NK coastline. Good weather, good clear shot."

"Yes," Hawke said, "that's the best one we got from them. Could you zoom in on that crescent-shaped bay? The one farthest north, just southwest of Chongjin?"

"Done," McCoy said, using two fingers to swipe a zoom. "Here? This the one, sir?"

"That's it."

Hawke pointed to the spot and said, "This bay is the point of insertion my team in London recommends we use. We have studied all the other options and concluded that this is it. It has the best access to the camp, the shortest overland travel through the mountains. This small bay is where we go ashore. Weather forecasts for the area are generally good for the next week. But on Tuesday, one week from today, there will be a moonless night. Obviously, we will all agree on that as the target date for insertion?"

"Agreed," everyone around the table said.

"So let's all take a good close look at the enemy defenses, shall we?" Fitz said.

He swiped his finger again, and an image of desolation appeared. They saw a long finger of land, by turns mountainous and barren, surrounded by the sea and a mountain range on one side and a wide river on the other. Endless rows of shoddy wooden barracks were visible, but they knew a good deal of the death camp was built underground to keep what happened there a secret from U.S. spy satellites just like this one.

"Fitz, are you and your team quite sure this is the camp where the escapee identified possible American hostages?"

"Why don't we ask him and find out." Fitz smiled. "Froggy, will you ask the colonel to step inside?"

Froggy went to the door as Stoke said, "Don't tell me you actually found this guy, Fitz?"

"Better than that. Ex-commando, South Korean army. Tough as nails, smart as bloody hell. I found him and I hired him—I had to talk him into leaving Stanford where he was in a doctorate program in political science. Wasn't easy, I made him an offer he couldn't refuse—the chance for a little payback time in North Korea."

The tall South Korean escapee walked in, followed by Froggy.

"Good morning," he said. "I am Colonel Cho Chang-ho. Please call me 'Cho,' easier that way. Welcome to Fort Whupass, gentlemen. Just a heads-up, we have no turn-down service and no pillow mints here."

Stoke laughed out loud. He already liked this guy.

They shook hands all around, and Fitz turned the meeting over to Colonel Cho. Hawke suddenly found himself feeling a whole lot better about the mission's chances for success. This man had been on the inside. And he knew, to put it crassly, where all the bodies were buried.

Cho flicked on a light stick for use as a pointer and began pulling up aerial images of the northern peninsula.

"The NKs run four of these camps, strung like islands in an archipelago running north-south the length of the interior of North Korea. They all look pretty much the same from above. Luckily, Commander Hawke, the CIA provided sat-photo close-ups of all four primary camps. This camp, six miles inland, was my camp. Kwan-li-so Number 25. Chongjin Political Prison Camp. I was there for ten years. I escaped into China by swimming across the Yalu River, seen here."

"And you had good reason to believe there were American prisoners there, Colonel?" Hawke said.

"I did. There were rumors all over the camp. But they were kept away from the general population. I never actually saw them—until a few days ago. I'll explain that in a few minutes."

"What are all the long rectangular structures?" Stokely said.

Cho said, "Barracks. Where the more privileged prisoners sleep. There are roughly three thousand prisoners interned here, making it the smallest of the camps. Camp 22, near the Chinese border, has over fifty thousand. The bulk of the so-called political internees sleep underground. A lot of them never come back up."

"Buried alive," Chief Rainwater said.

"Yes. Please take a close look at this CIA picture taken some years ago. Tell me what you think."

He swiped again, and an aerial image appeared. It was an extremely grainy black-and-white shot of three people walking across open ground.

"Notice anything?" Fitz asked.

"Children," Hawke said.

"Correct," Cho said. "The average height of a prisoner in this camp is something around five feet, give or take. Due mostly to the fact that they're on lifelong starvation rations. Most die ten to twenty years after entering the camps. This picture was taken five years ago, in 2009."

"The year Bill Chase and his family were kidnapped in Washington," Hawke mused.

"Yes, sir. This shot's dated one month after their abduction in Georgetown."

"Couldn't they be North Korean, Cho?" Brock said. "The kids, I mean."

"They could be, Mr. Brock, they certainly could be. That's what CIA analysts believed at the time. But I don't think so. There are children born every year in the camps, although very few are ever interned prior to the teenage years. But look at the body morph shapes on the two depicted. Much fitter than the other children, most of whom are walking skeletons, bags of chicken bones. While these two are normal sized, slightly taller, and clearly healthier. And a whole lot more meat on their bones."

"Americans," Stoke said. "Damn straight."

"Because of the timing of the sat shot . . . and because of the children's obvious physical condition . . . I am convinced that these two children you're looking at are none other than Milo Chase and his older sister, Sarah."

"I agree," Hawke said. "It only stands to reason."

"Let's go get those poor kids the hell out of there," Stoke said.

"Before those monsters bloody starve and beat them to death," Hawke said, his eyes suddenly gone hard with determination and a sense of renewed purpose. He knew the hostages were in there. With Colonel Cho by his side, he stood a damn good chance of getting them out alive.

He had it in for people who starved, tortured, and murdered children.

"Fitz, let's talk logistics a minute," Hawke said. "You've got a lot of men and equipment to move half-way around the world. How do you intend to accomplish that?"

"*Dumbo.* That C-130 you may have passed coming here. She's getting on in years, but our pilot, Froggy, makes sure she's airworthy. You just have to tell me where the sub will pick us up and we'll be there."

"I was just thinking about that. I know a remote place in the backwaters of the East China Sea. It's called Xiachuan Island. It's an old World War II Japanese air base with a serviceable eight-thousand-foot airstrip. The good news is it's completely deserted because of Japan's territorial dispute with China. I was intending to use it recently, land an F-35 Lightning there, but I got diverted by a relentless Chinese SAM missile, sadly enough."

"Sounds perfect, Hawke," Froggy said. "I'll plug Xiachuan Island's coordinates into our flight plan."

Fitz said, "Let's go over the camp's defenses, gentleman, shall we? Colonel Cho and I have provided a detailed analysis and have some preliminary thoughts on how to get in and out of the damn place once the sub puts us ashore."

The meeting went well into the night.

Chapter 57

The Cotswolds

"Hello?"

"Ambrose, sorry, it's Pelham."

"Good Lord! It must be after midnight, Pelham! You sound—"

"Someone's been murdered, you see."

"Where? Who?"

"Here at Hawkesmoor . . . and . . ."

"Alexei?"

"No, thank God. But his nanny, Sabrina, and . . ."

"Sabrina was murdered?"

"Yes. Apparently she died trying to save the child's life."

"Someone tried to kill Alexei, Pelham? Look here. I'm on my way. I'll be over there posthaste . . . How is Alexei? Is he hurt?"

"Wounded, but in no immediate danger. Superficial cuts to the head and hands. He's with me now, resting. There was a bird, you see, a raven, and— Listen a moment, Ambrose. I saw who did it. It was a woman. A young woman, late twenties, I'd guess. Blue silk dress. Short black hair, cropped straight across at the neck. I saw her going out onto the balcony window as I broke into the nursery."

"You broke in?"

"An axe. Locked from the inside."

"See her face?"

"Unfortunately not."

"Damn."

"However, I did manage to get the plate number on the rear of her car."

"Good show! What kind of car was it."

"A vintage Roller. Silver or light grey, I believe."

"By damn, I know that car! Big saloon. Saw two women driving it across the Fens one very foggy night. Never got the plate number. Tell me. Was the Roller a 1930s vintage?"

"Indeed it was."

"Plate number?"

"M . . . A . . . O . . ."

"M . . . A . . . O . . . As in Mao? Chairman Mao?"

"I never thought of that but . . . yes . . . I suppose that could be correct . . ."

"I'm ringing off. I need to get on to Cambridge Police, have them run a trace on that plate number. Pelham. You need to try and calm down. You need to get the child to hospital immediately. Have young Ian bring the locomotive around and drive you there! Now!"

"Was going to do that, but he seems relatively unharmed save a few cuts and scratches and—I think—"

"Take him anyway. I want an official police record of his admission and a log of his injuries . . . for the day this murder and attempted murder goes to trial. I say, did you mention something about a bird?"

"Yes, by God I did. A bloody blackbird. A gift from Sabrina to Alexei when she returned from her holiday in Cornwall. I'm sure she had no idea what she was introducing into this household. A predator bird trained to kill on command, for God's sakes!"

"Outrageous. Simply outrageous."

"Indeed. And to think this vicious creature has been perched right by Alexei's bedside in the nursery for days on end now! It had to be that woman who escaped who set the bird loose! She used Sabrina's silver whistle to coax it from its cage somehow. Ordered it to kill Alexei."

"Was that the first time the bird left the cage?"

"Not at all. Sabrina played with it all the time, tooting the little whistle to make it flit about the room, often perching on the foot of Alexei's bed. Harmless fun, I thought. This time it killed Sabrina and was attacking Alexei when I entered . . . and I . . . got the damn thing once and for all. Always hated that bird."

"Good God, Pelham. You must be a wreck. Shall I have Diana come and spend the night there? Keep you company?"

"No, not necessary. We'll spend the night in hospital. I'd better ring down to the stables and get Alexei over to St. Paul's Infirmary straightaway. He's started shivering . . . Gone pale as milk. Going into shock, I think . . . I hope he doesn't . . ."

"Go, go. Wrap him in a warm blanket and sit with him on the rear seat. Try to calm him. The trauma of seeing what that bird did to his dear nanny . . . Call my mobile en route if anything changes. I'll be in my car as soon as they pull an address off that plate. That poor Sabrina, that dear and lovely woman. This is one arrest I bloody well plan to make myself."

Ambrose gunned the Yellow Peril perilously quickly through the corners on the narrow and rain-slick county lane. It was a pitch-black night.

His yellow-tinted headlamps were not the very latest technology, better in fog than on a clear night like this. There were deer in these woods. Hit one at speed in his small yellow growler and he'd be done for himself as well as the deer.

He pressed on into the countryside.

He was headed for a small village he'd never heard of. Called Haversham and located about thirty miles outside of Cambridge proper. Inspector Cummings had given him an address to plug into his Garmin GPS and said he was headed to a country house, some drafty old pile or other called Ravenswood.

A blackbird, Pelham had said, attacked the child. Yes, certainly. A trained raven. It all made sense. The house was owned by a Dr. Moon. A well-respected professor at Cambridge, Cummings said on the phone. Chinese, actually. Hardly likely to be involved in a heinous crime like this one, he said. Ah. Well, it was all adding up now, wasn't it?

Watanabe had died a horrific death, subjected to an ancient Chinese form of torture called the Shining Basket. Perhaps the woman Pelham had seen escaping was someone who very well may have killed his old friend? Entirely possible. But he couldn't prove it. Not yet, anyway.

Why on earth had a distinguished professor tried to murder Alex Hawke's son?

Alex Hawke, who only half an hour ago had been on the telephone with Ambrose Congreve. Alex, furious about what had happened in his absence but under control, of course, wanting to leave Florida and fly back to England immediately . . . find whoever had murdered Sabrina . . . and remove the threat to Alexei.

He'd managed to calm his lordship down after a bit. Told him about the child's minor injuries, that he was spending the night in hospital with Pelham by his side, two men from Scotland Yard posted outside his door. That he'd already ordered massive security out from the Yard to put Hawkesmoor on a lockdown. The local constabulary was already doing a crime scene investigation while others were searching the grounds for any hint of evidence. Crime scene police were still with the murder victim, an ambulance on scene . . .

And then he'd reminded Hawke of the seriousness of his mission. He had the world on his shoulders again, and it was no time now to just slough it off. And, in the end, Hawke had agreed. But he demanded round-the-clock presence at Hawkesmoor from Scotland Yard Royal Protection starting tonight. Congreve had assured him once more that his home would be crawling with Royal Protection Squad men by daybreak.

Well before the child and Pelham returned home.

He mashed on the accelerator. 80 . . . 85 . . . 90 . . .

He was getting as much out of the old girl as he could squeeze. He looked over at his murder bag on the single seat beside him. The last time he'd opened it, at Watanabe's cottage, it was because he needed his gun. He had an idea he might need it again tonight. He reached inside, felt the reassuring cold steel, and withdrew the weapon. Also, an extra box of hollow-point cartridges, which he stuffed into the pocket of his coat.

Half an hour later, speeding through the woods, he was just slowing for a tight right-hander when he saw the huge black iron gates looming up in front of him. His headlamps played across them, and he caught a glimpse of the ornate word RAVENSWOOD fashioned out of gilded wrought iron standing atop both gates. They were both ajar, as if someone had hastily forgotten to close them.

He put his wheel hard over, skidded a bit on some wet leaves from the afternoon showers, straightened her out, and headed for the narrow opening.

There was a lodge to either side of the drive. When he was perhaps twenty yards away, two men leaped out directly in front of him, automatic weapons coming up. He tapped the high-beam button with his foot and flicked on the powerful searchlight mounted on his windscreen.

Something must have done the trick because they dove to either side as he sped right through.

He heard the chatter of automatic fire behind him and waited to hear the thump of multiple slugs slamming into the thin-skinned Peril's boot.

Or his own damn boot for that matter.

Neither happened.

He'd rounded a sharpish curve while heading into the deeper woods just as they'd opened fire. Dark clouds heavy with rain hid the moon. It was dark as devil's night, and without the powerful spotlight hinged from his windscreen, he would have had an extremely rough time staying on the road. At least the rain had held off for the nonce.

It was the longest private drive by far he'd ever been on. Where the hell was the bloody house? At this rate, he'd need a petrol station before he got there!

He saw lights.

House lights, flickering through the skeletal black trees. He slowed the Peril and doused his spotlight and the headlamps. Only a few more turnings and he'd arrive at the porte-cochere entrance.

Congreve slowed to a stop at the front of the very grim-looking residence of Dr. Chyna Moon.

There were only a few faint lights glowing from within.

He extricated himself from his machine and proceeded to walk down the gravel drive to the walled-in forecourt, the gate of which was open. Heavy drops of rain began to spatter the bricks, and he raised his beloved Swiss army knife umbrella, grateful Diana had once more insisted he bring it along.

The old silver Roller was tucked in between a vintage motorcycle and a pair of much sprightlier vehicles, an older British racing green Aston Martin DB4 and a shiny red Ferrari Berlinetta. Professor Moon was either a collector of vintage sports cars or she had guests who were. He went round to the long, louvered bonnet of the Rolls and laid his hand on it. Still quite warm. Faint ticking noises from within. No surprises there.

Ascending the wide steps to the entrance, he took his time. The murderer was to be found within these walls. No doubt the two armed thugs at the entrance had announced his arrival. He reached into his left-hand jacket pocket and pulled his snub-nosed revolver. Inserting it inside his waistband, he buttoned his tweed jacket over it.

He heard a muffle of voices from within. Two high-pitched female, one deep male.

Apparently, thanks to the minor gate episode, he was expected.

He rang the bell, then rapped smartly on the door with the stout wooden handle of his beloved brolly, the MI6 "Special Edition," as he now thought of it.

Chapter 58

Ravenswood

The front door was swung wide by a man who blotted out all light from within. A man with a voice that seemed to resonate from the bottomless pits of hell.

"Good evening, sir. May I help you?" he said.

This beast of a fellow had the flutiest English accent imaginable. He seemed a footman in the old sense, cutaway jacket with polished brass buttons, knee breeches, white stockings, and brogues. He had a sleek, bullet-shaped head atop his bull neck and massive shoulders. And, beneath brushy black eyebrows, two small black and stone-dead eyes that belied his wan smile. Ambrose had the distinct impression he'd seen this character somewhere before.

But where?

On the telly, that's where.

He had been some kind of a TV wrestler back in the mid-nineties. What was his name? Ah, yes, Optimus Prime. "The Brute," they'd called him back then. Who could forget him? This Prime looked like his true heart's desire would be to place his palms on either side of your skull and squeeze slowly but forcefully until you literally blew your top, volcano fashion. Ambrose forced a smile.

"Ah, yes. Terribly sorry about the hour. I would very much like to speak with Dr. Moon. Is she at home by any chance?"

"Whom shall I say is calling at this hour, sir?"

"Chief Inspector Congreve," he said, "of Scotland Yard. A matter of some urgency."

"Won't you step inside, sir? She's in the library, busy with her studies, I'm afraid. I'll locate Madame and ask if she is receiving."

"Thank you so much," Congreve said, stifling an almost overwhelming urge to add "My good man."

Optimus Prime stomped off down the hall and disappeared into the interior darkness. Congreve heard the squeal of a door, and suddenly an oblique rectangle of yellow light slid across the black-and-white marble checkerboard floor of the great hall.

Five minutes later, the famous brawler was back.

"Yes. Madame will see you now. She's waiting in the library. May I offer you some refreshment? A sherry? Brandy?"

"No, thank you."

"Right this way, sir."

"Good evening, Dr. Moon," Ambrose said, making his way toward the vast crimson silk sofa where she'd arranged herself rather grandly, as if she were sitting for a formal portrait. He was aware of a large number of tall glass showcases filled with beady-eyed black-birds perched atop realistic ceramic tree branches and inside smaller glass display cases in every corner of the room. And there was a lingering scent of perfume in the air. Shalimar. The very same fragrance he'd detected at Watanabe's cottage.

He said, "Terribly sorry about the appalling hour, Professor. Please forgive me."

"Not at all, Chief Inspector, not at all. I'm a night owl, as you can see."

She extended a long slender arm, encased to the elbow in tight emerald silk. Her protruding bloodred fingernails looked capable of plowing whole fields, and her many-jeweled rings glittered darkly in the firelight from the hearth. Her black eyes were ferocious, he noted, somewhat taken aback at their intensity.

He took the proffered hand.

Her handshake was like taking hold of a few little breadsticks in a silk sachet. She smiled, turning her face up into the light so he could get a look at her delicately rouged cheeks and colored lips, a practiced seductress of many conquests. And perhaps older than one might guess at first glance.

It was immediately apparent that this was not the murderess described as leaving the scene. This was an elegant woman of a certain age, not the pretty young thing in the short dress with chopped-off shiny black hair. The young woman Pelham had so vividly described.

"How do you do, Chief Inspector? To what do I owe the dubious honor of this wholly unexpected visit?"

"Ah, Madame. There's been a crime, I'm afraid."

"Really? What kind of crime?"

"Murder."

"The worst kind. Who was the victim?"

"A young woman of my acquaintance. She worked as a child's guardian. Miss Sabrina Churchill. She was a Royal Protection officer from Scotland Yard. A woman in the employ of the child's father, a gentleman named Lord Alexander Hawke. Shortly after midnight, his lordship's butler heard a commotion upstairs in the nursery. He rushed up to find the poor Churchill girl already dead upon the floor. She'd apparently been viciously pecked to death by some kind of killer bird, although it's too early to tell if that was the actual cause of death."

"How horrid."

"Yes."

"I'm so sorry to hear about all this, but, really, Chief Inspector, please tell me, precisely what it is that brings you here to Ravenswood?"

"Facts."

"Such as?"

"Upon entering the nursery, the butler in question actually saw the alleged murderer leaving the scene. She was in the act of climbing out a window onto a balcony that overlooked the car park. He got a good look at her. Also, a good look at the number plate on her car. The vehicle in question was a silver Rolls-Royce Phantom. Number plate reads 'MAO,' as in Chairman Mao. Sound familiar?"

"Indeed it does, Chief Inspector. That's my car."

"Have you driven that car this evening?"

"No."

"Where is that car now?"

"In the car park out there with the others."

"Does anyone besides yourself have permission to drive it?"

"Yes, of course. My dear butler and chauffeur, whom you've met, Optimus Prime. And my companion."

"Might I have the name of your companion as well?"

"Certainly. Her name is Lorelei Li."

Congreve was jolted by the familiar name but managed to conceal it. A lot of questions he'd harbored about the glamorous young *Times* stringer now tumbled into place.

"I see. Is Miss Li available? I would like to have a word with her."

"She's not available, I'm afraid. She retired early this evening, shortly after supper. Some kind of a stomach bug, I think. Running a fever. Quite ill. I wanted to call our local physician in, but she was having none of it. So I gave her a sedative and some warm milk and put her to bed."

"I see. And what time might that have been?"

"Who knows? Shortly after eight, I imagine. Yes, the clock in the center hall had just struck the bells."

"Where is her room? Does she live in this house?"

"Yes. A guest suite up on the third floor."

"And you say she's been in her room ever since eight P.M.?"

"She has."

"She is a suspect in a homicide. I must insist on seeing her."

"Perhaps if you'll come back tomorrow? We'll see if she's feeling better."

"Dr. Moon, listen carefully. Scotland Yard is conducting a murder investigation. A woman fitting Lorelei Li's description was seen leaving the scene of that murder less than one hour ago in an automobile now sitting outside in your car park. The bonnet is still warm, the engine still ticking. I checked."

"How very clever you are."

"Perhaps I may come up with a better suspect in days to come. Anything is possible. But right now your companion resides at the very top of my very own short list. Have your butler bring her down here for questioning. Now."

"Are you quite sure you wouldn't like something to drink before you go? A bone stiffener? Frightfully cold out."

"No, thank you. I came here to arrest Miss Li on suspicion of murder and that is what I intend to do. Based upon your lack of cooperation with this investigation, I may well charge you with being an accessory after the fact and obstruction of justice."

"The woman is ill. Why can't you believe the truth?"

"Because I don't believe a single bloody word you say."

She leaned her head back and expelled a never-ending plume of curling blue smoke.

"Oh, don't be rude. I begin to find you most annoying."

"And I begin to find you to be a woman aiding and abetting an alleged murderer. If you refuse to cooperate, you will find me a great deal more than merely rude and annoying."

"Odd, isn't it, when one has nothing to hide or conceal."

"I find that difficult to believe. As it happens, I already find you to be one of the most cowardly women I've yet to meet, perhaps in the entirety of my career in the enforcement of the law."

She laughed.

"Really. That's quite a statement, coming from a street bobby policeman. I've read your own dossier, you see. With all the details of your humble origins. Reminded me of a Shakespeare quote on the subject. Perhaps you know it?"

"Enlighten me."

" 'On what meat doth this our Caesar feed that he is grown so great?' "

Congreve didn't even blink.

"Professor Moon, I'm quite sure you consider yourself a woman of great intellectual and personal power. You exude a bristling confidence. You show bemused disdain for those, like me, whom you deem wholly beneath you. People like myself, who come from humble origins."

"Your humble origins are self-evident. Get to your point, for God's sake, assuming you have one."

"In all my professional life, Professor Moon, I have yet to meet a coward who wasn't cruel. And, since I think you to be capable of the most unspeakable cruelty, I believe you to be the most unspeakable coward."

"What cruelty? This is nonsense. I won't stand for it!"

"One of the most horrific implements of death in the fifteenth century. The Shining Basket."

"Oh, please. All this twaddle about baskets. At this late hour . . ."

"I'll not ask again. Pick up the bloody phone."

"Oh, for God's sake," she said, crisscrossing her long silk-encased legs and picking up the receiver of a black 1930s Bakelite telephone. "Optimus? Yes. There you are. Could you come to the library for a moment? Our unwelcome visitor has a little something he'd like you to do for him. Yes? Good."

"On his way?" Congreve said.

"On his way."

"What is this fascination with ravens, Dr. Moon? This room feels like a blackbird mortuary. Most curious. A hobby?"

"Oh, much more than that, Inspector. I import a very rare breed of raven from New Zealand. *Corvus antipodum*. Extraordinarily intelligent. Eaters of the dead, commonly referred to as carrion eaters, you know, feasting on dead animals, decaying meat. Hunger birds, I call them. Long considered a bird of ill omen, ravens are believed by some to be ghosts of murdered persons, or some kind of mediator animal between life and death. I suppose you find some of these things morbid or distasteful, but to me, they are creatures possessed of great beauty. Oh, Optimus, here you are at last."

The burly butler entered the large room and proceeded across the faded Persian rugs to position himself between the lady of the house and her guest. He kept his eyes on Congreve speaking over his shoulder to his mistress.

"You rang, Madame?"

"Oh, Optimus. How beautiful you are in this light. The chief inspector has a favor to ask, don't you, Inspector?"

"Indeed. My good man, would you please go to the third floor, find Miss Li, and bring her here to the library? I have a few simple questions regarding her whereabouts tonight."

"Sorry, sir. That will not be possible. She was feeling quite ill earlier and retired for the evening. A nasty stomach virus. She appeared in the pantry a short time ago and said she might run over to the twenty-four-hour chemist in St. Ives. Get something for it."

"In the Rolls-Royce?" Congreve said.

"No, sir. She indicated she was taking the Vincent Black Shadow."

"I take it that's a motorcycle," Congreve said.

"Indeed it is."

"Well," Chyna Moon said, "there you have it. So good of you to come all this way at such a late hour. Optimus, will you show Inspector Congreve to the door?"

"I am not leaving this house without speaking to Lorelei."

"Ooh, first-name basis!"

"Yes. I happen to know her. And I know she's in this house. If you refuse to fetch her, I shall arrest you both for obstruction of justice."

Chyna permitted herself a flash of anger.

"I think we are quite done here. I want you to leave, Chief Inspector. Now. Optimus? Remove him from my sight."

The big man made a move toward him. Congreve reached inside his jacket and pulled the revolver. He pointed it at the famous wrestler's heart.

"Lay a hand on me, Prime, and I will have your bloody head on a pike. I will—"

He never finished his sentence.

Optimus faked a move to the left, then got inside, clubbing Ambrose's gun arm down and away with a sharp and powerful downward chop of his left forearm. Before Congreve could bring the gun back up, Prime dropped away and kicked him on the point of his right elbow. Congreve felt like he had grabbed a threadbare power line with his bare hand. Red-hot wires ran up into his shoulder and down to his fingertips, and his arm went slack, half numbed.

The gun skidded across the worn carpet.

When the brawler lunged and bent to snatch it, Ambrose leaned back and drop-kicked him in the midsection with the steel-tipped toe of his custom Lobb brogue, something he would not have done in hindsight. A couple of broken ribs only galvanized the Brute.

Dr. Moon provided a smattering of applause as if from the audience. She was sipping brandy and watching the battle royal from the crimson sofa, the look on her face rife with amusement.

Roaring, Prime came back at him, swinging good punches. Congreve had somehow gotten shakily to his feet and was backpedaling, trying to put some distance between himself and his formidable adversary. He did manage to surreptitiously kick the weapon back into a corner behind him, and thank God Prime hadn't seen him do it. It was the only chance he had.

"Oh, Optimus. Look what he's done now," Dr. Moon said. "He's kicked the gun back into the corner behind him."

"I saw that, Madame. But thank you."

"For God's sake, don't kill him here. I do not want any blood on these rugs. It will never come out."

"No, Madame. I shall restrain myself."

"Please do," Congreve croaked.

Chapter 59

Ambrose could now lift his numbed arm, but he was a realist to the core. Pick your battles. Live to fight another day. He settled for taking the blows on his forearms and upper arms, protecting his head. This seemed only to agitate the Brute further, because he immediately threw an overhead right that hit the shelf of Congreve's jaw and knocked his mouth wide.

His knees went loose, and white rockets sailed behind his eyes. He bicycled backward, and only the wall kept him from going down on the spot. He hit it hard enough to jar the Old Master paintings hung above, the largest of which came crashing down, narrowly missing Congreve, with a corner of the heavy gilt frame striking his attacker on the crown of his head.

The wrestler roared in anguish if not pain. The man seemed immune to that human frailty.

Further enraged, Prime slashed down with the edge of his right hand, a diagonal blow catching Congreve on the side of his skull, just under the left earlobe. The famous detective melted down to the floor, his eyes unfocused, his legs jellied.

Then, blackness.

Congreve awoke on the cold, damp ground. When he could see, he discovered that he was out of doors; he was inside some kind of large wrought-iron cage or other. A towering thing that soared above him to heights lost to darkness.

He had no idea how long he'd been unconscious. Five minutes? An hour? He was extremely cold from the night air. He was on his back. He felt a huge weight upon his chest, but perhaps it was just pain. He had no idea how badly hurt he was. He worked his mouth. He tried moving his arms. Then his legs. He couldn't move his left leg. He tried again and heard a clink of chain.

His left leg was chained by the ankle to something—an iron stake pounded into the ground at an angle. He lifted his head to inspect his predicament.

In the shadowy realm beyond the cage he saw a tall silhouetted figure. She was peering at him through the bars. Chyna Moon. He couldn't see much of her face. But she was smoking a cigarette, and the glow of the orange coal made her black eyes flare every few seconds.

"I gave you an injection, something to bring you around, Chief Inspector. I'm glad to see you're feeling better. Methamphetamines are truly wonder drugs."

"Release me at once!"

"Tell me what I want to know and perhaps I'll do just that."

"I cannot imagine I have information of any remote value to you."

"Ah, but you do, you see. I want you to tell me all about your friend Lord Alexander Hawke."

"What about him?"

"Where he is, for starters? On my orders, my companion paid him an unexpected visit tonight. He was not in residence. So she had to wreak our vengeance upon Miss Churchill, that pathetic excuse for a bodyguard. And the child, of course. Poor dear."

"She told you she killed the child as well?"

"She did."

"Well, she didn't. The boy, no thanks to your murderous friend, was not seriously wounded. My friend Pelham interrupted Lorelei Li's plans."

"The boy survived? Well, well. She does lie a lot. No matter, the child can wait. It's Hawke I want."

"Why?"

"Many reasons. Hawke was fucking my sister Jet years ago in the South of France. She was quite famous in those days, a movie star much loved in China. But he tired of her. Discarded her, humiliated, like so much trash. And then he sent a giant black man to see my father aboard his houseboat in Hong Kong harbor. That night my sister ended up dead. My father holds Hawke responsible for the suffering of one daughter and for the death of the other. And then, of course, there's the little matter of Professor Watanabe."

"What's he got to do with this?"

"My father sent me a photograph, taken by one of his agents in London some time ago in Berkeley Square. My father had just learned that our trusted friend Professor Watanabe was a double agent. He'd been spying on us for MI6 for years. He had betrayed me. My father condemned him to death. He paid a terrible price."

"So it was you I saw that night."

"Where?"

"Near his cottage in the Fens one night. You and your companion were driving very slowly past his drive off the Carthage Road. That vintage silver Roller of yours. I followed you, but you lost me in the fog. Whatever were you two doing out there on such a foggy night?"

"Grouse hunting."

"I am not amused. My friend is dead."

"History's about to repeat itself. Unless you tell me where to find that bastard Hawke. My father grows impatient."

"Who is your father, anyway?"

"General Sun-Yat Moon. Look him up, if you miraculously live to get the chance."

"I will. Watanabe was one of my closest friends."

"Mine, too. So what?"

"I didn't kill him. I'll give you Hawke if you give me Lorelei. Where is she hiding?"

"Sorry. She knows far too much about my political activities here at Cambridge. Where is Hawke now?"

"On a business trip."

"Do you see what I have in my hand? Look over here."

"What is it?"

"A silver training whistle. I use whistles to call my little darlings to me when I need them. I gave one just like it to Sabrina Churchill when I gave her the raven as a gift—for the child, I told her. A very dangerous gift, but still. I liked the idea of a murderous creature introduced into a child's nursery. A hunger bird. Sitting innocently in a gilded cage, ever so close to Hawke's spawn. Day after day . . . waiting to be released."

"You're a monster, Dr. Moon."

"Well, we all have our little shortcomings, don't we? I'm going to toot my silver whistle now. You won't like it. My birds are merciless. They will pluck the flesh from your bones, the tongue from your mouth, and the eyes from your head. Like you, your friend Watanabe crossed swords with me and lived to regret it."

"Wait . . ."

"I tire of you. It's cold. I'm going inside to bed. Looks like rain. I see you're still clutching your precious British black rolled umbrella. I'm not all bad, you see. Wouldn't want you to die of exposure tonight when there are so many other, far more interesting ways to perish."

She blew the silent silver whistle, and the birds took wing.

"You're not even human," Congreve said.

"Cry me a river," Chyna said with a thin smile, just before she turned away and drifted off into the dark gardens drenched in cold moonlight.

The bird attack was instant and horrific.

He sat up to make himself a smaller target, brought his knees up under his chin, tucked his head between them down into his chest, pulled up the collar of his jacket and covered his head with his hands. All he could think about were his eyes. And that was unthinkable.

The first salvo of searing pain was immediate and excruciating.

The ravens, masses of them, were everywhere at once. Relentless, hungry carrion eaters. Meat eaters who ate the dead and dying. Seeking any morsel of flesh they could get at. He screamed at them and tried to bat them away, but it was no use.

This was no bloody way to die . . . but what could he hope to do in order to—

Mary Poppins.

The very special umbrella Hawke had ordered made for him at MI6! Where was it? He slowly removed his hands from his eyes and looked around desperately for the old girl. He saw it. Lying in the dirt perhaps three feet away. He reached out for it. Came up a foot short. The birds dove and dove. He was losing a lot of blood. Wounds to his scalp and forehead were leaking into his eyes. His eyes, his bloody eyes!

He rolled over onto his stomach. Stretched the chain taut with his left leg, the manacle cutting into the soft flesh of his ankle, yanking anyway.

He thought he had one more chance left in him.

He reached out with his right hand and began to claw at the dirt. Pulling himself closer one half inch at a time . . . finally . . . he almost touched it (Mary Poppins!) with his fingertips . . . close . . . closer . . . he had her in his grasp!

He clutched the high-tech lifesaver to him, elated. Despite the pain, he managed to roll over onto his bum and sit up. Flailing away at the hellish birds with his free hand, he depressed a glowing red button in the crook of the carbon-fiber handle. That button caused the microthin titanium-mesh umbrella to deploy instantaneously.

Now he had a shield capable, so Hawke said, of stopping at least a knife and perhaps even a small-caliber bullet.

He held the handle close to his chest and lowered the crown down near his head for maximum protection. His head and all his torso, as well as most of his legs, were now unreachable.

Still the shrieking ravens dove down undeterred. It felt like his umbrella was being bombarded with golf balls. Countless numbers of birds slammed into his protective shield at full speed and careened off the thin titanium skin. Many if not most of them were dropping dead to the ground all around him. And yet still they came.

His fingers found another tiny illuminated button, blue. There were advanced lithium-sulfur batteries inside the umbrella's tube, Hawke had explained with delight, capable of jump-starting a dead car battery. And thus the pointed ferrule at the umbrella's very top was electrified to serious voltage.

He pressed the blue button repeatedly and saw jagged flashes, a veritable geyser of blue-white electricity, arc upward from the finial in all directions, instantly killing anything within range. And showering the ground below with showers of white-hot sparks when he zapped the filigreed iron struts near the top of the aviary.

To a casual observer, it looked as if the world-famous criminalist had sought refuge beneath a small black teepee, one capable of firing jagged bolts of blue-white lightning skyward from its apex like some high-tech electrified Roman candle.

Inside the protective cover of his cozy titanium tent, Congreve inhaled the acrid scent of burning bird flesh and feathers with enormous satisfaction. Zapped ravens were dropping like flies all around him now and—what was that? Someone calling his name?

"Inspector Congreve? Inspector Congreve? Is that you inside there, sir? Under that umbrella?"

He raised Mary Poppins a foot or two, in order that he might be seen and heard.

"Of course it's me, Cummings, you bloody fool! Where the hell have you been, Inspector?" he shouted. "You were supposed to meet me here an hour ago!"

"Sorry, Chief Inspector, we had to—you see—we were held up by a lorry that jackknifed at a roundabout and—"

"Never mind all that. Just get me out of here! How many men have you got?"

"Six, including myself."

"Send four of your best armed men into that house. There are only two people in there that I know of, but both are extremely dangerous. One of them has just confessed to the murder of Professor Watanabe. Her name is Dr. Chyna Moon. The other is male, a psychotic wrestler by the unlikely name of Optimus Prime. Tell your men to take no chances with either. They're both mean as snakes."

"Yes, sir."

"Sabrina's killer herself lives inside that morbid house. She may still be inside it, but I rather doubt it. Her name is Lorelei Li, a stringer for the *Times* and a Cambridge grad student. I think she very well may have escaped via motorbike a short while ago. A Vincent Black Shadow."

"Any idea as to what direction she took, sir?"

"Yes. I seem to recall Pelham saying something about Sabrina visiting Lorelei at a cottage down in Cornwall. Nevermore, I think he called it. She's probably en route there. Pretty girl. Voluptuous, as they say. Late twenties, Asian, short black hair. Call it in."

"Very good, Chief Inspector. You appear to be bleeding."

"Of course I'm bleeding, you idiot. I say, Cummings. Are we going to sit around and talk all night? Or is someone perhaps thinking of removing me from this cauldron of death? No hurry, of course; I'm quite comfortable in here with these bloodthirsty beasts."

"Right away, sir! Constable Jenkins, cut away that padlock and let's get the chief inspector out of there, shall we?"

Jenkins hefted a pair of bolt cutters and went to work on the hefty padlock.

"I say, Chief Inspector," Cummings called out, "if you don't mind my asking. What is that strange contraption you're sitting under?"

"It's a bloody umbrella! What does it look like?"

"It does have a certain 'James Bond' air about it, sir, to be perfectly honest. All those special effects, I mean, the sparks, the lightning bolts . . ."

There came then another eruption from the umbrella, only this time it was not sparks but the raucous laughter of one Ambrose Congreve, glad he would live to fight another day.

Chapter 60

At Sea, off North Korea

A solitary and unblinking eye, black and hooded, emerged from the cold sea. The night sky was black, the sea was leaden, and that is all there was, save the eye moving slowly a few feet above the surface, leaving a rippled wave in its wake.

The eye slowed, then stopped.

It began to swivel counterclockwise, very slowly, making two complete revolutions. Then it paused and disappeared again, slipping unseen beneath the waves. The hooded eye had seen nothing interesting or threatening on the desolate North Korean beaches, nor any surface vessels on the sea. Nothing, and that was just enough.

It had been just ten days since the secret meeting at Fort Whupass.

Lurking below the surface, stationary at periscope depth, the USS *Florida* (SSGN728) was ready to commence operations. She was an Ohio-class ballistic missile submarine (SSBN) recently converted to a guided missile sub (SSGN) in order to insert SEAL platoons into hostile environments to conduct clandestine missions for extended periods of time ashore.

A stealth platform, she was designed, to use the SEAL motto: "To equip the man, not man the equipment."

"Prepare to launch two SDVs, Bash," the sub's skipper, Captain Ben Malpass, said to his young XO, Lieutenant Bashon Mann.

"Aye, sir. Launch SDVs."

Bash radioed the men working on the submerged deck. He then sent the periscope sliding back down into its well, a slight hydraulic hiss in the quiet of the control room.

"Prepare to launch, aye!" a crewman operating on deck replied over the intercom.

A minute later, Lieutenant Mann said, "Coming up on five minutes to launch, Skipper."

Five minutes later, a small, dark shadow slipped away from the submerged sub and headed for shore. It remained submerged, en route to a place code-named

Half Moon Bay. A few minutes later, a second shadow slipped into its underwater wake. Two twenty-one-foot-long submersibles, known as SDVs, or SEAL delivery vehicles, would rendezvous on the deserted and frozen coast of North Korea.

Launched from a tubular dry-deck shelter on the submerged sub's deck, the SDV carried its crew and passengers exposed to the icy water, breathing either from their scuba gear or the vehicle's compressed air supply. Aboard the two submersibles were a team of twenty-one men tasked with a mission that had been the subject of cabinet-level debate in Washington and at the highest levels of government in London.

The mission had very nearly been canceled until a courageous President David Rosow gave the last-minute go-ahead. The British prime minister, along with the director of MI6, had finally convinced everyone that this particular team of counterterrorist operatives actually had a fighting chance of pulling this thing off. All despite terrible odds and in the face of scathing resistance within the Pentagon and Naval Intelligence headquarters in Britain.

Rosow had made his decision based only on the heroic quality of the men he was sending into harm's way. The price of failure was incalculable. But these men, all of them, were a different breed. Hawke and his teams had long demonstrated a way of overcoming impossible odds; they had a track record of snatching victory from the jaws of certain defeat, and they'd done it time and again, year after year.

And now he was sending them into a country with which the United States was not technically at war, at a time when the slightest miscalculation could send the world hurtling toward catastrophe. "Godspeed, Hawke," Rosow had said the night before, speaking with the team leader on the eve of their mission.

"We can do this, Mr. President," Hawke assured him. "You made the right decision. Sleep well, sir. I'll keep you informed of our progress."

Hawke, Stokely Jones, Fitz McCoy, and Colonel Cho were the first four men ashore. They split up and made an immediate recon of the landing zone, making sure the designated LZ area was as deserted as their photo recon had indicated. Fitz went right, Stoke left, while Hawke and Cho went straight ahead up and over the sand dunes.

Hawke had wanted a dark night to go ashore and he'd gotten his wish. Stumbling once going up the sand hill, he flipped down his NVG optics. The world turned fuzzy green, but at least he could see where to put his boots. At the top of the dune he paused, turned, and looked back to sea with his binoculars.

USS *Florida* was way out there, her conning tower a thin black blip of a silhouette on the grey horizon line. Hawke could just make out two of the sub's five primary navigation lights: the rudder (white) and the port (red), winking at him in the distance. He swung back round to check out his objective.

His objective, the camp, was just on the other side of that mountain range.

Looking at the dense, endless blackness, he recalled a press unveiling of a U.S. Defense Department satellite image of the Korean Peninsula at night. The photograph showed the northern half of the peninsula completely in the dark except for a speck of light indicating the location of the capital, Pyongyang. South Korea's portion, in contrast, was aglow, its myriad cities alive with light. It was a dramatic depiction of the economic miracle that is Communism.

He smiled at Cho, and the two men turned to return to the beach.

When he stormed down the dune, he saw all the heavily armed men from both SDVs assembled on the beach. Hawke asked the men to count off and then radioed the minisubs. The two minisub drivers were standing by one-half mile offshore just in case it got spicy and he required an immediate exfil. He told them the mission team onshore was good to go, and that they could safely return to the mother ship. He reconfirmed the time and place set for the team's extraction and signed off.

He turned to the men under his command.

"You all know what to do. So let's go goddamn do it."

The little twenty-one-man army began the silent march inland. Their route would take them up through the mountainous region and across a narrow barren plain before they came to the dreaded *kwan-li-so.*

Number 25. The death camp.

Hawke raised the flat of his hand and brought the entire squad to a halt. They were halfway down a mountain, picking their way through ice-encrusted rock, loose boulders, and scrub. The temperature hovered around freezing. Fifty yards below was a small copse of trees, big enough to shield them from prying eyes; it was the last bit of cover they'd have for a while.

"Recon," he said. "Ten minutes R&R."

The men moved down into the woods, grateful for a few minutes' rest after the night's march. Hawke got behind a large boulder, rested his elbows on it, and looked through his binocs. The sky was turning pink.

He could see the gulag-style work camp with some clarity now.

At the main gate, a giant portrait of the late, unlamented Kim Jong-il looked out over acres of wooden barracks. This perimeter fence was studded with six tall wooden guard towers. Three men in each one with binoculars and automatic weapons, according to Cho. Hawke swung the glasses, searching for the sign the CIA had told him would confirm his arrival at the camp where the Americans were believed to be held. He saw it. A giant banner with huge red Korean letters that exhorted the workers: "Democratic People's Republic of Korea, to Victory!"

He calculated the distance from the tree line across the narrow plain to the camp perimeter.

They'd have to fan out and crawl on their bellies across a half mile of open ground.

He smiled to himself.

Nobody'd ever said this stuff was easy.

Chapter 61

Camp Number 25

FitzHugh "Lightning" McCoy was a sniper.

He was one of the most highly decorated snipers in recent military history and had even written a bestselling book about his experiences in Iraq and Afghanistan. Now, along with two of his best men, he was getting ready to take out the NK guards in the machine-gun towers.

They were in the woods, just above no-man's-land. With NVG telescopic optics, they could see the guards, not a few of them dozing atop the towers. Occasionally, the guards would fire up a searchlight and play it lazily around the perimeter. One could sense these were not men on a high state of alert. This was Norkland, for

God's sake! The home of the Norks! Norkland was what T&L called North Korea and its vast numbers of military rulers. Who in the world would ever attack a bunch of Norks out in the middle of bloody nowhere?

Fitz spoke in a low, deadly serious whisper.

"Take out the towers to either side of the main gate first. That'll be their wake-up call this morning. Then work outward along the perimeter. Remember, the colonel says there are three guards to a tower. But there's always one on a cot below the ledge where they catnap until relieving one or the other. I want three down before you move on to the next."

"Roger that, sir."

"Take out all those bloody searchlights, too. Just for good measure. Might encourage other internees to escape after we've gone. One can only hope."

Cho pulled Hawke aside.

Hawke's men were all still well hidden inside the copse of trees. Ahead of them, a wide stretch of barren ground with little or no cover. No-man's-land. No one could survive crossing that killing ground beneath the withering fire from the guard towers. The NKs used Type 73s, based on old Soviet machine guns, but updated and still effective.

Beyond the open ground stood the high walls of Camp 25.

"That open ground," Hawke said to Cho. "Was it mined at the time of your escape?"

"No, sir. Should have been, my opinion. Should have had heat sensors, pressure plates, all that and more. But the guards here are usually drunk and always lazy. This is the last stop in an NK People's Army officer's career. The only way to go from here is down. They've got nothing to lose, and they take it out on the prisoners."

"The worst kind."

"You been there, sir?"

"Some. Once when I got shot down over northern Iraq. Did about a month in one of Saddam's desert charm schools before I broke out. A longer stretch another time in a jungle hellhole on mainland China. Met some lovely chaps along the way. Unforgettable, really."

"Fitz says you're Royal Navy, Commander."

"Semiretired. I used to fly."

"What aircraft?"

"Harriers, mostly. But a lot of newer stuff more recently."

"Wait until I introduce you to Babyface," Cho said.

Hawke said, "You don't mean the Dear Leader himself? I thought he lived in some sick palace in Pyongyang."

Cho laughed.

"No, sir, I mean the camp commandant. That's what we called him. Babyface. Angelic little shit with the soul of a scarab. Likes-to-throw-babies-down-deep-wells kind of human being. You know the type."

"I take it you're not fond of him."

"He's the reason I'm standing here, Commander Hawke. He ripped my baby brother from my mother's arms and threw him down a well. Then he put a knife in my mother's stomach and twisted it until he found the uterus, killing both my mother and my unborn sister, too."

"Good God. I'm very sorry, Colonel."

"It's war, isn't it, Commander?"

Hawke looked away for a moment and said, "Colonel, as you know, after Chief's demolition guys blow the main gates, you and I will be first through the breach. As I said earlier, I want you to take me directly to the commandant's residence. We'll take a squad of four, including Froggy and the Alsatian gunner. One heavy machine-gunner fore and aft."

Cho nodded. "Babyface knows where the American hostages are. Based on what I know, the children will be aboveground and the mother below. Please leave that part to me, sir. I'll make sure he sees the sense in taking us right to them. He won't resist. He's actually a terrified little gnome playing God, lording it over this squalid corner of hell."

"All cruelty starts with fear. Or something like that. Seneca."

"Seneca. A great philosopher."

"Right," Hawke said, pulling out his hand-drawn map of the camp. "Show me his residence again."

"It's right here. The two-story house with his precious orchard of cherry trees around it. We called it the Teahouse of the August Moon. Guarded twenty-four hours a day. He sleeps on an outside sleeping porch located here. "

"You said there were land mines around his house?"

"Yes. But I know the clear path to his door. You'd think they'd move them around occasionally, but they don't. Lazy bastards."

"I'm glad you're here, Colonel. From the gate, that's, what . . . half a klick to his quarters?"

"About that."

"Stokely, Chief, Froggy, and Brock, you know what to do. Start searching the barracks one by one. Maybe you'll get lucky. I'll radio you as soon as we get their precise location out of the commandant. Meanwhile, keep looking. Capture a guard and make him talk. Find out in which barracks they're keeping all the children.

Get them out, not just the hostages, all of them. Alive. Whatever it takes. Yes?"

"Yes, sir," Froggy said. "Count on it, Hawke."

"All right then. As soon as Fitz has taken out those towers, we move out. Get your heads on straight and don't make any bloody mistakes. You guys are the best at this on the planet. You're number one. Go do it."

At precisely 0400, Fitz and the other two snipers began the process of reducing the six guard towers to smoking heaps of splinters. Their actions initiated a swift but confused retaliation. Unwisely, the main gate was now swinging open to expel an armored vehicle with twelve heavily armed troops in the rear.

"I've got zee muzzafookah!" Froggy said. He stepped from the woods hefting the shoulder-launched ATGM, an antitank guided missile light enough to be fired by one soldier.

"Take him out, Froggy!" Rainwater said.

The missile streaked upward trailing yellow fire, reached its apogee, and nosed over into a steep dive toward the oncoming armored troop vehicle. The driver swerved wildly but the missile was smarter: the impact was immediate and incredibly destructive. A loud *crack*, a blinding ball of fire, and thick black smoke rising from the unrecognizable hulk of wreckage. No survivors.

"C'est bon?" the Frogman said, smiling at Hawke.

"C'est tres bon," Hawke said, peering at the destruction through his binoculars. Suddenly, he pivoted left. "Heads up. Frogman! There's a second armored vehicle inside the compound speeding for the gate. Waste it, Froggy, while it's still within the compound. We'll use the chaos inside to cover our infil."

Hawke swept his glasses back and forth, assessing the unfolding situation.

Froggy lit off a second missile, and seconds later, another explosive *CRACK* and heavy flames and black smoke rising above the walls from within the camp. The two heavy gates slammed shut. Whatever resistance this "secret" death camp was capable of putting up . . . was now being implemented. The no-man's-land obstacle had been overcome. It only remained to be seen how much fight these desolate men had in them.

Hawke looked up. There was a new tinge of pink in the charcoal skies.

It was time.

"Go, go, go!" Hawke said, leaning in and giving each man a solidarity hit on the shoulder as he passed by. He was saying in their ears exactly what he had always said to them in times like this.

"Use this time, son . . . use the time . . . use it to get your head on straight . . . use this time . . . get your head on straight . . . yeah, that's right . . . focus, focus . . . you've got it . . . now keep it on straight . . . you too . . . okay . . . give 'em pure hell down there . . . okay . . . that's it . . . go . . ."

And so on they went.

Chapter 62

There was sporadic fire from atop the wall, but without the lethality of heavy tripod-mounted machine guns from the towers, it was mostly ineffective. Hawke, who, with Rainwater, was leading the Bravo squad, and Stoke, with Fitz and Alpha squad, approached the wide gates from opposite directions. They feinted once or twice, zigzagging as they ran, firing continuously at anything that moved along the wall.

"Alpha, this is Bravo," Hawke said into his headset.

"Copy, Bravo," Stoke said.

"Alpha, lay down heavy suppressive M-60 and mortar fire while we go in to blow the gate. Chief says give him three minutes to set the charge, another minute to breach. Follow us in."

"Roger that, Bravo."

"On my mark . . . four minutes . . . mark!"

Hawke thought Chief Rainwater had packed enough Semtex on Camp 25's front door to blow the gates of hell wide open. And when Thunder Team lit the fuse, he knew he'd been right. The massive steel slabs were blown right off the hinges, blown inward by the sheer force of the explosion. They gates themselves were lethal flying objects now, by-products of Thunder and Lightning's standard method of gaining entry to a hostile compound.

"Welcome to Norkland," Chief said, smiling at Hawke. "You can bet the Norks are shitting sizable bricks at the moment, sir."

Hawke flipped his helmet mike down. "Alpha, copy, Bravo is going in."

"Alpha, copy, got your six. Right behind you, boss," Stoke said.

It really was hell. Mobs of skin-and-bones prisoners dressed in rags, stumbling aimlessly around the compound in thin felt shoes or barefoot across the frozen rocky soil, zombies seemingly oblivious to the firefight going on around them. Already dead, Hawke supposed. If not, then certainly ready to die.

In the center of the camp parade ground, the flaming hulk of the armored carrier belched black smoke. There was some small-arms fire directed toward the invaders, mostly from windows in the buildings surrounding the square. And more serious machine-gun fire from the rooftop of a three-story building directly opposite the main gate.

Beyond the camp's main square, endless rows of grim wooden barracks stretched seemingly to the horizon. Somewhere in that warren of misery were two young American children who didn't belong there. Check that.

No one belonged here. No creed. No color. Nobody.

Bravo went left. Alpha went right, full run-and-shoot mode, laying down withering fire as they raced toward the bleak city of barracks.

Hawke's team took cover between two corrugated steel buildings facing onto the central square. He saw Stoke and Brock do the same thing, running alongside Fitz through a scraggy stand of trees toward a narrow street on the opposite side of the parade ground.

"What's that building?" Hawke asked Cho. "Machine guns on the roof."

"Officers' barracks. Married. Members of the 'loyal' class. Citizens with 'pure' family histories, no ancestral ties to South Koreans, capitalists, or Christians."

Hawke smiled at him. "The Great Cho: Google of Norkland."

"Guilty as charged." Cho laughed.

Machine-gun fire chewed at the dirt not thirty feet away.

"Chief, you and Froggy take out those gunners on the roof, lob some mortars up there. Then go in there and blow it. I mean level that building down to the ground. Colonel Cho and I are going to visit the commandant. We'll take two M-60 heavy guys to cover our asses. Your squad clears the immediate area. Basic search and destroy until we return. Ça va?"

"Mais oui, mon capitaine!"

"Teahouse?" Hawke said to Cho.

"Teahouse. Right this way."

They turned right at a dead end and hadn't gone a hundred yards when they found an abandoned jeep. Not a real American "Jeep" but one of the thousands the Norks had copied for their military. Hawke jumped behind the wheel, and the rest leaped over the side. Rainwater sat facing aft, a big M-60 cradled in his arms. He loved this gun. Officially the United States machine gun, the 7.62mm fires several types of live ammunition: ball, tracer, and armor-piercing rounds.

Cho sat up front with Hawke. They raced across the bumpy ground, swerving to avoid loose rock and random boulders.

"We're expected, right?" Hawke asked.

"Probably. Because of the twin explosions. But not necessarily."

"Why not?"

"Babyface doesn't like to be on the receiving end of bad news. He once shot a house servant on the spot for telling him the bacon was burned. So you'd think twice before informing him that nearly twenty armed mercenaries were taking down his camp piece by piece."

Hawke laughed.

"Twilight at the Teahouse?"

"Something like that."

There was a low concrete wall around the commandant's residence that Hawke had not noticed on the grainy satellite photos. Nor was he prepared for the size of the place. Surrounded by forests of black stunted trees, and a cherry orchard, it was like a large square blockhouse. Rather forbidding.

There was a winding and rutted dirt road leading through the cherry orchard. When the jeep drew within a hundred yards of the main entrance, Babyface's imperial guards popped up and began firing at them. Rounds found the jeep's hood and tires. Hawke cut the wheel hard right, hauling up on the emergency brake at the same time, creating a 180-degree switch in directions.

That put Chief Rainwater facing the opposition in position one: head-on.

He and Froggy opened up with both of the M-60s, and the effect was devastating. The deep bass *thump-thump-thump* of the 7.62mm armor-piercing rounds was enough to make strong men turn tail and hide, but the rounds slamming into the wall wreaked hell and havoc, turning the wall to a pile of rubble around the ankles of the few guards still remaining on their feet.

Just as the incoming fire from the residence ceased, gunners in the upper-floor windows threw open the heavy wooden shutters and trained their weapons on the jeep.

"Shit!" Cho said. A round had caught him in the deep right shoulder and almost spun him out of the jeep. Hawke jammed into first gear, his wheels spinning on the hard ground as he raced away and out of range. When the incoming rounds ceased, he swerved wide and returned to the Teahouse, staying out of range and circling around to the rear of the house and fishtailing to a stop.

Cho was bleeding badly.

"Froggy, field dress the colonel's wound, then follow us in. Cho, where the hell do I find Babyface?"

"His sleeping quarters are upstairs on the rear. No windows. But he has a secure office in the basement. Only his personal security is allowed down there."

"Chief, blow the rear door. We're going in. Clear left and right, then up the stairs. Move!"

Rainwater took the door out.

They went in low. Half dove left, half right. They caught a couple of guards shouldering their automatic weapons and took them out instantly with head shots. Rainwater was heaving smoke grenades, and the ground floor was filling up fast. He threw in a couple of stun grenades to add to the confusion.

Hawke found the staircase leading up near the front of the house. He flattened himself against the wall and did a quick-pick up the stairs. The plaster next to his cheek exploded, a big piece slashing a flap of skin loose. He put his head back against the wall, counted to three, and swung round with his automatic pistol at the ready.

He must have surprised the Nork because the guy was just going eyes wide when Hawke put two into him between the lamps and watched him tumble forward all the way to the bottom.

"Up here. Let's go. On me."

"Hawke! Behind you on the stairs, another one! He's locked on!"

Hawke dove and hit the floor rolling as rounds chewed up the floor around him. He came out of it with his gun up and put two rounds into the guard's chest.

"Clear," Hawke said, getting to his feet.

The squad, which now included Froggy and the wounded Cho, assembled at the base of the stairs. Froggy, carrying a machine gun slightly larger than he was, jumped to the lead and went up the stairs swearing and daring, challenging one and all to face the mighty Frogman.

One fool did so, and Froggy cut him in half with a sustained burst from the M-60 . . . *thump* . . . *thump* . . . *thump.*

Cho was right behind him, yelling directions to Babyface's quarters, a right, then a left at the top of the stairs. In a beat, all of them were at the top, looking for someone to shoot.

It was strangely quiet after all the fireworks.

Chapter 63

Pelham Grenville, on several occasions, had remarked that, in the absence of war, Hawke's spirits eventually went into decline. At times like this, right in the bloody heat of it, Hawke was forced to admit the truth of that sentiment. He was a warrior. Since his youth he had frequently quoted his great hero, Churchill, on the subject of war. "There is nothing quite so exhilarating as being shot at without effect." He was being shot at now, and he was exhilarated.

His blood was up.

The men, his men, went from room to room, heaving in smoke grenades followed by flash-bangs, killing or disabling the men who had surrounded, and were sworn to protect, the beloved commandant. Clearly, they'd sworn an oath to fight to the death because the thought of hands-up surrender didn't seem to be high on their option list when Hawke told them to throw down their weapons.

There was a corridor, short and wide, that led to a pair of ornate double doors. Oddly enough, there weren't two armed gorillas standing at port arms to either side.

"That's it," Colonel Cho whispered to Hawke. "His sleeping quarters. He's got to be in there and—"

Hawke saw the wide carved doors swing open. Out strolled a short and oval man in white silk pajamas with red piping beneath a crimson velvet smoking jacket. He had a gleaming bald dome, a bulbous nose, and tiny little pinprick black eyes with a glint of red in the irises. He was smoking a meerschaum pipe, even had a good bowl going. In perfect English, he said to Hawke, "Hello. May I help you?"

All with an unmistakably flirtatious smile.

A baby Hugh Hefner, Hawke thought.

Babyface. No mistake about it.

"We're just looking for someone," Hawke said, leveling his pistol at the man's heart. "Sorry about all the noise. Unavoidable, I'm afraid."

Rainwater, infuriated by the human suffering and horrific conditions he'd seen in the camp, took a step toward the camp commandant. He'd fixed his bayonet at the end of his rifle. He pushed the point into the man's protruding belly.

"What the gentleman is trying to tell you, asshole, is that we're here to blow up your shit."

"What do you mean?" Babyface said, genuinely puzzled.

"Means we come here to stick your dick in the dirt, boy," Elvis Peete, the team's comms specialist, said, firing a round into the ceiling over the commandant's head.

Cho added, "But first, we're going to need some information about the exact location of various people."

"No problem," Babyface, shaky now, said. "Whom exactly were you looking for?"

"You," Hawke said.

"Me?"

Hawke said pleasantly, "Do you mind if we step inside? We've just come down from the mountains. This hallway is quite drafty."

"No, no, not at all! Please be my guest. All of you. Can I get you some refreshments? Tea, perhaps? Whiskey?"

He gave a little bow and waved them into his bedchamber.

The bed was a massive four-poster. There was a gilded headboard depicting warring dragons and a lipstick-red satin bedcover. Babyface toddled over to his bed, got up on tiptoes, levered himself up, and plopped down on his belly before rolling over. He seemed to find his gymnastics amusing and Hawke said, "Well done!"

"Please, do take a seat, all of you. I have so many chairs."

There was a lot of eye-rolling and suppressed amazement, with the exception of Colonel Cho, who had obviously witnessed performances like this one in the past. It was clear that at first Babyface had no clue it was his old prisoner, escaped, and now, dressed as he was, an alien being, an American spec-ops warrior on a night raid in full battle regalia.

"Allow me to introduce myself, Commandant. I am Lord Alexander Hawke, come from England . . . and these men are—"

" . . . a real English lord?"

"As real as it gets," Cho said.

"I recognize one of your friends, Lord Hawke," said Babyface, Cho's identity at last dawning on him. "He used to be one of my students. Nice to see you, Cho. Have you been well since your relocation?"

No reply.

"Well. Be that way. You were saying, Lord Hawke?"

"Yes. I'm here at the request of the president of the United States and the Queen of England. They sent me here to your country in order to repatriate three Americans who are known to be . . . residents . . . here."

"Really. Who might they be?"

"Mrs. Katherine Chase. And her two young children, Milo and Sarah."

"Are you quite sure they're here? My bells are not ringing."

"Give us a few minutes," Cho said, the words dripping venom onto the floor. "It's going to sound like the Vatican on Easter morning around here."

The little demon smiled at that.

Hawke said, "What Colonel Cho means by that is, if I have to tear you apart one piece at a time to hear what I need to hear, I am more than willing to do so. We will not leave here without the three kidnapped Americans. And we are leaving here."

"My superiors in Pyongyang are aware of your act of war."

Hawke said, "Don't say that, it frightens the men."

Cho said, "Start with Mrs. Chase. Where is she being held? Now."

"How can I tell you? I do not know anyone by that name."

Cho looked at Hawke, a chilling look passing between the two men that looked almost prearranged.

Hawke nodded. Cho walked over to the bed and stuck the muzzle of his pistol violently into Babyface's right ear, twisting it so that blood began to flow down his neck.

"You and I are now going someplace quiet where we can talk. Get out of that bed. Now. Do you understand how serious I am?"

"Temper, temper, my boy, I'm coming."

He rolled off the side of the bed, gave a little leap, and somehow landed on his feet.

Hawke said, "Where are you taking him?"

"To his private study," Cho said. "It's just through that door there. This shouldn't take long, Commander."

"I wouldn't think."

Cho stuck the gun into the back of the man's neck and shoved him forward, into the adjoining room, closing the door behind him.

"Climb up on that table," Cho said when they were alone inside the small wood-paneled room.

"Why?" Babyface said.

"You'll find out. Do it."

The commandant, showing real fear for the first time, climbed shakily atop the heavy wooden table.

"Stand up. Turn around and face me. Hands behind your head."

"You don't have to do this, you know. I'll tell you everything."

"I know you will. But, you see, I want to do it this way. Where are you holding Mrs. Chase and the two American children? Milo and Sarah Chase. Tell me now. Lie to me, and it will be far, far worse for you. He meant what he said about taking you apart piece by piece."

Cho pulled a pair of needle-nose pliers from his web belt and held them up into the slanted light through the window.

"A little trick I learned from watching you, Babyface. Remember? Where are they? Twenty seconds . . ."

The commandant told him.

"Now another thing. Tell me. You said you remembered me, right?"

"You? Yes. Of course I remember you. Such a pretty boy."

"Good, I remember you, too. And what you did to me. So this one is for me," Cho said and fired a nine-millimeter round straight into man's right knee. The knee exploded in a misty red spray of gristle and pulverized bone. Babyface howled in agony and started to fall. Cho grabbed him, forcing him to remain upright.

"I said stand up there on the table! Hold on to the wall if you have to!"

"Please! Please do not do this! You—"

"Shut up. Do you remember my brother?"

"Y-yes, I remember him but—NO!"

"For my brother," Cho said, and fired a round that disintegrated the man's left shoulder. He howled in pain as his arm dangled loosely by his side.

"No more! Please!"

"Do you remember my sister?"

"Please! Stop! I beg you!"

"I'll say it again. Do you remember my unborn sister? We were all standing by the well . . ."

"Oh! I don't—"

Cho fired directly into his left knee. Babyface, delirious now, collapsed on the table, sobbing and shaking uncontrollably.

"And, finally, I ask you this," Cho said, jamming the muzzle of the automatic deep inside the wailing man's opened mouth, stifling his wailing cries.

"Wha—" he mumbled, wide-eyed with fear.

"Do you remember my mother?"

Cho emptied the magazine into the North Korean's head before he could even nod yes.

"I thought so," Cho said. "I do, too."

He slammed in a fresh mag, then leaned over and spat in the face of the corpse.

Cho opened the door and caught Hawke's eye.

"Yes?" Hawke said.

"He's dead."

"So I gathered. What did you get?"

"She's here. Mrs. Chase."

"Here?"

"In this house. He had her brought here for safe-keeping as soon as he heard the first explosions at the main gate. She's down in his basement safe room with guards. I made him call them and order her immediate, unconditional release to you. And to guarantee us safe passage out of the camp. He ordered a stand-down, effective immediately."

"Doesn't mean we won't have to shoot our way out."

"No, sir, it doesn't. Not a lot of military discipline here."

"Good work, Colonel. And the children?"

"Barracks Building 025. All the camp children live there, including the two Americans. The largest one, the one farthest north near the bend in the river. Second floor."

"Just a second," Hawke said, adjusting his lip microphone. "Alpha, this is Bravo, do you copy?"

"Copy, Bravo," Stoke said.

"The two Chase children are located in northernmost barracks, Building 025. Second floor."

"Building 025, second floor, roger that. On our way there now. How about the mother?"

"We've got her, Stoke. Still alive. I'll let you know. Go find those children. Over."

Stoke was first to find the two children. They were barely alive. Dressed in rags and huddled on rancid straw in the last room he searched. He was shocked at their appearance. In Hawke's Lightstorm dossier, he'd seen youthful photos of both Milo and Sara recovered by the FBI. Two young, vital, healthy, and happy American kids. Each had grown a couple of inches, but their hair was almost gone; they were just two little shadows in the process of fading away.

Mostly it was their hollow, sunken eyes. They looked like small adults on a starvation diet. No way to tell the boy from the girl except for size. Milo was the youngest and the smallest.

He bent down and said to the boy, "I'm here to take you home."

"Who are you?" the boy said, drawing back, terror in his eyes at the sight of the giant with the booming voice. Stoke saw that he was trembling.

"A friend of your father's."

"You don't know my father," he said, distrust clouding his features. He clearly didn't trust anyone.

"I know who he is."

"Our father is dead, anyway. What do you know?"

"Is this your sister?"

"I'm Sarah," the young girl said. "What do you want?"

"I want to take you home." Stoke smiled.

"They'll kill you if you try to leave. They shoot everybody," she said.

"I have a gun, too. I will kill anyone who tries to harm me. Or you."

"You speak American, don't you?" Milo said. "It's funny."

"I do. I'm an American soldier. I rescue people like you. All the time."

"When the guards come? If they hear us talking to you, they'll beat us."

"My soldiers have seized control of this place. No one will ever hurt you again here. You just have to trust me. Look at this." He handed Sarah a folded picture he carried in his wallet.

"Who is she?" Sarah said.

"That's my niece in Miami. Sofia. She's your age."

"She's pretty . . . so . . . we're really leaving? You're taking us home? I don't believe you."

"But I am. We'd better get going, too. There's a boat waiting for us out there."

"What about all the other little children here?" Milo said. "Can they come?"

"Our mission here is to get you guys and your mom out safely. But we're going to liberate as many children as we can. Lead them down to the river before we go. It's shallow enough now that they can swim or wade across and escape into China. We will shoot anyone who tries to harm those trying to escape. Do you understand?"

"Are we crossing the river, too?"

"No. You two are going home with your mother. On an American submarine."

"Our mother?" Milo said.

"They told us our mother was dead," Sarah said. "That's why we never see her."

"She's not. I just spoke to someone who's with her right now."

"I don't believe you."

"You will. Wait and see."

"What's your name?" Milo asked.

"My name is Stokely Jones Jr., son, but you can just call me Stoke, okay?"

"Okay, Stoke. Nice to meet you and . . . MOM! Mom, you're okay! You're alive!"

Just as the boy stuck out his hand, Alex Hawke and Colonel Cho walked into the room. They had their arms around the children's mother, supporting her, as she was too weak to walk. When she saw them she sagged and tears filled her eyes.

"My darlings . . . I thought you were . . ." she managed to say before she staggered and broke down completely.

"Mom! Mom!" both children cried and ran to her.

She dropped to one knee and embraced them both, hot tears running down both cheeks as she pulled them as close to her as she could, not daring to believe this moment was really happening.

Chapter 64

At Sea, Aboard USS Florida

Alex Hawke made his way forward along a cramped companionway toward the sub's sick bay, ducking his head to miss the bulkhead every time he entered a new watertight compartment. USS *Florida*'s sick bay was located just aft of the forward torpedo tubes. He was greeted with a smile and a cheery "Morning, sir!" by all the young sailors who passed headed aft, everyone on the boat feeling good about the hostage rescue mission just completed.

And it was a good feeling.

In the six hours since they'd been back aboard, sailing in enemy waters, the three Americans they'd rescued had been under intensive care. Hawke's team had four casualties. Despite his shoulder wound, Colonel Cho was now leading legions of freed death camp captives on a march to safety across the Yalu River and into China. Many of the older prisoners would not survive—but most if not all of the children would.

Three other badly wounded men, including comms specialist Elvis Peete, had been in surgery and were now resting comfortably. At Hawke's behest, the U.S. secretary of the navy had included in the ship's roster a physician trained in the care of rescue victims suffering severe deprivation and major trauma. So, even at sea, the Chase family was getting the best care possible.

Hawke had been reading a new CIA dossier on Chase in his bunk when the ship's telephone on the bulkhead rang. He picked it up.

"Hawke," he said.

"Commander. It's ship's medical officer, sir. Mrs. Chase would like a word with you. She's drifting in and out of the sedative I've given her, so I'd come as quickly as you can."

"How is she?"

"I'd say you didn't get her out of there a minute too soon, sir. She had just about exhausted her resources, physically and emotionally. Malnourished, dehydrated. Multiple bone injuries. Systems in the process of shutting down."

"She'll recover?"

"Oh, yes. A lot of heart, that woman. Already survived far worse than most endure in a lifetime."

"Please tell her I'm on my way."

"Will do," he said and hung up.

A medical orderly opened the patient's door, and Hawke ducked his head, stepping inside.

"Mrs. Chase?"

"Yes . . ."

"I'm Alex Hawke. I'm so very glad to see you awake. Are you feeling any better?"

"Oh. You're the one who . . ."

"Yes."

"How are my children?"

"Being very well looked after. Weak and hungry, of course, but they're going to be fine. I looked in on them an hour ago. Milo says he would very much like some ice cream, please, and Sarah wants pancakes, but the doctors want to go slowly and—"

"I . . . I really don't know how to thank . . . I never thought we would be . . . that the children and I would . . . ever see one another . . ."

The tears came, hot tears of relief, tears of grief for their years of suffering . . . tears of remorse for all the lost time. And perhaps a few tears of joy that, somehow, she and her children had hung on just long enough to survive.

"Can I see them?"

"Of course you can. As soon as the doctor—"

"Please . . . uh . . . sorry, what is your name?"

"Alex."

"Please, Alex. Sit down a minute?"

"Delighted," Hawke said, pulling a chair up to her bedside.

Her voice was tired and strained, but she clearly had something she wanted him to know.

"There's one more of us, you know. My whole family was taken that night."

"Yes."

"My husband. Bill Chase."

"I know."

"Are you here to . . . to find him, too?"

"We are. My comrades and I are here as part of a joint U.S./U.K. operation to rescue your entire family. Tell me, Mrs. Chase, do you have any idea at all where your husband might be?"

"None. I've written letters over the years. All censored, probably never sent. I haven't seen or heard from him since the night we were taken . . . my birthday, you know. I don't even know if he's still alive. My guess is not."

"He's alive, ma'am."

"Oh! Are you . . . certain?" Her eyes brimming, she reached out her hand to him. He took it.

"I am. I saw a picture of him taken just last week. He was photographed leaving a government building in Shanghai. The Ministry of State Security. The Chinese Secret Police."

"Was he alone?"

"No, Mrs. Chase. He was being manhandled by two secret police thugs. Hustled into a waiting car. CIA operatives followed but lost him in traffic. Both CIA and U.K. intelligence officers, like myself, are working day and night to locate your husband. So that my team can go in and get him out. It's only a matter of time."

She was silent for so long, Hawke thought perhaps she fallen prey to the sedative.

"Alex," she said sleepily.

"Yes?"

"I have something. It may be nothing. It was given to me by a Chinese woman in the camp. She had been arrested spying on the North Koreans for the Chinese Secret Police. On the morning of her hanging, we were all lined up to witness as always. We parted to let her through and she saw me, caught my eye, and nodded. It was odd. Almost as if she recognized me. As she pressed past me, she slipped something into my hand.

The guards never saw it. I managed to hold on to it all these years, hoping it was worth something, a talisman, something to believe in, you know?"

"Yes, I do."

"It's in this little pouch around my neck. Could you remove it?"

"Of course."

She raised her head and Hawke gently lifted the thin braided necklace. The pouch was small and made of leather, faded and cracked.

"Open it," she said.

He tugged at the drawstring, and something fluttered out onto the bedcovers.

A tiny scrap of paper, folded many times, about the size of a postage stamp.

"What is it?"

"I don't know, really. It's a single handwritten word. I don't even know how to say it. It's a word I've never seen before . . . but . . . I swear to you that it's written in my husband's handwriting. . . . Read it out loud. I want to hear how you say the word. It's been . . . my . . . private incantation all these years. My last shred of a connection with what my life had been."

"Xinbu," Hawke said.

"The 'X' is pronounced like a 'Z'?"

"Yes. It's Chinese."

"What does it mean, Alex?"

"I've no idea. But I do promise you this, Mrs. Chase. I will find out and tell you before the sun goes down. Please rest now. I'm going to visit my men who were hurt at the camp. Then I'll check on the children again. See how they're . . ."

She was asleep.

One hour later, Hawke was back at Mrs. Chase's bedside. In his hand, a printout of a flashpoint message just arrived from his old colleague Brickhouse Kelly, director at the CIA. Alex pulled up the same chair and sat beside her.

"It's a very good, good thing that you believed in your talisman all these years, Mrs. Chase."

"I believed in hope. Tell me what the word means, please, Alex."

"Xinbu is a semitropical island. It's located in a remote corner of the South China Sea. It's primarily a resort haven for the Communist Party and military elites, but here's the hopeful part. It's also home to a major Chinese army weapons design facility."

"I see."

"Here's why I'm so hopeful. In recent years, the Chinese have been leapfrogging the West in terms of their military technological advances. The world is at a frightening place right now, Mrs. Chase, far more dangerous than the one you left behind."

"And you think Bill has something to do with that?"

"He's the reason for it. He's been sending us coded messages. Using parts of weapons he's designed, in the hopes that we'd find them. We did."

"Do you think he's a traitor?"

"No. I think he's been placed under enormous duress. I think the Chinese have used you and Milo and Sarah as a sword to bend him to their will. He did what he did only because he put you first."

"When his torturers learn what happened at Camp 25, about our rescue and all the freed prisoners, they'll kill him."

"No. He's far too valuable. And his work is not finished. But they have a problem they're not yet aware of."

"What is it?"

"Me."

"What do you even mean?"

"They think he's safe from me. And he's not."

"What are you going to do?"

"I can't really give you that kind of information. But I can tell you this. Right before I came to the sick bay I told the captain of this sub to change his course. We are now sailing for Xiachuan Island. We have air transport waiting on an abandoned airstrip there. It's a short flight over water to Xinbu."

"May I ask, what is it that you do, Alex?"

"Fairly straightforward, Mrs. Chase. I go after bad people. And I go after good people. I hurt the former and help the latter. Like you and the children."

"Thank you."

"And, with any luck at all, your husband."

Chapter 65

There was a rap at the door.

Hawke opened it and a fresh-faced young orderly saluted him. "Sorry to disturb you, sir. The captain requires your presence in the wardroom. I'm instructed to tell you that it is urgent."

"Tell him I'll be right there."

There were two sentries posted outside the wardroom. *This is serious,* Hawke thought as he was ushered inside. His suspicions were confirmed when he saw all the ranking officers seated around the large green baize table. And the president of the United States speaking on a large monitor, obviously a real-time feed. Hawke swiftly and silently took a seat and listened to what the very grave American president had to say:

"Captain Malpass, I cannot possibly overstate the urgency of this matter. Iwo Jima is gone. Disappeared. General Moon says Okinawa is next. God knows what's after that. Pearl Harbor? Christ, Los Angeles? They are launching those goddamn Centurion ICBMs from the seabed. So it's obvious there is at least one more of those unmanned submersibles out there in the Pacific. Hell, if not more than one."

The sub's skipper said, "Mr. President, Commander Hawke has just joined us here in the wardroom. I won't ask you to repeat everything, but if you could briefly reiterate General Moon's demands?"

Hawke was jolted upright.

General Moon? A name from his bloody past with a lot of unhappy memories attached.

The president said, "Certainly. At 0300 hours this morning I was informed that there had been a military coup in China. President Xi Jinping and his cabinet have been arrested. General Sun-Yat Moon, former head of Ministry for State Security, and now with the full support of the entire military establishment, is running the show. He immediately issued an ultimatum. We have twenty-four hours to agree to comply or he launches a third Centurion at God knows where on the U.S. mainland. All U.S. and allied forces must withdraw from South Korea, Japan, and Taiwan within seventy-two hours. The *Theodore Roosevelt* carrier battle group withdraws from Okinawa and the Pacific region within six days; likewise, the Seventh Fleet and the Fifth Fleet with two marine divisions en route to the DMZ in South Korea. And the list goes on for another two pages. Let me stop a moment. Any questions so far, Commander Hawke?"

"Thank you, Mr. President, I do have one. The Chinese Centurion Project clearly lies at the very heart of this crisis. Defuse that and you defuse Moon. My colleagues at MI6 believe that the Centurion USV was designed for China by Dr. Chase. Is that your belief?"

"Absolutely. Got his name all over it."

"I read in one of the classified White House dossiers about a built-in fail-safe system on board the USV. A way to destroy the vessel should it ever be in extremis. Is that accurate?"

"Yes, it is. There were forty missile silos aboard the *Gaius Augustus*. The forwardmost silo to port had a missile in the tube but no hatch cover for launch purposes. A young naval officer who'd been aboard her sat right here in my office and told me he was convinced it was a fail-safe self-destructive device to be used in cases of submarine malfunction or should the vessel fall into enemy hands. And I believe him."

"As you may know, Mr. President, I am currently en route to Xinbu Island to attempt the hostage rescue of Dr. Chase and—"

"Sorry, did you say Xinbu Island, Commander?"

"Yes, sir, I did."

"Thank God. CIA has just identified that island as General Moon's headquarters. A top-secret Chinese military installation. It's where he's doing TV statements and interviews and issuing all these goddamn ultimatums from. Also, we just learned, it's where Langley believes he's holding Chase. We're looking at Xinbu in real time here in the situation room right now, via satellite."

"I'll wave to you when I get there, Mr. President."

Rosow smiled.

"How in hell did you know about Xinbu Island before I did?"

"Mrs. Chase, sir. Luckily for us she's now aboard this submarine with her two children."

"Lucky doesn't begin to cover it. Listen, Commander Hawke, I'll go to war with China if I have to, but there will be countless millions of casualties and a world spun out of control. So timing is critical to say the least. Get Bill Chase the hell out of there and find out how the Centurion fail-safe works. He designed those submarines, so he damn well knows how to destroy them. With them off the board, Moon has zero leverage in the Pacific."

"Yes, sir. I understand."

"It's literally the only way out of this death spiral, Commander Hawke. Five minutes ago, I didn't think we had a way out."

"I understand completely, sir. Get him out and get the codes. Chase and I will make every effort to destroy the Centurions together. How long have I got?"

"Until noon tomorrow, Greenwich Mean Time. At which point I have to pick up the phone and call General Moon. I will have two choices: agree to dismantle America's military might in the Pacific in order to avoid global nuclear holocaust, or tell him to go fuck himself. I prefer the latter. This guy is telling the world that the United States is in decline and it's only a matter of time until our demise. We need to send this crazy bastard an unmistakable signal to back the fuck off, pardon my French."

"I suppose in that case you'd better wish me luck, Mr. President."

"Son, listen to me very carefully. Because this, and I mean right this minute, is a moment in time that will define history for the next two or three decades, perhaps centuries. Believe me when I tell you, our whole nation wishes you and your men Godspeed and good luck, Commander Hawke."

Chapter 66

Xiachuan Island Airstrip

Hawke got his first real glimpse of *Dumbo* at dawn.

He shook his head in wonder. The thing looked enormous on the tiny World War II airstrip. The matte-black camo paint of the after-fuselage and tailplanes was riddled with bullet and cannon shells, an aileron appeared to be shredded, the port outer engine was saturated in oil, and the cockpit Perspex was shattered and starred in a dozen places.

A week or so ago, he'd invited Froggy to join him for a couple of beers at the Sunset Beach Bar on Islamorada. Froggy would play an important role in the success of this mission and he liked to get a sense of his key guys.

He'd asked him, "What's the most important lesson you've learned about flying combat in all these years, Froggy?"

"Always make the number of safe landings equal the number of takeoffs," the little French battle tank had responded with his big grin.

He smiled and climbed aboard the behemoth, the last man to do so.

"Everybody all strapped in?" the pilot, Froggy, said over the intercom.

"Aye-aye, Captain!" a couple of hard-asses in the rear responded. The hulking beast began to roll, slowly picking up speed. The intercom crackled again, the captain speaking.

"Folks, I know you have a choice in air carriers here on Xiachuan, and so, on behalf of myself and the entire crew, I'd like to thank you all for choosing Air Dumbo for your transportation needs today."

It was a joke, a very old Thunder and Lightning joke, but it still made them all laugh.

"Good morning, ladies!" Froggy shouted.

"Good morning, sir!" everyone aboard shouted in unison. Just before the big black C-130 Hercules roared off down the crumbling, weed-infested runway, Froggy added, "Now drop your cocks and grab your socks and get ready for takeoff!"

The nose lifted, the big aircraft rotated. The thunder of the mighty turboprop engines was deafening as they clawed the air for altitude.

In the cockpit, Froggy was just getting warmed up. "Since our route of flight today will be taking us over water, federal regulations require me to inform you that, in the unlikely event of a water landing . . . the cheeks of your ass will act as a flotation device."

More hilarity in the back of the bus.

Laughter was a rarity when it came to nut-cutting time in a high-risk mission like this one. But it was a damn fine way to start one, Hawke thought. Fitz McCoy was the one responsible for morale in this outfit, and he and Froggy did a hell of a job. Hawke looked at his watch and then at Stokely Jones. He smiled. Stoke was in his pregame warm-up mode, head back, eyes closed, the big bright red pair of Beats headphones Fancha had given him clamped on his head; he was more than likely listening to Marvin Gaye or Barry White.

Most of the men were seated in rows of canvas sling chairs that lined the cavernous fuselage interior. Some were spread out on great greasy pallets scattered about the steel floor, playing cards or reading dog-eared paperbacks by Cussler or Flynn or W.E.B. Griffin.

In the dim light of the cavelike C-130, the troops were mostly alone with their thoughts. The Big Dance, they were all thinking, because this one really was for all the marbles.

Just for fun Hawke turned to Harry Brock, who was sitting right next to him. Man with the thousand-yard stare, the one the Yank GIs had invented in what they called "The Shit," also known as Vietnam. Brock was endlessly checking and rechecking his weapons, gear, and ammo.

"What are you thinking about, Harry?" Hawke asked a surprised Brock.

"Corvettes?"

Hawke had to laugh. Perfect.

"Really? Me, too," Hawke said.

"Really?" Brock said, his face lighting up.

"No. Not really, Harry," Hawke said. "Is that what you were really thinking about?"

"No, sir."

"So? What?"

"I dunno. Look. I know you think I'm a fuckup. Hell, I guess I am. But what I was really thinking was that . . . in this world, you don't get to live free for free . . . You don't get that without working for it. Not just the things we do, insertions like this, but just find a way to work for it somehow, do something to keep the lantern lit. Know what I mean, sir? I mean, we've all got to earn it every single day. Right?"

"Right."

Hawke looked at him a long time. This was not the Harry Brock he thought he knew so well.

"And . . . the way I figure, Commander, all this shit we're in, guys like you and me? The truly deep shit, like this insertion, I mean. For me? It's like this shit was always out there waiting for me. And I suppose I was always waiting for it. Like a, I dunno, a hill to climb every day, I guess. Other side? Like Syria? The North Koreans? They got no rules, but—somehow—we've managed to hold on to them. That make any sense, sir?"

"Yeah. It does, Harry. Makes a hell of a lot of sense. Now, you settle down. Get your head on straight. You hear me?"

"Getting it straight, sir."

Their insertion into China Naval Base Xinbu had been methodically planned aboard the sub while en route to the air base at Xiachuan Island. They'd looked at CIA-generated thermals and sat images of the installation. They'd studied topography, the defenses, the guard changes, until they could no longer see straight. How the hell to get in and how the hell to get out. Ultimately, it had been decided that the best way in was airborne. A HALO night jump, high-altitude, low-open.

HALO minimizes the time men spend floating down in their parachutes, which is when they are most at risk from enemy observation and fire. HALO jumps are done from about thirty thousand feet. Nobody hears the aircraft approach at that altitude, nobody sees the jumpers coming. At such a high altitude, it is necessary to use minibottles of oxygen and a mask to remain conscious. Altimeters on the parachutists' wrists—every move is precision timed.

Fifteen miles before the jumpers reach the target, out they go. Nobody sees them that high up is the idea. They use flat chutes as parasails to steer through their descent. The team free-falls for as long as possible, straight down through the radar detection zone, and then the men pop the chutes and begin long, controlled glides downrange into the LZ.

Using the newly acquired White House satellite images of the Chinese military installation's location on Xinbu, they had identified a pretty good landing zone. The designated LZ would be a high mountain meadow located two miles from the base perimeter fencing.

On the seaward side of the base, Hawke had seen images of a huge complex of hardened concrete bunkers with no visible opening to the sea. This, he knew, was so that Centurion submarines could come and go unseen by sats or surface eyes. He'd also gotten flash traffic from his U.S. Navy contact inside the White House that a wolf pack of six Yong class subs had left Xinbu sub base at 2200 hours. They were steaming straight for the USS carrier *Theodore Roosevelt*.

According to his inside guy, the president had told the *TR*'s fabled skipper, Rabbit Christiansen, "You better get ready, Rabbit, because that Chinese wolf pack is all over your ass. They will be picking you up on their screens by 0500. They mean business, son . . . this is WAR!" Half an hour later, his navy guy had messaged him again.

It was official.

The Chinese subs had cornered the besieged carrier battle group. The United States of America had gone to DEFCON 1. This state of maximum readiness carries the exercise term "Cocked Pistol," meaning nuclear war is imminent. During the September 11 attacks, the United States reached DEFCON 3, standing by for an increase to DEFCON 2, the highest level ever used, which never came.

At DEFCON 1, you were teetering on the brink, one foot in the abyss.

Like the big engines under her wings, hours and hours aboard *Dumbo* droned on. Two hours had passed, then three. Hawke could feel the men's emotions spiking as the drop zone rapidly approached.

In what seemed like no time at all, the jump/caution red light illuminated, and the jumpmaster was pointing at Hawke.

"Saddle up, Commander," the rangy kid said. "Skipper's going to dip down to thirty thousand feet now, reduce our airspeed, and then we go."

"Five minutes out," Froggy's excited voice boomed over the intercom. "Conditions at the LZ, good visibility, no SAM installations visible, no combatants, all clear. I'm turning over control to my copilot now, boys, getting my chute on. I'll see you on the ground!"

Brock touched Hawke's forearm and said, "Look, if this doesn't go well for me? My luck runs out tonight? In the marines, all I was interested in was mission success. Getting it done and getting my guys home safe. Sir. That's all."

"Just do your job, Harry, you'll stay lucky," Hawke said. "Duty. That's all I ever ask."

"Just like the rodeo cowboys say, ride it to the buzzer."

Hawke stood up, almost invisible in his black camo jumpsuit plated with Kevlar body armor. He checked his weapons for the last time. HK 9mm submachine gun. A Sig Sauer 9mm sidearm. Both with suppressors. Grenades, stun and smoke, plus Willy Petes, the white phosphorus grenades hung like grape clusters from his web belt. Terrifying to an enemy and incredibly lethal. He was carrying a lot of gear, but nowhere near the weight of the men who'd be going out with the M-60 heavy machine guns.

Weight was a big problem in the thin air of a high-altitude jump. Some men jumped carrying a hundred pounds of equipment. He didn't envy them.

"Two minutes!"

The huge ramp at the rear began to grind down and soon *Dumbo*'s interior was filled with an icy roaring wind.

"Ramp open and locked," the jumpmaster said, and Hawke walked out onto the sloping ramp, the cold wind tearing at him.

Time to go.

Ride it to the buzzer, cowboys.

Chapter 67

Xinbu Island, China

The jump alarm bell signaled one minute to drop.

Hawke would be first out. He used the time to turn the impending scenario over in his mind: fitting all the individual jigsaw pieces of the strategic plan together as quickly as he could until they popped up as a cohesive story. Beginning, middle, and end. He couldn't vouch for a happy ending, but he could always vouch for an end.

Of course, no war plan ever goes like it's supposed to. But he'd gotten into this last-minute prep habit during his Royal Navy flying days and it had served him well. And just as the last puzzle piece popped into place—

The jump light flashed from crimson to green.

Hawke glanced at Stoke, gave him a big thumbs-up, and strode all the way out onto the lowered ramp.

"Mind your head, boss!" Stokely shouted over the roaring wind. Hawke instinctively looked up. There was a good twenty feet of clearance above him.

"Go!" the jumpmaster shouted.

Hawke stepped out into thin air.

The freezing slipstream body-slammed him like a wall of ice.

He sucked it up and relaxed into his long free fall, watching the earth spinning crazily up toward him, trying to memorize the island's geographic details as they flashed by. Then, in what seemed like no more than a split second later, his flat chute deployed automatically and beautifully, an event always cause for brief but profound celebration.

He'd occasionally had a chute deploy ugly, and it was always most unpleasant.

He began a series of controlled and ever-tightening spirals to slow his speed for the rest of the way down. He was on a glide path toward the two-hundred-square-yard patch of meadow, the landing zone known forevermore as LZ Liberator. Stoke had code-named it aboard the sub.

Descending through three thousand, Hawke could now make out the purple-black silhouette of the mountainous basin where the target meadow was. The bowl of night was black, filled with cold, pinprick stars and drifting strands of cloud. Off to his left, a large white marble structure he recognized. The Te-Wu Academy for assassins. Then, to his left, he saw the huge white bunkers of the Centurion submarine complex and, finally, a large ultramodern four-story building he knew to be the newly constructed Weapons Design Center, or WDC.

Perhaps Bill Chase was in there at his drawing board right now. Burning the midnight oil in the service of a madman. CIA had told him that if Dr. Chase really was in residence on Xinbu Island, there was a very high probability that he could be found working and living in that building. The WDC, on Hawke's map, was a quarter of a mile from the intended insertion point, the spot where they would breach the perimeter.

It was certainly possible. At the very least it was a good place to start. The ground came up fast, but Hawke tucked his chin in, bent his knees, manipulated his risers, and managed to stay on his feet.

He gathered his chute. He heard canopies fluttering high above and looked up to see a host of falling angels, the brave men who would march beside him into battle, each one of them prepared to make the ultimate sacrifice on this historic do-or-die night.

Hawke adjusted his helmet headset. "First Knight, this is Lone Eagle, copy?"

"Roger that, Lone Eagle, copy." It was Stoke. The newly anointed "First Knight." Stoke now informed strangers that he was the first member of his distinguished Harlem family to attend college—and the first to be knighted by the Queen.

Hawke said, "Boots on the ground, First Knight. LZ Liberator all clear."

"LZ clear, roger that. I have you in visual contact, boss. Better duck, here comes the cavalry, over."

He and Stoke would lead the two eight-man squads, code-named Lone Eagle and First Knight. Usually, in HR ops like this one, they would divide and conquer. Tonight was different. There was no way of anticipating the degree or concentration of resistance they would encounter.

Hawke, who trusted his instincts in these situations, had early on told Fitz and Chief Rainwater he believed they stood a better chance of survival if they stayed together as a cohesive unit. In the face of unknowable opposition, he wanted to present the enemy with a unified force, one with enormous combined firepower.

Two minutes later, Stoke was standing beside him, cutting away the remains of his chute.

"Boss, you know what they say about the best-laid plans?"

Hawke looked over at him. This wasn't going to be good news.

"Yeah?"

"Froggy's comms guy, Elvis Peete, he just got a radio flash from CIA Langley. Seems a Chinese army military medium-range transport, an IL-76MD, just lifted off from Ching Li air base on the mainland. She'd boarded heavy artillery and at least a hundred spec-ops paratroops, the best they got, badass storm troopers. CIA is certain the destination is Xinbu Island. Flown in specifically to protect this new leader, General Moon, and his fleet of Centurions. En route now."

"Christ. Flying time from mainland to Xinbu?"

"Langley operations estimate the IL-76 will arrive here over target at 0400 hours. Enemy boots on the ground at 0430. Our guys up against a hundred heavily armed storm troops? Goatfuck, boss, really bad odds."

Stoke looked at his wristwatch.

"We got less than sixty minutes before they show up."

"Radio the sub. Get the skipper. Tell him to advance the offshore exfil up one half hour to 0415. Say I want those two SEAL delivery subs off the beach at 0400. Got it? Not a second later."

"Copy."

Stoke made the call, listened, and looked at Hawke. "Skipper says he'll make it happen."

Hawke had other things on his mind already.

He said, "Look down there. What do you see?"

He indicated the vast enemy compound spread out below them.

"Looks quiet," Stoke said, his Zeiss binocs sweeping from right to left while they waited for the rest. From this elevated vantage point he could see the entirety of the installation below.

No reply. The man was thinking. Finally, he said, "They have to know we're coming, Stoke. That's why Moon called for the paratroops. But if they're watching for us on their radar, because of the HALO jump, what they don't know is that we're already here. Right?"

"Or . . ."

"What?" Hawke said, silently counting off his men as their boots hit the ground.

"Or, somehow, they do know, boss. Whole thing's a trap. They want us trapped inside their perimeter when all those mainland airborne troops arrive. That's what Chief Rainwater thinks. And . . . oh never mind. Just idle bullshit, boss."

"What does he think, Stoke? Tell me."

"Well, I don't want to say anything. But."

"But what?"

"The chief is conjuring up the Chinese updated version of Custer's last stand at Little Big Horn."

"Seriously?" Hawke said.

Hawke cocked his head and looked at him through narrowed eyes. Stoke knew what was next. Hawke's really bad Gary Cooper imitation.

"I ain't no Custer," Hawke said, dead serious.

Stoke laughed. "Hell no, suh, no, you ain't!"

"How's Brock?" Hawke said. "Seemed spooked right before the jump."

"Told me out on the ramp something about his pucker factor. Said it was spiking a little bit, that's all."

"Pucker factor? What the hell is—?""

"Don't even ask, boss, trust me."

"I do. Assemble the troops, let's move out. Now."

Chapter 68

Ten minutes later, Hawke's men were rapidly moving down the rocky shale mountainside in single file. The footing was dicey, a lot of slipping and sliding, but they were moving double time because of the newly adjusted time parameters.

Hawke had started the mental countdown clock in his head. They now had less than fifty minutes to fight their way inside the perimeter and locate the target building. Then they had to locate Chase. If the hostage was still alive, extract him. Get the auto-destruct codes and fight their way to the heavily protected Centurion sub base and wreak such havoc as they were capable of with Chase's help.

Finally, fight their way to the end of the rocky point

where the SDVs would be waiting offshore. And escape to the sub before the overwhelming force of crack paratroops had a chance to stop them.

Nearing the bottom, they entered the good protective cover at the foot of the mountain.

They'd identified the area in the sat photos, large clusters of boulders the size of automobiles with a clear view across the strip of open land to the camp's stockade fence line beyond. Stoke handed Hawke his high-powered Zeiss binoculars.

A hundred yards inside the fence was a tall steel watchtower, fifty feet high and four sided at the top with a large high-powered searchlight on each corner of the rooftop. Tripod-mounted heavy machine guns were placed on all four sides.

From the aerial views, the tower had looked like some kind of shed on the ground, because all you could see was the roof. Now it was a serious obstacle that must be dealt with. Hawke silently signaled for Fitz to move up. Fitz and his trusty RPG, a rocket-propelled grenade launcher.

"Can you take that tower out from this distance?" Hawke asked him.

"Is Dublin a city in Ireland?" Fitz replied.

"On my signal," Hawke said. "Wait for it."

Concertina wire topped the eight-foot-high fence.

Inside that fence, running the length of it, Hawke knew, was a two-lane asphalt track that encircled the entire compound. Studying the sat feed on board USS *Florida,* he and Stoke had spent hours timing the perimeter guards' rotation schedule, over and over, until they knew they could count on it. They'd been watching a real-time feed from one of the U.S. military satellites now whirling by above them.

The rotation worked like this.

Two armored troop carriers, each with twin tripod-mounted machine guns in the rear, and carrying eight heavily armed guards, traveled around the perimeter in opposite directions. Every four hours, the two squads were relieved, new men took their places, and the cycle started all over again. The trucks traveled at exactly twenty miles per hour.

It took nearly half an hour to complete the twisting circuit, which looped out around the sub base located on a thrusting rocky point to the seaward side of the military base.

Stoke was on recon, watching the patrol vehicles now patrolling the six-mile-long circuit through high-powered Zeiss glasses.

"On my mark . . ." he said.

The armored vehicles passed each other wordlessly, the officers saluting each other. A moment later, both trucks had disappeared around a curve. Stoke was monitoring the sweep second hand on his Rolex. He knew precisely long it would take for the two vehicles to pass each other on the opposite side of Xinbu Base.

At that precise moment, when the guard trucks were as far from the invaders' insertion point as possible . . .

The minutes stretched out.

"Mark!" Stoke said, and Hawke tapped Fitz on the top of his helmet.

With a huge *WHOOSH,* the RPG fired. It left a trail of dense white smoke as it streaked toward the target.

Fitz never missed.

Where the tower had been, a blinding ball of yellow, orange, and red. A huge fireball created by the explosion fifty feet in the air. The sound reverberated off the mountainside and lit up the ground around it. Then came a rolling blast wave even Hawke could feel on his face.

"Go, go, go!" he shouted.

Rainwater had already packed C-4 explosives on a twelve-foot-wide section of stockade fence. He pulled out his iPhone and triggered the second blast in as many minutes.

———

Now the eighteen-man hostage rescue team began to race across open ground to the insertion point in the fence. It had not been chosen randomly. It was at the farthest point from any physical structure within the perimeter.

It was also the farthest point from the guard barracks and the hulking marble monstrosity that was the Te-Wu Academy for young assassins. Not to mention home to its headmaster and new leader of the People's Republic of China. Hawke's old enemy. A man whose daughter had once tried to assassinate him. A man who had recently ordered not only Hawke's own death, but that of his beloved son. A man responsible for the death of a lovely young woman beloved by his son: Sabrina Churchill.

General Sun-Yat Moon.

Chapter 69

The auditorium went quiet as the general crossed the stage and made his way to the podium. The walls of the academy's Great Hall were hung with battle flags and portraits of China's great military heroes. A huge monitor behind General Moon carried a heroic image of the general's face with the scrolling words *CHINA SHALL RULE!* superimposed over it in countless languages.

Moon was impeccably dressed in his customary snow white uniform. He wore mirror-polished knee-high riding boots. Every ribbon, cross, and battle decoration he owned was pinned to the snowy white breast of his brass-buttoned jacket.

Moon gazed out at his flock. The eager faces of the young assassins, the proud faces of their teachers, instructors, and trainers. He smiled. This was a far cry from his own graduate ceremony at Oxford: all the raucous youth, the dour faces of the dons, the ancient architecture, the palpable weight of British history, the old-world feel of it all.

He smiled at his private thought: that was the old world.

This is the new world.

This is my new world.

"Good evening, ladies and gentlemen," the general said, leaning into the microphone in his breathy, soft-spoken way.

"Or should I say, good morning. I confess I am filled with mixed emotions. I have served Te-Wu Academy as headmaster for nearly twenty years. I arrived on this island with only one thing. A vision. A vision to create the world's very first school for what I shall call 'the dark arts' of interrogation and political elimination.

"I recruited the best teachers on the planet, men and women who had served our nation with distinction around the world. And then I began recruiting the first class. Graduates of that class still serve our nation, bringing honor and glory upon us as well as themselves . . . I mentioned mixed emotions. Let me explain, please.

"This is probably the very last time I will address a graduating class . . . No, no, please be quiet and let me continue . . . Address this class and also all the faculty and instructors here with us tonight. Because of my new government and party responsibilities, sadly, I will be leaving you. Leaving my beloved academy to fill a slightly more exalted post in Beijing."

They laughed, and he paused for a moment to let the laughter die down.

"I will assume the official mantle of the presidency one week from today. And so I have decided that this class, your class, will be graduating from the Te-Wu not in June, as is traditional, but a bit early this year. As a matter of fact, it will be tonight. This very night will be your final examination, as it were. I have assembled all fifty of you here for a very special graduation assignment.

"And so I ask you. And I want to hear your answer. Are you, each of you, ready tonight to meet your final challenge? Shall you serve?"

"We shall serve!" the audience roared in unison, getting to their feet, repeatedly thrusting their right fists into the air and stamping their feet. "And China shall rule!"

"Shall you serve?" he exhorted them.

"We shall serve!" they replied.

"So China shall rule?"

"China shall rule!" they shouted to the rafters, stomping their heavy boots even harder.

Moon smiled and spread his arms wide, as if offering a papal benediction. As they continued to chant, the fluttering image of the Chinese flag on the massive monitor behind the general faded away.

"I want you to take a very close look at this man."

Moon used the remote to bring up a new image. It was an old color portrait of a handsome English naval officer in dress uniform. Jet-black hair, piercing blue eyes, strong jaw. Boyish good looks, late twenties. Some of the females in the class sighed audibly, as if the officer were some kind of British royalty or rock star.

"His name is Alexander Hawke. Remember that face. British, former Royal Navy officer, now a counterterrorist operative with British Intelligence, MI6. This is the face of the enemy. This is the face of the man who dishonored my daughter Jet. The man who had her sister killed aboard my own houseboat in Hong Kong many years ago."

The audience was too shocked at this personal revelation to react.

Moon leaned forward and snarled into the microphone.

"But tonight I will exact my revenge. Or rather, you will exact it for me."

Shouts and cheers erupted then that filled the entire Great Hall.

"Shall you serve?" Moon cried out.

"We shall serve! We will serve! We will serve!"

He waited for them to quiet down and then he said, "Hawke is here. On this our island. Now."

The audience expelled a collective gasp.

"Hawke, along with a group of battle-hardened commandos, has breached our perimeter. Our academy, our military installations, our very home is under attack. Your assignment is obvious. The death of all invaders. If you are successful, you will all graduate with honors and the rank of full colonel in the Te-Wu. On this very stage. Tonight. But. If you should fail . . . it shall be deemed an act of treason. You will all hang. At dawn."

Numb, shocked silence.

"As that electrifying American Benjamin Franklin so eloquently put it, 'You must all hang together, or assuredly you shall hang separately.'"

Moon smiled the smile of a beneficent uncle, pressed his hands together as if in prayer, and continued smoothly.

"On your seats tonight, you found a sealed envelope. Do not open your envelopes until you have left the auditorium. Inside each envelope is a picture of one additional target. Do not be surprised if you recognize the face. It is the face of one of your instructors or perhaps one of your classmates upon whom I look with distrust and disfavor."

At that moment, one of the elderly instructors, his face distorted with fear and panic, leaped from his seat and raced up the aisle toward the doors at the rear.

"Let him go," Moon said, chuckling softly. "He won't get far. Now, one final word. In exactly one hour, some of my fiercest ground commandos will parachute into this compound to defend me and this military installation. So you have until the first army boot hits the ground to complete your final exam. Good luck. It has been my profound pleasure to lead you all these years. Shall you serve?"

"We shall serve!" they cried.

"Shall China rule?"

"China shall rule!"

General Moon bowed deeply from the waist and then stood tall. He raised his right fist in triumph and his words rang out and filled the hall: "Then bring me the head of Alexander Hawke!"

Chapter 70

Their footsteps crunched in companionable unison over the hard-packed sand. They were kitted out in the latest ceramic exoskeleton combat suits; they were black, hot, and heavy, but for a close-quarters interior firefight like Hawke anticipated, they offered the best protection available on the planet.

The eighteen men had agreed to a rendezvous at a small building in the shadows of the Weapons Design Center. Fitz, on a prelim recon, had found the Annex, separate but connected to the main building where they believed they would find Dr. Chase. At 0400 hours, the building showed not a single light, the sharp square angles a black silhouette against the starry sky.

The Annex was unlit and unlocked and would offer them brief cover while Hawke and Stokely gave the troops a final brief before they stormed the WDC.

"Huddle up, guys," Stoke said into his headset, holding up a cell phone. "On me."

They all gathered around him. He raised the iPhone so they could all see the screen.

"What is it, Stoke?" Hawke asked.

"Something our comms guy, Elvis Peete, here just downloaded from Langley. A thermal-imaging fly-by video CIA wanted us to see. Good timing, huh? I just watched it and now I know why. See the time code? Shot just one hour ago. Take a look."

He pushed play. The video was grainy black and white but remarkably clear for something shot from so high above. They were looking down at the target building. The Weapons Design Center was dark, not a window lit on any of the floors. Just like now. Five seconds into the film, a white panel truck skidded to a stop in front of the building's entrance. The driver and a passenger jumped out and went around to the back of the truck. They opened the rear doors and one man climbed inside. The driver reached in and started pulling. Out came the limp body of a male. Unconscious. Or dead. The driver had the ankles, the other man had the wrists.

"Holy fuck, it's him!" Harry Brock said.

"How do you know?" Stoke asked him, hitting the pause button.

"Bill Chase is six foot four, remember? Look at that guy. At least that tall. How many guys over six feet tall you think holiday here on Xinbu fucking Island, Stoke?"

"Harry's right," Hawke said. "That's Chase. Play the rest of it, Stoke."

On the screen, the two men carried the sagging body up the broad steps and into the building. Lights on the ground floor went on. Six figures came outside and stood guard at the entrance, three to either side. All holding automatic rifles. They stood aside as the body was carried in.

A minute later, long enough for an elevator ride, the lights on the top floor illuminated. A minute later, the lights were extinguished. Right after that, the two men exited, climbed inside the panel truck, and drove out of the frame. The six who'd guarded the door in their absence moved back inside the darkened building. The lights shut down and remained off. Just like they were now.

Stoke said, "Target is lying unconscious, possibly dead, in a room on the top floor, left side front, end of the corridor of the central elevator bank. Thank you, gods of the Central Intelligence Agency."

"Modern warfare," Brock said proudly. "My guys are the shit, right?"

"Damn straight," Stoke agreed. The video was literally a gift from above.

"Shitfire," Chief Rainwater said. He was standing in the open doorway of the Annex.

"What is it, Chief?" Hawke asked, putting a hand on the big man's shoulder and peering out.

"Two armored troop vehicles. They must have heard us blowing shit up, and now I'd say they've seen us. Both headed this way at full tilt."

Both men screwed up their eyes in automatic reflex as the fierce glare of powerful oncoming headlights struck them, the flare path arrowing out into the darkness.

"Fitz! Froggy! Take an RPG position behind that pumping station out there. Wait until both trucks close to within a hundred yards and then take them out simultaneously. Don't let one veer away. We don't have time to bloody deal with those assholes now."

The two men hefted their RPG tubes and raced off into the darkness. Two minutes later, two fiery and nearly simultaneous explosions blossomed up into the star-dusted darkness.

"Good shooting," Hawke murmured under his breath as Fitz and Froggy reappeared on the run.

"Chief," Hawke said, looking carefully at Rainwater, "you and Froggy ready to go blow that sub base off its foundation?"

"You can be fairly sure we ain't taking a couple of hundred pounds of Semtex and C-4 home with us, Commander Hawke."

"Good. How long will it take you to rig the complex?"

"Maybe an hour."

"You've got forty minutes. Figure thirty. Set the timers to blow the complex exactly at 0430 hours. Got it? Move out!"

The two saboteurs, the big Comanche and the squat little Frenchman, ran off into the darkness.

Stoke said, "Only six guys waiting in there in the dark to guard our guy? I'm not sure I buy that."

Hawke said, "I don't buy it either." He glanced at his wristwatch. "We've got fifty-four minutes to find and identify the hostage, dead or alive, blow up that sub pen, and get the bloody hell out to the far end of that rocky point. Alive enough to rendezvous with the sub. And hopefully before that planeload of commie commandos lands on our bloody noggins. Let's move."

They double-timed it up the steps to the entrance, splitting at the double doors, Hawke's team going right, Stoke and his going left. The men flipped their night-vision goggles down and waited for the two squad leaders to enter the blacked-out building. The plan was simple. Hawke and Stoke would clear the ground floor before anyone else entered as they'd done it countless times before.

Stoke kicked the thick glass-and-stainless-steel doors inward. He and Hawke went in together, avoiding the doorway's kill zone at the center. They dove left and right, hitting the floor in a roll. They came out of it, back on their feet, with their automatic weapons ready to fire, sweeping left to right and back again. It looked empty. There was a wide center staircase to the first floor and—

"Oh, hullo," a disembodied voice said, in perfect Oxbridge English.

Hawke swung around, his finger tightening on the trigger. Somehow someone, a woman, had gotten behind them! Early thirties, close-cropped black hair. A BBC, his mind insisted. A British-born-Chinese. She smiled and said, "Sorry, the power's out. May I help you?"

Some kind of receptionist? Hawke wondered. Bizarre. And then he thought, *She looks oddly familiar. Where? When?* He focused on that but couldn't pull it up, nor had he time to worry about it.

"Show us where to find Dr. Chase. Now." Hawke took three menacing steps forward and lowered his MP5 barrel until it was opposite her defiant heart.

"Who? I'm sorry. We have no one here by that name." Incredibly cool and confident under the circumstances. Definitely not a receptionist.

"I have zero time for you. Tell me where he is now or I cannot guarantee your safety."

She just smiled.

"Lock down on that woman," Hawke said to Stokely before turning away. "Shoot her."

"No problem," Stoke said and raised his silenced automatic.

"Last chance," he said to the woman. "Where is he?"

There was a muffled *pfft* from above. A bullet grazed Stoke's hand and the 9mm pistol flew from Stoke's bloodied hand and clattered across the marble floor. At the same instant, Hawke felt a stinging sensation in his right earlobe. He put his hand to it and came away with a bloody smear.

"Up there!" Stoke shouted as he and Hawke peered up into the darkness. They were in some kind of open atrium, like those Hyatt airport hotels, open center to the roof, balconies going all the way around the inside of the building on every floor.

The lobby lights went on with a bang, like a master switch had been thrown.

Hawke swung back around. The young woman was now standing, half hidden by an open door, still smiling at him in oddest way.

Hawke hesitated a beat; then he saw her hand dive inside her jacket.

"Gun!" Hawke shouted.

The space filled with the jackhammer chatter of his weapon. He fired a four-round burst that almost chopped her in half and she pitched forward to the floor, the gun in her right hand. Hawke flinched at the sight. He killed his enemies for a living and he did it with a ruthless efficiency appalling in its single-mindedness and thoroughness of execution. But he rarely killed without regret, nor without the most bitter self-condemnation. Still, he carried on, consoled by the knowledge he killed simply that better men might live.

He'd seen six figures emerge from the entrance when Chase's body was delivered. If the scientist was dead, his mission was over; he needed only to confirm the death and they could get the hell off the island. He'd knocked one enemy down, so five remained up there.

"Chase is up here," a man's voice echoed from the top floor. Again, English. They looked up again. No one there.

Hawke signaled to Fitz, five fingers for the number believed to be waiting for them upstairs.

The squad moved inside the lobby behind Fitz like a rolling black tide of utter destruction. "A bloody tomb in here, ain't it?" Fitz said, looking up at all the white marble.

No one replied to that.

"Bad choice of words, maybe," Fitz muttered.

Chapter 71

"Watch out!" the scrawny Tennessee mountain boy, Elvis Peete, cried out in pain. "Someone's up there on the third level with a gun and—"

Elvis hit the floor, already dead, gouts of blood pumping from a stomach wound.

Stoke got a glimpse of the guy up there, just a kid, really, trying too late to duck away. He put one through his forehead. Guy fell forward over the railing and plummeted downward. Three of his guys had to step aside to avoid being hit by the falling body.

He landed with a sickening thud at their feet, spattering their combat boots with soupy blood. He was on his back, blood seeping from his mouth and nostrils, his dead eyes staring up at nothing.

"What the fuck?" Brock said. "This dumb shit's wearing a coat and tie!"

Hawke nodded imperceptibly at Stokely. The two men each plucked a dangling pineapple from their web belts, heaving the two stun grenades simultaneously on the count of two, up to the second-floor balcony.

The twin blasts, the horrific *BOOM,* and the blinding flash of light were deafening within the marble interior. And disorienting to anyone within immediate range of the blast.

"Okay. Let's move," Stoke said, starting up the stairs after Hawke.

"Go right," Hawke said, going left himself at the top.

As he mounted the top step he saw someone to his left dart back inside an opened door. He tossed a smoke grenade, bouncing and rolling it; it stopped just outside the door, the fuse loudly hissing. Another well-dressed figure, male, stepped out in order to kick the grenade away when Hawke shot him through the heart, swung the still-chattering M5 machine gun upward to a man firing down on his troops from the balcony above, saw him crumple, half his chest torn away by the tearing slugs.

Suddenly, it came to him.

He stepped to the rail and shouted across the open atrium to Stoke and his men.

"These guards? All bloody Te-Wu, Stoke!" he said. "Assassins from the Academy! So you men mind your heads."

Stoke answered with a long burst from his weapon.

There was an open door at the corner.

He could see armed folks, men and women, all stacked up, waiting to come out and engage the invaders. Did it make any sense? Maybe they were highly motivated, crack shots, expert marksmen. But he saw fear. Terror. And panic on their youthful faces. Some kind of suicide do, or something? But they were trying to kill him and his guys, and so he opened fire.

Do the thing you fear and the death of fear is certain.

The first guy to die fell back against the next in line. Stoke fired again. The man fell back against a young woman who pointed a gun at Stoke. And so he continued to shoot, his teeth clenched tight until his jaw ached.

Suddenly another door was flung open, then another and another. More of them. Like the others, armed with pistols, few machine guns. Boys wearing coats and ties fighting highly trained commandos wearing full body armor! Nuts! A guy fired at Stoke just as he took a knee and one of Stoke's guys went down, his throat making horrible gurgling noises. What could they do? Kill or be killed, that's all. He and his men returned a withering barrage.

Stoke was beginning to wonder how many more of these kids were in the building. They were every-where. These kids were outgunned and obviously not at all used to close-quarters combat. Well, assassination was a one-on-one kind of killing. In the privacy of a hotel room or a dark alley. Not this kind of shit.

That's when a guy who'd been on the ground feign-ing death jumped up in front of him, firing wildly. Stoke fired once, twice, three times, wordlessly and with great care. The force of the powerful rounds at such close quarters lifted the man off his feet, smashed him against the wall, pinned him there for one incredi-ble second, nailed against the wall as if in spread-eagled crucifixion. Then he fell to the floor and Stoke stepped over him to find Hawke in the melee and somehow put an end to this slaughter. He'd now lost three men, with more wounded. And he was winning the damn war.

Hawke, meanwhile, was advancing up to the third floor. He and Fitz, with Brock bringing up the rear, mounted the steps. The third-floor galleries were empty except for countless expended shells scattered everywhere.

But not the fourth floor. Not empty at all.

All four sides of the atrium gallery above were lined with the Te-Wu, men and women standing shoulder to shoulder, their pistols and automatic rifles aimed at the men pouring up the stairs. A last stand—Hawke could see grim determination on their mostly terrified faces.

Hawke paused on the steps.

"Don't shoot!" Hawke shouted up at them. "Listen to me. You people don't have to die here tonight. Lay down your arms peacefully, raise your hands where I can see them, and I will make sure you get out of this building alive. All I want is Dr. Chase. Turn him over to me, and I have no more business with you or anyone else on this island."

"Who are you?" a glowering mop-haired chap with burning black eyes shouted down to him.

"My name is Alex Hawke. I am—"

"Hawke! We will give you Chase," another man shouted, "but we want you, Hawke! Even trade."

"Show me Chase and we'll see."

"We don't trust you, Hawke," said a young woman who couldn't have been over twenty.

"I don't think you've got a whole lot of choice. So either you bring him out here where I can see him or—"

Hawke never finished the sentence.

The woman simply pulled her trigger and shot him. The bullet got lucky and found a seam in his armor plating. He felt a red-hot blast of pain in his left side, one that spun him around and down. Fitz put three bullets in the assassin's head and dropped to cover Hawke's body with his own.

His men opened fire on the gallery above with a vengeance. People, a lot of people, started pitching forward over the railing, dead or dying, and landing with sickening thuds three stories below.

"Is it bad?" Fitz asked him.

"Hurts, that's all. Went right through me. Let me up. Woman tried to kill me. It was personal, Fitz. I saw it in her eyes. Get the hell off me, I can't breathe."

"Not till I stop the bleeding."

"These people are zombies, Fitz. Like the walking dead; they act like they've got nothing to lose. I'm tired of this crap, and we're running out of time. These goddamn automatons want to die so damn badly, heave a dozen or so Willy Pete grenades up there so they can go out in a bloody flaming white phosphorus blaze of glory . . ."

Chapter 72

They were all dead. Fifty of them maybe, Hawke thought, maybe a lot more. Charred bodies stacked on top of more bodies. He waded through them, his left hand pressed against his wound, sickened by the stench of burned flesh, making his way to a room at the end of the long corridor where he prayed he would find Dr. William Lincoln Chase.

"What are you gonna do if Chase ain't in there, boss?" Stoke said, as they paused outside the door.

"Just shoot me," Hawke said and pushed inside.

"You already shot," Stoke said, right behind him.

Chase's home was an anonymous small bedroom with an adjoining toilet, a writing desk, and built-in bookcases overflowing with scientific tomes and military history. Engineering drawings covering the walls. Models of unrecognizable weapons . . .

There was a man lying faceup on the single unmade bed in the corner.

It was Chase.

Hawke bent over him and pressed three fingers to his neck, checking the carotid artery.

"Dead?" Stoke said.

"Alive. Probably drugged. Quick, soak a washcloth in cold water in the sink. I'm going to pop an amyl nitrate under his nose. That should do the trick. What time is it, Stoke?"

"O420, boss. We gotta move. Now."

"Dr. Chase? Dr. Chase? He's coming around," Hawke said, cleaning the hostage's sweat-greased face with the damp washcloth. "Here, help him sit up."

"Who the . . . who the hell are you?" Chase said, his voice fuzzy with narcotics.

"Dr. Chase, my name is Commander Alexander Hawke. Royal Navy and MI6. How are you feeling, sir?"

"Lousy . . . I . . ."

"Sir, I've got to get you out of here. Let me quickly inform you that your wife and two children are safe. They are now en route to San Francisco aboard a U.S. Navy destroyer."

"What? They're out? My God, how?"

"A long story. Can you get on your feet?"

"We'll see, won't we?" he said. Hawke and Stoke each took an arm and helped him up. "I seem to be operating under my own power again. Where are you taking me?"

"Home, ultimately. But we need to stop at the submarine command and control ops center."

"Why?"

"Moon has launched a series of attacks using the Centurion missiles you designed. Iwo Jima and Okinawa were completely destroyed. He's now threatening to take out Pearl Harbor, sir. We need to stop him."

Chase said, "That sonofabitch never told me he was already launching them."

"How many Centurion subs are out there, sir?"

"Eight. Four in the Pacific, four in the Atlantic."

"You lost one in the Atlantic. Seven more Centurions. I believe you built a fail-safe self-destruct mechanism into each sub, is that correct?"

"I did."

"You memorized the codes?"

"Of course."

"That's why we're going to the ops center. Once you've destroyed the seven Centurions, I'm going to blow that building up. We need to get moving. Ready?"

"Ready?" Chase said. "Seriously?"

Hawke smiled. Yeah, he was ready all right. "Any luck with the jeep?" he asked Fitz.

"Managed to borrow three."

"Good man, Fitz. You may have just saved our asses." Hawke looked at his watch again. He was conscious of every passing second now.

The three jeeps, overcrowded with passengers, raced across the sand toward the sub bunkers.

"Which entrance?" Hawke yelled at Chase, jammed up front between him and Stoke.

"Far left. That's where CCC, Chinese Centurion Command, is located."

"Command and control? Where they monitor and control all the unmanned subs at sea?" Hawke yelled. "Right?"

"Right."

Hawke cranked the wheel hard left and spun his tires. All three vehicles fishtailed to a stop at the entrance, sandstorms whirling about them, and the men jumped out and sprinted full up the broad steps leading to the entrance. Hawke and Stoke ran more slowly, still helping a slowly reviving Chase to keep moving.

Once inside, Hawke said, "Which way?"

"Follow me," Chase said, taking off at a run. The news that his family was safe and that he might soon be freed from Moon's living hell seemed highly motivating.

He'd been broken on the wheel. Now, he was the wheel upon which his adversary would be broken.

Hawke ran after him, everybody overtly conscious of that big ticking time bomb overhead, the one flying in with overwhelming reinforcements from the Chinese mainland.

Chase checked up outside two stainless doors with a keypad entry. He pressed his right palm against the sensor and the doors slid apart. "All the way to the far end of the corridor," he said. "That's what they call the 'War Room.'"

The room was very cold and very dark. An undercurrent of electronic humming. You could see silhouettes of men at control consoles, staring up at the big monitors above them. Hawke and Chase stole through the darkness, counting down the minutes and seconds that remained to them to complete their mission.

Chase grabbed Hawke's forearm, stopping him.

"That's him," he whispered. "That's Moon."

"Which one?"

"At the center control module. White uniform and . . . wait . . . He's initiating another Centurion missile launch! That's Honolulu. He's got bloody Pearl Harbor up on the monitor. God, Hawke, we have to stop him!"

Hawke turned and motioned for all the men to advance into the room, all at ready arms. They strode forward warily and stood in a semicircle behind Hawke, Chase, and Stoke, ready to kill anything that moved . . .

"What's the—" Stoke said, but Hawke silenced him.

"General Moon," Hawke called out. Loud enough to be heard, but calm.

He could see from the general's posture that he'd gained his attention. The man got to his feet, turned, and said, "Continue with the launch sequence," to an older navy officer standing next to him. Then he saw Hawke and Chase. Betraying no visible emotion, he began to walk toward them. Hawke held his weapon loosely at his side, ready for anything.

"Good evening, Commander Hawke. It's been a long, long time. I see you've met my colleague, the good Dr. Chase."

Hawke said nothing.

"Have you completely lost your mind, General?" Chase said, trying to remain calm. "You're about to start World War Three, you goddamn maniac. There'll be no world left for you to rule . . ."

Moon's face was suddenly twisted in a rictus of rage.

"You think we are starting this? Did we invade the West? Did we enslave millions to opium? Did we carve your territory into bits and pieces to give away to our friends? Answer me! Are you really so ignorant of history?"

"Ancient history."

"Two centuries of humiliation and hardly ancient by our standards. We should have done it sooner, Dr. Chase, but we had not the means. When your enemy hands you a sword, you use it. And you handed me this Centurion sword, lest you forget."

"Right, General. My friends are here to help me take it back."

"Never! You're too late. No one can stop me now. Even you, Hawke. You're a walking dead man."

Hawke ignored him and spoke very calmly. "Dr. Chase, I want you to abort that impending Centurion missile launch on Honolulu. How long have we got?"

Chase looked up at the red digits whizzing by on the countdown timer. "Five minutes and counting."

"Go do it."

"I wouldn't try that if I were you, Dr. Chase," Moon said, moving a step closer.

"Why not?"

"Not enough time to enter the fail-safe codes. And because the only sensible thing for you and your men to do is surrender. If you don't, I can promise you that every last invader on this island will either be dead or imprisoned in a matter of minutes."

"Really?" Hawke said. "Just how do you intend to do that? We've already killed all your adoring Te-Wu acolytes. The remaining men here are no match for us."

"True. But any second a Chinese military C-130 will roar overhead. One hundred crack Chinese paratroops will float to earth. How many of you are left in fighting condition? Ten? Fifteen? I don't fancy your odds. There's no place to run on this island, Hawke. We'll hunt you down like dogs. Hang you from hooks in the trees."

Hawke raised his sidearm, leveled it between Moon's eyes.

"You murdered my son's guardian and tried to murder my son, General. Reason enough to kill you on the spot."

"It's war. You killed my daughter tonight!"

"Hell are you talking about?"

"Liar! I watched you do it! On the security cameras . . . the beautiful black-haired woman who stopped you in the lobby tonight . . . my darling Jet."

Hawke, amazed, said, "That was Jet?"

So . . . his old lover. The woman he thought he'd recognized back there somehow . . . the young Te-Wu assassin sent by Moon to kill him years ago . . . in a hotel room in the south of France . . . yes, of course it was her.

Jet Moon.

"General, listen carefully. If you try to prevent Dr. Chase from aborting that launch, you'll be the second member of your family to die by my hand tonight. You have five seconds to decide."

Moon's eyes bulged, and color rose in his face. But he said nothing to his men.

"Dr. Chase," Hawke said evenly, never taking his eyes off the countdown, the general, or his armed men ranged around the room. "Abort the Centurion launch. Now! Fitz, go with him and watch his back. Shoot anyone who interferes."

Chase brushed past Hawke going to the console and Hawke felt a clumsy tug on his thigh holster and knew in an instant what was happening. Chase had snatched his assault knife.

"No! Dr. Chase! Stop!" he said.

Chase lunged toward General Moon, his face contorted with hatred, screaming at the torturer his wife and children had suffered under.

"You miserable little monster!" he shouted at Moon. "You monstrosity! You stole my life. Now I'm going to—"

Stoke was closest to Chase. His big hand shot forward like a piston and clamped around the doctor's wrist, tearing the knife from his grip and handing it back to Hawke in one single, fluid, and blindingly fast motion. Chase screamed in frustration and lunged for Moon with his fists flailing.

Shots rang out as two of the general's personal security bodyguards moved forward, reacting instinctively to this attack on the exalted new leader of all China. Hawke, to his horror, saw that Chase was nanoseconds from death despite all that had been done to save him. Without him, half of Honolulu's population would disappear in seconds.

He fired into the first bodyguard's brain and brought his gun hand down on the other's wrist, snapping it before he could squeeze off the fatal round—

"Dr. Chase, you have exactly sixty-two seconds to abort that missile destined for Honolulu," Hawke said. "Do it! Move! Fitz, you, too!"

Chase and Fitz bolted for Moon's console panel.

"Stoke, you guys disarm and cuff everyone remaining. Get them all facedown on the floor. If they resist, shoot them."

Now came the unmistakable roar of a giant Chinese C-130 approaching overhead, flying at low altitude, filling the air above Xinbu Naval Base with a hundred parachutes . . . shit . . . he looked up at the digital launch clock, the red numbers flashing toward 0045. . . .

They weren't going to make it.

He saw a hidden knife suddenly flash in Moon's hand.

And he heard the big C-130 roar now directly over his head.

One hundred crack Chinese paratroopers were now hitting the silk. An overwhelming force against fifteen or so left to him . . .

Battle-weary soldiers of fortune.

What was it he'd promised Stoke earlier?

"I ain't Custer."

Chapter 73

Moon, desperate, hate filled, came at Hawke with the knife above his head. Stoke raised his sidearm. A dozen automatic weapons were now locked on Moon's heart.

"Leave him alone!" Hawke yelled at his men. "I can take care of him."

Roaring, the big martial arts expert launched his body at Hawke, driving him back against the wall, and slashing down with the dagger. Hawke feinted to one side and deflected the blade, ducking inside the powerful punch that followed. Still, Moon's knee came up under Hawke's chin, hard, and his vision blurred. When Moon went for his gut with the knife, Hawke dove forward and caught an ankle, hugged it to his chest, and spun with it. Moon started to go down but turned, kicked Hawke viciously in the forehead with his free foot, and tore loose. Hawke staggered.

"My daughter Chyna will make your son suffer before he dies," Moon said, getting to his feet. "No matter what happens here tonight. I promise you that."

"Your daughter Chyna is in London in police custody, General, charged with murder. Probably being waterboarded by MI6 officers as we speak. Or hadn't you heard?"

Moon, enraged, was back instantly, throwing a barrage of punches that felt to Hawke like being hit with round rocks. Hawke staggered back, and the man launched himself into the air in some kind of strange scissor kick, coming at him feet first. Hawke slid sideways along the wall, snatched at the lower of the two feet, and whipped it as high as he could. The first thing to hit the floor was the back of Moon's head. He rolled up onto his hands and knees, shaking his head.

Hawke stepped forward and drop-kicked him again. Moon rose up and came down hard on his back, rolled up, and as he came halfway up, Hawke chopped down viciously with the flat edge of his hand, a blow to the face that flattened his nose, breaking every bone, a sickening crunching sound.

Moon dissolved to the floor, blood gushing from the center of his face and blinking slowly like a lizard, eyes out of focus, done.

"Stoke, cuff the general's wrists to that overhead support beam," Hawke said, glancing over at the launch clock, the big red numbers scrolling down to—0012—

"Twelve seconds! Chase! Can you stop it?" he cried out.

"Yes . . . one more thing and . . ."

The launch warning alarms all fell silent. The clock had stopped at 0007. Chase sat there at the console staring up at it, breathing hard and bathed in sweat.

Hawke raced over to him, put a hand on his shoulder, and said, "God bless you, Chase, you just might have saved a million lives on the island of Oahu."

Chase came out of his chair.

"Commander, I've got to destroy the rest of the Centurion fleet! Moon has preprogrammed the remaining subs in both the Atlantic and Pacific to launch all weapons at primary urban targets in Britain and along the U.S. West Coast. L.A., San Francisco, Seattle. Launch codes have been initiated. He was just finalizing their codes when we entered and—"

"Dr. Chase. We have no time. This entire complex is about to blow sky-high. Where are the self-destruct controls for the fleet of Centurions?"

"Over there! That whole panel is dedicated to the seven remaining subs and the 280 ICBMs aboard them. You can't blow this place now, Hawke. To do so is unthinkable."

"Good Christ in heaven. How long to destroy them?"

"How long have I got?"

Hawke looked at his watch just as he heard Chief Rainwater and Froggy cry out from entrance to the control room, "Hawke! For God's sake, you've got to get out of here now! We set the timers. At 0430, in less than six minutes, this whole damn place is going to blow!"

"You've got four minutes, max, if we want any chance to get out of here alive," Hawke said to Chase. He was already at the control panel, working furiously, punching in codes on seven different screens, his hands a blur across the keypads.

"I built these fucking things; I am more than happy to die destroying them."

"I'm not leaving without you."

Chase ignored him, working furiously. He screamed something Hawke couldn't understand at four of Moon's young Chinese scientists, who immediately sat down on either side of the American and started punching code as rapidly as humanly possible.

"Evac all your men from the complex, Fitz," Hawke shouted over his shoulder. "The SEALs' minisubs will have already arrived offshore to ferry you all out to the sub. Get down to the beach and start swimming to the

SDVs. We'll be right behind you as soon as we're finished here."

"Aye-aye, sir," Fitz said, and gave the order for his men to evacuate the CCC building.

At that moment, four of the first Chinese paratroopers to land burst inside the control room, firing wildly.

Fitz and Stoke shot them all dead where they stood, and Fitz and his men raced out into the night, carrying their dead and wounded, no man left behind.

"You'll be taking fire from above, Fitz!" Hawke called after him. "Take out as many of those spec-ops paratroops in the air as you can on your way to the beach!"

Fitz grinned at him and nodded his head.

As Hawke had predicted, Fitz found the sky overhead filled with moonlit white mushrooms, a hundred parachutes streaming down from a star-filled sky. The instant he and his men emerged from the CCC structure, lead rained down on their heads.

"It's done!" Chase cried out, leaping up from his station at the console. Seven codes on seven monitors flashing "TERMINATED" on the screens above. Seven wailing alarms went silent, and seven identical digital readouts wound down to 0–0–0–0. Hawke glanced at his watch.

In less than ninety seconds, the huge submarine base and weapons complex surrounding them would be reduced to rubble.

"To confirm. All seven Centurions terminated, Dr. Chase?"

"Every goddamn one of those monsters, Hawke, and the three hundred and twenty nuclear weapons inside them are now vaporized on the deepest part of the ocean floor. A few tsunamis in the forecast, but that's about it."

Hawke looked over at General Moon, at his hand-cuffed wrists high over his head, suspended from the steel beam, a lethal mixture of fear and furious frustration flashing in his black eyes. A vengeful Chase was hovering in close, his right hand squeezing the general's throat, barely under control.

Chase said, "You told me once you were a man of destiny, isn't that right, General?"

"I am!" Moon managed to croak.

"Just not quite the destiny you contemplated, is it? IS IT?"

Moon whipped his head around and summoned a jungle roar that sounded primeval. An animal, now, in his death throes.

Hawke had seen and heard enough. He stepped directly in front of Chase, pulled the American's hand away, and got right up into Moon's face.

Hawke's voice was low, low and cold.

"General Moon. I don't know how to say 'Sayonara' in Chinese, unfortunately. But I do have one last thing to say. Your assassins murdered the American president. Tom McCloskey was a good, honorable man whom I considered a close friend. His widow and his immediate family are still in hospital, fighting for their lives. All wounded during your despicable and morally reprehensible attack on mourners at the president's gravesite."

Moon was writhing, seething.

"Say what you're going to say . . ." he spat out.

"And now, from that very grave, with a little help from me, the late president returns the favor. Rather a fitting ending, isn't it?"

Moon hissed back at him:

"You expect me to beg, Hawke?"

"No, General Moon, I expect you to die."

Hawke, Chase, and Stokely Jones dashed out of the seaward entrance of the CCC building. He could see Fitz and his men racing toward the very end of the rocky point beyond, pursued by paratroops who'd already landed and being fired upon by those who had not. Fitz and company were returning fire over their shoulders as they ran, darting and weaving across the rocky headland toward the curving sandy beach, beckoning white in the waning moonlight. Hawke saw to his relief that there were a lot of men in the sky hanging motionless in their harnesses and floating to earth.

Some of the invading troops were deliberately landing on the rooftops of the sub base and taking up firing positions there. Bullets whined and spanged the rocks around them.

Hawke saw Froggy and Rainwater had stayed behind. They'd taken up a position about thirty yards behind the last of the retreating commandos. They were firing from behind some large earthmovers to cover Fitz's retreat with their two big M-60 heavy machine guns. *Thump-thump-thump-thump*, like a deep rumble of thunder. They were laying down heavy suppression fire at the advancing ground troops, the men on the rooftops, and also firing up sporadically at the remaining descending paratroopers.

It was enormously effective, but their position was still dangerously exposed from the fire raining down from above.

Hawke and his two companions raced ahead, firing at anything that moved, until they reached Froggy and Rainwater's position.

"You've got to go," Hawke said to them, ducking behind a bulldozer. "In sixty seconds, all those paratroops still alive are going to be on the ground and racing this way. No bloody way we can hold them off . . ."

"Just get Chase safely aboard the SDV," Rainwater said, his finger still on the trigger, firing full auto. "Froggy and I'll cover your retreat as long as we can. But we'll be right behind you!"

"He's right," Hawke said. "Stoke, you go. Take Chase. Get him to safety. Rainwater, Froggy, and I will remain here and help cover your backs."

"Boss, you can't—"

"Don't argue, Stoke; just get Chase to the sub alive!" Hawke said, and, crouching low, he began firing single, very precisely targeted sniper rounds at the silhouetted soldiers up on the roof and those still suspended in their harnesses and floating to earth.

Stoke and Chase had just bolted for the beach when their world shook to its core and the whole of Xinbu Island seemed to turn a red-hot shade of white.

A massive series of explosions shook the earth as the enormous reinforced concrete structures lifted into the sky, blown to bits by the countless satchel charges laid by Rainwater and Froggy around the interior and exterior of the CCC complex. Black smoke and plumes of red-orange-yellow fire reached skyward, licking at the bottoms of the lowest clouds scudding by. All the

Chinese rooftop commandos died in the collapse, and many of the troops on the ground were killed by the radiating blast. Even more were killed by the giant chunks and bits of falling concrete thrown high into the air and now raining down upon them.

"Good bang for the buck, lads," Hawke said to the two men, allowing himself the very briefest of smiles between bursts of getting the lead out. All that fell to him now was to try to get off this godforsaken island alive. If he didn't, so be it. He was untroubled and unafraid. A memory of Admiral Lord Nelson's last words aboard the HMS *Victory* came to him:

I thank God that I have done my duty.

Chase was safe. Moon was dead, his terrifying weapons destroyed. Mission accomplished, and all the rest of it was gravy. He looked at his two comrades and added, "Demolition of that magnitude often makes a good diversion, too. I suggest we get while the getting is good."

"D'accord," Froggy said, smiling his agreement.

"Leave that fucking gun behind!" Rainwater said to Froggy as the Frenchman got shakily to his feet, the big gun cradled in his arms. "Too heavy! You can't run with that monster in your hands."

"Mais non!" Froggy said, hefting the thing. "They'll pick it up and use it on us, Chief!"

"Hell with it, let's go," Rainwater said.

And so the three men ran, the little Frenchman staggering along behind, going as fast as his short legs could carry him with the heavy gun cradled in his arms. There were still rounds being fired at them, not as many as before, but still, very lethal slugs of lead were whistling overhead.

Hawke finally had the crescent-shaped beach in sight when he felt the absence of Froggy behind them. Glancing over his shoulder, he saw no sign of him.

"Froggy!" Hawke called out. "Come on, let's go!"

"Shit," Rainwater said. "Must have fallen or gotten hit. I'm going back for him."

"No, you're not, Chief. Keep moving. I'm the one responsible for the safety of every one of these men, not you. Go. That's an order."

"Merde!" they heard Froggy's faint cry of pain; he'd gone down somewhere, a hundred yards or so back there in the gloom, among the scattered rocks.

"Shit is right, Frogman," Rainwater said. "Good luck, Commander!" Then the Indian warrior turned and bolted for the beach and the submarine waiting offshore.

Hawke ran back, darting this way and that, firing blindly toward the winking muzzles of the oncoming paratroops, his eyes scanning the rocky ground, calling out Froggy's name.

He heard another soft moan a few yards to his right. The little guy was facedown in a puddle of water on the rocky shale, arms and legs akimbo, his beloved gun beneath him, a dark stain spreading across his back.

"Froggy?" Hawke said, dropping to his knees and getting his arms under the Frenchman. "You still with me, mon ami? I'm getting you off this beach."

The Frogman croaked out a little laugh, said something in such a hoarse whisper, Hawke couldn't make it out over the approaching rattle of automatic fire.

He hefted Froggy's considerable weight, got to his feet, and started moving rapidly toward the sea, looking down into the little Frenchman's fluttering eyes.

"Stay with me, Froggy! Hold on, damn it! Keep your eyes open. What did you say back there?"

"Bienvenue, mes amis, au paradis!" he whispered.

Hawke mounted a rise, a rocky outcropping that overlooked the little bay riffled with whitecaps and the sandy beach thirty feet below. He saw a narrow crevice in the rock, with a sandy path leading down to the crescent of shoreline beyond.

He paused for a brief moment before starting down.

His eyes were fixed on the far horizon.

The distant burning star of fire inched up above the earth's dark rim. Rising, the sun sent its first brilliant, white-hot rays streaking across the heaving wave tops, splashing color over the water's surface, creating radiant streaks of deepest blue. In the distance, the silhouette of the black submarine waited for him, the welcoming twinkle of tiny red lights visible fore and aft along her hull.

The fresh sea air on his face was good in the cool blueness of the morning. It carried a sharp bite of salt along with its promise of a brand-new day.

It was going to be a beautiful day.

"Come on, Froggy, let's go home," he said, and carried the dead man in his arms down to the sea.

Epilogue

CHRISTMAS EVE

It was Christmas Eve.

Lord Alexander Hawke was standing before his dressing room mirror, singing.

Just a few bars, mind you, of his favorite holiday carol. He sang while he brushed his hair and finished donning his white tie and tails. Tonight he and his son, Alexei, were off to attend a very fancy Christmas Eve feast.

This festive event was hosted every year by Lady Diana Mars and her fiancé, Ambrose Congreve, at their home, Brixden House. But, this year, it was much more than a holiday feast; actually, it was a prewedding celebration for the happy couple.

The wedding would be tomorrow, on Christmas Day.

Despite having to dress up like a penguin, Hawke was decidedly cheery on this very special evening, for any number of reasons:

It had been snowing all day long.

His dearest friend in the world, Ambrose Congreve, was finally getting married in the morning.

And it was the night before Christmas!

The little boy in him still loved Christmas with all its trappings and traditions. His own little boy had his back to him. Alexei was standing at Hawke's third-floor dressing room window, his puppy right beside him, gazing wide-eyed at the magical scene of rolling ice-cream hills in the muffled silence of the eternal snow.

The storm had begun earlier that morning, great feathery white flakes that stilled the world; hushed it, made it ethereal and dreamlike.

As the first flakes fell, Hawke, who had adored snow since childhood, prayed the storm would never cease. To his delight, it had not.

It was now dusk, and as the setting sun reached across the white-breasted Cotswolds hills with slender violet fingers, Alexei said, "Don't stop singing, Papa. I like that song."

Hawke sang, "'May your days be merry and bright . . . and may all your . . .'"

"Keep going, Papa!"

"Sorry, forgotten the rest of the lyrics." He was no Bing Crosby and hated hearing himself murder such a well-beloved tune.

"What is a white Christmas, Papa?"

"It's a Christmas, darling, just like this one, when the whole world is white with snow."

"Isn't every Christmas white?"

"No, not anymore. Long ago, yes. We had ever so much snow then, when I was a little boy. I can never remember whether it snowed for six days and six nights when I was twelve or whether it snowed for twelve days and twelve nights when I was six. I do remember I made a snowman and my cousin knocked it down and I knocked my cousin down and then we all had tea with Pelham under the Christmas tree."

He looked out of the frosted window to the clock on the roof of the stable. It was a few minutes before six. They had best get cracking or they'd be late. He was, after all, Ambrose's best man.

The back country roads were icy. He was taking the Locomotive because of better traction on wintry drives and because Alexei liked to sit in the rear all by himself on the enormous backseat and play with his puppy, the irrepressible Handsome Harry.

Hawke was still at his dressing mirror fussing endlessly with his white tie. Always a chore to tie the damn things, and usually Pelham was there to help him. But since Hawke and Alexei were off for a two-night stay for the wedding, he'd given the dear fellow all of Christmas week to go visit his relatives in Wales.

"Will we see reindeer where we're going?" his son asked.

"It's Christmas, Alexei, anything is possible."

"Even Uncle Ambrose getting married?"

Hawke laughed at his precocious boy. He looked so adorable in his dark blue velvet suit, short pants with white kneesocks, and patent leather shoes.

"Quite right. I did say I wouldn't believe it until I saw it, didn't I?"

"Is it fun? Getting married?"

Hawke gave a start.

He'd started to say yes, but then he flashed on a deeply suppressed image from his past. It was his new bride, Victoria, dying in his arms, an assassin's bullet finding her heart on the steps of the chapel where they'd just wed. He willed the nightmare vision away, shoved it roughly aside. He moved to the window seat, sat down, and took the boy onto his knee.

"More than fun! It means you have found someone you love more than anyone else in the world and you wish to spend your whole life with them."

"Did you and Mama ever get married?"

"In our hearts we did."

"What's that mean?"

"We couldn't get married. Some very bad people took your mother and you away from me and—for a very long time I thought she was up in heaven. With you."

"She's in Russia."

"I know."

"Why don't you go there and marry her, Papa? So you can spend your whole life with her?"

"You know what, darling? Maybe someday, when you're older, I will do just that. You and I will go there together. And we won't leave Russia until she agrees to come home with us."

"And then get married to us. Forever."

"And then get married to us. Forever."

The day's last golden light was fleeing the western skies. The old Locomotive chugged up the last hill before descending to the right-hand turning into the grand gates of Brixden House. It was the wedding of the season and Hawke expected tout le monde would turn out for the affair. Assorted Royals, of course, but also the upper echelons of London society, a few boldface film people, the press, the media, et cetera.

"Look down there, Alexei!" Hawke said as the big car breasted the hilltop. "Looks like a winter wonderland, doesn't it?"

Alexei pressed his nose against the window, staring down at the sight of the Brixden House and gardens decorated for Christmas.

Hawke had caught a glimpse of Diana's great house and grounds spread out below them. There were over a hundred rooms in the house, and it seemed that every single window was blazing with light. The great evergreen trees lining the long drive were strung with countless fairy lights, leading one from the gate, through the woods, all the way up to the main entrance of the house.

It was enchanting, and not just to a four-year-old boy.

The sight of such splendor was not merely breathtaking, it was joyful. Hawke knew just how much love there was between his oldest friend and his bride-to-be. He'd never known a couple more perfectly suited for each other or who made each other so happy . . . a tinge of regret was tugging at his heartstrings still.

Would he himself ever find such happiness again?

The receiving line snaked up the grand staircase and all the way into the grand ballroom on the second floor.

Inside the house, it was all a glittering affair. Hawke had never seen the house look quite so lovely. There was greenery everywhere he looked, flaming candles and Christmas decor of every description on sideboards, mistletoe in the bookcases . . . he looked down at Alexei's upturned face . . . a smile full of wonder.

"Let's go this way," Hawke said, and peeked through a cracked door into an empty reception room off the Great Hall.

"Coast is clear, let's make a break for it," his father said. Alexei held his hand all the away across the parquet floors and beneath the brilliantly illuminated chandeliers to a set of floor-to-ceiling bookcases lining the far wall.

"Watch this," Hawke said as he reached up and pulled a large leather-bound volume of antique maps from one of the shelves. There was a whir and then a steady rumble.

"Daddy! It's moving!"

"It is, isn't it?"

The twelve-foot-high section of casing swung open. Behind it was a polished brass door set in the wood-paneled wall. Hawke pushed a button and the door slid into the wall.

They quickly entered the small elevator and watched the bookcase swing closed after them.

"What do you think of that?" Hawke asked, pushing the up button.

"Can we do it again?"

"Of course we can. We'll come back downstairs this way. So no one can see us, of course. We're on a secret mission, you know."

"I love secrets."

"Me, too. Like father, like son. Okay, here we are, all out. Let's go find Uncle Ambrose."

The grand ballroom was packed solid. An undulating sea of fashionable men in formal attire and women in glittering costume, perfectly coiffed and festooned with diamonds that rivaled the long row of glittering crystal chandeliers high above. In the center of it all, a magnificent Christmas tree soaring at least thirty feet into the air. Alex hoisted his son up onto his shoulders so he could see this wonder.

At the far end of the room a stage had been erected. A full orchestra was playing Christmas carols mixed with Cole Porter. Hawke and Alexei made their way along the edge of the room, dodging dowagers and waiters bearing trays laden with sloshing flutes of champagne. He had spied Ambrose ducking out onto the terrace for a smoke. You could hardly blame him; hosting a soiree like this was exhausting work.

"I thought I'd find you out here," Hawke said, approaching him from behind, Alexei still riding his shoulders. The snow was falling softly, and the powder squeaked amiably underfoot.

"What? Oh! Hullo, dear boy. And you, too, Alexei. Merry Christmas, laddie!"

"Merry Christmas, Uncle Ambrose!"

"Aren't we the lucky ones? A white Christmas this year!" Ambrose exclaimed.

Alexei said, "Does St. Nicholas come down your chimney, too? You have so many; how does he pick the right one?"

"He always finds it, and I should not be surprised if there's something under the tree for you in the morning. How are you, Alex? I must say, few men look better in white tie and tails."

"I am very well indeed on this jolly occasion. How are you bearing up?"

"One of the reasons I adore Diana is that she's the load-bearing pillar during these affairs. My only role is to play the affable host. Do you have the ring?"

"Of course. How many whiskeys have you had? It's going to be a long evening."

"None of your bloody business!"

"It is my business. The best man's job is to get you to the altar in presentable shape."

"Let me see the ring."

Hawke produced the little velvet box from his waist-coat pocket and opened it.

"Isn't it lovely? My mother's, you know."

"Oh, I know. I retrieved it from the bottom of the sea after your boat sank in Bermuda, remember?"

"I shall never forget that, Alex. Now, listen. I was looking for you earlier in the receiving line. One of our guests would like a private word with you." Hawke's smile faded.

"Don't tell me Sir David wishes to discuss business on Christmas Eve."

"No, no. It's not C, believe me. I would forewarn you if he were up to his old tricks. He's in the third-floor drawing room, swapping war stories with diplo-mats and all your MI6 cronies."

"Who on earth is it, then?"

"I was asked not to say. Waiting for you in the library now, as a matter of fact."

"Ah, well, this better be good."

"I think that will all depend on you."

"Aren't you the man of mystery? Will you take Alexei with you? He needs to shake hands with his hostess. And get him a Shirley Temple or a glass of milk? I shan't be long, I assure you. No matter who this mystery man may be."

Hawke made his way up the grand stairway and turned right. The library at Brixden House was one of the most beautiful in Britain, the room where he spent most of his time when visiting Diana and Ambrose. The door was cracked, and he pushed inside the gloom, his curiosity much aroused.

There was, of course, a huge fire crackling in the open hearth. That flickering orange light provided the only illumination on the walls and shadowy furniture.

"Hullo?" Hawke said.

Silence.

"Anyone there?" he said.

He waited. Ambrose playing some kind of a prank?

He was just about to pull the door closed when—

"Merry Christmas, Alex."

A disembodied voice had come from deep within one of the two winged chairs facing the fire. It was a woman, obviously, vaguely familiar, but he didn't really recognize the voice.

"Merry Christmas, yourself," he said. "Whoever you are."

A woman rose from the chair closest to the fire, her back kept to him. The firelight was lustrous in her swept-up auburn hair. He couldn't make out her profile but he saw the beauty of her long neck and pale white shoulders.

When she at last turned to face him, there was a knocking in his heart that made him feel suddenly weak.

"Hello, Alex."

"Hello, Nell."

He stared at her, poised and elegant in a simple black silk evening dress, a single strand of pearls around her neck. She looked lovely, just as he always remembered her.

"Fancy meeting you here," he said, taking a few steps into the room.

"I was in the neighborhood."

"You look wonderful."

"As do you."

"Can a man buy a girl a drink?"

"Already got one. One for you, too. Gosling's. A double. The ice is melting."

"Sounds enticing."

"Come sit down. There's a chair here for you, too."

"I'd be delighted."

He sat down beside her, unsure of what to say. The silence stretched out, and he picked up his drink and took a sip.

"Missed you, Lord Hawke," she said quietly.

"Missed you as well, Miss Nell."

"This house is cold. Are you cold?"

"No. You?"

"Hot is more like it."

"That's my girl."

"I meant the fire. I was so terribly sorry to hear about poor Sabrina. That ghastly woman. Lorelei Li. I knew her once, you know."

"We still haven't found her."

"So I've gathered. She can't hide forever. Not with Ambrose Congreve hot on her trail."

"He's got the bone in his teeth, all right," Hawke said.

"Aren't you going to ask me what I'm doing here?"

"What are you doing here, Nell?"

"I've moved back to England, for starters."

"Really? What about the job in Washington? The British embassy?"

"Left it."

"What about the handsome young diplomat you married?"

"Never did get around to marrying him. Left him, too."

"Why did you do that? You were so in love."

"I've learned a lot about love."

"I'm hopeless on the subject."

"Falling in love is a certain madness, Alex. It's volcanic when it erupts, then, eventually, it cools. When it does, you have to make a decision. Two people have to decide whether their roots are to become so inextricably entwined that the merest thought of parting is inconceivable. That's what real love is. Not breathless desire or lying awake all night longing for someone's touch. But true love, the kind that endures."

"I'm afraid I don't understand, Nell."

"Love itself is what is left over, Alex, when being in love has burned away. Doesn't sound terribly exciting, I know. But it is!"

"It broke my heart when you left."

"Mine, too. It's why I came back to England. I'll try to unbreak both of our hearts if you'll let me."

"What are you saying, Nell?"

"I want to come back to you, Alex. If you'll have me."

They stood for a long time out on the balcony, entwined, oblivious to the blowing snow swirling around them. Hawke kissed her neck, her hair, her lips, startled beyond measure at the depths of his loneliness now revealed. And how ravenous he was for her.

He held her even closer and stared down into her eyes.

"Is this love, Nell?" he whispered.

"No, darling," she said. "This is just the beginning."

Acknowledgments

I would like to acknowledge the help of three people without whom this book could never have been written: Lucinda Watson, Peter Lampack, and David Highfill. I thank you one and all.